… I speak in grief,
Not exultation, for I hate no more,
As then ere misery made me wise. The curse
Once breathed on thee I would recall …

… If then my words had power,
Though I am changed so that aught evil wish
Is dead within; although no memory be
Of what is hate, let them not lose it now!
What was that curse? for ye all heard me speak.

Percy Bysshe Shelley, *Prometheus Unbound*, Act I

ARTHUR MAIMANE

Hate No More

Kwela
BOOKS

c/o Kwela Books
28 Wale Street, Cape Town 8001;
P.O. Box 6525, Roggebaai 8012

An earlier version of the novel, titled *Victims,* was published
in the United Kingdom by Allison and Busby in 1976

Photo on cover by Jürgen Schadeberg
Cover design and typography by Nazli Jacobs
Set in 10 on 13 pt New Baskerville
Printed and bound by NBD, Drukkery Street,
Goodwood, Western Cape
First edition, first printing 2000

ISBN 0-7957-0102-0

Prologue

He stood on the periphery of the crowd, alone but at ease with himself within the enveloping bustle of the ballroom. This new and glitzy hotel had quickly gained popularity with the in-crowd: the brand-new – what? An amused grunt in his chest as he wondered what to call them, these citizens of all races who had so happily taken over the reins of power, replacing the monochrome rulers of the past.

The glitterati? No. That's got no political weight – no dignitus. How about the nouvelle demimonde? Gratify those among this gilded bunch with sophisticated pretensions – gained overseas with a capital O, of course! – from their time in European exile. Picked up a smattering of French, and now superior to those other exiles who spent their years just north of the Limpopo or, worse luck, east of the Lebombo Mountains in Maputo. Poor and dusty liberation centres that sorely lacked the sophistication and glamour of metropoles like London, Paris, New York – even Moscow and East Berlin, for God's sake, he chuckled silently.

But, of course, all of them above us stay-at-home 'inxiles'. Lusaka better than Maputo, because time spent there suggested, at least, a nodding acquaintance with those members of the ANC's government-in-waiting who now had offices inside the Union Buildings and the ministerial complex on Parliament Street in Cape Town.

Now – come on, man! he scolded himself. Being spiteful because you've never been out of the country isn't like you, Phil: not cool, my *brikaid.* None of that reverse snobbery for the returnees and these others who've become jet-set tourists since their elevation into politicals and corporate executives. Yes, okay, he apologised to himself. But, dammit, they do love dropping place-names and showing off their expense-account finery and big-time connections. Why, they crowd into this hotel at the slightest excuse because it graces the leafy northern suburbs their mothers had known as domestics and washerwomen.

Its popularity has overtaken the Carlton's, and that ancient monument to golden wealth – tallest building in Africa, remember! – has been forced to close its doors; downtown Jo'burg suffers from an infestation of violent criminals, while the leafy northern suburbs still have a semblance of safety … Which exile was it, on a scouting trip after Madiba's release – "just checking out this new scene before I make a firm decision" – walked goggle-eyed into the Carlton? His first time in the kind of place he remembered as a 'Slegs vir Blankes' reserve. And said, after he recovered, the lounge bar still looked and felt – "all these black faces, my brikaid!" – and sounded – "all this loud talk and uproarious laughter, man!" – like the shebeens he'd known way back.

Now, those voices have been modulated by big money and high office, political and corporate. And their networking is discreet and costs more in this epicentre of high society that looks like a prison from the outside.

Philip Mokone's solitary and sardonic humour veered towards irritation when his wandering eye recognised the threat that he was about to be dragged into the networking circuit. Heunis Swanepoel was heading his way, and looked as if he were quickly briefing a woman who had to be his wife on the socio-political need for her to be introduced to yet another of these black men dominating this official function.

The décolletage of her evening frock was too low-slung for her age, and the bony shoulders it bared didn't cause a twitch in his loins. The belief that they're all so fucking delectable hasn't changed … but now wasn't the time for that, old man, he scolded himself as he averted his eyes from bare white flesh and put out five fingers to shake the meaty hand of Heunis Swanepoel. A younger man but much bigger, and Philip had to look up at what could've been a rugby second-row forward in youthful times, when apartheid generously provided all the good food and other benefits to which Heunis was entitled by birth. What chance do our boys, still raised on pap and vleis, have against them in a scrum?

"Howzit, Philip?" Swanepoel was saying, then quickly turning to his wife without waiting for a response. "And now you get to meet the man, skat – Mister Philip Mokone, chairman of –"

"Please, Heunis – asseblief, meneer!" He was cut off, and Philip let go the sweaty ham of a hand imprisoning his fingers. "Not those formalities, man!" He softened the sharp tone with a smile for the wife, and offered his fingers to her painted talons. "That's only the second time he's called me that 'mister' thing, you know. And why tonight – when this is supposed to be an informal toenadering of the –"

Swanepoel smirked. "Informal or not, Philip, it's still an official function! And since you're the chairman – sorry, meneer – chair, hey?" he laughed, "of our portfolio committee ... You know."

"What, Heunis?"

"Well, a member of the opposition has to show respect for one of the best leaders in the Gauteng legislature!"

Philip took a silent but ironic bow. The man's coming on too strong, he was thinking as the wife gushed at him, still pumping his hand. Long fingers that would've stroked ecstasy into any lucky man when she was still young, lissom and pneumatic. Even if the boobs were only the size of apples.

"And you know what?" came the rhetorical question. "Heunis says you're such a good chair, because even if you ANC people have this big – this overwhelming – majority in the Legislature and also in Parliament ..." She paused for breath, then continued: "Heunis says you're still fair and sometimes even – er, impartial?"

"Why not?" Philip grinned, regaining his hand and wondering if those tapering fingers still electrified Heunis. But then distraction nipped in from a different direction. Was she being so – well, whatever – because her oke was planning to defect from the Democratic Party? Another seeking sanctuary in the ranks of the rulers who could – maybe would – stay in power past the four decades of Nat rule? Does Heunis want to climb aboard for a safe seat on what his motor-mouth party sneers at as a gravy train? A staff-rider who didn't want to lose his footing and fall onto the rails under the speeding train? A lot of township would-be *klevahs* had fallen victim to that death-defying trick. Their running along the train or bus was fine, but they couldn't break from its increasing rhythm and swing on board while fare-paying *moegoes* gasped.

"Yes," he was saying to her and smiling. "Why not indeed? We have this 'overwhelming' majority as you say. So why not be kind to the DP and the rest of the opposition? Even if Heunis and his fellow democrats – so-called, Heunis," he added, giving Swanepoel a sardonic grin. "You believe, don't you, that democracy means always sniping at us, right?"

Swanepoel frowned, hurt by the rebuke, which Philip softened: "The way Tony's leading your verbal charge – shooting from the lip and hip – you've got a chance to win big in the '99 elections, since Marthinus is still dumb-struck at becoming leader of the Nats."

"You really think so?"

"But Thabo's not going to be so full of reconciliation as Madiba."

They laughed and chatted for a while, but then Swanepoel's eyes started to wander, seeking another political trophy. He led his wife away to continue his networking campaign.

Philip exchanged the empty glass for another from a passing waitress, whose cleavage promised dusky pillows for a night of bouncing passion. Whoa, boy, he reminded himself: You're getting too old for such lustful thoughts. The nights are long gone when cherries could whisper that there wasn't much sleep in your bed, lover boy. Not quite past it; but this free-flowing booze at the tax-payers' expense is giving me ideas …

"Ja, *timer*," a half-jeering voice drawled behind him. "Yeah, man. I know just what you're thinking about – sies! Old as you are, but sharp eyes still roaming the room and sliding over dangerous curves. Altyd ander mense se cherries – neh?"

He turned slowly, sensing trouble in the casual challenge. The wizened face was vaguely familiar, and the sneering manner a give-away: they had to have been young together in another, distant age. In Sophiatown, when a jeering and sneering attitude to life was favoured by the *wake-up* as a defence against all the brutalities of apartheid. A careless bravado against unfair odds, and bred by a bitter cynicism.

"If I'm a timer, my brikaid, what about you – hey?" he asked the elderly man. Had to hang tough with the insulting bastard or be given a hard time. "I've still got hair on my head, ou toppie – and you're a cheese kop!"

The man grinned, stroked his bald head and said with a disdainful laugh: "Okay – but maybe you dye yours, eh? So you can still get a bit of *skondaai*, neh? But not as much I hope – and all fucking free! – like when you were a pretty boy in Soph'town! These days even politicians have to pay for young cherries. Right?"

Another insult, but the man was still smiling – once the crucial difference between friendly teasing and a challenge that could not be ignored. And yet another challenging insult: "Not so pretty now – hey, Nice Time Phil?"

"And not as ugly as you, brikaid." Tone flat, voice quiet, and the responsive insult ignored: level terms.

"But I have to look at your ugly face in the papers – and even on television."

Who the hell is this short-arse bastard? Obviously a klevah from Sophiatown, who sounds like he could still hold a grudge from the old days, when I was resented and threatened for enticing cherries from guys like him? Times when knowing thine enemies was a necessity of life – only way of staying alive. Those faint scars on his bald and gleaming head suggest he was the kind I had to stay on sort-of-friendly terms with to avoid too many dust-ups. One of *die manne* – the *majita* – who wielded three-star knives. Definitely not one of *die real manne* who carried Mausers and Lugers: like Chanam, who called himself the Durango Kid and opened fire at will to prove he was a really bad-bad outlaw.

"Yeah – you don't remember me, do you, *nice-timer*?" the man sneered. "Just because you're a sort-of big-shot politician, now? A defender of democracy! You of all people, hey – Nice Time Phil!"

"Like just said, your ugly face was out of sight a long time, my brikaid."

"I'm not your fucking brother!" But, again, the man laughed. "You really mean you don't remember me from the old days, Philip?"

"Those 'old days' were forty years ago – and more."

"But I remember you, jou moerskont!"

"Because, like you say, you see my – hey, wait a minute! Of course I remember you – jou lae luis!"

Philip laughed away the insult as, suddenly, the recognition switch clicked in his head, the memory banks whirred and focussed on an angry, youthful face on the dusty streets of a Sophiatown since razed to the ground for being a 'black spot'.

"Not your ugly mug, but I remember that voice – who can forget the fucking noise you made?"

The man grinned, happy at last and now expectant.

"Of course you're not my fucking brother, jou moerskont," the elderly politician went on, using swearwords that had not passed his lips for decades. "Just a *tsotsi* called Boykie Eightpence! Right – old-timer?"

They laughed and embraced, then stood apart and stared at each other, noting traces of the passing years on faces and bodies. And laughed even louder the second time. Faces turned, frowned and stared, but the elders were lost in memories that had to be funny and tragic, good and evil.

"Ja – die's ek, *my ma se kind*!" said the man whose nickname marked an incident – most likely a crime – in his youth. Boykie Eightpence tapped his own chest. "But this is not any kind of Boykie now – eight pence or even one hundred rands, you hear me, pretty boy? Otherwise I'll fuck you up – right now and here in front of all these *situations* who respect you. Mister fucking Politician!'

Philip held up his arms in mock surrender.

"Ja, ek *notch* jou, groot man," he said, pretending fright. "I mean you know we situations were always poep-scared of you tsotsis!" Philip laughed, bringing down his arms. "Me – sommer now a situation, eh?"

"I didn't say you were a situation, just that – Oh, what the fuck? Just a blerry klevah but not so fucking clever! Slaved for *laanies* while we – die real manne, die majita wat notch ..."

"Mugged old men and moegoes straight from the farms?" Philip sneered.

"Nee, man! You know we had just one target, man – laanies met groot *ching*! Not poor darkies – no money there!"

They laughed, but this time like boys sharing a secret, dirty joke.

"So?" Philip asked. "What're you called now, Boykie Eightpence?" A malicious grin at the pained expression that flitted across the other's face. "I mean, nobody ever knew your real name. Except, maybe, your mother."

"Why tell everybody your secrets? Some of us had sense, klevah!"

"The guys who went to school with you just forgot. So – what's the big secret, Boykie?"

"Don't say that, man! I'm a businessman now – successful. And use my real name." A sly, malicious glint in the eyes: "No slave mentality, you see – sticking to a laanie name like Philip."

"I like it, Boykie."

"Nhlanhla – no more Boykie."

Philip laughed at the politically correct man. "So the good luck is still with you, eh! Making a lot of honest money at last?"

"I was born lucky. Why d'you think they gave me the name?"

"But what happened after they bulldozed Soph'town and we were moved to Meadowlands? Never saw you there, after their guns made a joke of that song of defiance – 'ons duck nie, ons *phola* hier'."

"Me – do what those fokken *boere* tell me? Never, man! So, we all had to duck from Soph'town – they had the guns, like you say. But my family went to phola in Alex. Freehold property there, jy notch! Not like tenants in that fucking Meadowlands. Where you all had to put up coloured rags outside those matchbox houses because they looked the same. And the streets had no names – just long numbers nobody remembered!"

"We learned to remember them, Boykie." He held up an appeasing hand as the other's eyes flickered in anger. "Sorry – I mean Nhlanhla," he smiled. "You know, I didn't even know you were a Zulu."

"Who cared in those days. Didn't mean shit – except to moegoes straight from the platteland!"

"And now – where does the successful businessman phola?"

Offhand but proud: "In Kelvin – and, man don't –" a wagging, warning finger: "and don't call it 'Alexandra Extension' like some of you guys who've moved into these big-time, leafy suburbs! I also got a big house with a swimming pool, you know." He sneered, "We're all laanies now, jy notch!"

Spiteful grin: "But can you swim these days?"

Indignant: "What you think! Where could we learn with no swimming pools?" And proudly: "But my grandchildren are getting good in the water ... And you, Phil?" That sneer again: "A big mansion, I suppose – maybe two swimming pools and tennis courts in Sandton, eh? And all of it from all the taxes we pay?"

The politician had heard enough gravy-train jokes and snide remarks, and replied quietly, "I don't steal from anybody – just like I don't drive a delivery bakkie any more – Boykie Eightpence!"

The man born lucky only grinned at the implied rebuke.

"But I'm doing okay, my ma se kind," Philip added, grinning back: If you can dish it out, you've gotta swallow it too, my mother's child.

"Somebody told me once – years and years ago, man – that by some miracle you uplifted yourself and became a lawyer. I couldn't believe it, man – you?" came another sneer from the wizened face that was still as outraged at life, at everything, as it had been when they were growing up in Sophiatown.

"No, Nhlanhla – you're right. Just a legal clerk in one of the first practices – companies, I mean – of black lawyers. After Mandela and Tambo opened the fortified gates."

"I know about 'practices', man – give 'em a lot of my business, you know." A calculating pause: "And I suppose that's where you started getting into politics – 'activist' in the UDF, or maybe the SACP." A sly wink: "Because with the commies, white girls skondaai anybody. Whatcha-ma-call-it – free love?"

"Sort of, Nhlanhla – but not that communist crap. I only really got into politics – became your 'activist' – in 1976. After my daughter, my eldest girl, went missing during the Uprising. A lovely girl – so bright and beautiful that ..."

"She wasn't the only kid who disappeared those days, Phil," he was consoled while lost for words. "Did you find out what happened?"

"Found her body in a mortuary – in a stinking pile, my brikaid. After searching for a whole, bloody week. A bullet, maybe two, in her back."

"Those fucking *gattas*!"

"I still miss her, you know. More'n twenty years, and I still miss her."

"No other kids?"

"Oh, a couple of boys – also in business like you, now."

"So what're you complaining about – with two boys doing well?"

Philip laughed; but sadly: "I'm not a Zulu who believes only boys can –"

"Tribalist!" Nhlanhla jeered and smiled. "And I'm not a sexist either, you know. But, hey – what about that kitchen girl you – sorry, man! Your beautiful wife, I mean?"

Philip laughed. "You must've also eaten *dogs' meat* when you visited *sheilas* working in the kitchens. We all checked out the avenues – *die Avies*, remember? – for talent."

"And that's where we now live!"

"Right – residents in suburbia, and Betty has her own kitchen girl – except they're called 'helpers' these days. No more sneaking in through the back gate and staying out of sight in the tiny room hidden behind tall bushes at the back of the garden."

"I didn't have to do that, one time," Nhlanhla grinned, smug and proud. "I had this *weebit* who worked for the Japanese ambassador in Pretoria – which got me diplomatic immunity from police raids! That mansion was foreign territory, you see!" A sly look and grin from the one-time tsotsi: "But now it's you – the klevah who sold *back-door* stuff – now you're almost above the law! Right?"

"No way! Not me, man. I told you I don't steal from –"

"Hau! But you're now a big-shot, right? A member of ... pouting chest and mimicking an overbearing manner: "... the Gauteng Provincial Legislature! You make the laws, brikaid – right?"

"Make them but I don't –"

"And all just because your darling little daughter was killed by the cops?"

Philip's response was sharp with asperity: "You fucking ...!" But then aborted. He took a deep breath and grinned as he would have back in the old days when playing it cool was the thing: "Okay – Boykie Eightpence. You're right – once a crook, always crooked. Right?"

Nhlanhla only laughed.

"And fuck you too, moerskont!" Philip snapped.

The highly respected senior provincial politician walked away from the successful businessman. Only momentarily overwhelmed by the raw emotions of days long gone. When they were both young, brash – and criminals by necessity and intent to varying degrees. When the overpowering emotion in him had been a frustration he attempted to spit out in several ways, most of them physical.

And fathered kids – no, dammit, sprayed his seed recklessly – among nice-time girls, and half-decent ones who didn't know where to go when the seed flowered. And no thought for the buds that bloomed from his careless loins. Weeds, really, and best forgotten. Except, maybe, one of them. He would always wonder about her. What was her name again?

Chapter 1

It was a warm night in Johannesburg. A scarf of diaphanous cloud was strewn across a sky glimmering with stars. A rising wind rustled through the trees along a busy avenue in Hillbrow: then still a trendy and fashionable flatland, home of the young but advantaged – the first step towards a house in a leafy suburb farther north, where the air was scented by blooms from one's own garden. Beyond the brow of that next hill and down to Joubert Park was the city's golden heart, pumping lucre.

The sough of the wind against the apartment buildings, the murmur of leaves, the purr of big, gleaming cars ... the sounds of a city night chorused into an exhilarating, limb-loosening expectation within Jean Ryan. The wind dragged her dress against her thighs, and she felt glad – to be alive, to be beautiful, to be young.

Who was the poet who wrote, 'to be young was very heaven'? But that was about events centuries ago – the French Revolution? Who cares. But he was right, Jean thought. It would indeed be very heaven if Patrick were home and I didn't have to make up excuses to get out of the flat. It was stifling, after another day alone inside.

The street lamps formed pools of light on the twin pavements sloping down the gentle hill. They massed into a bright cluster and detoured round the big, flower-filled traffic island, then straightened out again into military precision to march up the other hill and over its rounded brow. Then down into the garish fairy-land of night-time Johannesburg, where she and Pat could've been dancing in some nightclub.

It was a beautiful and peaceful night to be out, though.

Jean paused at the entrance to the alley between the apartment buildings, eyes dreaming about what lay beyond the hill in the money-pumping city. Sucked the soothing, caressing air into her body with the contentment of a Highveld evening. She raised one arm languorously above her head, then brought the hand down to press into the back of her neck, fluffing her yellow-gold hair with sensuous movements.

She felt unaccountably happy and free. She wanted to laugh and sing.

If only Patrick were home now. She'd hurry back and – she giggled to herself at the pictures flitting into her mind as sudden desire inflamed her limbs. He'll be back soon enough, my girl. After a bachelor evening out and full of alcohol – not drunk, but loaded for more than he can handle. So loaded he has to go on and on and on, before – and often enough he doesn't make the fyndraai, as the Boers say; but I do, on and on ... She almost laughed out loud this time at the thought of him and his exciting frustration while she went through ecstasy after ecstasy. If only he were home, now. But he's not, and I'll have to wait.

The waiting would be so much easier if we had children for me to fuss over ...

She broke off that thought. A sudden emptiness at the return of the nagging knowledge: they could not have children. Perhaps some day, please God, one day soon ...

Don't you start on that, now, she admonished herself firmly. Too beautiful a night for self-pity. Back to the flat, now; that luxurious but empty flat. Make that hot chocolate that was the excuse for coming out to buy milk, when you should know better. Still some Natives lurking about, despite the police patrols. If only it was safe enough to go for a real walk: a stroll through these quiet streets, on this beautiful night ...

Hah! A walk! This is Jo'burg. Only the foolhardy and the criminal walk these streets on any night. It's dangerous enough just going round the corner for this milk.

She turned away from the street into the familiar darkness of the alleyway. Forty steps – don't forget those three rubbish bins, now; and turn left through the little gate into the small backyard of the apartment building; then ten steps to the foot of the back stairs, thirty steps up, and home. Empty home.

It was a dank and smelly alley, but she preferred it tonight to the front entrance where her mood would be destroyed by the polite smiles and hellos, the stiff nods and those eyes that refuse to show recognition: the neighbourly rituals of the foyer, lifts and corridors. She wanted to spare herself, and maintain the mood the night air had instilled.

She walked past the first dustbin, then took an easy, long-legged stride across the faintly-seen puddle near it. She walked a few steps further – then her heart missed a beat. There was some other person in the alley. Don't panic now, she told herself as her body was enveloped in a cold fright. You don't have exclusive rights to this alley.

But a strange man in the alley with me. And black …

It was pitch dark. She could sense the familiar landmarks through her fear. She could also sense this unknown, frightening presence. She walked steadily, carefully on: you mustn't be frightened; and don't show it if you are. Don't look back.

She was weak and dizzy with apprehension; a foreboding of the terror she expected to descend on her at every laboured breath. Recriminations swamped her mind. Why did you have to come out at all? Couldn't you do without your precious hot chocolate for one night, after all the warnings? Patrick's made you promise so often to keep yourself safe.

And why come down this horrible alley? Why not use the front door like everybody else? Preserving a mood! You stupid romantic!

The peaceful contentment permeating the warm, starry night for Jean Ryan did not find its way into Philip Mokone as he walked along a darker side-street of whites-only Hillbrow after dark. He was restless; brimming over with nervous energy like he used to be when he drove for the travelling salesmen, who regarded him as a machine attached to a steering wheel. After driving all night on the Benzedrine tablets his white bosses solicitously fed him – "dankie, my baas!" – before trying to sleep in the car loaded down with the samples he'd be flogging in the morning, bright and chirpy.

He told himself he was not that tired or hyped up tonight. Just annoyed. No – irritated, frustrated. He hadn't seen the girl after all. Well, he had seen her; but that hadn't been the idea. He had wanted to do more than just see her. All that cajoling and planning; but then the white woman, her Missus, suddenly decides to have a party. That's the trouble with going after domestic servants: the Madam's whims come first. That's the trouble with being black, he corrected himself: all whites come first, the bastards.

So now on the way home to Sophiatown. And he was not going to let them make him unhappy. It wasn't the thirteenth or thirteen hundredth time they'd messed him up and he wasn't going to give them that satisfaction. Maybe he was just tired. Driving the delivery van through those ruts called streets in the townships, and having to drag out a smile and patter of bright conversation for those incompetents playing at being shopkeepers. Feeling sorry for them, while he played at being a proper salesman after his promotion. But having to threaten them for prompt payment because the cashier – that other first-class white bastard! – had threatened him ...

He told himself he could not really be exhausted if he'd been looking forward so much to seeing the kitchen girl in Lower Houghton – a wise-up cherry to be working for high-class laanies. That kind of 'seeing' needed plenty of energy. Maybe just waiting for her in that tiny, stuffy room at the bottom of Madam's garden had done it. Couldn't even open a window, just in case some blue-eyed bastard glommed him.

Well, so it was going to be one of those Sophiatown nights, followed by a hangover tomorrow. But first the long walk, miles and miles, from bloody Houghton and across town to the bus rank on Diagonal Street. And dodging cops all the time, bloody gattas. Not such a fucking long walk to the Noord Street rank. But that's if I lived in Alex, way north and out of town in the bundu – and who wants to live with those moegoes who're proud they don't have street lights, and call it their 'dark city'? Only moegoes are that stupid! Soph'town, anytime: stamping ground of the only real klevahs and *die really real manne*! Kofifi, home of die majita.

Probably worse than a hangover, he grinned to himself, if he was lucky and could *skep* – pick up a girl in one of the shebeens. Those nice-time girls don't let you sleep, man. Ah, yes – Christmas every night in the kaffir city, he jeered at himself. Don't these black bastards ever stop boozing and rutting? He almost laughed out loud, remembering the expression on the red, congested face of the dispatcher, good old Baas Benade, at the wholesale company he worked for. They had promoted him to dizzy heights for a kaffir because the locations had become too dangerous for white salesmen.

Make a good propagandist for the government, talking like that – thinking about us like them. People of the civilised world, listen good! We barbaric, smelly black savages are very happy under the jackboot of apartheid. So please don't criticise, condemn, blackball – no, white-ball? – or boycott our beloved whites-only government, we beg you!

Just ask our respected and admired leaders, our masters and teachers, to make it an offence for our own women, all of them known to be promiscuous, to be kept out of our beds by the whims of white women. White women who arrange endless parties so they don't have to go to bed with their men. The poor, flat-arsed, ice-cold bitches! As long as we have booze and women, dear misinformed people of the world, there's nothing more we could want. Equality? Freedom? What for? Heaven can wait, man! After all, people of the world, we're only a few years down from the trees, don't you know? Please just give us another thousand years to learn about civilisation. While the white-man-boss gives us a paternal kick in the backside and lives off the fat of the land – our land, of course, that we so happily exchanged for the Bible and servitude. A very fair and civilised exchange! They can have this world, and we'll have the next, the missionaries have assured us pagans.

Aah …! What's the use? Philip sneered at himself. That's the way the ball bounces, and that's how it will continue to bounce. And the cookie crumbles. Just forget the bastards and live the best way you can. As good a life as possible. Good? What does that mean, Mister Mokone? Not Bible-good, of course. So what else can it mean? Aah, forget it. Leave that philosophical stuff to Boykie and Desmond. You're going to have a few drinks with the boys – well, maybe several – and, if you're lucky, end up in bed with a frisky filly.

A bedding a day keeps the blues away. Sing the blues, if you like; or drink, screw and fight them away. I don't want to wake up tomorrow with – how does the song go? The blues standing by the door and still not gone …

He smiled, his angular face assuming a saturnine expression. He straightened his slim body from the slouch his thoughts had made him adopt, and padded along on crêpe-soled shoes: hands deep in trouser pockets and a stylish, narrow-brimmed Battersby hat tilted rakishly over his eyes.

He turned left in Hillbrow and walked along the wall of one of the huge apartment buildings. His step was now jaunty, and there was a smile on his lips – puckered for whistling a blues tune he preferred to remain unheard. He slowed down, wary, when he saw a laughing group of white people come down the stairs of the brightly lit entrance to the apartment block. He did not want to have to stop and openly concede them the right of way – an adjustment that had become almost automatic behaviour for his kind.

His timing was just right, as it almost always was for these covert assertions of his personal dignity. He passed a few feet behind them as they massed at a car in the line parked at the kerb. One of the women turned to laugh into the face of the man behind her; but the flirty smile burgeoning into laughter froze momentarily when her eyes met Philip's, beyond the man's broad shoulders. She spoke in an amused, loudly jeering voice:

"What's he so cocky about?"

Other heads turned to stare at Philip, who looked straight ahead and pretended he had not heard. One of the men supplied an answer:

"The kitchen maid's just given him a taste of the master's whisky."

They laughed in a chorus of voices whose tones were more spiteful than amused. Several interjected explanations and comments into the jeering laughter:

"Do you think that's all he got? I bet he slipped in a quick stiff one between the soup and the meat!"

"Of course, yes – they don't think of anything else!"

"I heard that –"

Philip would hear no more. He was not sure if he shut out the insults, as all black people learn to do, or if the voices had become an indistinct, hysterical babble as he walked farther away. He did not alter the pace or jaunty manner of his walk; if he had, he felt, their spite would have been gratified. And if he stopped or openly reacted, he would probably have been assaulted: "What're you standing there for, kaffir?"; "Why're you looking at the Missus, hey, you fokken black bastard?"; "Hey, are you listening to our private talk, kaffir?"

But they were in a good mood, and perhaps it would only have resulted in an almost light-hearted kick in the pants to send him on his black way.

Hope you got your kicks, white woman. Who d'you say can't think of anything else? Hope it'll add some excitement to yours tonight, just thinking of me banging away between servings. Don't you get your – aah, the hell with all of them! Bastards. Forget about them.

They're only important eight hours a day. Just keep out of their way the rest of the time, and lead your own life – which isn't so bad if you can forget some things and ignore others.

He turned left again, into a broad avenue whose street lights were fragmented and dimmed by the trees; giving the thoroughfare a darkling, brooding atmosphere. He knew it well and did not have to look down its gentle slope to the traffic island or up the reverse slope to the horizon. There, he knew, the pulsing glow of the city's fun-time lights would be, mirrored in the clouds above. He walked at a slower pace now, the jauntiness jeered out of his step.

He saw her standing near the entrance to the alley, with a gracefully arrogant tension about her stance and sensuous body that made his first reaction one of simple, manly admiration. Then three words wiped the appreciation from his mind: another of them!

What's she standing there looking so proud for? Aah, maybe just a prostitute waiting for cruising Romeos in their American cars. Naa! Just one of them. Proud, high and mighty: another white goddess. Gazing up at the sky like – whatsamatter, white woman? D'you have to pray to the moon for it, now? No man to ... ? Got one, but he's no good at it?

All that arrogance, that superiority and contempt for us: the rutting kaffirs who've got it round the clock. Maybe I should volunteer my services, poor bitch. He laughed.

Yet he slowed down further. Why not? Teach them all – No! Don't even think of it, my *bra.* Hang for something so stupidly crazy? Nothing's worth that – *die hangpaal.* Wouldn't be any fun in it, anyway. But that's what they think of us: ever ready, and especially for white meat. Yes, and that's no reason to prove them right. Though she – they, all of them – deserve to be dragged down into ... aah, forget about it, bright boy. You crazy?

His mind registered her disappearance into the alley, but only moments after she had gone. He was glad she was gone. Now he would not even have to bother about these crazy thoughts teasing his mind. Yet it did not disappear with her, this crazy idea. It bobbed to the surface each time he thought he had submerged it. When it did, he was frightened and excited. Because each time it came with an increased urgency and attraction. It was a short and furious battle, during which he cursed and observed the hardening of this urge to rape the unknown woman, the symbol.

I won't do it, he told himself angrily. I can't do it, dammit! But why not? an inner voice asked. What've you got to lose? They'll hang me, that's all – and it's a crazy and evil thing, he admonished the temptation. That pampered body, those perfumed white thighs ... No! I will not. What's so important about whiteness? Those nose-in-the-air bitches, ball-breakers! That's why they deserve it, the insidious inner voice said. This is your one chance – take it! He shuddered at the image of himself thrusting between the white thighs for the first time ever.

No, dammit! Your last chance, Philly. Don't let it go. Why should you leave her? Hell, you can get away with it, man! You're a klevah and you can do it, boy. And not just because she's white meat, or anything stupid like that. But because she's one of them. Just to show them what you think of them. You'll never get another easy chance like this, man! But who wants to do such a thing?

His mind was in a turmoil of excitement, fear and challenge. Show them you're not afraid; show them they're not the extra-specials they think they are.

A moment of painfully clear realisation flashed through his mind as he approached the dark mouth of the alley: the consequences of such an action, the frustration and humiliations of his life. What did it matter what happened to him? Why the hell shouldn't he do it, and to hell with everything else?

He turned sharply into the alley, refusing to look cautiously about him or even ahead. A small portion of his mind still hoped she would have vanished completely from his life. She had not.

Jean Ryan reached the narrow servants' gate that led into the courtyard of her apartment block. She rested on bruised hands and torn knees. Her head hung low between her shoulders: the long, yellowish hair trailing down to the rough, pockmarked tarmac of the alleyway.

Can I crawl up? How many rough, concrete steps? She tried to concentrate and remember their number, ignoring everything else – the pain, the exhaustion, the numbness, the residue of terror, the misery, the humiliation. After what seemed an aeon she decided she could not drag herself up the steps. The street, she thought. People driving, some still walking. Still early. What time is it? The thought of looking at her wristwatch made her head whirl – a dizzy idea. Maybe it's stopped, anyway. Time has stopped. It ought to go back.

Slowly, painfully, she crawled back. On past the rubbish bins, through the puddle she had stepped over so easily – how long ago? Crawled on torn knees towards the illuminated darkness that was the pavement, safety, rest … Not rescue. Too late for that.

She stopped just beyond the entrance to the alleyway. The scarf of cloud that had been flung across the stars was torn; its rolled-up shreds tumbled before a rushing wind. The trees moaned under the pressure of the wind and their leaves crackled with a harsh, frightened sound. The pools of light seemed further apart, their march down to the traffic island and up the other hill wavered and staggered. A car squealed and roared round the traffic island and up that hill towards the city lights.

The street and pavements were empty of people.

Rest, now. In the light and safe. Nothing worse can happen. Over, everything. Finished, absolute. Rest … then perhaps move further into the street lights. Drown in a pool of murky light. A little rest, first. Now.

She rolled slowly, painfully onto her side. Then settled on her stomach. She pillowed her head on limp arms. The yellowish hair spread out on the pavement, a lesser pool of incandescence. She closed her eyes slowly, wearily. But in the darkened theatre behind her burning eyelids, dazzled scenes of humiliating horror flashed and jerked and spun. Dizzying her. She fluttered her eyes open in wild relief, away from that theatre of cruelty. A violent shudder convulsed her body and a sobbing moan escaped puffed lips. A moan that was ragged and filled with despair.

Philip left her spread-eagled in the filth and darkness at the end of the blind alley. He walked slowly, carefully, towards the light of the pavement, concentrating on brushing the dirt off his clothes. Refusing to think or remember what he had just done. He stopped within the alley's entrance, reconnoitred the broad thoroughfare: empty. Then walked briskly down the street, close to the walls of buildings and away from street lights. No problem if this was a dark city like Alexandra: plenty of lights here for the laanies …

Well, I've done it. Showed them. What, my ma se kind, *ngoana oa mme*? a new voice asked inside his head. A head whirring with exultation after the body doing it – the unthinkable. Well, of course showed 'em that – aah, the hell with it. I did it! I can't call it back. And I'm glad I did it. And now let's forget about it and stick with staying alive. But he could not forget. Was he really glad? Had he enjoyed it – her? Hah! How could he, that cold bitch who lay there in the filth like a dead fish or something? He had not wanted to enjoy anything, anyway, or expected to. Rape? Dammit, he'd refused an invitation once in Sophiatown because he'd known there would be nothing to enjoy. Some poor plaas-sheilas on their days off from slaving on the farm ...

No way was he going into that tsotsi scene. He was a klevah, and called Pretty Boy Phil by plenty of nice-time babes offering all that they were showing. To which he responded, come *duze*, baby ...

There were also other reasons for not getting any kicks in that stinking alley. But he couldn't put his finger on them, not yet, anyway. But, one of his voices whispered, there had to be a difference between this and the Soph'town invitations: this had been a white woman, dammit. There should've been more to it – not enjoyment, but pleasure from defiling her. Them. Show the lot of them that – what? Well, teach them a lesson. That we don't do it because we expect the immaculate whiteness will – oh, fuck it! How the hell would any of them, would she know the difference?

Just drag her down; that's all. Into the muck. Your muck in which your *botho* has drowned, pretty boy? No, dammit, not my muck. I still have humanity, ubuntu! I'm as good as the next decent man, and I don't have to drag anybody down to my level. It's their muck – they created it for us, didn't they? Give them a taste of living down in the gutter. On their backs in filth.

He stood on the brow of the hill and looked down on the bright, harsh lights of Johannesburg, City of Gold: Gauteng, Egoli, where everybody scuffled for a living. A long walk still to Diagonal and the buses, but he should be home in another hour or less. But, he suddenly remembered, there was danger for him on those bright-lit streets. If she's been found, squad cars with tall radio antennas will be picking up every black man in sight. The usual suspects – Christ!

He looked quickly down at his smart, *dogs'-meat*-seduction clothes.

They were not suspiciously soiled. But that wouldn't make any difference to the gattas. He was black, and they would pick him up.

So what to do? He couldn't think as fast and clearly as he wanted to – or should, being a klevah, born and bred in Jo'burg. He needed a drink, and fast. There was so much to think about. Maybe just get drunk. He looked at the buildings about him and recognised one of the apartment blocks. There was a shebeen on the roof of that one, he remembered; in bloody Verwoerd's 'location in the sky', populated by domestic servants who lived in rooms so tiny the beds were high up on bricks, so they could store their boxes underneath.

He would lose himself among all of the boozers.

Philip was wrong about the shebeen's location. It was not on the roof but in the basement garage. Had to walk between lines of shiny cars and knock at a small, plain door. And the joint was not run by a kitchen girl: the door was opened by a small, heavily-moustached old man who glared at him with truculent suspicion.

The unknown interloper mumbled an apologetic explanation for his unknown face and unexpected presence. He was allowed into the over-heated, dimly lit boiler room, and said a friendly good evening to the few customers in the shadows. Asked for half a jack of brandy, and when the pleased janitor brought it – his other clients could only afford to *gazaat* for a nip – Philip offered everybody a drink. Not much: a symbolic tot into the extended mugs. He needed most of it for himself.

So you wanted to defile her. And there she lay in the muck, the only sign of life ragged breathing, eyes shut. Maybe unconscious. Didn't hurt her, though. Not a virgin. No, not that kind of hurting. Not a physical thing, but a – a ...

Aah, forget it and drink up.

The squad cars are already picking up every single darkie on the streets. She's started squawking, and even if she's still knocked out by the shock and humiliation, they'll know what happened and go hunting.

They'll hang me. No, they won't get you, man. Just another black face.

He sighed into the mug full of cheap brandy. Funny thing is, I'm not afraid. Not really. Don't want to get die hangpaal or anything; but I really don't care. Only worry is their angry red faces poked into mine and the bullying questions. The beatings in the charge office and the cells. I won't tell them a thing, the bastards. I've been there before – we all have.

His skin crawled: not with fear but revulsion at his anticipation of the humiliation. The rage of his arrest – come on, jou fokken kaffer; the kicking and bundling into a charge office – vinnig, jou moerskont; the crude interrogations – let's see your fucking smelly great cock; the beatings; and, finally, the trial with his friends amazed that he could do such a thing ... The hanging would come as a relief.

It would all of it be such a shaming violation of his privacy, those preliminaries to that plunging moment inside Pretoria Central. A privacy made more delicate by uncertainty about his motives for the rape and, now, his reactions to the deed. He did not want to try or be forced to think or talk about it. If only they would shoot immediately they arrested him – that would be the easiest way out. He'd look so stupid if he tried to answer their questions, explain it all. How could he? Even if he wanted to; which he did not want to do even to himself. Maybe put up a fight, then they would be happy to shoot him. No: try to escape and they definitely would. If he put up a fight they'd just mess up his face. Escape. Mmm? No. He could not give them that satisfaction. Then there was the if: if they caught him, knew it was him, had definite evidence. They might round him up with all the other suspects, but that would not mean that they could ferret him out as the perpetrator from all the others. Nobody could give evidence against him. Not even the goddess: it was pitch dark – and we all look the same to them.

The Flying Squad car shuddered to a stop at the entrance to the tall block of apartments. Six policemen tumbled out of the rocking car, the whip-like antenna swinging, doors slamming, feet pounding across the pavement and stomping into the thick-carpeted foyer. The shrivelled janitor watched the invasion through eyes lit by a frightened fascination and respect. He was waiting at the bank of lifts for their arrival. The lift doors whispered shut behind the crowding policemen, who stared at their shine with bleak impatience. The gilded cage rose smoothly towards the roof, bearing its cargo of Law and Order – hard-eyed with legal righteousness and bitterness towards even the janitor – a fear-tinged resentment of all black men. 'Die swart gevaar ...'

The fear and resentment bore down heavily on two of the policemen: they were black, and the fury and bitterness of their masters-cum-colleagues did not exclude them. They were part of Black Manhood and its presumed violation of White Womanhood.

They feared the fury of the white world they had sworn to protect. And resented black men whom they had been browbeaten to believe were obvious suspects for any crime. Tonight, only a black was capable of such an act against the sanctity, the very fount, of their white rulers. It had to be a black man whose folly had them standing so self-effacing in this Europeans Only/Slegs Blankes lift. Their fear and resentment would drive the brutality they would inflict on this roof and any other tonight. The need to prove yet again to their masters and mentors that they were on the side of Law and Order and were, at the very least, equally infuriated by this presumptuous violation.

On the windy, gravelled roof, the policemen spread out in pairs without a word. The whites unbuttoning the flaps of pistol holsters, the blacks taking a firmer grip on their batons, winding leather straps around thick wrists. No need for instructions: each one of them had been on countless similar raids. Six more gattas came pounding up the back stairs – the goods lift stopped on the floor below – and crunched off among the low, box-like structures with tiny, high windows that housed the population of this location in the sky.

The beams of torchlight cutting through the darkness were duplicated on the roofs of neighbouring buildings as the guardians of Law and Order, and especially White Womanhood, rounded up all black men for the night's outrage. Their orders had been simple: round up all suspicious Natives – which meant all African men, for which one of them was not suspect from the moment of his birth?

They banged on, and kicked at, the flimsy doors.

"Open up!" white policemen barked. "Police!"

"Open the blerry door, you black bastards!" black policemen shouted.

Inside the tiny, stuffy rooms voices responded: cursed and grumbled in undertones. What's the trouble this time? We had a raid just last night … The bloody police! Why don't they go after the tsotsis murdering and robbing in the township streets? Afraid! Lazy! Stupid! The police! Just pests!

Doors were unlocked from inside and kicked open from the outside. Swords of light stabbed into the cubicles: flashing over rumpled beds, on the decoratively cut-up newspapers covering packing boxes fashioned into dressing-tables and chests of drawers; reflecting on slivers of discarded mirrors. Eyes stared with blinded resentment as the Law pushed at half-naked bodies, lifted blankets and peered under beds:

"No man tonight, eh, Annie? Don't they like you any more?"

Stiff fingers jabbed at hairy and hairless chests:

"Pass, you black bastard! Permit to be here! Tax receipt! All right, jong! Into your blerry clothes and outside with the other crooks!"

Half-dressed men were shoved, punched, dragged and kicked out of the airless cells into the wind-blown lanes between the bleak structures. A shoe was missing, a shirt – "What sock, jong? Get the blerry hell out. Didn't you hear me?" They were marshalled together near the stairs, but stood apart: alone in their humiliation, self-consciousness, anger and fear.

The dragnet had been cast wide over Hillbrow. It extended to the boiler room, in which all the liquor had miraculously disappeared at the first sounds of the raid. Philip and all the other men were herded out and into a police van.

The long, narrow charge office at the station was crowded with dishevelled, frightened, close-faced men. Black policemen glowered under helmets as they pushed and jabbed their prisoners into long lines. White policemen glared icy-eyed from under peaked caps, sorting out genuine domestic servants – the 'rou kaffers uit die platteland' – from the closed-faced tsotsis; it was a well-known fact that all city-bred kaffirs were criminals – past, present or future.

The large charge sergeant with a bushy moustache spoke into the final silence. One of you, he told them, has just raped a woman – a white woman, damn your donkey-sized cocks! It'd save police-time and all of them their health if the perpetrator came forward right now. They were going to get him, anyway, even if they had to twist all their bloated balls. Then they'd teach him a lesson. To stick it only to black whores – which he'd never have again, anyway; because he was going to hang and shit himself. If he stepped forward now, he'd be doing himself a favour. Because they'd be blerry angry when they got him. And if any of you bastards know who he is, you'd be doing yourselves a favour, too. Pointing him out – now. "Because, kêrels," the sergeant said with soft menace after the threats, "we're going to work on all of you tonight, tomorrow and the day after tomorrow. Until we know who did it. If we still don't know, the Missus will come here and point him out at the ID parade."

He grinned. "After that – after that, julle swartgat bliksems! – we shall see. Hy sal sy ma sien for forcing the Missus into the shame of looking at all your fokken lelike vuil gesigte!"

Philip stood relaxed in the sweaty tension, listening absent-mindedly to the threats and vilification. His emotions suspended, but eyes resting on the florid hate-filled face behind the charge desk. But barely saw the man. He'd been in other charge offices, and had heard such language often. In the past he'd been choked by an impotent anger. Never been able to flatter and humour as other klevahs did to avoid the impersonal brutality. Too choked by anger to force out the familiar phrases and be let off with a kick in the backside for infringing one of the countless paper offences that fenced in black lives.

But if he was given a beating tonight – as he would be – it would be the first time. His luck was overdrawn, and maybe he deserved it.

Yet he was not afraid nor angry. His only emotion was an odd kind of pity for the sergeant and his gang of enforcers. But he felt sorry for the men who were going to suffer so needlessly. For himself, only puzzlement at the absence of a catharsis that should have followed the violence he had brought down on an unknown woman. Her only identity was the colour of her skin. And that should have erased the half-hidden fury he had lived with for twenty years or so, since he had begun to perceive the contempt for his own colour in the society about him.

A fury that had increased and festered with the years. And had tonight warped his sense of self. What was left of his masculine pride.

The catharsis had been within reach, tonight: that must have been his forlorn, unconscious hope. But it had eluded him, and he was left with an uncomfortable void in which flitted bats demanding answers to new questions. So he listened to the sergeant without the familiar, impotent anger. Only a curious detachment. And realised that he was no longer afraid of these gattas. All of them, and the oppressive power they represented and of which they were brutal tools.

He pitied them. Themselves and what they represented.

Chapter 2

Philip Mokone lay in the corner of the cell furthest from the steel door and the leaking slop bucket that stood near it. His knees were drawn up to his chest to relieve the pains in his stomach and sides from the beating by the police. That assault had not been too bad, compared with some he had heard about. Too few policemen and too many victims for a thorough going-over, he decided. No broken bones, and they had not touched his face. He was grateful that the courts now took enough interest to act if a policeman was crude enough to make the beating obvious by hitting the black prisoner about the face and head. Philip was vain about his good looks.

The pains were not too bad, either; as long as he lay curled up like this on the straw matting that was his bed. He could take it. The worst beatings would start after they had narrowed down the suspects to a few: when she had identified whatever number looked the most likely villains to her. That was a gamble he would have to take; nothing he could do about that. Though he was certain she could not pick him out alone with any certainty. Too dark and she was taken by surprise. Scared. But he might still be among the finalists even if only because she thought he looked like a rapist. He listened to the groans and muttered curses of the other prisoners who littered the cement floor of the cell.

He was certain there would not be any more brought into this cell; too crowded already. So he could sleep now, if he wanted to, without being disturbed by the clanging of the steel door, the groans and thud of falling bodies. He did not think he would be able to fall asleep even in the most comfortable bed with all tonight's tangled thoughts going through his mind. Things he had not thought about for years, ever since he had been forced to leave high school and begun the painful process of blunting his sensitivities and ignoring his unfulfilled ambitions and ideals. He did not need ideals to be a chauffeur; in fact, that kind of thing was a downright disadvantage. It just made a person want to protest against the brutalising stupidities of the system, which was a dangerous thing to do – and pointless.

Now here they were with him, these thoughts; all crowding back into his head with additions and complications. He smiled at the phrase: it sounded like a problem in maths. Emotional mathematics. Where's all that logic you were supposed to learn from it?

Oh, it probably helped to get you promoted from chauffeur – no, dammit, just driver! – for a white salesman to become one of the first black salesmen. But without your own chauffeur, of course. And no comfortable car: a light delivery truck to tool around the townships picking up tiny orders from hole-in-the-wall shops. No need to bother with big, idealistic ideas about right and wrong, vengeance and compassion. That's what you need now: fluency in all that philosophic jargon. Boykie would have all the answers. So would Desmond. Haven't seen much of them lately. Must go and – what makes you think you're going to get out of here, sonnyboy?

You raped a white woman. Why? In vengeance. Let's examine that proposition. Like a lawyer: I put it to you that you cannot avenge yourself against a race by raping one of its women. Are you, the defendant, suggesting that's what all those horny kaffirs who've been hanged every year, as the law demands, were trying to do?

Leave that kind of talk to Boykie and his shyster-lawyer boss. Look at it straight. Well, the first question is – did they really do it, the rape? Weren't they framed, as one of us here tonight might have been? Didn't some of these white women only yell rape when they were found out breaking the law and the social traditions of supremacy? Or – well, he interrupted himself: you weren't any of those things. No excuses. You are guilty. You took the decision and acted on it in a moment of ...

Decision? Hah. You call that a decision? An impulse. That's more like it. For no reason that I can put my finger on, anyway. Or an accumulation of reasons that go back beyond the day of my birth. Why should we let them continue bossing us around as if we aren't human too? We've got to show them we're human beings. By behaving like an animal – worse, my dear Phil? Well, maybe. Make her feel what it's like to be forced to behave like an animal. Drag her through this dirt we're supposed to enjoy. Foul her – befoul her. Can't do it to all of them, so one has to serve for the rest. She and her sanctified sisters.

The immaculate founts of their hated race. He had cursed her inwardly as he spewed his vengeful seed into her, wanting to lecture her on the meaning of what he was doing. But what could he have told her?

He only knew that when he saw her standing there in the dark, proud and sensuous – with that provocative pride they all seemed to display in the presence of all black men, even the ugliest – he had suddenly seen rape as the fulfilment of his need to assert himself.

A violation not so much of the woman and her luscious body, but of her being, her intimacy. A defiling of the wells. The first tenet of white supremacy decreed that she – her sex, White Womanhood – was the ultimate human perfection in all the world and the envy of all other races. He had felt, in his head not his loins, that this would be the ultimate violation of the idol.

But he was not satisfied now; he felt cheated. There had been no elation, no sense of achievement. There had never been, even in the dark alley. Was that why he did not care so much if he were found out and hanged? The question brought a wry smile to his face in the darkness of the cell, malodorous from the stench of the overflowing latrine bucket and the fetid smells of his fellow prisoners.

I've got a legal way to commit suicide any time I feel like it. Just walk up to the nearest police station and confess. No: just tell them in the morning right here. Or right now – bang on that steel door and demand their attention.

Get it over for all these poor bastards crowded on the floor, groaning and nursing their outraged bodies, because of me. Am I sorry for them? I don't know. I don't think so. They'll survive. It's not their first night in a cell for just being black. But if she identifies one of them? Unless he's got plenty of evidence to prove where he was, he'll hang. A white man's word is better than a black man's, any day, and a white woman's is not only sacred but fatal. Aah, they can prove where they were – don't have to worry about that.

But what if the lamb chosen for the slaughter can't? Will you raise your hand and say, "I'm sorry, Baas, but the Missus is mistaken; it was I who did it to her"? Will you? They wouldn't believe me, anyway. Get my teeth kicked out for calling a white woman a liar. Yes, but that shouldn't stop you. Why not? Hah. Who's a hero in here? Not me. Anyway, it won't happen. But if it – Okay, let's wait and see.

Her eyes fluttered open, one at a time. Somewhere above them a whitish mass floated and undulated. She saw it through a blurring mist that made it difficult to identify. She tensed her body, slowly, against the weariness drugging it and her mind. Then she blinked her eyes rapidly and stared again … It's a ceiling. Where? Whose? Mine is blue in the flat. A lovely robin's egg blue.

The eyes swivelled down and past her narrow nose, over the blanketed mounds that must be the firm breasts she was so proud of, and between the outward sloping peaks that would be her feet. The legs she was equally proud of – slim but shapely – were slight ridges spread apart under the blanket. She scissored them sharply, knees knocking together, as she remembered. When the nausea from the sudden movement had receded, her eyes looked beyond the foot rail of the bed and focused on a nurse sitting at a discreetly lit table near the door. The nurse was knitting, her eyes half-closed: intimate memories.

Jean Ryan sighed; a ragged sound. The nurse lifted curious, compassionate blue eyes from her knitting, over the foot rail, the peaks and mounds, and rested on the wan and still beautiful face on the white pillow. She rose from her chair, placing the knitting on the enamelled table, and walked to the bed.

"Where am I?" Jean asked. Don't be silly, a voice spoke irritably inside her head: obviously in a hospital!

"The General Hospital, Mrs Ryan." The nurse smiled. "Just sleep and rest. You'll feel much better in the morning."

"Morning … How long since – have I been here?"

"Oh, just a few hours," the nurse replied lightly. "But don't worry about that now. What you need is sleep."

"What's the time?"

"A little after four o'clock. It'll be morning soon. And you'll need all your strength, then. When the police come and want to talk to you."

A shudder passed slowly through Jean's body, rising from her legs and inflaming her pelvis before spreading to colour her neck and cheeks. Her head moved in slow jerks from one side to the other.

"I don't want to talk to them … to anybody … about anything …"

The smiling face suspended above her wavered, fragmented and floated upward, merging with the white, blurred mass that was the ceiling. She closed her eyes and her body relaxed. She was asleep again.

The nurse straightened the bedclothes, then returned to the small, clinical table. Poor woman. Quite beautiful, too. Lovely hair – glorious colour. The brute had taste, you can say that for him! The risks of beauty … no. They want any white woman. She can be bloated or even leprous, and they'll want her as long as she's white. Black, fucking devils. Don't they get enough from those big-bottomed, melon-breasted whores of their own!

But perhaps it was a white man. A bliksem who's been admiring her for ages? A scorned admirer! Yes, that could be it. She's lovely enough to drive any man crazy. How exciting!

The nurse's eyes brightened, then glazed as if entranced by a Technicolor screen conjured above the bed of the violated woman. The screen shimmered with the passion of Scorned Love driven to ecstatic violence and poetic vengeance … No, she told herself firmly, disappointed. It could only be a Native. No white man would do that. Only those bloody kaffirs.

The meaty-faced detective seemed too large in the private room. His heavy, rounded shoulders appeared to push at the ceiling; his well-worn grey flannels clung to huge thighs which threatened to burst their seams. A sweat-stained hat covered the bedside table.

"My name is Viljoen," he was saying in a voice that rasped with the habitual growl of officialdom. "Detective Sergeant Viljoen of the CID."

He paused, his rusty-brown eyes wandering over the small room, avoiding the turned-away face and blanketed body. He felt awkward and somehow defenceless in this atmosphere.

"I realise, Madam, that this is going to be difficult for you. But it has to be done as soon as possible, Mrs Ryan."

"I understand, Sergeant," she replied in a small voice.

"You see, we need the facts quickly. These black skelms – we got them packing the station right now – they can be blerry – sorry, tricky you know."

There was an audible – she was certain he could hear it – click in her head. She had been unable or afraid to think coherently since waking up a second time from her stupor. She had succeeded in retaining this drifting, unthinking wakefulness by refusing to see her husband. She could not refuse to see the detective; and now he had succeeded in penetrating the protective screen.

And what he had just said brought back the question she had asked in the dark alley when she was numb with disgusted terror: who is he? Was this official assumption that he was black correct?

"You mean you've arrested some Native boys? Because of me?"

"Oh, yes, Mrs Ryan," he said with proud satisfaction. "Rounded them all up last night, soon as we found you. They're cluttering up the cells now and eating too bler– too much." He smiled at his own awkward humour. "Been working on them since we caught them. But they're stubborn, you know. Like donkeys, stupid and stubborn. So you'll have to come to an identi–"

"But how do you know it was a Native, Sergeant? Did I say so last night?"

The brick-red furrowed brow above the bushy eyebrows wrinkled, the eyes narrowed. "Wasn't it?" he asked in surprise.

Who else could it have been? she asked herself. Nobody else could do such a thing. It must have been. But why me, you black devil? Of all the women in Johannesburg – in the country – why me? I hope they hang you! But you don't know that he was black, Jean. How can you accuse a race when you're not sure?

"I don't know, Sergeant," she answered listlessly, moving her shoulders in an irritated shrug. "It was all so – such a horrid mess. I didn't see him. It was dark. Then when he – he … I closed my eyes. Tight. I didn't want to see anything."

"Didn't he say something? They usually do, you know – swearing and all that."

She thought back, forcing herself to remember what she wanted most to forget. "I don't think so."

"They usually do," he repeated firmly. "A lot of dirty, filthy things. But he smelled, eh?" he asked hopefully when she remained silent.

"I suppose he did … or I smelled fear. Perhaps the rubbish in that filthy alley. But any man who'd do such a thing would surely be smelly?"

He grunted. "But when you struggled with him – you felt his lips, his nose, his hair? Hey? Fat lips, flat nose, korrel hair?"

"I didn't struggle, Sergeant," she answered wearily. "I was terrified. Paralysed by fear."

He gave a short, angry bark. What kind of woman is this one, dammit? Not defending herself – her honour?

"How long was it from the time he left you to the time you were found?"

"I have no idea. None!" she said sharply, reacting to the unspoken disapproval that was in his tone and manner.

Sergeant Viljoen grunted again. "Look, we got about fifty of these boys in the chooky up the hill. It must be one of them. Now, all you got to do is come and look them over. Just point him out. We'll do the rest."

His eyes watched her hopefully as she thought over his offer. He hoped she understood. She must know that they had to charge somebody. We can't let them get away with it. No woman would be safe. All you got to do, rooinek woman, is point him out. The next thing he knows, he'll be kicking at the end of a rope in Pretoria Central. And shitting himself. Come on, now, Engelse vroumens! Do your duty. We must be avenged!

"It wouldn't be any use, Sergeant Viljoen," she replied, gathering her dignity about herself as a protection against his disapproving manner. "I couldn't identify him, ever. And I couldn't stand it – to look at fifty horrid faces like that. Especially with him possibly one of them. All of them knowing. The shame ..."

Would kill you, hey? But his John Thomas didn't. Ag, these bloody genteel, rooinek English! Why didn't you all stay on your blerry genteel island? The shame! Can't stand it! How d'you think we feel about this, Mrs Ryan? If she had been Mevrou van der Merwe, a good strong Afrikaner girl, she'd have fought the bastard off. Scratched his blerry fucking eyes out! And if she failed, she'd damn well understand and point him out.

"But –"

"It's no use, Sergeant. Will you please go now? I'm tired."

She knew she had disappointed him. More than, in fact. And this pleased her a little; she had noticed when he had stopped addressing her as "Mrs Ryan". Talking to me like I'm a Native girl!

He could not go just yet, he explained with heavy sarcasm. There were details he must have for his docket:

Full name? Jean Griffiths Ryan. Age? Thirty.

Married – how long? Eight years. How many children? None.

Ha! A blerry mule on top of everything else! Probably asked for it, the bitch.

Husband's full name? Patrick Sean Ryan. Occupation? Real estate – partner in a real estate company. His age? Thirty-two. Places of birth? Johannesburg.

"Now. If you don't mind, Missus," he rumbled, glaring at the prone victim. "Can you tell me exactly what happened? Hey?"

First time he's looked directly at me, she thought. Is eye contact necessary for the interrogation? And what if I do mind the boorish manners of the Boer? Will he go away if I do mind? Of course not, so gird your loins, sore and aching or not.

"From the time you left your flat," he was saying. "And why you left it – went out into the dark when everybody knows the skelms are at their worst?"

"I'll try, Sergeant," she sighed.

It was late afternoon and she sat up in the hospital bed, a mound of pillows propping her up. Examining the face of Jean Ryan in a mirror. A beautful face, but a little drawn, the green eyes forlorn. But still the face of the Jean Griffiths she had always known and smiled at in myriads of mirror as she grew up and, finally, became Jean Ryan. There would be no scars: just the bruises on your palms and knees, she reassured herself. The real wounds and scars will be inside, but I must ignore them. Forget last night – try to. Become the same again, if they'll let me. Will that ever be possible, dear God? It has to be! If one tries hard enough, one can be anything one wants to be – happy, desolate, wholesome, scarred. Just had a nasty experience that has taken something from your being, Jean. Discard the nastiness, fill up the loss, and return to a normal life with Patrick.

Patrick! She had succeeded in keeping him out of her mind for quite some time now. Just as she had succeeded in keeping him out of her little refuge, this private hospital-room he was paying for. But she could not keep him out much longer. One can't hide from oneself or other people. How does he feel about this ghastly business? No. The question is: how does he feel about me? Does he still love me? Want me? How could he? The defiled woman. But it's not my fault! Why should he hold it against me? I didn't rape myself! You knew the dangers, though, as that Sergeant Viljoen charged during his interrogation right here in this room.

Going out alone at that time of night. Why did you, then?

It was a beautiful night. That's not good enough. I needed some milk. You could have had something else, instead of chocolate. The cocktail cabinet is bulging with alternative sleep inducers. Don't like drinking alone, that's why! Water and a pill? Oh, all right! I was bored and it was a beautiful night.

Alone all day, as usual: the pampered young matron, recognised by sales girls in the best shops. Then expected to be happy alone all evening. Or at least content, while he tells smutty stories with the boys, or clients. Or listens to talks about property at a business dinner. Business! Isn't the day long enough for that? Must I also spend the nights alone in an empty flat?

"The night was made for loving," some poet has declaimed. Ha! Not in this country. Not if you go outside and a prowler with a hard-on spots you. And all because your loving husband thinks it's more important to be with the boys, or make what he stuffily calls 'new business contacts'.

Does he think I'm just a – Now, Jean! Now, now. Don't be unfair to Patrick. You didn't have to stay home. You've got friends. And there's his family, who'll now think ... Don't you think about that, my girl.

There are cinemas, the theatre, the – oh, shut up! Go alone and see everybody else having fun together? I prefer staying home. I want to like staying home. I'm a housewife, aren't I? Why should I want to escape my own home to the cinema or the homes of other people? Inconvenience and embarrass them? But you did. That's what going out for the milk was – an escape, a diversion. Only for a few minutes. And are you really a housewife? There's the girl. She does all the housework. What do you do, housewife? Aren't you just a glorified kept woman? A licenced mistress? Maybe; but that's because I don't have children. And that isn't my fault, dammit!

The arguments swirling in her mind had taken away her immediate misery. But now she'd touched on her most vulnerable point. Children ... to have a baby, to be a mother. She was still not reconciled to being childless after all these years of marriage. Perhaps if the lack had been in herself? No; I'd have hated myself for not giving him children.

Patrick! Are you furious with me, darling? I'm sorry. I wish I were dead. How can you ever hold your head up again? How can I? When everybody'll be pointing fingers and whispering behind our backs?

But that's not the worst. What about us? Can I ever look you straight in the eye again? I feel so ashamed. Like ... like something that should remain hidden under a flat rock. I'm dirt. How can you ever want me again? Will I be able to, if you do? Oh, why did this happen to me, God? Why me? What did the filthy bastard want? He couldn't have wanted me. Not like that. No person can. But what's going to happen to us, Patrick? Please help us, God. I'm so afraid. So ashamed. Help him especially, dear God.

There was a quick knock at the door, and someone opened it without waiting for a response. Patrick Sean Ryan entered the private ward and she closed her eyes. How dare he come in here without warning me! Oh, God, please give me courage.

He was a tall, slender man with a long, sensitive but indecisive face. The grey eyes were filled with a self-conscious sadness, as if he had spent time before a mirror composing his face in the proper expression. There was self-pity, too, as he looked down at Jean's tightly shut, quivering eyelids in the pale, tensed face. My poor darling. My poor, violated – the word wiped all sadness off his face. He reddened and a bitter anger suffused him as his mind conjured up the violence that had led to her lying here. Oh, the black bastard! She lay under him in that filthy alley, and he ...

He sat down in the chair beside the bed.

"Don't you want to see me still, Jeanie?" he asked in a voice soft with pleading and hurt. "You mustn't feel that way, darling. It wasn't your fault."

She remained silent.

What does one say at such a time? That you forgive her? No. What would you forgive her for? Tell her that you are wild with fury over such a thing happening to her?

"I love you, darling," he said hesitantly. "I'll always love you. Please look at me, Jeanie. Tell me how you feel."

"I'm all right, Patrick." Her voice was flat and her eyes remained shut. But the tension was receding from her face. "At least I think I'm all right."

"The doctor says you can come home this evening."

She did not say anything.

"Why don't you look at me? Please open your eyes, darling."

Slowly they opened, and the tears that had been dammed behind the eyelids flooded her cheeks.

"I'm so ashamed, Pat. You aren't angry with me?"

"Of course not, my darling. Not at you." The hardness returned to his voice and face. "What I'd like to do right now," he said in a strangled voice, "I'd like to get my hands on the black bastard who did it."

She felt so sorry for him. Poor Patrick. And he too thinks it was a Native. It must have been, if they're all so certain. But white men do it too. This isn't logical.

"Paddy," she said softly. "How d'you know it was one of them when I don't?"

"Of course it was!" he said sharply, staring at her in shocked surprise.

It was no good. No point arguing with him. Why upset him? And it probably was, anyway.

"I suppose it was one of them, Paddy."

"Are you certain – really sure, Jeanie – that you couldn't identify him? Sergeant Viljoen says –"

"I've told him and all of them already, Pat," she said impatiently. "It was dark, he grabbed me from behind, I was frightened, I closed my eyes, I ..." she paused for breath and glared at him. "Must I be interrogated all over again? And by you?"

"I'm sorry, Jeanie. I didn't mean to upset you. But you must try to remember, darling. It's very important. He must be found. And hanged!"

Chapter 3

The wake-up young men and women of Sophiatown – the klevahs who in slang referred to the tiny location as Soph'town and Kofifi, to confuse un-wake moegoes – stood talking or laughing, sat whispering or laughing. And all of them swayed gently or tapped their feet to the beat of the jazz booming from the huge, highly-polished radiogram which dominated a corner of the shebeen. All of them drinking, while a few had set aside their glasses to sort-of-dance to the music: alone or in couples tightly clasped to the other's bosom. The dance shuffle and sensuous movements were minimised so they hardly moved: come duze, baby, but be cool …

Cool klevahs and their babes, but below the surface, a high-strung gaiety was palpable in the room. An undertone of suspended tension; a truce in the amorous and physical hostilities engendered by living too close in the crammed location. Those hostilities could be resumed later; or never again, or immediately – depending on developments brought on by booze. But at the moment what mattered most was that they all enjoy as much as they could this unexpected and no-cost nice time. And to hell with everything else. Heaven can wait, my broer, whatever those missionaries said while they talked us into giving up our freedom!

Philip leaned against the edge of the table, as highly polished as the radiogram that was the centre piece of the imbuia-wood furniture suite. His right hand jerked forward, and the neat brandy in the glass he held sloshed towards the rim; but he saved the *mahog* by quickly tilting his hand. He gulped some of the cheap and fiery liquid, then bit his lower lip to gauge his state of drunkenness. Not bad; still comparatively sober, he decided. His eyes rose from the table and its litter of bottles he was paying for and wandered about Maisie's classy joint. Maisie was an imposing, large lady who presided over the shebeen like a social dictator. Her big boobs, battling up-lift bras, looked like cannons – which got her a nickname that was only whispered by most of her clientele: Battleship. Only a few, like Philip, could use the name to her face – but with a smile, or else even they would be on the receiving end of the shebeen queen's sharp tongue.

Any indiscretion, or what Maisie thought was an indiscretion, and you're on her banned list, boy, just like the tsotsis who can't get even their noses into Maisie's; and that would be social suicide.

He squinted blood-shot eyes – no sleep that could be termed restful last night – and looked around at his uninvited guests. Enjoying his impromptu nice time simply because these nice-timers were already on the scene when he arrived. He's just announced with a crazy flourish that he was buying. No gazaat today, gents, and just keep your hands out of your empty pockets, julle *baekie-vangers*! A few had turned hostile at being called freeloaders; but those who knew this crazy bastard had asked: why the generosity? And burst into derisive laughter when he replied it was to celebrate his release from Hillbrow police station that afternoon. Maisie had only grinned, shaking her head at this one's unpredictability: the only thing predictable about Nice Time Phil, she knew, was that he was unpredictable. But a sweet boy – when sober. The friends in the crowd had laughed, but nobody debated his need to celebrate: a free drink from anybody was a free drink any day, *mzala*! If he wished to celebrate a routine event already experienced by almost all them in the room or anywhere else in Kofifi – well, then, heaven can wait, man!

Arrest and release, or conviction, was a natural hazard: born to be harassed, if not to be bad. Didn't deserve more than momentary attention if it was for less than, say, three months. But if Pretty Boy Phil – hey, *wena*, don't give him such a big smile, baby! If he wanted to celebrate such an ordinary thing – well, it was his money. The klevah was only living up to his reputation as a nice-time boy. He could afford such craziness because he made extra ching by diddling his company and selling some stuff back-door – lucky bastard.

But they were not interested in his real reason for the celebration, or his motives for anything he did. Questioning anybody's motives was not only rude but suspect: why the fuck do you want to know why, eh? Curiosity kills more than cats, s'tru's God, my ma se kind. Die Here hoor my!

He squinted against the glare of the lights in the smoke-filled room.

All the nice-timers having a very-very good time, because it was only once in a blue moon they didn't have to gazaat the same amount towards buying a bottle of mahog, which was then carefully doled out by a *skinker* using his fingers to mark equal measures of brandy. Only splurged their *mazooma* on clothes that were *can't-gets*. A week's wages for a hat imported from Mossant in France, Battersby in England, Biltmore and Stetson in America. Wake-up clothes beyond the reach of most of their neighbours, but not these denizens of Soph'town: the arbiters of fashion, morals and slang in Jo'burg, and therefore the country.

Weetie die taal, man! No whitey understood their language, and any moegoe who tried to speak it made mistakes. It was an ever-changing mixture of Afrikaans, English, Yiddish and the vernaculars, but with certain words and phrases sacrosanct to certain strata of the wake-up. To outsiders – the laanies and moegoes – they were all tsotsis who wore tsotsi clothes and spoke this confusing tsotsi-taal. That's why these outsiders got into trouble and were looked down upon.

Confusing a klevah with a tsotsi was an insult to both groups: the former despised the latter, but maintained diplomatic relations with them. It would be suicidal to show their scorn, because tsotsis were criminals who assaulted, stabbed and robbed moegoes of any colour or race. And not only in the dark of night.

Maisie's joint was popular with the wake-up: no tsotsis allowed, and any differences of opinion were settled elsewhere. And unlike some of her rivals, Maisie didn't sell *korea*: brandy or gin, whose volume was multiplied with additives such as methylated spirits, tobacco soaked in water for colouring, and, for way-out dronkies, plain water.

Philip nodded his appreciation of the smart establishment. And smiled when his eyes caught those of Boykie Nine Years across the crowded room. Slouched in a corner, talking and laughing: relaxed, with the security of two walls behind his back and two cronies on either side. Yet still scrutinising the crowd and evaluating each change of mood, each new alliance or disenchantment, through hooded eyes.

There were countless children and young men named Boykie and Boy – pet names for unimaginative mothers' sons – and the only way to differentiate them was to add a definitive adjective or phrase. Among the many Boykies Philip knew was his childhood friend, Boykie Courtroom, a chief clerk for a white lawyer whose clientele was exclusively black. A burly man in a flower-patterned shirt from Hawaii and a narrow-brimmed hat from England – can't-gets – was called Boykie Nine Years after a prison term for some forgotten crime. One of his first murders, Philip thought; but it could also have been for burglary with violence. Anyway, it was the only name he was known by. Proper names and surnames were used by the police or their informers – and situations, of course.

Boykie winked, and Philip raised his own glass in salute, holding onto the smile. Hail to die real manne, he said to himself. Keep timing with them and you live happily – and longer. Boykie must've been talking to Maisie in the kitchen when he arrived. The hard man called Nine Years – and, unlike The Battleship, not annoyed by the nickname – spoke across the room in a jeering, sing-song drawl that was soft but above the music's level.

"Hey, klevah," the man said. "What you doing that to me for, hey?"

His voice brought down a hush among the nice-timers.

"Toasting you and your sidekicks, Boykie – saluting your bizness," Philip replied in a bantering tone.

"What the fuck do you know about my bizness, Pretty Boy?" the burly man growled; the voice lower. And the listeners moved aside and out of the line of fire that was, so far, only verbal. "You trying to be clever with laanie toasts and shit like that, eh? Maybe you think this is your mother's wedding?"

"Don't talk about my mother, Nine Years," Philip replied.

His tone also hardened, as he released his first shot in what he hoped would be only a verbal fire-fight. Had to *keep timing* with three of them here – and the rest of the gang somewhere else in Sophiatown. But I live here and can't let him insult my mother. Otherwise this could be the first step to being run out of town.

"Okay, okay. Forget that, my ma se kind," the gangster laughed, and a silent sigh of relief was palpable in the room. "But you sound like you're becoming a situation," he jeered. "Going to start talking English to us? Wearing a tie?"

Philip laughed, his tone again bantering rather than ominous:

"You know I wear a tie when I'm working, Boykie. And I speak English to the laanies – you wouldn't understand."

The man grinned and snorted; and a few brave listeners murmured appreciation of the banter.

"But the toast was not a laanie thing, my ma se kind," Philip went on, returning the brotherly compliment. "Just showing you there's still plenty mahog, Nine Years." But then the brandy he'd consumed made him suddenly reckless: "Even with you baekie-vangers trying to bankrupt me!"

"H-e-y …! "one of Boykie's sidekicks said, dragging out the word in a mock-surprised whisper. "What, hey? What're you saying, klevah?" – that word turned into an insult. "Suddenly we – and I mean we, die real manne, Pretty Boy – ons is baekie-vangers, hey? Well, I'm sorry, my broer. We didn't know we were poor low-lifes. Just tell us more, man."

The earlier tension at the start of the exchange with Boykie had been lulled by banter. But ears always attuned to danger recognised the new challenge and threat in the sibilant voice. Eyes jumped from Philip to Boykie, then to Boykie's crony, calculating the possibilities of a dust-up. Anxious eyes searched for Maisie, who could be her own bouncer if so inclined. Surprise as they looked at Philip, wondering at his reckless use of the most insulting term in a shebeen: baadjie-vanger, free-loader. To a man of Boykie Nine Years' reputation for wanton gang violence! All three real manne were most likely carrying Mausers or Lugers; bullets could be flying, soon. Only Maisie could stop that, or a grovelling apology from Nice Time Phil …

"Aaahh," Boykie said, dragging out the dismissive sound with amused disgust into the silence. "Leave the klevah alone, Jerry man. Maybe he suddenly became a quarter-millionaire, or something. Maybe he carries two forty-fives, now, and wants to take over from the Durango Kid."

Philip ignored Jerry. His eyes had remained fixed on Boykie Nine Years throughout the challenge. They had been schoolboys together, once upon a time. He knew – hoped – that this normally friendly acquaintance would accept the insult as the congenial riposte to the reference to Philip's mother, a much more serious insult. Jerry also had a reputation, but Philip was confident he could deal with him if it came to that, which he hoped it would not. A fight with one of Boykie's gang would unnecessarily complicate an already delicate relationship. Such relationships with gangs were useful. They offered a certain amount of protection to klevahs teetering on the razor's edge between victimised respectability – the besuited, tie-wearing situations – and the down-trodden masses, harassed by a vicious, vindictive underworld.

"Hell, man. Me in the quarter-million, Boykie?" he asked lightly, voice falling and rising in the sing-song, casual rhythm that separated the wake-up from all the *cattle*. "You know I'm just one of the *oxen* working for the laanies, boy. Only die real manne like you got the pluck to go for the quarter-million! And you notch we're all waiting for you to move up there, Nine Years – so you can walk in here after a payroll job and say, 'Maisie, fill up the table my sister!' Then we can have us a real nice time – not my small-fry thing like tonight. Eh?"

"Hah!" Boykie laughed, eyes opening wide in mock shock. "You think I'm a fool, gonna spend my dough on ...?" A hand swept contemptuously at the crowd. "Aaah, never mind, my *laaitie*!" He smiled as Philip's ironical flattery registered, the outer edges of his eyes crinkling. "You're buying tonight, that's all. Even for a stupid reason – getting caught in white-by-night Hillbrow, chasing some sheila from the farms!" His finger jabbed at the watching women. "What's wrong with these cherries, you got to go eat dogs' meat in the kitchens?"

Approving giggles and thrust-out chests from some of the nice-time girls.

"These ones are expensive – and I wanted something fresh, Boykie."

"Anyway, the quarter's for educated whores' sons like you," he was told. "Me, I'm just a pick-and-shovel boy."

"No – hit and run," Philip grunted. "Forgotten the geometry we learned at school, Nine Years?"

"Ag, shut your trap, klevah. You're asking for *shaandies*, and you're going to get yourself into a real mix-up," Boykie said, sounding a casual warning.

Philip knew he was taking chances with a gangster who killed and maimed people casually for saying much less – or nothing at all, just staring at him. But the danger signals need only go up if the rude tone of voice turned silky – a red light he was not certain he would heed on this night. He, too, had a reputation for seeking trouble on occasion, when the frustrations gnawing his guts would suddenly cause him to shed his mantle of the bantering, seductive Nice Time Phil.

But the devil-may-care mood enveloping him this night was something else. Something strange and a bit frightening. He was brimming with an exhilaration that was in some manner also frustration. The bravado of a man with nothing much to lose, and still desperately in need of a catharsis.

"Okay, groot man," he said in mock awe, holding up his hands protectively. "You know I'm scared of you! I'll even pay you protection."

"Now, moerskont. You're really speaking into your mother's –" Jerry began, the sibilance of his voice thin and sharp.

But he was cut off by Boykie Nine Years: "You must really stop looking for trouble, Phil." The jeering gone from his voice and replaced by puzzled concern. "We like drinking your money, my mother's child.

So don't talk like that, my laaitie. Because, you see, then you won't be around much longer."

"Okay – but I'm not your laaitie. I'm nobody's little boy."

Boykie grinned, nodding. "Now, groot man – why don't you tell us what really happened in Hillbrow last night, eh?"

Philip shrugged: "Aah, nothing much."

"Like yesterday morning when you refused as usual to queue for a bus?" he was teased. "As if your father owns Putco – right? A staff-rider! When're you klevahs going to learn to respect the law?"

Philip joined in the general laughter: "Why should I queue when they know I got a friend like you?"

Boykie shook his head: "Stop clowning, man."

"I was picked up in a Hillbrow shebeen – you know, one of those dogs' meat joints," he said with sudden reluctance. "In one of their raids."

"Oh, I see!" Boykie responded in awed tones. "So just because you spend one night in chookie after they drag you out of a kitchen girl's bed for not having a special pass, you want us to waste your wages – and what you steal from the Jew as a part-time, back-door salesman?"

"Not just a ordinary raid, bra Boykie," a young man piped up respectfully. "I also got picked up. The gattas were catching every darkie 'cos a Madam was raped."

Boykie turned away impatiently from the young man to stare back at Philip with malice. "Rape! Just the kind of thing you'd do, you bloody greedy bastard! Screwed all the nice skondaai in Soph'town, so now you turn to laanie Madams! 'Something fresh', that's what you said! Don't you know they hang you for that, bliksem?"

"I don't –"

"Was she nice?"

Philip pulled back his lips in a disgust that was genuine, deep down. "Me? One of those ice-cold bitches who just lay there like dead fish?"

"Plenty done it and got hanged already," a voice said.

"Kitchen boys, those!" another voice began. "Plaasjapies who believe white propaganda that white meat is –"

He was cut off by a female voice. "What about that Orlando boy – Boetie Sevenpence?" she asked in shrill indignation.

"Ag, him?" the second man retorted with contempt. "Just a *war-time* klevah, that one. Six years off the farm! He didn't notch Jo'burg like we do, *ousie.*"

Boykie waved for silence with his empty tumbler: "You haven't really answered my questions, nice-time boy."

"Look, Nine Years," Philip said, his voice suddenly vicious. "If any of those ice-cold bitches ever sent me an invitation and opened their thighs – I'd stick a bloody big candle in it! That's what I think."

And may the Lord forgive me for the lie. If it is a lie, because –

The indignant woman made a rude noise with her lips and laughed jeering disbelief. "I believe you, my brother! I believe all of you when you say things like that! But we see you watching them on the streets of Jozi – hungry eyes!"

Philip joined in the laughter – defensive from the men – and after further accusations and counter-accusations, the familiar subject was abandoned.

Drinking, flirting and dancing recommenced. Heaven could still wait, the brothers were having a nice time. Who needs to rape a laanie woman when there's all these nice-time sisters wiggling their arses and pushing out their tits?

Boykie Nine Years, Jerry and some other young men in the shebeen were die real manne. The real men, as distinct from die manne or majita: terms reserved for klevahs when their patronising betters who didn't have to clock in each morning wished to be complimentary. Those terms were preferred to klevah, which could have undertones of derision, depending on the tone in which it was used. And only the ignorant and foolhardy would ever call Boykie Nine Years and his unemployed but well-dressed comrades tsotsis – hooligans who were the lowest level among the wake-up, and robbed black people for their paltry pay packets and valuables.

Die real manne only concerned themselves with white victims, for they were respectable – and made real money. But then there were real men and really real men. The aristocrats of the underworld who relinquished robbing delivery trucks to the Young Americans, the Berliners and other gangs; and suburban burglary – with and without violence – to Boykie and his brethren.

Philip looked across the room at one of die real manne, a dandy who proudly called himself Joe Florsheim. Chatting up one of the girls and probably telling her how much he had paid for his new pair of gleaming, two-toned Florsheim shoes. I must ask him to get me a couple of those new cashmere sweaters, Philip told himself.

On the other hand, Philip thought as he continued his observations of his guests' faces, we also have situations here: clerks, schoolteachers and so forth. Though these are not really situations – more like klevahs, but not in the same class as us, die manne. These have a good sense of self-preservation, and don't look down their noses at the rest of us. Or speak English all the time, like proper situations – "Well, you see, my friend, the situation is ..."

By being situations without behaving, dressing or talking like them, they should have long and comparatively safe lives. They're not victimised for just being intellectually superior, or resented for showing off. Such high-handed behaviour was expected from whiteys, who were hated for it but protected by their distance, apartheid and the country's law enforcement agencies. The situations were not, and all the resentment was vented on them.

Boykie Courtroom should be here, Philip thought. The ultimate wake-up situation, and really a klevah, he kept his distance without turning the rest of die manne against him. I'd really like to see more of that clever bastard, after last night ... but he doesn't like shebeens, much. Drinks in his little palace of a room – booze his white friends buy him from bottle stores at half what we pay here, lucky bugger. That's when he's not drinking in the suburbs; with those liberals he knows through that lawyer he works for as a clerk, interpreter, translator and *mabalane.* Just fancy drinking with your boss!

Maybe I should go round and see him on Sunday. That's a good idea.

"Hey, klevah!" Danny the Drunk said in a loud, reedy voice and slapping Philip on the shoulder. "You're Mister Money tonight, ain'tchu? So, how about some more booze for the boys? We're running low, pal – we're running low!"

Philip turned with sudden irritation rising in him. A malicious anger surmounted the irritation as he glared down and took in the slight body, glazed eyes and empty grin of the young man tottering at his side. Why the hell does Maisie allow him in here?

"Why don't we see your money for a change, dronkie?" Philip snapped. "Didn't I hear you small-timers snatched purses on Tuesday? Drunk it all already?"

"Hey, whatsa matter with you, klevah?" Danny demanded, his voice trying to harden but cracking instead. His right hand swung and rested on his hip pocket. "Since when's what we do your business, hey? You been playing the big shot tonight, man. So just go on and –"

"Aah, never mind, Danny," Philip said in a tired voice. "I've just come back from the cells and don't want to go back for you. So leave that knife in your arse pocket. Dangerous for you, carrying a three-star, you know."

He turned from the glowering young man and called to Maisie – watching all happenings from near the kitchen door – for another bottle of brandy. For a wild, triumphant moment he had looked upon Danny as the release he so sorely needed for his pent-up feelings. But there was no percentage in demeaning himself by beating up The Drunk – even if Danny had done his share of stabbing and robbing the usual, frightened victims.

Maisie came back into the room, waving the bottle of mahog above her head.

"Here you are, you baekie-vangers!" she shouted angrily above the din.

"Here's some more booze for you – the last bottle from my *leshetla*, the Number One Nice-Time Boy!"

No offence was taken. Maisie was a tall, heavily-built and handsome woman in tight-fitting clothes over gargantuan curves. The prominent breasts that seemed to be jutting ahead of her cleared a path through the revellers as she approached the table.

"Aah shuddup, Battleship!" a voice retorted behind her, followed by hesitant laughter from different parts of the room.

She wheeled sharply in the direction of the voice, greater anger emblazoned on her face. "Which son of a whore said that?" she screeched. "Does he want to pass back through his mother's cunt? If he thinks –"

"Okay-okay, Maisie," Philip said in a placating but amused voice.

"We all know you carry a gun, my sister, and we're all afraid of you. So just hand over that bottle before you waste it on somebody's head."

She wheeled back towards him at the table.

"And why don't you shut up and go home, Phil? You've wasted too much money on these tsotsis who make me so angry sometimes."

He smiled at her. We're opposites, he thought. I only get mad if they call me a klevah when I get drunk. But she hates that name only when sober. When she's *poegat,* she's the first to use it: caressing those sixteen-inch battleship guns with a lewd pride. Aiming them all over the place. Ah, the girls, the girls … women! Shebeen queens and the nice-time sisters who work in factories and even laanie kitchens, but dress better than their Madams. Why? Because they get their clothes back-door – at a fraction of the price shown on the tag – from the guys who go door-to-door in the locations.

As Philip slopped brandy into glasses eagerly extended towards him, the door opened and one of the nice-time sisters squealed her delight. Philip turned with the others and looked up. Two men stood at the door, smiling benignly at the gathering. Carefully and exquisitely dressed in soft-textured suits that were much less flamboyant than those of the other men in the room; snowy-white shirts, with precisely knotted silk ties held down by jewelled clips; and narrow-brimmed hats held carefully in leather-gloved hands.

"Oh! Die really real manne! The quarter-million boys – die ouens, man! Die majita …!" chanted the praise singer who had squealed her welcome, her eyes fixed on the two men. "Howzit, bra Nick? Mister Ronnie? Are the Cadillacs outside, majita?"

Oh, the really real men in their fifty-guinea suits and fifteen-guinea two-tone shoes!

"Okay, my sister – *alles is dolly. Alles is singali,*" Ronnie grinned and spoke quietly, giving the girl a pat on the shoulder. "Thanks, my sister. But be careful, ousie – we don't want to get shot dead by your boyfriend one dark night."

"Or right here, right now, my groot brikaid!" a male voice half-jeered.

The soft-spoken Ronnie turned and smiled broadly at the roars of laughter. "And how're the nice-timers? Giving it stick, eh, Maisie?" He looked appraisingly at her large and preening self. "Fill up the table, my big sister. We don't want to spoil the nice time."

Ronnie slowly pulled out a pigskin wallet – from his back pocket like us poor anybodies, and not from inside his jacket, Philip noted. A Mauser or Luger nestling in the pocket of that loose-fitting jacket? That's where American torpedoes keep their *gats,* I've read in Peter Cheyney's books.

The elegant man placed two five-pound notes negligently in the top of Maisie's blouse, between her huge cannons.

The girl was at it again. "What did I tell you?" she squealed. "Now that's how the quarter-million boys do it! Didn't I tell you! And we're really going to drink, now! The best mahog you've got, Maisie!"

The shebeen queen glared at her and walked out of the room.

"And you better shut up, baby, or I'll send you home," her boyfriend said, grabbing her elbow and pulling her towards him.

"Hey, Ronnie!" Philip called as the two men glad-handed their way into the crowded room. "What's all this fill-up-the-table talk of yours? What do you think's on the table, eh?"

The two smooth men, whose status in the underworld demanded respect throughout all Jo'burg townships, turned towards the half-indignant voice and laughed – amused by the cheeky bravado. Everybody else in the crowded shebeen laughed, amazed by such ingratitude. Laughter all round that did not include Philip Mokone.

He had intended to be outraged, and not just indignant. He'd half-changed his mind as he started to speak. What was the point? He'd already made a half-enemy in the jeering exchanges with Boykie Nine Years; but both would've forgotten the half-threats and half-insults when they bumped into each other at a *stokvel* the following weekend.

Tangling with the quarter-millionaires would be like something else. Suicide. Not physical, because he knew that was all romantic bullshit inspired by reading too much Peter Cheyney. Of course these two – smooth operators and not torpedoes – didn't weigh themselves down with gats hidden in specially reinforced inside pockets. They carried heavier weapons than Lugers and Mausers on Fridays when they were working, dressed in overalls. Tangling with them now, tonight, would be social suicide in the world of the wake-up.

He would lose face in the upper strata of die real manne. Miss a lot of inside information and invitations to exclusive parties. And the cherries would no more shine take-a-good-look-at-what-I-got smiles on him. Quizzical and pitying looks from the wake-up, and out in the cold with no bullet-proof protection from harassment. Just one of the masses – the oxen. Not a klevah, not a tsotsi and not even a situation. Even those squares would be uneasy in his presence if he tried to sneak into their circle with Boykie Courtroom and Desmond as his sponsors. Sneered at them too often, no halfway about it.

So he'd just about kept his timing and not quite insulted die really real manne. Kept it light, no serious offence taken ... but there's got to be something suddenly wrong with me, behaving like a crazy *plaasjaapie* who doesn't know and understand the protocols of life in Sophiatown.

And Nick's reply was a voice that was far from soft, like his partner's, and half-jeering in the Soph'town style. Tough, no-nonsense voice; but polite:

"Put your money away, onse brikaid – if you got any left in your *gatsak.* We heard it's your nice time, boy – the word's out there," he gestured with a gloved hand towards the excluded world. "We just want to contribute. Isn't that so, Ronnie?"

"Of course we must contribute!" Ronnie agreed with mock surprise at the very thought that it had not been expected of them. "Aren't you our friend, Phil? A nice, pretty boy like you? And, anyway, you can't really afford to throw ching away like this, boy."

"That's just what I was telling him before you came in, Nick," Maisie said in a severe voice as she returned, bearing a tray loaded with bottles of a better brand than the Mellow-wood she'd been serving to Philip's impromptu guests.

"You hear that, Phil?" Nick asked, grinning. "This kind of thing costs serious money, my laaitie ... I mean, kid, you're an honest young man. Working for – what? Five pounds a week and –"

The rest was drowned in a new burst of laughter. Jeering laughter from mouths already slavering in anticipation of drinking free and classy mahog.

"Aah, go ahead and take over. But I'm not your laaitie, Nick – or anybody's kid. And just don't think I'm going to drink your lousy brandy. I'm coming into Maisie's bedroom with you for the moonshine you're gonna sneak away in there to booze. Julle hoor my, Ronnie?"

Drinking whisky with them, away from his own hijacked guests, would show these others that he was on the inside track and wasn't just another baadjie-vanger like they were. And moonshine would be a rare and expensive treat – what Boykie Courtroom so casually boasted he drank with his liberals out there in the suburbs. Scotch, blended or single malt, whatever the difference was; Irish whiskey, with that unexplained 'e'; and bourbon from Kentucky, or was it Tennessee?

"What can we say, brikaid?" Ronnie laughed indulgently. "You know we're shit-scared of you, nice-time boy. Anything you say, groot man!"

"Now you're talking like die really real manne," Philip laughed. "But I'm not coming. Some of us got to work tomorrow – turn the wheels of industry for a lousy fiver or something like that."

"You don't have to remind us, klevah!" Danny the Drunk retorted waspishly. "We know it's getting too fucking late for all the oxen!"

There would be at least one highly-polished Cadillac convertible parked outside in the dark; but safe as houses, because all likely thieves knew the owners; respected and admired them – and feared the consequences. Everybody in the townships who could notch the scene knew which of the high-living and big-spending payroll robbers owned the Cadillacs, Mercuries and Buick straight-eights. Limousines that were driven at very low speeds on the streets with die really real manne aboard would be greeted with black hands waving and pursed lips whistling shrill appreciation. And on the city streets, white faces glared suspiciously and wondered why the police did not arrest these arrogant Natives. They couldn't have come to drive such luxuries by honest means.

The problem for the police was that paymasters insisted they couldn't identify the 'boys' who robbed them on Fridays – because all kaffirs looked alike. Cheeky kaffir boys who somehow had the brains, can you believe it, to stage well-planned and precisely executed armed hold-ups.

The boys came away with thousands of pounds, and the romantic notion in the townships was that each haul amounted to a quarter of a million. They were considered the elite of the underworld: socially above die real manne, above factions, gang wars – and jealousy. Always well-dressed and polite; and never a thought of making any black person a victim.

Philip smiled contentedly and looked about the smoke-hazy room. They were all here as usual at Maisie's, representatives of the best of the multiple, contradictory and overlapping social strata of the ghettoes. They lived jammed tightly and explosively together, these varying and often hostile classes who were supposed to enjoy living like sardines. By legal enforcement they were on the same social level to the white ruler who swore they were identical to his cold-blue eyes. This enforced classlessness did not fulfil the political potential that theorists might read into it. Instead of a solidarity of the oppressed masses, there was a heightened and resented awareness of the differences evident beneath their blanket of oppression.

On the following morning Philip Mokone walked slowly into a noisy, fume-filled courtyard, crowded with delivery vans and the piles of merchandise he and the other Natives milling about were to deliver for the wholesale company. He waited with detached concern for his stomach to tighten into the usual ball of anger over the routinely nasty scene with the chief dispatcher. Benade – Baas Benade, as the bastard insisted he be called – was the bane of his working life. Convinced that they were all loafers and shirkers by nature, he would never accept any excuse for absenteeism. Several of the guys hoped to meet him alone on a dark street some lucky day.

But the ball failed to bind Philip's stomach. He remained relaxed and even indifferent. He'd keep timing, this time, unaffected where it mattered by the loud, harsh insults Benade yelled so often. Maybe it's because I have an explanation even he can't kick against. It's their laws that have us arrested. But he knew a good excuse would not help; vindication would only turn the dispatcher from unbelieving anger to infuriating sarcasm.

The dispatcher ignored him, standing above them all on the edge of a platform curving about the loading bay. He looked over Philip's head, shouting harsh instructions at the loaders and drivers, cleaving the air with the clipboard he held in one hand. When Benade finally decided to take note of yesterday's absentee, his manner took Philip off-guard.

"What the blerry hell're you standing there for, hey? Hey? Why aren't you in your dust coat and ready to drive the blerry van? Why – oh, Jesus Christ, man! Must I tell all you black bastards how to do everything? You want me to show you how to poke your blerry black whores too?"

The tirade was from an unexpected tack, but the venom was as usual. And the anger that flooded Philip was sharp and clean, without the fear and resentment of past incidents. He stood looking up, savouring the emotion, trying to explain it to himself.

"Well? Why the hell don't you say something?"

The emotion pulsing through Philip's body showed for a moment on his face before he regained control. His face returned to the closed expression that so many white men found exasperating and infuriating, or a justification for their conviction that all Africans were imbeciles.

"I wanted to explain why I was absent yesterday," he said, avoiding using the man's name to spare them both the wrangle over Philip's constant refusal to address him as Baas: a prerogative demanded from all Africans by white men, even if not in their employ.

"You think that interests me? You think I'm surprised when you swartvelle stay away? Ha! I know you bastards too well! Loafers, the lot of you! One day's pay docked – that's all!" Benade grinned, thin lips showing uneven teeth. "That you understand. And you stay away again – no job! Verstaan jy, jou donner?"

"But it wasn't my fault ..." He stopped, checking the resentment building up in him. Why bother? What difference would it make? And, anyway, wasn't it his fault?

"Oh, yes? What happened?" Benade asked, thin, red face sneering down and low voice heavy with sarcasm. "Your mother died again? Your uncle, grandma, cousin, whore – hey? Or maybe you were arrested. That's never your fault, is it? Laws interfere with your criminal instincts, don't they?"

Philip looked up into the mottled face with a new wonder that swamped the residue of anger still in him. Is this what's been making me mad and unhappy all these years? These fools and their cheap, frightened theatricals? He felt an urge to laugh at this man and at all of them – and at himself for the self-inflicted tortures of the past. He wanted to make some gesture: say something or do something to show that he was not afraid any more. Never again! Yes, I'll call him Baas, voluntarily and freely. Surprise the bastard with my new freedom – of expression, if nothing else. It won't be the admission of inferiority I've always resented. Not any more. And if this capitulation pleases him, more's the pity. For them.

"As a matter of fact, Baas Benade ..." He wanted to laugh at the amazed look and suspicion which flushed the thin face. "I was arrested." He pointed at his split lower lip: "That's what the basies at the station did to me."

"Ha! Being cheeky again, hey? Why didn't they knock your blerry block off?" But Benade's curiosity was aroused. He particularly enjoyed bawling out this cheeky, half-educated bastard; but the kaffir was one of the best boys he had – give him a desk job, if he just wasn't so blerry cheeky. Thought he was almost as good as a white man. Never been in trouble before. Now he says he'd been arrested. A pass or permit – night pass – offence, and he'd have been out after paying the ten bob or whatever-it-is they get fined.

Benade was curious, but did not want to show it. It would lower his dignity to be that interested in a kaffir. The two men, baas and boy, stared, each waiting.

"Well?" Benade finally asked. "What was it?"

A shrug and puzzled reply: "They thought I might have raped a woman."

"Don't you bastards do it all the time?"

"A white woman, Baas Benade."

"What!" The thin face was suffused by indignant fury and work came to a standstill around them as ears flapped. "A white woman! You fucking black bastards! You ... bastards! Why didn't they twist your blerry balls off?"

"They tried."

"Look, you blerry black swine! Don't think you can talk to me cheeky like that! Who d'you think I am – you are?"

"I thought you wanted to know."

"Did they get the fucker?"

"No. I don't think so."

"Black bastards," Benade muttered. "A blerry – a white woman!"

The intense washed-out blue eyes examined the yellow-brown face below as if they had never seen it before. "Did ...?"

He could not finish the sentence. Instead he whirled and glared at the listeners. "What's you fuckers standing there for – loafing again, hey? Voetsek, julle!" The men dispersed, slowly, and Benade turned to look down again at the impassive face below.

Go on – ask me, Philip jeered inwardly. Why're you afraid? Aren't you always afraid? That's why you call our women whores, isn't it? Want to fuck them, have for centuries, but scared stiff – no, limp – by us, now. Go on: ask, damn it!

And Philip knew that if Benade did ask him, if he completed his question, he would tell him the truth. The dread knowledge spread a chill between his shoulder blades. A legal means to commit suicide, he remembered telling himself two nights earlier in the stinking cell. Suicide by regulation hanging. I almost did it, too. Naaa ... this one would just think I was being cheeky again. Parmantig – his favourite word. But I must be careful.

"Get to work, jong," Benade said in a flat, tired voice.

No, boy, defeated, Philip thought as he sauntered away. Triumphant, but puzzled by his own new and unexpected behaviour.

Chapter 4

"**H**owzit there, Philip? Howzit my brikaid!"

The hip greeting among klevahs came short, sharp and clipped, with the wake-up sing-song lilt to it.

"*Heita,* Fats ... Peppy ... Howzit, Fred," he replied, stopping near the three klevahs who sat on the edge of a veranda that ran the two lengths of the corner store. Gabardine and cotton trousers with sharp creases were hitched high over shining two-tone shoes and they sat on snowy-white handkerchiefs, freshly ironed shirts standing away from their bodies.

"Aah, is dolly, man," Fats said in the slow, soft and impersonal manner that marked a sort-of modesty among the wake-up when they spoke of themselves. "Only there's getting to be too many dogs in Soph'town."

"Yeah," Philip admitted in the same tone. "Heard you had some shaandies – a dust-up last night." One was not supposed to show interest in another's affairs until invited to do so, unless it was a close friend. He was nothing of the sort to any of the three men he had casually waved to as he walked past their customary perch for observing the location's passing show.

"Ag – just one of these war-time klevahs, jy notch," Fred said with off-hand disgust at the memory of the johnnie-come-lately from the bundu who'd attempted to assert himself as one of die real manne. "Six months here, and they think they notch everything and everybody. If they haven't seen you before, you're a no-count. So he gets into some argument with Peppy – and you know Peppy," the young man grinned.

"Doesn't take crap from nobody," he went on, digging an elbow into Peppy's side. "This was at the Cabin in the Sky, you understand, my brikaid – and you can't let some moegoe give you lip in there. So, Fats borrowed a three-star blade from some tsotsi, but the Durango Kid was there."

"And that moerskont can't stay out of anybody's fight, the bastard," Peppy added. "Says oxen like us – just because we've got jobs – don't know how to handle no-counts. So he takes over."

They laughed, each with a clear image in his mind of the crazy bastard who had this penchant of firing the two pistols he almost always carried. Just like the real Durango Kid in the movies.

"So Chanam fixed him?" Philip asked, using the gunman's given name. Looking up the noisy, crowded and sun-splashed street as if he didn't have much interest in the outcome of the dust-up.

"I don't think so," Fats grumbled. "You know these plaasjapies – tough, you understand. Three bullet holes, and he still runs away."

"Used to chasing hares on the farms, you notch," Fred explained.

"Maybe the fokken dog bled to death somewhere," Peppy suggested hopefully.

After a few more off-hand exchanges Philip continued along Victoria Road. Sunday afternoon and the narrow main street seemed to have drawn the uncounted thousands of Sophiatown onto its pot-holed tarmac and dusty pavements. People streamed up and down in their Sunday best, mingling, weaving, stopping, turning, talking, laughing, shouting. Young men leaned like languid sentries against the walls of stores, or sat on the edges of their verandas – narrowed eyes scanning the passing crowd, nodding at some familiar faces, waving at acquaintances, shouting a casual profanity at friends. Girls and young women – in tight skirts, flared skirts, demure suits, caressing frocks – walked hurriedly on their own, provocatively in pairs and trios, confidently with boyfriends who were confident in friendly territory; or nervously if he was a situation or an ordinary garden-variety working ox. Older people in this promenading, vividly coloured crowd carried themselves with slow dignity that tried to ignore the tension emanating from the sharply-dressed, cold-eyed sentries. And those others who walked broad-shouldered, even if thin, and bumped into likely victims: tsotsis in search of shaandies.

A seemingly gay, casual parade of the inhabitants of Sophiatown – a Sophiatown doomed too soon to be a pile of rubble; the best known, best loved, most feared and most hated ghetto in all South Africa. Most of them proud to belong here; but many trying to look like they belonged, and many afraid because they did belong – and could feel and isolate the underlying danger that never eased. Seemingly casual, but aware of the back-prickling, foot-hurrying, eye-swivelling undercurrent of spontaneous, instantaneous, half-expected and explosive violence: a carefree yet cautious skating over the thin ice. A semi-conscious readiness to flee from any sudden outburst, an unprovoked stabbing, a shooting, a gang fight, an abduction, a robbery, an arrest. Under the eye of a hot sun they walked with their fears, smiled their confidence, talked through their wariness. A resigned expectation of trouble – for anyone but, please God, not for me; not today, not this year.

The green buses with yellow stripes sped, roared and honked. Cars braked, revved engines and nosed through the jostle; bicycles tinkled their bells, swerved and weaved. A jungle: the animals promenading for the duration of an unwritten day-of-rest truce that could be revoked without warning; treading softly, shuffling, hurrying uncertainly.

Philip turned into Ray Street, and after a few yards into the drunk-leaning gate in a high, disintegrating corrugated-iron wall that had been painted red generations earlier. Behind this screen was another world of courtly drinking: small groups were dotted about a forecourt whose red earth had turned black from constant floods of dishwater and home-brewed beer: *skokiaan, barberton* and *se bapa le masenke* – only groping along zinc fences would get them home – or *s'qeda viki,* which kept imbibers drunk for the rest of a penniless week.

A man stood woozily at a corner of the battery of lavatories, his feet sunk in the pool of urine to which he was adding. A few braziers smoked between the groups of drinkers. Children played around them, and women hurried from their customers to the hidden holes of illegal brew whose heavy, cloying smell permeated the air.

Philip approached the first door in the row of one-room family homes enclosing the yard. He knocked and a loud, belligerent voice from within demanded:

"Who's it?"

"Me, Boykie. Philip."

"Oh, you!" The lock turned and the door opened. A very black, broad-smiling face above a stocky figure appeared in the crack. "Howzit, Phil!" A toothy-grin examination of the visitor: "How's the sharp dresser, eh? Come on in, boy! Come on in!"

Like the rest around the yard, the room was small and dark; but cool with curtains drawn to keep out Sophiatown. A room as small as others around the yard, but not cluttered from too many people and their possessions squashed too close. A quiet, other world from that outside. The throb of muted jazz, the gleam of polished furniture: cosy and with an easy atmosphere that encouraged quiet chats.

An ice bucket stood on a low table holding a bottle of white wine. A book case held neat rows of records, 78 r.p.m. and the new-fangled LPs, near a portable player. Battalions of books stood to attention on shelves set high on the walls above the furniture. And glossy magazines were scattered on chairs, tables and the double bed. This was the solitary retreat from the world in which Boykie Courtroom held court for rigorously selected friends.

A thin man, younger than the host and his new visitor, was collapsed in an easy chair near the record player. Long legs sprawled, a glass of wine in his negligent hand, and a smile on an angular face, the head nodding to the music.

"Hi, Phil!" the younger man laughed.

"Howzit, Desmond."

"Take the weight off your feet, klevah. And have some wine, boy! Have some chilled wine!"

Boykie, the out-of-place legal clerk, paused in his bustling about the room – he never could be still – and glared at Desmond. "'Have some wine,' you say – eh! Who the bloody hell d'you think buys the wine you're soaking up and offering around?"

Desmond grinned, and the tirade continued: "When're you going to learn some manners, you up-country bum?" Boykie plonked his stocky self on the bed, shaking his head at the impertinence. Then turned impatiently to the new arrival:

"Come on, Phil! Don't act like a stranger, even if I don't see you often enough. Take off that can't-get Palm Beach jacket – and the weight off your feet, as this clodhopper has already told you. Make yourself at home, man!" He grinned – a burst of sunshine in the darkened room.

Desmond laughed, refilling his glass and becoming the object of another glare. "You're going to get yourself ulcers at a woefully early age, Boykie," he said. "Why don't you resign yourself to living with black barbarians like me, eh?" He laughed again, a loud hiccuping sound.

Philip removed his cream linen jacket and laid it, carefully folded, over the back of a vacant chair. He undid the top button of his flower-patterned shirt as he sat down. For the first time in days – since that night – he felt completely relaxed and at ease.

He waved away the glass of wine Boykie had filled after grabbing the bottle from Desmond and was holding out towards him.

"That's for white hobos, man," Philip grinned mischievously. "You know I don't drink that stuff."

"Aah, you're just another barbarian!" Boykie scolded. "Only drink rot-gut mahog! I don't have any brandy – good brandy. Desmond and some greedy pigs cleaned that out last night. You offer these kaffirs a drink and they've got to finish the bloody bottle!"

"Brandy?" Philip asked. "I don't want a hangover on blue Monday."

He rose from the chair, reached out for his jacket, and withdrew a flat half-bottle of whisky from its inside pocket.

Desmond laughed yet again and rubbed his hands in exaggerated pleasure. "Now that's a man's drink, boy: moonshine! Eh, Boykie?" He turned to the bringer of illegal nectar: "These intellectuals and their wine, Phil – ugh!"

"Aren't you one too, Des – a member of the black intelligentsia, as your liberal friends called you?" Philip half-jeered. "All those books you're always carrying around like a mobile lending library."

Boykie and Desmond were accepted by the klevahs, but were on a quite different level from the closed-faced young men Philip had been speaking to on Victoria Road. Different, too, from Philip's type, who fluctuated from the near-violence of shebeens to the quietly desperate dignity of the situations' respectable world. Desmond and Boykie were, basically, situations; but wake-up and treated as such. Then, again, these two almost-klevah near-situations were citizens of a fringe world – where the black intelligentsia fraternised with those white liberals who did not fear the ostracism of their more upright friends and neighbours.

Most black men, and almost all whites, who made this illegal contact across the colour bar now termed 'apartheid' did so through political organisations. But Boykie and Desmond were comparatively apolitical, and had made their entry into this world through their intellectualism and employment.

Boykie was chief clerk to a left-wing lawyer, and Desmond was one of the brighter reporters on the only newspaper for Africans, the *Golden City Post,* that was read by liberals. Boykie Courtroom was a situation by nature, and a klevah by design and the necessity to survive in Sophiatown, which provided most of his employer's clients. And also a Black Intellectual – as the white liberals told him with congratulatory enthusiasm. Living on these various levels at the same time had engendered in him an impatience with his kind, different from that of the average situation. He was impatient with what anti-apartheid politicians termed 'the masses' and tsotsis sneered at as 'the oxen' – people who dragged behind in the obstacle race for emancipation. These people he ignored, but he was forced by the might of the Law to live among them. He had created his own, cloistered world of books, music and art he'd been introduced to by his white mentors, and for which he had developed a desperate craving. Being able to discuss and appreciate their civilisation made him acceptable to these arbiters of all that could be good.

His impatience turned into eruptions of anger at those who, like him, had been allowed to get a seductive glimpse of life on the privileged side of the colour bar, but were not sufficiently impressed to also adopt the mannerisms of enlightenment.

Such a dissident was the younger and irrepressible Desmond. Boykie had given Philip up long ago. He had tried to lead his childhood friend into this twilight where black and white were a concessional grey, but Philip had scoffed with bitter sarcasm instead of being grateful at this chance and privilege of having white friends. He hated them too much, and Philip's attitude had led to an estrangement. They were still good friends, but Boykie felt that Philip laughed at him when he enthused about the dinners and parties he attended in the suburbs – almost always the wealthiest suburbs, and most of the participants Jews.

A *jewish* situation for Boykie – as klevahs said when they were pleased. And, boy, he'd made conquests among Jewish girls! So 'fascinated' by township life that a few had spent the night in his 'absolutely fantastic' room – which he called a bedsitter, in the English manner – after trawling shebeens with evocative names for new and 'extraordinary' experiences.

No skondaai was worth risking six months' in prison for contravening the Immorality Act, Philip had thought. That is, if she did admit to the gattas she'd opened her thighs with pleasure and not under duress – plain rape and what you expect, Sergeant …

But Desmond! Boykie despaired of him, and at times detested the out-of-town boy. Yet he could not break a friendship that sprung up after meeting at one of these 'mixed' and illegal parties, when they'd realised they had so much in common apart from knowing the same liberal crowd. Desmond was one of a few Africans Boykie could 'communicate' with; but so damned immature! To him apartheid was a joke, as was the painful sincerity of the liberals, who went out of their way to make Black Intellectuals feel at ease and display their own lack of racism.

"Well, Mister Wonderful – how's the girls these days?" Boykie was asking, smiling too broadly. Attempting to hide his unease at the rare, and so unusual, visit; and using the popular song for a jibe that was also a compliment. "I hear that's what they call you, now, Phil – after they get a taste of your bedside treatment."

Desmond burst into new peals of merriment: "No, boy, not bedside!" he corrected. "In situ, Boykie – inside the bed!"

Boykie flapped a dismissive hand at Desmond, who was slapping his skinny thighs in applause at the witticism the older young men ignored.

"Oh, they're still tossing their curves, Boykie," Philip answered, smiling lazily. "You know how it is. One night of inspired screwing, and the word gets around."

"Yeah – and not just once, you greedy bastard. Always had the pick of them," Boykie said, the envy almost hidden by lewd admiration. "Remember those little girls at school? And the times you've denied everything, or your parents had to pay damages?"

Philip's eyes narrowed, and he winced in pain to recall and then reject the memories of his three – or was it four? – unknown, illegitimate children. One phase of his life he'd pushed far back into his memory. Good as forgotten. There were probably more than four, but he'd so emphatically denied other charges – lately in a threatening manner – that a few girls, and recently young women, had turned to other men to share their intimacies.

"The good thing these days is that nice-time sisters know – or should know," Desmond temporised, "how to take care of themselves."

"If they're not already barren, the bitches," Philip remarked.

Desmond burst into more laughter, ignoring, more likely not comprehending, the warnings Boykie was signalling at him. Boykie had noted the flicker of hurt and anger that glinted in Philip's eyes: not in a mood to boast about his conquests.

"You mean girls like Virginia – don't think I didn't see you two that night last week, Philip! You mean they're mules?" Desmond asked in disbelief. "With bazooms like – almost like the Battleship's! I mean, boy – a dairy cow like that?"

"She's got two children, Desmond," Boykie cut in dryly. "She doesn't need any more problems. And you – cheeky laaitie! – are likely to end up in casualty, talking like that about people's girlfriends."

"Oh, Philip knows I didn't mean to."

"I know, Des," Philip stopped him. "Like all the times you want me to line up some cherries – the bigger tits the better – to pose as pin-ups for your lousy paper."

"What's wrong with that?" Desmond asked, chuckling to hide his defensive tone. "Any guy should be pleased to see his cherry in a bikini – showing everybody else what they're not getting."

"Hah!" Boykie snapped. "What you and your photographers hope to get into! Dazzling these stupid girls with chicken-feed glamour, so before they know what they're doing, they've opened up for you? Haven't you boys learned yet that they're all the same under the clothes?"

"That knowledge hasn't stopped your rampaging, Boykie," Desmond laughed.

"It's all this showing off of naked thighs I don't like," Philip observed, and his friends exchanged a questioning glance: is he another of these sexual conservatives? "I'm not worried that any of my girls find themselves in bed with one of these goats. Not my chicks! The glamour won't dazzle them."

"Why?" they asked, overlapping.

"They know what they get if they do that," they were calmly told.

"Now that's one thing I don't understand about you, boy," Boykie said, voice hesitatingly reproachful. "Beating up girls, I mean. I've heard a few funny stories, you know. And they don't sound like you at all. At school you were the one who used to interfere when some bum –"

"That's how many years ago?" Philip smiled. "People change, you know, Boykie. Just look at us now. Who'd think you and I were inseparable? But now you're Boykie Courtroom, the intellectual. And me? I'm Nice Time Phil, the delivery-van driver."

"Salesman, isn't it?" Desmond asked.

And Boykie smiled. "You're making twice the money I make. Who wants to buy back-door legal briefs?"

"And there's problems of bulk transportation, boy!" Desmond added, slapping a bony knee. "I mean, those documents are bulky – apart from unintelligible."

"I suppose that's another thing that worries you about me, Boykie?" Philip asked, but it sounded like a statement. "You think I've turned into just another of those minus statistics Whitey draws up – and you despise. Me another darkie who steals at work and sells back-door. You think we're criminals – well, maybe just crooks?"

"Well," Boykie said slowly, his earlier unease returning. They had drifted too far apart for him to speak as frankly and forcefully as he once could. Especially to questions in that softly mocking tone in Philip's voice – talking like die real manne when they're offended; manoeuvring the unwary into words that justify assault.

The thought chilled Boykie, but he shook it off. That wasn't quite the sibilant tone, he decided. In some cock-eyed way, he really does want to know – a judgement from me of his attitudes. Signs that Philip was turning more and more into one of them, the amoral, were there. His violence was not confined to erring girlfriends ... Boykie wondered how long it would be before Philip slipped off the razor's edge he was teetering on, and into the unequivocal nether world where daylight killings were only a shade worse than the wanton, casual assaults that took place daily.

Walking the razor's edge was a delicate way of life. Always the danger of slipping into a straddling position, when the sharp edge would cut deep into a moral groin with efficient indifference. And it could be more difficult for their relationship, if Philip fell to the other side. Whatever drove Philip to this irrevocable fall might turn those frustrations against Boykie with a spiteful bitterness reserved for childhood friends. And that would inevitably thrust Boykie into the despised and harassed, because respectable, world of the victims. In his case, that of the situations.

"Well," Boykie repeated carefully, but Desmond cut in, unaware of tension.

"You see," he imitated, "the situation is like this ...!"

The skinny younger man laughed, amused by imposing on Boykie the mantra that had given situations their jeered-at label. Boykie turned on him with an anger generated by his fears:

"Shut up, you little pip-squeak! If it wasn't for me when you arrived from Port Elizabeth, you'd be just another situation – and suffering like they are!"

"Never mind the kid," Philip said gently. "Go on, Boykie. You know you can say whatever you feel – I won't be offended. There are times, you see, when all of us need truth more than anything else. I have you for that, my ma se kind."

Boykie gave him a long, speculative look, then. But he still chose his words carefully, eyes ranging from Philip's immobile face to a study of his own fingers that he laced, unlaced and re-laced.

"What you're doing, Phil – you and everybody else who's got the chance, the opportunity – from your jobs ... it's morally dishonest. Theft always is, whatever the justification – even if in this case everybody talks about it as 'just taking' instead of stealing. And Desmond's newspaper makes the sly suggestion that you're all just Robin Hoods. Taking from rich whites to sell half-price to poor blacks."

"What!" Desmond objected, but grinning. "We don't do that! Have you forgotten the paper's owned by a white capitalist? You think just because he talks race equality and all that crap he's going to let us write that it's right for our people to steal from his fellow tycoons?"

"But you do, Desmond," Boykie said with unusual patience. "All these exposés – so-called revelations – you publish. Aren't you glamourising gangsters and back-door salesmen?"

Desmond the reporter shrugged and sipped whisky.

"Anyway, Phil, as I was saying … there's justification, when you look at the issue politically. We don't owe them any loyalty because of the way they treat us. But it's still morally wrong, and I wouldn't do it even if I had the chance. You must understand me though, boy. I'm not condemning anybody."

"Because even you buy back-door, Boykie," Philip commented. "You got a Hector Powe suit from the Young Americans a couple of weeks ago."

He pointed: "And that's how you've built up your record collection. You get them back-door."

"That's true, Phil," Boykie acknowledged, smiling. "I did, I have – and I'll continue to buy. I like nice clothes, we all do – but we can't afford them when they don't pay us what we deserve."

"So in fact we're doing you a favour? Taking the dishonesty off you? Because receiving stolen property isn't as bad as doing the stealing?"

"You see, Phil," Boykie began, eyes on fingers, "there's a personal morality involved. I mean –"

"There you go again, Boykie!" Desmond exclaimed, wagging an amused and accusing finger. Boykie turned to glare and he held up his hands in mock surrender. "Okay, Okay, I know I'm just a kid compared to you greybeards, boy. But you must give me a chance. This is an intellectual discussion, and age doesn't count – especially if it's only about five years. Hey, Phil? Am I right or not?"

Philip wanted to laugh, amused by the abrasive relationship that seemed to exist between these two members of the intelligentsia. He nodded. "I don't know about 'intellectual discussions', Des," he said.

"You're the one who carries the books. But go ahead and make your contribution."

Desmond looked quickly across at Boykie out of mischievous eyes, then spoke. "I know you used to be Boykie's bosom buddy; but I've come to know him better than you do now. He likes arguing as much as I do, but only when's he's on the winning side. When he's not, he brings out this collection of clichés like 'personal morality'."

"Give me an instance, wise guy!" Boykie snapped.

"Well, take your attitude towards your white friends."

"Our white friends, you mean!"

"Hey – that reminds me!" Philip said, trying to draw them away from what he could see was going to be a bristling, hair-splitting haggle. "There's some things I want to know about these liberal friends of yours. I mean, for instance, do they really like inviting you to parties and meals – dinner – in their houses? Or are they only ..."

He stopped, uncertain about the 'or', and Boykie turned slowly, smiling knowingly. "But you know you're not interested in them, Phil. You've laughed at me too often when I've tried to explain what I think you now want to know."

"What's that?" Desmond demanded.

"Why don't we talk about jazz instead?" Boykie said. "Or the latest films showing at the Odin?"

"But I am interested, Boykie. It's kind of all of a sudden, but I am. Now."

"That's the last thing you should be, Phil," Desmond warned. "Just keep laughing – at us, I mean," he added quickly as Boykie swung round to him. "We take ourselves and all this Good Race Relations crap too seriously. It's all a joke, really."

"You're still too young to understand these things, Desmond. All right, not too young," Boykie conceded as Desmond opened his mouth to protest. "But you lack a proper perspective. If you'd grown up in a place like this, instead of some mud-hut village near Port Elizabeth, you'd realise what it all means. You just don't understand how important it is that those of us who get a chance must show these whites that we're as good as they are."

"By drinking wine," Philip said with an ironic smile, pointing at the empty bottle in the ice bucket. "By reading big books of philosophy," he added, waving his hand negligently at the rows of books high on the walls. "By listening to Bach instead of Basie, Debussy instead of The Duke ..."

"I like that alliteration, boy – congrats, Phil," Desmond chortled. "I didn't realise you'd even heard of them!"

He was ignored. "What you don't seem to appreciate, Phil, is that they choose the standards," Boykie said. "We live in a world where white equals good, and black equals bad and barbaric. So whatever claims we make for equality – for goodness – are going to be judged by the standards they have set."

"Why must they be allowed to choose the ground?" Desmond demanded. "What makes them think their standards are better than our traditions? For a start, our morality is much better than theirs. And I don't mean this hotch-potch, catch-as-catch-can non-morality of the locations. I mean the morality – the cultural traditions and morality – of our forebears."

"So you still want to measure the spear against the rifle?" Boykie said in an irascible voice. "Have you forgotten what happened in the 'Kaffir Wars'?"

"Of course not – and that was only technology," Desmond laughed. "Firearms started in China, anyway. And inventing the wheel has nothing to do with civilisation or culture. But I mean, does appreciating a Picasso make a person 'civilised'? Is Picasso any better than, say, Gerard Sekoto – famous in Paris right now? Or, going centuries back, the Bushmen who did the cave drawings? And, anyway, do all whites appreciate Picasso, Bach or what-have-you? They're all supposed to be civilised. But just being born with a white skin doesn't make them civilised."

Philip grinned, thinking of Benade the dispatcher. "I know a few who think they are, Des. But, man, one look – one word – and you know otherwise."

Met them at the police station too, he bitterly remembered.

"But how else can we show them?" Boykie asked, despairing. "They control the world and choose its standards. After all, we want the things they have, don't we? The advantages, the know-how, the –"

"All I want from them," Philip interrupted, "is that they leave me alone to make my own life as I like! I'm sick of their –"

"I want them, Phil – all these things they've got," Desmond said. "But not at the price they're demanding. Boykie can't afford to tell them he doesn't really like Mozart, because they'd just nod wisely and take it as proof that we all need a thousand years to catch up with them."

"I prefer Bach any day!" Boykie grinned ruefully.

"It's a stupid, crazy world we've made for ourselves, us so-called Educated Natives," the reporter went on. "No wonder tsotsis victimise situations. Trying to discourage us from all these useless attempts to be like whites. We never will be, and they don't think we'll ever be what they like to call 'civilised' – not the most liberal of them, I tell you!"

"All right, wise guy," Boykie said. "I won't argue. Just tell us your solution. What must we do?"

Desmond laughed. "I don't have any solutions, but I do have my personal viewpoint ..." He stopped, shaking his head with sad recognition. "There I go too, hiding behind the magic word 'personal'! Anyway, what I mean is that I don't feel I'm under any obligation to prove anything to anybody. If they think I'm inferior, that's too bad. And if they think I'm equal, fine. No amount of proving is going to change anything. Arguments aren't going to change anybody's prejudices."

"So we just sit on our black backsides and hope that one day they'll come to think we're equal!" Boykie snapped, voice sarcastic. "How mar-vel-lous!"

"But, Boykie," Philip said, "don't these friends of yours already think you're as good as themselves?"

Desmond laughed and waved his arms, then pointed at Boykie. "Go on, boy. Answer him!"

"They do, Phil," Boykie said hesitantly, aware of Desmond's mocking eyes. "On the whole, they think we – most of us that they've met – are at least getting there. That's why when they have mixed parties they bring others, so that they, too, can see for themselves."

"Yet even though we're such civilised, well-mannered ambassadors – we sip our cocktails, not gulp them, we nibble at their tiny sandwiches, not guzzle them – they want to believe we're exceptions, boy. We're not representative. But!" Desmond held up an ironic finger, "They insist on regarding the lowliest, illiterate kaffir as the true representative of us all."

Philip turned to Boykie. "So then, my bra, the programme calls for all you Black Intellectuals to personally convert all two-and-a-half-million of them?"

Anger and defeat in Boykie's eyes as he looked steadily at Philip, while Desmond went into another paroxysm of laughter.

"You see?" he said finally. "All you wanted to do was make fun of me. What's the point of trying to explain things to you? You've got your mind made up already. And as for you!" he snapped, turning to Desmond. "What d'you find so funny, you laughing hyena? Why do you go to all the mixed parties if you think it's all so crazy?"

"To drink all that free whisky, of course!" Desmond grinned. "And screw their women – I definitely approve of their way of proving that they've got no colour bar!"

Philip looked quickly up at a Picasso on the wall to hide his interest.

"I've told you often enough, boy," Desmond said in what passed for a serious tone. "I know what I am, and I don't care if they agree or not. I'm not looking for their, er, acceptance. I'll just play the game so I keep on getting their invitations."

The boy's not so stupid or crazy, Philip told himself. Just that annoying laughter at every bloody thing gets to me.

"Tell me more, Desmond," Philip said aloud, an intense curiosity stirring within him. "Why don't you care? Don't you want them to believe –"

"Oh, I do – I want them to. But I'm not going to waste my time on proving it to them. If they're too stupid to realise their prejudices have no logical premise, that's their problem."

"I think I dig what you mean," Philip said slowly; wondering if he would find the right words to express himself without giving anything away. "Not everything, of course, since I'm just a van driver, you understand."

He smiled, and Boykie stared suspiciously at him. "I don't dig you, old buddy," he said.

"I was picked up in a raid a couple of days ago, you see. But d'you know what I felt – how I felt about all those white cops cursing and beating us in the station? Usually I'm mad as hell. But this time I was sorry for them."

"God forgive them, for they know not what they do," Desmond intoned.

"No – not that way, Des. I pitied them for what they are, I think."

"Hey!" Desmond exclaimed, and jumped excitedly from his chair, offering his hand. "Congratulations! Congrats, boy!" he shouted, wringing Philip's hand. "And welcome to the company of the few – the liberated few. You pitied them! Boy, you don't have to worry about a thing, now. You've made it!"

"What d'you mean, he's made it?" Boykie asked, irritated.

"I mean he's free!"

Desmond threw his hands up and wide.

"Freer than even our beloved Prime Minister himself. He's above prejudice, don't you see? He's not competing any more, boy. Don't you understand that when you pity people it's like despising them? And you only despise inferiors. Don't you see, Boykie? You hate your equals or superiors, but you pity and despise inferiors!"

He stood in the middle of the room with the muted jazz piping out of the record player and stared with pleasure and wonder at Philip. "I shouldn't even say welcome to you, Phil," he added, slowly. "Because I haven't quite made it. Not yet."

"You're talking a lot of bull," Boykie commented.

"I think you're wrong," Philip told him. "If you pity people – or despise them, as you say – you don't go out of your way to revenge yourself on them. Do you?"

"What kind of revenge?" Desmond asked, the sharp eyes of a reporter probing.

"Well," Philip started. "Take, for instance … the case of a black man who, let's say, rapes a white woman … to show them what he thinks of –"

"That's humiliation, boy," Desmond interrupted. "What else do you do to a person you despise but to humiliate?"

"Nonsense!" Boykie retorted. "That kind of hostile act is an attempt at assertion. And that doesn't result from a superiority complex. A superior being has no need to assert himself."

Philip sat back and listened to the excited argument over what Desmond grandiosely termed "the dichotomy of rape".

You bloody, stupid fool! Almost gave yourself away, didn't you, you moegoe, you war-time klevah … Philip scolded himself as he walked back along Ray Street. Oh, you tried – you think you tried – to complicate it and all that nonsense. But it stuck out a mile who you were talking about. Better be careful or you'll be sitting in the death house at Pretoria Central. Not legal suicide, but from talking too much, asking too many questions. Boykie isn't stupid – hy notch alles, man – and that boy Desmond has some kind of instinct. A war-time from PE, but hits the nail on the head where even Boykie is muddled by living on too many levels.

At least things are beginning to clear up. Humiliate – humiliation, is the word. Show her and all of them what I think. Never lust, but something else.

So pretty, dainty and nose-in-the-air. At least I didn't grab just any ugly thing simply because she was white. Wiggling her arse even in the dark – they do it all day, like they were doing it against a wall. And staring coldly at, or through, us non-people for looking at them like they were women instead of sacred symbols to be worshipped from the gutter. We're not people to them. Calling a cop just because we look at what they want us to look at. Crimen injuria – that's what you 've just done, jong! Just look at me, you stinking kaffirs! Look at something you'll never get! And if you look too boldly, or I don't like your face, I'll have you arrested! All so high and mighty. Queens of the universe protected by kings. Drag them into the gutter they've kicked us into and make them taste the muck. Into the lowest, stinkingest depths. Hurt her pride – defile it – smash that master race confidence. Make her feel some loathing for herself.

But maybe I've only made her hate us the more. So what? When they hate instead of just despising us, then maybe they'll begin to think of us as people. Not just grovelling tools whose only use is living for their convenience. Next time she sees a black man she won't be impersonal or contemptuous.

Yet if only she'd fought back! Just struggled a bit. Not to excite me, as Desmond claims is what rapists like to happen. Then I could really have made her feel every single thing. Instead of lying there like a piece of wood. Ice-cold fish. In a trance like it wasn't happening to her. Not experiencing every single second of her degradation. But then if she didn't feel anything, it wasn't such a terrible thing you did. An insidious and insinuating voice chortled in his whisky-fuddled head – Boykie had, after prolonged hesitation, reluctantly dragged out a bottle of his special ... But that means I didn't succeed – not the success I wanted and expected. Failed. Where's that feeling of exultation, of achievement? And why the hell am I cracking my head over it all? Why do I remember? Why speak to myself, if nobody else, like this?

How did that poem go? *I speak in grief, not exultation as I did ere misery made me* ... What next? Something like that. Who was the poet? English and young, no experience of the real world. Not my world, anyway ...

Chapter 5

She heard the key in the door, as she had so often in the past with affectionate anticipation; then the door opening and closing – a softer sound than in the happy past, and no cheerful shout announcing his return from the day's labours. She looked down at the jewelled wristwatch that had been an anniversary gift from him. He's on time, as he's been every working day since that horrible night.

She sighed, and her eyes moved listlessly back to the scene outside the window of the apartment. The setting sun shot fiery streamers across the western sky, throwing the tall apartment blocks of Hillbrow into sharp silhouette. Below, in the street, streams of cars crawled and growled north out of the city centre, where their occupants had earned more money, towards luxury and security in the leafy northern suburbs. Roaring, squeaking and smelly Native buses shot the other way back into the city, to pick up more unskilled workers to take home to Alexandra township. That was somewhere off the main road to Pretoria, but never actually seen by her – a dreadful slum, she'd read. But that was not her problem. She had enough problems of her own, caused by one of them – or so everybody thinks ...

Through a gap between the buildings a little to the left of her window, she could see the untidy bulge – a carbuncle to her eyes – on the brow of Hospital Hill, beyond which the city lay. An earthen heap called The Fort, but called Number Four by the Natives, she'd heard somewhere. The awaiting-trial prison for brutes, where the cause of her problems should be locked away by now, if she'd not been so stupidly, so completely, frightened out of her wits. A little way beyond The Fort, on the city side of the hill, was the hospital she'd been rushed to that horrible night. A shudder quivered her body as she remembered. Her eyes came quickly away from that horizon and back to the street below her window. But she could not get away from the memories. There had been few cars that night, that beautiful, calm night that had turned into a nightmare. She knew that if she leaned a little out of the window she would see part of the alleyway. She did not want to see it again, ever.

A hand rested lightly on her shoulder, and lips touched her neck.

"Hello, darling," his voice said.

"Hello, Patrick," she whispered, leaning her head against his arm. "You're on time."

"I don't ever want to be late again," he said slowly. He walked past her and leaned against the window, looking down at her where she sat like an old woman. "What kind of day did you have?"

"Quiet," she told him.

"It must be terribly dull."

She did not say anything, but looked up into his troubled face. The old firmness and confidence has gone, she thought. Traces of self-pity, now. Uncertainty. And it's all my fault. Everything we say now is either about that night, or has undertones, memories of it. We must not be so morbid. But what to do to exorcise that horrible night?

"This won't do, Jeanie," he said in a voice that tried to be firm, but instead held a plea. "It's been over a week, now, and you're still obsessed with it. You sit in here all day and brood. You've got to snap out of it – just got to, darling. And you can't forget it if you just sit around here, refusing to see anybody or even talk to them on the phone. I want to forget it too – we all want to; but we can't even make a start while you go on like this."

Tears came into her eyes. With a quick movement she placed her hand over his on the window-sill. "Oh, Pat! Why did this have to happen to us – why us? I'm so sorry, Paddy. I've shamed you. What are people saying?"

"Nothing, Jean! Can't you understand?"

"Nothing? Really?"

"Nobody's laughing at you or at us. You've got to get this idea out of your mind that everyone's snickering. Everybody's sorry – even the Native boys at the office. My driver said – oh, what's the use?"

"They're only being nice because … But don't you know, can't you guess what they say behind your back? How they feel inside? They smirk, Patrick! I know! And I can't stand it … I can't!"

"Oh, stop it, Jean. You're being silly. We have good friends and they'll stand by us. Everybody'll have forgotten about all of this in a few weeks – but only if you will let them, Jean. Only if you will!"

"I just can't, Pat." Suddenly she thought she knew why – and what must be done if she was to forget. "I can't forget while we live here," she said, looking up at him and hoping he would agree. "Not in this flat, this building, this – this everything! I've got to go away. Some place far from here."

His face told her this was impossible, and she changed: "Maybe only for a few weeks. Go somewhere I'm not known. Where I can pick up my life again, remember who I am … Then I can come back. Don't you see, Paddy?"

He laughed with sudden relief at this simple proposal. He went down on his knees beside her chair and took her hands in his. They were trembling.

"Is that all you need, Jeanie?" he asked happily. "A holiday? Of course you can go away, darling. Tomorrow, if you like. What a bloody fool I've been! Why didn't I think of this? Of course you must go – to the coast somewhere. Anywhere! Hell, even flirt with all those muscle-men who pretend they're *Charles Atlas*. After all, I won't be around for them to kick sand in my face – eh?"

"Paddy!" she scolded gently, stroking his hand.

He laughed. "Anything, my love! Anything, if it'll help you regain your self-confidence. Within limits, of course!" He chuckled, waving an admonishing finger. He kissed her hands and looked up into her smiling, tearful face. My God, how beautiful she is, he thought, the depthless sadness in her eyes tearing at his insides.

"When do you want to go? It's too hot for Durban, so somewhere further south. In the Cape? Knysna or George, eh? Get one of those little beach cottages and soak up the sun; burn out the past, eh?"

"As soon as you can arrange it, darling," she said softly, pleased to see him looking happy again. Relieved. Please, God, she prayed, please make it work. For his sake, please. "I love you very much, Patrick."

"I love you too, my sweet." He rose and glanced at his watch. "I think I can still get the travel agents before they close for the day. You can leave the day after tomorrow, I'm sure. Fly down and –"

"Pat?"

He stopped on his way to the telephone and looked back at her. "Yes, Jeanie?"

She bit her full lower lip, looking helplessly around the room. He started walking back to her. Slowly, his face shedding enthusiasm. "What's the matter now?" he asked, the voice hardening.

"When I come back, Paddy – you won't be here, will you, darling? I mean you'll have moved us into some other apartment. Far from here. The other end of town. I don't want to even pass near this place – through any part of Hillbrow – again. Can you do that?"

He grinned. "You seem to forget that my business is finding homes for other people, darling. What good would I be if I couldn't find a nice place for my own wife?"

Jean Ryan packed and prepared for a hiatus from everything on a sunny beach on the Indian Ocean – or was it the Atlantic – coast?

And while she lounged and read on the train she had preferred to flying ... while her luscious body turned a honey gold in the sun and her hair bleached to spun gold ... while she loafed and tried not to think beyond the next page of whatever she read ... life went on as usual six thousand feet up on the Highveld, and at its heart in the City of Gold.

Boykie Nine Years wore dirty blue overalls over his suit and, like any other delivery 'boy', pedalled a green delivery tricycle down a street in Doornfontein, the garment factory section of the city. He knew all the streets intimately from past excursions with his gang, who in the city looked quite different from their appearance in Sophiatown: anonymous working oxen, not dapper klevahs. He was keeping several car lengths behind a growling cab and its trailer with the legend 'South African Railways' stencilled on their sides. The trailer was piled high with long rolls of cloth wrapped in heavy paper, bearing labels that declared they had been imported from Europe: can't-gets that wouldn't be so exclusive when the suit-lengths were tailored at the factory. At the summit of the pile sat a wizened old white man, keeping rheumy-eyed guard over the precious consignment. It would not be long now before the other white man driving the combination would park as near as he could to the entrance of a factory, enter it with the way-bills, and return with black labourers who would cart the rolls into the cutting rooms under harsh warnings to be blerry careful.

Boykie knew the drill for deliveries at least as well as the guard. His eyes flicked from one side of the street to the other, checking on his ouens. Jerry walked along the pavement to his left, keeping between the tricycle and trailer. He also wore a khaki dust coat over his normal, sharp clothes, which placed him several cuts above Boykie in his guise as a common 'boy'. And Billy Mauser strolled along the right-hand pavement, without any particular disguise and on a level with the trailer.

The trailer double-parked on the quiet street. The driver climbed out, carrying the way-bills on a clipboard. He hurried round the front of his cab and entered the high, blank-walled factory. Boykie pedalled slowly on, swung his unwieldy vehicle to the right as if to pass the trailer. But he braked and stopped alongside it on the street side, so close that the guard perched on top of the consignment could not see him. In a moment he heard Jerry's drawl from the pavement side of the trailer.

"Ek sê – Basie," he sneered, "what's the time, eh?"

The rheumy-eyed guard took time before he deigned to respond. He coughed, spat onto the pavement, and said, "Quarter to four – kaffir."

The coarse voice continued after a few moments' silence: "Well? What you blerry standing there for now, boy? Get on and deliver what you're paid for – loafer you."

Jerry laughed; a lazy, contemptuous sound. "I think your cheap watch ain't no good, basie."

"Don't call me basie – I'm a baas, boy!"

" I bet you paid just ten bob for it, Groot Baas! That's all you fucking poor-whites can afford."

"Hey, you kaffir!" the guard spluttered. "You talking to me like that?"

"That's right," Jerry sneered. "And what you going to do about it?"

Boykie heard the guard's angry coughing and swearing as he blundered above him: bastard could fall off his perch. Then Jerry's voice jeering a challenge: "You wanna fight, you old stront – hey? Come on down here, then, you son of a whore! I'll fokken kick out the last teeth you got left down your stinking mouth!"

"You black bastard!" the old man half-wailed.

Boykie glared at the small crowd of expectant black faces that was gathering at a distance. They looked quickly away or hurried off. He beckoned to Billy Mauser watching from across the street, and as the sidekick approached he quickly cut through one of the ropes tying the consignment down. The watchers on both pavements were familiar with the scene, and grinned as the pair began sliding out one of the heavy rolls of cloth.

They loaded it into the large, green bin between the two front wheels of the tricycle while Jerry continued to exchange obscenities with the guard.

"Ah, fuck off, jou lae luis!" Jerry suddenly shouted the warning signal. "I got no time to waste with you, jou moerskont."

They had three rolls in the bicycle's bin, and Boykie pedalled away without a sideways glance at the amused spectors. He passed Jerry and saw the delivery driver cossing the pavement behind his sidekick. Billy had crossed back to the other pavement and jiggled his hand at the watchers in a gesture that was a greeting and, if necessary, also a warning.

Monday morning, and Desmond sat with other senior members of the *Golden City Post*'s editorial staff in the editor's office for the first news conference of the week. They had already completed a post-mortem of the previous day's paper, and were considering possible stories for the next issue. The news editor leafed through his diary, reading out routine assignments: political meetings, juicy divorce cases, contraventions of the Immorality Act by disgraceful white men who consorted with black kitchen girls; a follow-up to one of the campaigns that gave the paper a reputation for public service – and annoyed the government. These and others were discussed and decisions made on their handling.

"We still haven't got anything for the front page," the Scottish editor said. Grinning wickedly, he added: "Pity high government officials don't try to sleep with black – I mean African – women more often, eh, Desmond?"

"I've got something that might make the front page, Jimmy," Desmond said as the laughter subsided. "Needs some investigation, still; but I think it'll make it."

"Well, tell us, old boy," the editor instructed. "Our fingers are slipping off the edge of the cliff, man!"

"Well, seems there was this black man with five children," Desmond told them, his voice deadpan. "Anyway, he had some kind of argument with his white-man-boss. He was immediately fired, of course. Then when he went to have himself signed off, the boss scrawled across two pages of his pass book, 'Any person who employs this Native must be crazy' – or words to that effect. Didn't even give him a week's pay in lieu of notice."

"Well?" the editor demanded. "That's not much of a story, is it? Not even a filler paragraph."

"The point is," Desmond said patiently, "who's going to employ this poor father of five kids with that kind of recommendation on his pass book?"

"And he had no right doing that," Henry, the black news editor, added. "If he wants to write a reference, good or bad, he's supposed to do it separately. All he's meant to enter in the pass book is the date his employee was discharged. Without giving reasons, Jimmy."

"So, you see, Jimmy," Desmond took up the explanation, "this kind-hearted boss has condemned this poorly-paid father of five kids to the ranks of the permanently unemployed."

"Unemployable," a voice muttered.

The editor had reddened at the irony in Desmond's voice and now glared at the mutterer: "Can't he tear out those pages?"

"Ah – good idea. But that, unfortunately, is a criminal offence!" Desmond replied. "Wilful damage to government property. We pay for these dompas books, yet they remain government property."

"I still don't see much of a story in it," the editor said, holding back his temper.

"Probably not front page, Jim," Henry conceded, "but it's still a good story."

"Bad news," the mutterer added.

"Maybe a news feature – a spread on this kind of thing. If this man can't get a job within a specified period, he'll be endorsed out of the

Jo'burg magisterial district. He'll have to go back to the reserves, even if he was born right here."

"Can't he go back to his boss – I mean his former employer? Get him to change it?" Jimmy asked.

"He did – protested at the time it happened," Desmond countered, smiling at the discomfiture of his editor: an immigrant who'd arrived from Scotland with what he believed to be liberal values and attitudes. But then why, the reporter had always wondered, had Jimmy Mason chosen to bring his family down here – if not to escape a freezing climate and enjoy the benefits of apartheid under blue skies?

"And," Desmond continued patiently, "the white-man-boss told the poor man – sorry, boy – that's just what he'd intended: have him kicked out of town."

"I can't believe it. No man would do a thing like that on purpose."

"But he did, Jimmy. They do it all the time."

"He must have meant it as a joke."

"Not a very funny one. Too sophisticated for us niggers."

"Don't speak to me like that, my boy!" the editor snapped. "Are you forgetting who I am?"

"No, Mister Mason," Desmond replied. "I know who you –"

"I'm your bloody editor! That's all I meant!"

"And this is supposed to be a black newspaper, Mister Mason. We don't have to apologise for the evils of white people."

"Who's apologising? If you can prove to me –"

"If I may say so, Jim – Mister Mason – you have the rather unfortunate tendency of feeling you have to defend the white man to us. You take all his guilt onto your –"

"You're fired!" Mason exploded, letting go of his temper. A pause, and then he added: "I could fire you for that, you know that?"

Philip almost killed a man one morning – blue Monday in Sophiatown, when heads spun and were dizzy from weekend hangovers.

He joined other klevahs at the terminus, where the buses belched gagging diesel fumes as they idled, loading passengers, and then roared off in blue-black clouds of smoke. They ignored the long, patient lines of people dragging themselves off to work in the city: only oxen, moegoes and lesser klevahs queued. Philip belonged to that elite which was so close to the status of die real manne that Putco's queue marshals, conductors, dispatchers and inspectors were happy to do them small favours at no cost to themselves, thereby guarding their own status and health. Die manne chatted in a group at the head of the queues, and casually selected the crowded buses they would ride for free into town, crammed near the narrow doors and steps.

But occasionally one of the bus company's men baulked at such a liberty being taken by spies he didn't notch. Such a one was the broad-shouldered conductor who stood in front of Philip that morning, barring his way onto a bus that was fully loaded and about to depart. A relief conductor from one of the other townships – and thus almost a moegoe in Sophiatown terms. He must regard himself as a real man in Alexandra, Orlando or wherever he'd come from, Philip told himself, to hang tough and try to throw his weight around in Kofifi. He believed he could choose those to whom favours were extended.

"Not on my bus, spy!" he told Philip, who stared and tried to smile.

This kind of rebellion happened to most klevahs at some time or other with some Putco slaves. Either the man didn't know the klevah, or had taken a sudden dislike to a particular guy he felt he could, at long fuckin' last, resist. For Nice Time Phil this was one of those familiar times when a stifling rage knotted his stomach and rose like bitter bile from his guts to block his throat. Made him want to vomit, and spill out the racist poison implanted in his guts. Times when his very being was suddenly outraged for no reason evident to others. But the cause could only be brooding on the frustrations of the life he – they all – led under the yoke with which the white-man-boss had saddled them: what Boykie Courtroom called the monkey on their bowed backs. So pent-up with an impotent rage that he welcomed any violent release.

But this time was different. Not a reckless impulse to violence, but a strange and calculated coldness in his reaction to the public affront from the unknown bus conductor. So strange that he tried to speak lightly, determined to ignore the insult of being called 'spy' and avoid what he feared would follow.

"Okay, my brother, my brikaid," he smiled. "Don't be like that, man." Voice hoarse and tight. "We're all pals around here – ons notch mekaar."

"Not you, sonnyboy," the conductor sneered, slant eyes screwed almost shut. "I don't like your kind – a situation trying to make out like a klevah."

"Ag, China," the bus driver said through the window of his cab. "You're wasting time, man. Let him get on."

"Not this son of a whore," the conductor insisted.

Philip could feel the eyes of the people encircling them watching, waiting for his reaction to these insults. He did not have to fight to retain his standing with them. The man was bigger and must have a reputation where he came from. He could still turn it all into a joke and shrug it away. "Okay, Charles Atlas, I'm scared of you," he could say, and perhaps add that some other day ... Instead the cold rage within pushed him beyond the point of no return.

His voice turned sibilant as he asked the sneering man: "You're serious, neh?"

"What did you think, spy? You think I got time to waste on punks like you?"

"You want a fight," Philip said, "for a three-penny fare?"

"Not a fight, dog. Just kick you back into your mother's –"

Philip lunged forward, the conductor brought up his fists – and was kicked in the groin. The slant-eyed man called China knifed forward and down towards the pain and was kneed in the face. He staggered back against the bus and Philip kicked him again in the groin. The man screamed and fell in a huddle onto the ground. A hot, triumphant rage spread over Philip's body, swamping his earlier cold anger. He pulled back his foot to kick the man in the face in the approved manner: the heel of his highly-polished, two-tone Jarmans splitting the broad nose –

But he was stopped by a hand grabbing his shoulder. He swivelled round, expecting an ally of the conductor. But it was Jungle Joey, who grinned and offered the long-bladed knife he was named after.

"Don't spoil those nice shoes, klevah," Joey said, casually. "Take this jungle and show us you could be one of the real men – one day!"

Philip grabbed the knife and turned back to the huddled man. A gasp rose from some of the women craning forward for a better look. The conductor lay on his back, knees drawn up to the pain; staring with pop-eyed fear at the descending knife. At the last moment Philip deflected the knife and it stabbed harmlessly into the earth near the conductor's shoulder. He looked down into the frightened face, then staightened up.

He still had the presence of mind, as he handed back the knife, to smile and drawl, in the approved, casual manner: "What's the use of doing five years for a dog like this one?"

Joey laughed, pulled out a handkerchief and started polishing the dirt off his jungle knife. And Philip pushed through the crowd, towards the taxi rank. He felt cold and stiff-jointed. He was not certain what had stopped him from the act that his every fibre craved. Was it that, as he lay there, the conductor reminded him of that blurred, frightened, sacrificial face in the dark alley? Maybe simply that he could not go that far – not yet.

If that was the price of admission to die real manne, it was still beyond him.

And Danny the Drunk died in action that day on the city streets.

Philip heard the story in a Fordsburg shebeen, one of whose main attractions for the real, and really real men was the occasional availability of the daughter of the house. A not-too-pretty but overly voluptuous Lebanese girl – officially white under apartheid – who served drinks, swapped bawdy jokes in 'die taal', could be petted on a shapely behind and, when she felt like it – or for whatever unknown reason she had – would take one of them to her bedroom. Openly, without fear of arrest under the Immorality Act.

The story was that Danny the Drunk and his gang were on patrol in Jo'burg's streets. Peeping into white women's purses as they shopped, in search of a fat roll of pound notes. They found one such and followed her through several shops, strung out in line behind her flat arse, according to their roles. Danny, as usual, led the gang. He snapped her handbag open on the crowded pavement. The next in line loosened the purse inside, the third raised it almost out of the voluminous and gaping handbag.

Then Danny, only half drunk in the morning, came round for his second pass – the swoop. He lifted the fat purse out of the handbag and was about to pass it back down the line when a hand clamped down on his left wrist, the one that held the purse.

He swung round to face what looked like a Spingbok rugby forward and, without pause, pulled out his three-star knife – much shorter than a jungle – and slashed the heavy face lowering down at him. The grip on his wrist relaxed, he broke away, and the chase was on. The sight of the long, blood-stained knife cleared a path, and Danny ran. He weaved and ducked under a few restraining white hands and skipped over outstretched legs – the knife slashing, the purse in his other hand.

The chase went down several streets, past gaping faces and shouting voices. And a few sympathisers tried to confuse and interfere with the chase. But the bleeding Springbok and a white cop would not be diverted.

Danny had never been an athlete and, with his drinking and smoking, he could not hope to run very far for his freedom and the only life he knew. He finally slumped into a doorway and faced his pursuers, out of breath and weakly brandishing the knife. And the cop – Jou moer se gatta! he gasped at him – shot him dead.

Chapter 6

Patrick Ryan stood apart from the expectant throng on the station platform. He was successful at hiding that he was much more excited than any of them – and nervous. Why the hell are there so many people waiting here? How is she – recovered? How must I behave? Mustn't make a single mistake … must be careful; don't want to start a relapse. I musn't … hope to God she's recovered, damn it!

The steam engine hissed along the platform, black and gleaming with brass. The driver looked down with a brightly blue, supercilious eye at mere mortals who had started to wave handkerchiefs at their yet unseen beloved. The windows of the first two ancient wooden coaches were jammed with African, coloured and Indian faces; but held cautiously back until they had passed the white section of the platform. Then necks stretched out of the windows, grinning and calling out greetings to friends and family. Patrick glared at the vari-coloured faces, and the whites about him jeered, grimaced or were imperiously unseeing. The gleaming steel coaches for the white passengers followed and delighted squeals, waving handkerchiefs and hands accompanied by welcoming shouts filled the air about him. Patrick searched the faces suspended above him with dread and rising excitement.

He only saw her as she climbed down the stairs at the end of the coach, holding an overnight bag in one hand. She paused on the lowest step and looked enquiringly over the jumble of grinning, expectant faces. His chest was suddenly too small for his heart as he stared at her. She's so beautiful! Oh, my own darling! Her face and bare arms were a honey brown and the yellow hair had turned tawny, with streaks of straw from bleaching by the seaside sun. The low-cut summer dress clung to the firm moulds of her body, and the breasts had a fullness he did not remember from the ten years he had known, desired and adored her.

He wanted to push through the crowd, punch and kick them out of his way, to gather this desirable, beloved body into his arms. Jean! Dear God, how I love you, my own Jean! But he contained himself and made his way slowly around happy reunions. His knees were fluttery when he finally stood near her, smiling inanely as her face lit up with relief and pleasure.

"Hello, darling," he greeted quietly, placing his hands on her elbows and kissing her lightly on the forehead.

Her body tensed. "Kiss me, Paddy – kiss me hard!" she implored in an urgent voice. Then threw herself at him, arms clamping around his neck. She opened her lips and kissed him with a passion that embarrassed and flattered him. A few faces nearby turned and smiled approval.

"Oh, Patrick! Paddy – Patrick!" She breathed the chant, pressing her cheek into his neck. "I'm so glad to be back! I'm sorry I didn't write; I couldn't. But you still love me, Paddy! I can see it – feel it," she giggled, looking up at his face with flirty eyes. "How I've missed you and waited to come back, my darling. How I've dreaded this moment, from the time I left you. I wished I hadn't gone because I was so afraid of coming back to just this moment. But now I know everything's going to be all right – I know, my love!"

She would have babbled on, her voice slowly climbing the scale towards hysteria; but he stopped her mouth with a kiss.

"Now, Jeanie, now ..." His fingers pressed into her bare forearms, and his eyes stared with misgiving and anxiety into her brimming eyes. "You needn't tell me everything just now, darling. Wait till we get home."

"Yes," she answered softly, a tremor crossing her face. "Of course you're right, Patrick. I'm being silly." The light in her eyes dimmed and almost died. His eyes searched her face, and saw that it was pale under the honeyed tan. She hasn't forgotten yet, he told himself with a sinking heart.

"Now let me tell you about our new home," he said as he guided her through the dispersing crowd, trying to sound carefree as the people around them. "It's in a nice area, I'm sure you'll be pleased to know – Parkhurst, in fact. A quiet, shady street without the noise and hustle and bustle of Hillbrow. And I haven't bought much furniture yet because I'm sure you'll want to do that yourself ..."

He stopped and drew a long breath. Light-headed from his breathless attempt to close the gap that had yawned between them with that dimming of her eyes. What's happening to us? Is this how we're going to live – being careful not to say the wrong thing, letting her get hysterical because her eyes die when I restrain her from gabbling away like a lunatic?

Jean liked the flat. It was spacious, sunny and elegant. In a quiet and tree-lined street, as Patrick had promised. Most important, in a suburb she'd only driven through or past. She was certain none of the people she knew lived nearby.

But Patrick watched her anxiously and with rising hope as she cautiously relaxed, slowly snuggled into her surroundings and began to purr like a cat that is stroked after its tail has been stepped upon. The glow he'd noted with relief, pleasure and desire at Park Station returned to her sun-bronzed cheeks; a lively spark shone out of her greenish eyes. Patrick sighed in cautious relief, and also began to relax.

But still he had to be careful. He could not risk the confusing tensions, doubts and self-pity that would come with a relapse. There had almost been one her first morning in the new flat, with her insistence on cooking him breakfast in a strange kitchen. A silly business about his organisation of the kitchen being disorganised. But they had quarrelled. And he vowed afterwards that he would let her have her own way. For some time, anyway. Not that he'd ever dominated her. In good time, he would be firm.

The straw had broken when she told him, with great enthusiasm, that to re-organise the kitchen and their new and promisingly cosy life in Parkhurst, the maid he had hired must be dismissed.

"This is a new beginning for us, Patrick, and I want to be a real wife. Do all the cooking, sewing, cleaning and scrubbing myself."

Of course he objected. Who'd ever heard of such a thing? What were Natives for if not to serve? He didn't want to find her worn out when he came home in the evening. And when would she find the time to see all her friends again?

"I want you to live again, Jeanie. A new life doesn't mean drudgery. You can't hole up in here and – and vegetate!" he said and immediately realised it was the wrong word. So he appealed: "You belong outside in the sun and fresh air, my darling. Not cooped up in here like a – like ..."

He stopped and stared at the face that had lost its enthusiastic, burgeoning housewife's smile. Like a prisoner – somebody hiding. Was that it? Was that what he had wanted to say?

In the end he had given in. Anything to make her happy and forget, he told himself, grimly. But I'm going to get her out in the evenings, he firmly assured himself, if it's the last thing I do. But not immediately, of course.

The second unsettling incident sneaked up on him and left him remorseful, excited and ashamed. Her third night back, and they were lying quietly in the twin beds of the spacious bedroom. Each steeped in speculative thoughts about the future, and pretending to be asleep. She had spoken in a small, desolate voice.

"Pat," she had said into the darkness. "What's the matter, Paddy?"

He was immediately alarmed, and had raised himself onto an elbow, peering at her through the separating gloom.

"What d'you mean, Jeanie? Nothing's the matter."

She was sitting up in her bed. "Then why don't you make love to me? Don't you want me any more? Am I too –"

He was out of his bed at the end of the first question and his lips smothered the last, which would to be too terrible to hear. An hour later she was sleeping quietly in his arms, and the bed that should have been too small was not. He remained awake and wide-eyed, asking himself why.

Why hadn't he done it the first night, when he'd thought she looked so gorgeous and desirable as she alighted from the train? Surely it wasn't because – I just didn't think ... Still she was still too ill to ... But maybe subconsciously I had not ...

He searched his mind for a long time, first in a mortified flood of shame, and then slowly, carefully, trying to find out. Why?

That was the last unhappy incident for a long time.

She was radiant the following morning. She looked younger, like she'd been when they met and fell in love ... after the first time they made love. No – like she was after I married her. The first morning of our married life? No; she looks better than that.

When he left for the office she clung to him at the door after his brief kiss, kissing him with the same frightening and flattering passion she had shown on the station platform, and that had burst into dazzling, ecstatic fury during the night and as the new day was dawning.

It was a long time before she could bring herself to dress. She wandered around the apartment, savouring the nakedness of her body under the silken night-dress and negligee. When she finally went into the bathroom she stood naked before the full-length mirror and stared at herself with amazement. The sight of her body had always pleased her; but what she stared at with such amazement was its fullness and her breasts. They had always been beautifully rounded, but today they seemed – yes, and they felt – fuller, too. The best surprise were the nipples. For years, now, they had been flat, giving the roundness of breasts that Paddy adored, and she was so proud of because of the adoration: a decapitated look. Now they stood out: eager to be caressed and kissed.

She passed light fingers tenderly, lovingly over them – and a lubricious smile wreathing her face. Only stopped when they began hardening under her touch. She giggled, wagged a finger at herself in the mirror – naughty-naughty girl! – and turned on the taps for a sudsy bath.

When Patrick returned from the office, she wound naked arms slowly around his neck before he could close the door, and kissed him. She lingered thoughtfully over the kiss, indulgently curbing the passion flooding her body and pleased by the responding excitement of his caresses – at first surprised hands clasping her body, and then laughing as he stroked. The door was open and the curlers in her hair hurt his face, but he did not care; he was pleased, happy. Then he stood back and studied her face with soft, satisfied eyes. She was wrapped in a new and diaphanous negligee – not the one from the morning – and he could see she had nothing on underneath.

He kicked the door shut, watching her shining, freshly-washed face for the teasing invitation to follow her he had last seen – when, on their honeymoon? But it did not appear.

"Why the curlers?" he asked, trying not to show his disappointment.

She laughed gaily and kissed him lightly, briefly on the nose.

"We're going out, silly!"

"Oh?"

"See?" she said twirling away from him. "I'm not the least bit 'worn out and exhausted' – as you said I'd be without a maid. And now the housewife demands her reward for the day's labours of love. Well? What d'you say, darling heart?"

She looked up into his grinning, acquiescent face.

"Into your glad rags, my boy – and let's paint this li'l ole town red! A nice, Irish red! No – green's your Irish colour, isn't it?" she giggled. "A Welsh red, Paddy – my colour."

It was not until they were in the bedroom that her infectious gaiety began to wear off and doubts chased round in his head. But he would not clarify these doubts to himself. She was so happy, like a little girl. I mustn't spoil it for her. I dare not. He remembered the dimming of her eyes on the station platform.

If she feels like this, fine – I'm with her.

But they avoided the fashionable places which, they reassured each other, would be crowded. Somewhere quiet and intimate: a romantic atmosphere for our second honeymoon. Who wants crowds and bright lights? Not us!

She sat enthralled in the car as they drove into the city, staring at the dazzling, flickering fairyland of lights as if she had never seen them before. She had not seen them for only six weeks, but it felt like a lifetime.

The Italian restaurant they settled on was dotted with reassuringly unfamiliar faces, illuminated by flickering, and so intimate, candlelight. They held hands across their tiny table, lips sipping imported wine, and eyes smiling. Then her greenish eyes hardened into marbles of jade as a man with an unbelievably black face – twice as black as the maid she'd gotten rid of, to avoid them as much as she could – smiled blindingly around at the patrons as he came out of a side door near the kitchens.

The black man walked softly, but with too much confidence for her liking – an unbelievable familiarity among white people. Can't be a servant, with that cocky walk, and the way he's dressed: in a tight-fitting black silk shirt and black trousers that tapered to black-and-white shoes. No jacket, and the goatee on his chin was indistinguishable from the midnight colour of his face. What's he doing here? He walked to a corner of the bistro and skipped onto a small dais she hadn't noticed. A spotlight lit up the tiny stage and he sat down on the lone chair. Away from the dim lighting over the tables, that smile still blinded: out-dazzling even the spotlight.

The very black man picked up a guitar from its metal cradle waiting in a corner of the dais. The instrument gleamed even brighter than his teeth. And, without a word of the introductory spiel loved by showbiz folk, the entertainer began to strum its strings. Playing slowly and softly, as if noodling the notes only to himself as he warmed up for a rehearsal. Casual chords that floated around the restaurant and were, after a while, recognisable as the melody of a love song: a sentimental, evergreen standard. And then came the whispered lyrics of the song – talked in hushed tones, rather than sung. The voice was a soft, rich bass that had a smile much more subtle than the toothy dazzle on his face before he started playing. No expression on the face, now; no grandstanding for an audience that might as well not have been present.

But she was there – and responding deep down to the music. At his first appearance, Jean had wanted to look away from this terribly, frighteningly black face in a white restaurant. Get away from it – leave the restaurant as fast as she could, whatever the embarrassment. Then, as he strummed the strings and whispered about yearning love and requited love, she felt free. Reminded herself that she was free, now that Patrick had reaffirmed his love for her and hers for him.

She could look at the guitar-player, and at all of them, from the yellow and ochre-coloured ones to the blackest. Because Patrick still loves me, and that's all that matters.

I'm free and he's going to be free too.

Her eyes remained on the black entertainer, the first she'd ever listened to, and her eyes were quizzical.

The boy – no, the man – performed beautifully. In fact, he's very good. She suddenly realised she'd never before thought of Natives – Africans, whatever – in this manner: evaluating them as individuals, rather than utilities always available when needed and otherwise ignored. And he's not really ugly, she thought. Very black, but with nice features ...

Oh, no! Not that, now. Don't go to the other extreme! Not after what's happened – not you, of all people!

But I don't really know if it was one of them. Do I?

She stopped a waiter, glanced quickly at Patrick, and asked, "Who is he?"

The waiter's eyes followed the nod of her head and he smiled: "His name, Madam? General Duze. Good singer for a darkie, hey?"

She was affronted by the young man's patronising qualification, but a greater urge was to ask – How can he have General as a name? That for a start. Of course they did have some odd names, like Wiseman and Godson, courtesy of the missionaries she supposed. But General? Yet the uneasy surprise in Patrick's eyes discouraged further inquiry.

The days and nights that followed were a happy haze of love, joy and amazed contentment. They stared at each other in constant, delighted wonder; with a new and thrilling knowledge and recognition. For hours on end – sometimes even a whole day – there would be no echoes of that ghastly night they so desperately wanted to forget. When the memory did intrude they made frantic attempts to obliterate it with loving and laughter.

For Patrick, office hours at the estate agency were leaden-footed, and the minutes of lunch breaks, when he rushed home, too fleet. For Jean the hours they were apart were a timeless, drifting hiatus in which memories of their time together were suspended like gossamer glinting with sunlight. The hours were also a time of expectation, and a planning of possible new delights and discoveries.

God! That it could ever be like this!

Jean blossomed. Her face retained vestiges of the seaside tan as it softened and rounded. Her hips fought the seams of close-fitting dresses. Her breasts jiggled provocatively, demandingly. Her eyes glowed with an inner peace, and were brilliant with joy at being alive when she smiled and laughed.

She was not just his wife, but the essence of woman, Patrick thought. Breath catching in his chest as he watched her walk about the apartment.

He could not keep his hands from her luscious body.

How long can a honeymoon last? Their love was still in its dizzying orbit on the Wednesday evening when Patrick opened the door, his eyes already crinkling at the pleasure of her rush into his arms. But she was not in the tiny hall. He looked around.

"Jeanie?"

"I'm here," after a long silence.

The voice from the living room was flat and unfamiliar. No, he'd heard it before. His body turned cold at the memory.

The premonition, the recognition, had been correct. After the flatness of her voice, he was not surprised to find her seated at the window, as in the Hillbrow flat. Only the room had changed. She wore a house coat and bedroom slippers. Her back was stiff and she did not move as he walked towards her.

"What's the matter, Jeanie?" Myriad fears whizzed round in his mind as he stood looking down at her – again. "Aren't you feeling well, darling?"

He tried to turn her head away from its sightless gazing out of the window, but her neck muscles tensed. He would not force her.

"Don't make me look at you, Patrick."

"But what's the matter, Jeanie?" he asked in a voice rising with apprehension. "What's gone wrong now? Has – has anybody ...?"

"No, Patrick; not that." She spoke in a slow, toneless voice. "I wish it were only that." Then her face turned to look up at him, tears streaming out of eyes that were forlorn, pleading, apologetic. "We've been very happy these few weeks, haven't we, Paddy? Happier than ever, happier than anyone has a right to be? The luck ..."

"Yes, darling. Very happy. And we deserved it, my sweet." He spoke softly, kneeling beside her chair and placing his arms round her ripe body. "We've been happy, and we can always be happy."

She tensed and recoiled at the feel of his arms. She pushed them away. "Don't do that, Patrick. We must talk."

Protests and pleas rushed onto his tongue, but he clamped them back. He rose to his feet, pulled up a chair and sat near her, his knees almost touching hers.

"We've been so happy, Patrick!" she sobbed. "So happy!"

"So what's wrong now, Jeanie? Tell me – for God's sake, please tell me!"

"It's finished, Patrick."

"Come on now, Jean! You love me, I love you. That's the most important thing, and while we have that, nothing's finished." He paused and took a deep breath. "Now, if you'll only stop being so melo–, well, so ... talking in riddles. We'll get to the bottom of this. Talk it over like grown-up people."

"I went to the doctor this afternoon, Patrick." She laughed mirthlessly. "That's what young brides are supposed to say to their husbands, isn't it? I prayed for so many years to be able to say those words to you. Then gave up. But now I can say them, Patrick. I'm pregnant."

Her eyes gazed steadily into his, waiting for a reaction. His face was blank.

"You know what that means, don't you?" she asked quietly.

For a moment – a dizzy, mad moment – he'd almost jumped up and whooped with joy. Then his body went numb. It had been drummed into him by enough specialists that he could never be a father.

"Damn," he said. "Damn it all! Damn everything to hell!"

His voice rose in a shriek, and the words writhed and shot out of stiff, bloodless lips. "The black son of a whore! The rutting –"

He choked on the words and stopped, eyes staring blindly. "Why?" he sobbed. "Why? Why, damn it?"

And why, she bitterly asked herself, had it taken her so long to even suspect that she was pregnant? After all, she was not a child. She should have known soon enough – what with all those gynaecological books she had studied so avidly, searching for a ray of hope. Was it because she had given up hope of having a baby such a long time ago that the blossoming of her body and missing periods had not raised the alarm? She'd missed them before, and nothing had ever come of that hope against hope. So why should she have taken any more notice this time? Unused machinery gets erratic, she told herself with grim irony. But there had been the other signs, this time: the blooming ripeness of her breasts, the filling out of her curves …

Oh, what does it matter anyway? At least the delayed knowledge gave me a few weeks of a joy I did not think could ever be found in this horrible world. Now I can say I have really loved with all of myself, and been loved for all of myself – even if it was all false. I know, now, what it feels like.

And for that I'm grateful.

Chapter 7

Patrick Ryan lay in his bed, tense and miserable. He did not want her to know he was awake, or if she was herself. And if she was asleep, he did not want to disturb her. If he could only blot out the shock of that terrible night, and the revulsion of this evening. Perhaps he could sleep, then. Restrain the urge to go out into the streets right now – this was about the time, wasn't it? – and kill the first black bastard he came across. Like in Hillbrow, these streets in Parkhurst were for white people. Any black walking them at this time deserved to be killed. He had to be a criminal – burglar, mugger, potential rapist … or a fulfilled bastard.

He lay on his side of the bedroom filled with guilt at the revulsion that had flooded his body after his initial shock and impotent fury at her announcement … Pregnant! By some horny black bastard! Just as well we have twin beds, or I would've had to … Was that why he'd bought them? And not bought a double during their weeks of bliss? He really must ignore these crazy thoughts pushing, nagging, scratching, whining for admittance into his consciousness.

Sleep, come on; sleep, damn it! Those slow hours plodding through the apartment, her eyes accusing him of the revulsion he felt towards her. He must forget those eyes, too: forlorn, pitying and calculating. In the morning – or tomorrow evening – they'd talk. Now sleep. Forgetfulness.

Maybe a stiff drink will help. Sleep in the arms of Morpheus – no, the other one: the Greek god of boozers. Bacchus – that's him. But that would be cowardly and wouldn't really be much use. Melodramatic. And I'd probably wake her when I sneak out. But how can she sleep, anyway – knowing? And feeling it inside her … Of course she doesn't feel anything, stupid! Yet. Still, how can she – why can't I sleep if she can? I need the bloody rest for work tomorrow!

"Patrick?"

The voice from the deeper darkness a few feet away was flat and lifeless: as it had been when he got back from the office.

"Patrick, I'm sorry."

"Don't …" He cleared his throat with a harsh sound that tore at the darkness and echoed in the corners of the spacious bedroom. Why the hell isn't she asleep – why aren't I? "Don't worry now, Jean. Sleep."

"He could have been a white man, Patrick."

White! Was that supposed to make any difference? Like bloody hell. Of course there's a difference, but does it matter? You've been raped. You're pregnant. And I'm – what? A cuckold? No, a patsy. White? How could she even … It couldn't be …

"I'm so sorry, Patrick."

"Please sleep, Jean. Don't worry."

Another dark hour or more crawled by as they lay silent in their small, dark world. Too quiet to be asleep. Separate worlds, now.

"Jeanie … couldn't it be …?" No way could it be a miracle achieved during the nights of bliss in the too-narrow bed. "Wasn't it somebody at the coast?"

He lay tense, listening to her sudden, broken sobbing. Soft, tired sobs. Bastard – shouldn't have said that. And what if it were a holiday lover? A Charles Atlas on the beach who couldn't kick sand into my eyes? Still wouldn't make it my baby. Doesn't make any bloody difference, white rapist or lover.

Abortion. That's all there is for it. The sooner the fucking better.

That's what I should've told her. Right now, this evening. Instead of just sitting around moping. Avoiding each other's eyes. Get rid of the bloody thing. And then? Go back to the old life, of course. Sure? Can't recapture the glory of the last weeks, of course ... but maybe we can. If I could feel like that about her, after the revulsion of that night, then ... No. There was some of that, even then. That's why I didn't do anything when she came back from the coast. She had to ask me, first. And it was marvellous. If it could work then ... But why was she so much more sexy – no, sensuous – than she'd ever been before?

His skin crawled over raw nerves at the question. Why was she? Don't be stupid, man! Because of the black bastard – the tiny bastard of a monster growing inside her. That's why! Her body filling out and legs spreading like they'd never opened before. And poor, stupid me diving right into somebody else's mess. What a wonderful lover you thought you were! Cashing in on some stinking, randy black bastard's ... Oh, go to sleep, can't you? Do you want to drive yourself crazy?

The next day Patrick left his estate agent's office early for lunch. He visited two specialists. Neither of them would say definitely that the possibility of a miracle didn't exist – a miracle that had made him able to become a father.

He had pretended to be making enquiries for a bet that he and some friends had made. The first doctor hadn't blinked at the explanation, but the second was about his own age, and had smiled thinly, knowingly: he'd already heard them all. In such a case, he'd told Patrick, somebody else would have been doing the hypothetical husband's work for him.

Patrick arrived home resolved to get down to brass tacks after that second humiliation.

But his resolve was dissolved by the atmosphere in the apartment. She was cold and distant, making him feel that even an enquiry about her well-being would lead to a scene. He did not want a scene. Some other night, maybe, and I hope she can be adult enough, then, for us to work it out without any hysterics.

I hate hysterical women!

She felt his wavering, and waited for him to initiate the threatened discussion. But he did not. She was grateful for the respite – this extra time to sort out her own emotions and rationalisations; but at the same time she pitied and despised him for not having the courage to take the initiative. They went to bed early after a cold supper.

Jean lay in her bed, quiet and relaxed. There was no tension in her body, as there had been the previous night. Then she had expected him to bring up that word at any moment ... abortion. He had not, and tonight she'd known he wouldn't, either. So she had time to think. No decisions, but having overcome the trauma of the previous day she could – she hoped – look dispassionately at her situation.

First, he doesn't love me any more. A resigned admission of what she had realised in a flash the previous evening, when he had stared at her in horror and revulsion. That instant knowing had haunted her all night and all of this day. Now it was a fact. No need to hope any more. It was all over, as she had herself told him yesterday. He loathes me now; must shudder when he thinks of those recent nights and days. Men! Disgusted by the thought of having slept with a woman pregnant by somebody else; someone else's dirty water, as they say. Yet they don't expect women to be disgusted, when they leave their pregnant wives' beds for those of others. They are immaculate, we never are.

But how can he hate the memory of those days and nights? The most glorious anybody could ever wish to have? I don't. I won't. Whatever happens, however hateful he becomes. I'm glad I had them, whatever the reason for our heightened love and sexuality. If the rape was responsible, the catalyst, then I'm – no. Don't think like that, now. Just about what a wonderful lover he's been.

A lover at the coast! How dare he think that I – after all these years! I could have had my pick of the very best. But no: I was a faithful, loving wife. So now he suggests – doesn't actually accuse me, but suggests ... Surely he knows how I felt then, about all men? Rape doesn't make you love men. All right, he might have thought it, about a lover – but to say it! Perhaps I should've said I did have one, if he's that stupid. For whatever consolation he'd have got from the 'confession'. Now he'll leave me. Pack up and go back to his mother. I've disgraced them all, the immaculate Ryans. All such good, decent, upstanding citizens that it couldn't happen to them. If they were raped, they couldn't ever become pregnant. Oh, no – their ovaries are so discriminating, didn't you know?

But am I to blame? Whose fault is it that we don't have children? Oh, what's the use. We've gone over that before, so leave it alone. The point now is you're going to have a baby. On your own. No father. A bastard. In both senses. A black – no; a coloured baby. A half-white, half-black bushman. Bushbaby. You don't want to make jokes now. Even if its father – was it really a Native? A white man? A coloured, perhaps? Or an Indian? No, I'd have smelled his curry breath. I don't know. Does it matter? The point is – yes, I know, I'm going to be the mother of a bastard. What an awful word. Now I know what it really means. At least he won't know what he's done to me, thank God.

You've been used, Jean Griffiths Ryan. Truly and foully used. Like a lavatory, a repository; like a wall in a dark corner. No, like a bush – a weed that can flower and bloom and blossom after being nurtured by the foullest of water. A piss pot. That's what you are. A smelling, overflowing, fly-covered bucket like the Natives use in their shanty towns. Used and discarded. By a faceless, nameless, colourless beast. Used, then left to germinate, flower and bear fruit on the dung heap. And nobody wants the fruit. Germinate. You've done that at last, you poor old weed. Conceived – the human word. Aren't you pleased? Isn't that what you've been praying and hoping for all these years? Your dream's come true, sweetheart.

You're going to be a mother. Hip-hip hurray. Good old Jean. You can depend on Jean to do it the unusual way. Conjugal bed not good enough for her fertility. Has to be a dark, stinking alley, didn't you know? Just like any mongrel bitch in heat. Except she, the pedigreed bitch, is going to have a mongrel. How quaint.

What are you going to do with it? Keep it? Give it away? Suckle it? Yuck! Who'll have a dung-heap flower? Very cheap, madam. A flower is a flower is a flower … no, a weed. Will you, Mrs Patrick Ryan? Are you going to let it distend you for another … let's see … six months? Buy maternity frocks and suits, eat for two and make sure you get all the right vitamins? Go to a pre-natal clinic? Are you going to do all that? Are you? Come on, now – answer! Eh?

But I don't have to do any of that. There's always abortion …

The hands of the bedside clock had merged when she opened her eyes. Twelve noon, high noon. Do not forsake me, oh, my darling ... What will I do if he leaves me? She slid slowly out of bed. Weak and dizzy, sick headache and queasy stomach. She stopped in front of the mirror and bleary eyes studied her body. She bent slowly, cautiously down, trying to keep her head up; with eyes staring straight ahead she gathered the full skirt of the nightdress in her hands and straightened up. She peeled the garment upwards and slowly over her head.

It was a beautiful, desirable body, she decided after long, thoughtful moments. Any man would want it. But none will, now – if they know what's in it. Nothing much showed, yet; nothing definite anyway. But the heaviness of the breasts, the fullness of her face, the voluptuous curves of her hips: these were Nature's signs, her message of what was to come. It's inside there, whatever it is: growing and taking shape with every minute. Just give it time and it'll make itself felt and seen. Before it pops out. If you let it ... Are you going to? You've always envied those big-titted, sway-backed, piano-legged matrons bulging all over, gasping and grunting like God-knows-what as they waddle proudly down the streets. Envied even the most awful, blotchy complexions, puffed-up faces, bulge-veined legs and all. Wished you could change places with them. Now you don't have to. You're going to be one of them, my girl. Can be one of them. And better looking, too. Be like the pretty ones you've seen; delicate dolls, bright-eyed and – oh, to hell with all that! You won't be bright-eyed, that's definite.

What are you going to do? Are you going to let this vileness grow inside you, form and take life?

"I've been thinking, Jean," Patrick said as he dropped the newspaper he had been reading.

She watched him carefully as he lifted his glass and took a swallow. His fourth drink that evening. All stiff and straight whiskies. I suppose they've done the trick, she thought bitterly. The curtain has risen, at last, the cue has been given.

"I've been doing a lot of thinking," he said into her silence. "Since you told me. Of course you must have realised – immediately, as well – that there's only one thing to be done."

"What?"

"Abortion."

Easy, isn't it, he scolded himself. One word. That's all. Why didn't you say it before?

"But, Patrick – Isn't there a chance it could be yours? The remotest, least-considered chance? After all, we've had some marvellous nights … like never before."

"No, Jean. It can't be mine."

"How do you know, Patri–, Paddy?" she pleaded breathlessly. "Everything changes, doesn't it? Wounds heal, broken flowers grow again … Couldn't you – with time, with the years, with this new thing between us … Couldn't it have brought about a change? Couldn't it, Paddy?"

"No it could not!" He barked a short, bitter, embarrassed laugh. "I've seen nothing but doctors – again – since you told me."

"Oh."

"That's the only way to find out, isn't it? Scientific proof."

"Doctors! Tests! Science! D'you all – you and these precious men of science – do you forget there's a God above? A God whose ways aren't always clear to man? A God who made you, and can change you? They could be wrong, Paddy. It could be your child, Patrick! Our reward – our consolation for that horrible night."

As she listened to his bitter and angry answer, Jean realised that she'd for the first time acknowledged something she had refused to recognise. Through all the bitterness of the past hours it had been there: somewhere, deep in her mind, but she had ignored it. She was pleased to be pregnant. The pure fact was a pleasure, an excitement. But only if and when she could divorce it from its causation. She also knew that these emotional arguments – this grasping at straws by her – justified the bitterness of what he was now saying.

"Since when have you been such a devout believer in God, Jean? And a stupid believer in miracles, too? Can you remember the last time you even entered a church? The last time you went down on your knees anywhere to pray? Or even standing up – a serious, sincere Please-God-help-me prayer? Your Welsh forefathers might have been God-fearing, but you're supposed to be too sophisticated for all that tribalism, remember? So let's be realistic and reasonable. There's been no miracle and there's no bloody hope of any! God didn't decide that you must first be raped – crucified, if you want to be Biblical – for me to become a father. You're just the victim of an ordinary, kitchen-garden type of rape by some kitchen boy, some Native. And now you're pregnant. The father of that thing in your belly – some black swine who's still boasting to his pals over gallons of skokiaan about what he did to you. We've got to get rid of that thing, Jeanie – and the sooner the fucking better."

First time she'd heard him swear, but her tremulous voice spoke into the silence: "I suppose one of the doctors you've been seeing is an abortionist. You've already made an appointment."

"No, but I've – why're you speaking like that, Jean? Don't tell me you're – good God, you're not even just ... No. It can't be!"

"I may not be devout, Patrick," she said stubbornly, "but I still remember the Ten Commandments. 'Thou shalt not kill,' Paddy. That's one of them. And your Church, Patrick – that superior Church I had to be converted to before you'd marry me – if I remember correctly, it has very strict edicts about conception, contraception and abortion."

"To hell with –" He stopped, holding his breath. I don't have to blaspheme. "Let's not confuse the issue, Jean. Let's leave the Church and Commandments out of it. This involves just you and me, and not some sanctimonious celibate priest who can't –" He checked himself again. "Let's just leave those edicts and restrictions out of this. If we start bringing all that in, we'll be in shit street before anything –"

"You don't have to use filthy language," she cut in, grabbing at anything she could use to fight him.

"Well, damn it, Jean!" An explosion that bleached his long thin face, turning it deathly pale. "Never mind my fucking language, the sanctimonious Church, miracles and all that – that bullshit! Let's stick to the important things, here and now. There's just one thing to be done, and you're fucking well going to do it! You're going to get rid of that damned thing as soon as I can arrange it!"

They glared at each other across the darkened room.

"I'll think about it, Patrick," she said coolly into the silence. "No, don't say anything more, now. There's nothing more you ..." The frosty manner dropped away, and she was crying. "Give me time,

Paddy, please! Time to think – just a few days, Paddy. I'm so confused!"

Hours later, she turned towards the wall as he entered the bedroom. He walked softly, carefully, and with the deliberation of a man whose brain does not have full control over his limbs. She listened to the heavy, uneven breathing as he fumbled at his clothes and, finally, stumbled into his bed. At least he'll be fast asleep soon. I won't mind the snoring. It'll mean I won't have to pretend to be asleep. I can relax, and think. I have to think.

About what, dearest? There's nothing to think about. He's right, and whatever's brewing in your head and distending yor belly is crazy and wrong. There's only one thing to be done, and you've got to do it. There aren't going to be any miracles, and there's no alternative. You've got to get rid of it, cut it out like the cancer it is.

But I've never been pregnant before. Whatever he thinks about my devoutness, I've prayed hard and sincerely all these barren years. For just this one thing to happen ... All right, perhaps I can't have the baby. But can't I continue the experience just a little longer? Just to know I'm pregnant for a few more days, weeks? I can make myself forget how it happened, and just experience it. This is my only chance of this experience, and I don't see why I should be rushed. Of course the perfect thing would be to go ahead and have it – forgetting how it came about, mind you – and then give it away. Just to experience that ultimate fulfilment of being in labour. I'm not afraid of the pain. Perhaps that is asking too much, but just two or three weeks more; maybe even a month – six weeks. It would surely still be safe then to have an abortion. Surely if Patrick loves me he can sacrifice his pride for just another six weeks?

Of course I'm disgusted at what's happened to me. But do I have to be – about it? It's completely innocent. We're both of us innocent and didn't ask for all this to happen. So how can I be disgusted at the poor thing? And it's part of me, isn't it? It's more mine than whoever the brutish bastard was. That's somebody to be disgusted at, to be spat on, kicked, hung, drawn and quartered. We two are innocent and part of each other. The responsibility is mine and I can keep it as long as I like. Within safety limits, of course. There's no need for this great panic.

Chapter 8

Betty Nkosi entered the noisy room and placed a large tray on the table's edge, between two of the young men seated at the table, resting the other end of it on her curvaceous hip. She gave the klevahs a quick, inspecting glance, and passed a practised hand over the mass of shiny curls her hair had been processed into with hot irons, as she carefully placed plates from the tray on the starched table-cloth. The wake-up and smartly dressed young men hardly glanced a her as they talked, laughed and passed the plates laden with generous portions of chicken, boiled rice, carrots, potatoes and beetroots along to their friends.

There were good-natured complaints about the food: "Not your cooking we know, my sister; but these are small portions your stingy cousin is feeding us today!" Betty only smiled at them and left the room, self-conscious because she knew some eyes were casually examining her retreating curves.

The usual furnishings of a room that, in Sophiatown, was usually the only home for a whole family, had been removed and a score of chairs added for the stokvel to which all friends and supporters would be welcome later in the day. It was still early Sunday afternoon, and the young men Betty was serving were the dozen or so members of the stokvel her cousin Tami belonged to. It was his turn to gather the mazooma provided by his self-help society, one of many in Sophiatown and all other locations and townships. Wake-up young men and women had drifted in and out of Tami's rented portion of the house at all hours since Friday's party – which had started at sundown – and all friends and casual supporters would be welcome again after the member's ceremonial lunch. And there'd be plenty of them for the Sunday night climax that would further multiply Tami's income. He was a popular klevah who made a point of patronising other stokvels, guaranteeing himself a thirsty and free-spending crowd. For this, as a bachelor, he required the assistance of Betty and other sympathetic women.

Now was the exclusive interlude for members, who were gathered for the customary free lunch, all drinks extra, my brikaid – jy notch, mos. On arrival, all members had ceremoniously signed the stokvel register and given Tami three pounds: their dues. It wasn't much of a jackpot, but was supplemented by the food and liquor sold to other patrons throughout the three-day duration. Profits of as much as a hundred pounds were made by popular hosts who, like Tami, patronised other such parties each weekend, and spent liberally.

Betty had reluctantly agreed to make her first appearance on this climactic last day, after insistent pleas from Tami – if only to serve the ritual luncheon, mzala. But she suspected he only wanted to show her off – the mzala he'd been showering with presents since her arrival in Jo'burg; but so far keeping her at a distance from Sophiatown's fast lifestyle.

Said he wanted to display her subtle beauty in the best light – and yet warned her against the skelms who were denizens of his beloved Kofifi. She was fond of him too, and prepared to fulfil the family obligation he pressed on her; but it was her curiosity about these famous and notorious parties that had drawn her away from a comparatively sheltered life. There were stokvels in Orlando where she'd grown up; but she'd avoided their drunken violence, and the chance of being tainted with the reputation of a nice-time sister. But this one was different – her cousin was desperate for her assistance, and Tami would protect her from any unpleasantness. He was respected and even feared among his kind, and it would be useful for it to become common knowledge in Sophiatown that she was his mzala.

Especially, she now mused, among these klevahs who believed Orlando was inhabited by vulnerable moegoes because it was way out of town. A municipal encampment of drab and identical matchbox houses with, Soph'town people observed, "long-long numbers nobody can remember – and no street names!" A camp for *magoduka* from the farms, isolated on a barren veld "somewhere near Roodeport – and that's a plaasdorp, man!" While their Kofifi was freehold, a short bus ride from town, had street names, and was surrounded by white suburbs.

She was removing empty bowls that had been piled high with custard and jelly when Philip Mokone arrived, and was greeted by friendly and not-so-friendly teasing: "You're too fokken early, klevah – since when are you a member, eh?"

Betty studied him with unexpected interest – only curiosity, of course – as he grinned and hurled back insults at the merry men. Wearing a sky-blue cashmere jacket over a black shirt: stylish combination, and a jacket she'd admired in a Levinson's window display quite recently. Wondering who'd be mad enough to pay the price on the tag – many pounds, nineteen shillings, eleven pence and three farthings. Why didn't these *makgoa* just give the price in pounds, since it was only a farthing short of what they wanted? Playing with us dom kaffirs.

And now here was a klevah wearing it with just the right shirt – and not a cheap shirt, either. She wasn't surprised, only certain that he'd not paid the shop price; not for the sharply-creased Palm Beach trousers and cocoa-coloured Panama hat tip-tilted on his cocky head either; nor for the two-tone Jarmans on his feet. Many months' wages at Levinson's, Wings and other fashionable stores where white salesmen treated the majita like people, not Native boys. But surprised – pleased? – by the taste with which he'd selected the back-door clothes.

But then she noticed the watery eyes and the slight stagger as he crossed the room, shaking hands with those who'd uttered friendly jeers, and finally slumped into a chair. Drunk. At three in the afternoon. A real nice-timer! She was surprised by her anger, as she carried the tray out of the party and into the room across the passage which Tami had borrowed from a neighbour for the duration of his stokvel.

As the afternoon wore on and more non-member supporters walked and staggered into the room, Betty observed the handsome young man referred to – mockingly by some, with half-jeers and sneers by others – as Nice Time Phil and Pretty Boy.

There was something different about this nice-timer that made the loud voice, the flashing of pound notes and his other exhibitionism seem incongruous. He was dressed as sharp as – better than – any of the others, spoke the same jargon, swore in their bantering tone and was just another klevah; a particularly handsome one, she conceded, but seemingly just an ordinary, Sophiatown klevah. Yet there was something about him … something desperate, she decided. Trying to enjoy himself – forcing himself to, almost. As if he would never have other chances for nice times. And something else about him, too: a suggestion of quiet depths, and a sensitivity violated by this role of a money-squandering ladies' man.

His drunkenness must be an attempt to live up to the role and be like the others here, she told herself. He was one of them, all right, but not of them; trying to break loose and out of the lonely silence of his shell. She was sure those gathered about him, talking and laughing as they gulped down the liquor he offered so expansively, were also aware of his difference. There was something self-conscious about them when they talked to him, or laughed too hard at what he said. They don't really like him. No, not quite that. They accept him but don't understand him. So they're uneasy with him.

These impressions came to her disjointedly, between taking orders for food and squeezing her way back through the drunken crush. She worked efficiently, laughed with the guests in her restrained manner, and threw back saucy rejoinders to their casual, explicit advances; but her eyes kept darting back to him, quizzical. She was beginning to feel an angry but protective compassion towards him, wanting to shoo off the grinning, loud-laughing spongers – die baekie-vangers. And tell him he did not belong here with them. Then, when their eyes met, his were cold and hard, with a jeer in them that made her feel uncomfortable and conspicuous.

"What're you looking at, ousie?"

His voice cut harshly across the room, the challenge in it hushing others. Heads turned quickly, warily, warned of impending trouble. A dust-up! Shaandies with this unknown and almost prim woman who was Tami's mzala, as their host had been warning them all the time.

"You!" he was saying, dragging out the word and pointing a wavering but accusing finger across the room. "You with the little apron – sister! Why've you been looking at me like that all the time? Like you're a schoolteacher or something? You think I'm – I'm ..."

"Heeey, klevah," Tami's voice cut in, casually menacing, as he pushed through the crowd. "I don't want any dust here, nice-time boy. If you're feeling strong, try somewhere else. That's my cousin, man" – he glared around the room – "and anybody who gets funny with Betty is kicked right back into his mother's womb." Tami stood short and squat beside her, the smile on his face belying the threat in the soft-spoken words. He was not an imposing figure; but then physical strength did not matter, and was often a liability. What did count was how good – or how willing – one was at ruthlessly utilising the various, available weapons. Tami was, as judgement went, an honest and good man; but he had a reputation – and that counted most.

"Okay, Tami. But I don't like the way she looks at me," Philip replied stubbornly. "Like I'm a schoolboy who's pissed in his pants!"

Not meant as a joke, but the roars of laughter that followed, led by a relieved Tami, broke the tension building up in the room. Philip, butt of the joke, looked around at them, bewildered and annoyed by their amusement.

"Trouble with you, Phil," Tami drawled, "is too many of these molls" – gesturing with some contempt at the glamorous, wake-up women – "run after you. Jy weet, my brikaid? So now every time a girl looks at you, you think she wants a skondaai."

There was another burst of laughter, but only from some of the audience. And Betty was surprised by the malice in their voices. She told herself she should not be surprised; a man who was successful with women, as this one seemed to be, would never be popular. And this one less so, because he was a puzzle to them. Why do they accept him? Why hasn't he been killed? Or cut across the 'pretty' face? Because of the money he throws around? Maybe a reputation?

"Aah, molls!" Philip sneered. "Who cares about them!"

"Yeah, that's what you say now. But you better watch out, Pretty Boy," a tall, broad-shouldered man lounging in a chair near Betty replied in a cold voice. "If you ever try your funny tricks – talking English and all that Yank crap – with my girls … it's the coffin for you, my mother hears me."

She watched with trepidation, but fascinated by the instant change in this Philip. An indefinable, subtle change, yet visible to her. He seemed to draw into himself, his lips twisting into a smile that had something manic and hysterical about it: the smile of a man who suddenly sees release from his personal devils.

"Your girls? Which ones, eh?" he asked in a voice that was spoiling for a fight. "The ones you force just to smile at your ugly kisser? You call them your women? Aah, fuck you, man! I'm not scared of your guns and knives, tsotsi! And if ever – and I don't think it's going to happen – but if I ever want any of them …"

What followed was confused, and Betty was never able to sort it out. The men lunged at each other, but Tami grabbed the bigger one and dragged him out with the help of others. Philip followed, violently brushing off restraining hands. She felt like hitting him over the head with the tray she held, exasperated by such stupid and senseless provocation of a man who was bigger and obviously dangerous, behaviour she instinctively felt was beneath him.

She was one of the few who remained in the room while the rest rushed out to watch the outcome of the dust-up livening the stokvel. She hoped and prayed beneath the excited babble; prayed that this poor boy whom so needed help and protection from himself should not be too seriously hurt. Her prayer was seemingly answered, as the crowd wandered back in. Disappointment on some faces. Then, after what seemed an interminable period, Tami led in the two combatants. They smiled warily at each other while Tami hurriedly poured them brimming drinks on the house. But it was plain to her that the enmity between them remained.

"Trouble with you educated punks –" she heard the bigger man grumble before he was cut off by Philip, who placed a hand on his higher shoulder.

"That's just the trouble with you, my ma se kind," Philip said, laughing. "The only school you know is five years in Number Four on Hospital Hill, and then Blue Skies on the East Rand."

The man shrugged off the friendly hand, ready for renewed battle.

"Oh, don't get excited now. I'm as scared of a gun as you are," Philip grinned. "So don't take offence, my brikaid – my brother!"

An hour or so later, Tami brought the poor, lost boy into the kitchen, and Philip apologised in a manner that made her want to pat him on the head – or was it put his head to her breasts? – and tell him everything would be all right. If only he would not torture himself so much!

And even later in the evening, he found her in the borrowed room that served as kitchen for the party, while she was washing up glasses. She was surprised, because she'd seen him depart much earlier. People came and went, but she'd still not expected him to come back. She returned his smile hesitantly, watching his face carefully in the flickering lamplight.

"I'm really very sorry, my sister," he said, using the term with the proper tone of respect, instead of the sarcastic mockery with which he'd shouted at her across the room earlier. He seemed sober, too. "You don't know how sorry I am, ousie."

"That's all right, Philip. Just forget it, please."

"I don't even know your name."

"Betty. Betty Nkosi."

"And you're Tami's cousin?"

"That's right."

"But you don't live in Soph'town. I've never seen you before."

She laughed shortly. "Do you know all the girls here?"

"Well, all the pretty ones."

"Now I know how you get them."

"Where d'you live, Betty?"

"In Orlando. I suppose now you think I'm a moegoe cherry, because I don't live in wake-up Sophiatown."

"Oh, no! I know quite a few wake-up people out there. It's not a bad place. Just too big and too far away, maybe. All those municipal houses that look the same – you get lost easily, you know."

"Not us – we don't," she smiled at him. "And they've got numbers, or haven't you noticed, nice-time boy?"

He grinned back: "I've gone there sober as a judge, you know. But such long numbers – five and six figures. And then the streets've got no names."

"Once you get used to it, you don't get lost."

"But I bet I'm going to get lost, coming back," he said.

She looked at him quizzically, and he smiled disarmingly. "I mean, I'd like to take you back tonight. I've borrowed a car, and you don't have to worry. I'm sober and a professional driver. But I'll still get lost getting back to Kofifi – and the next time I try to come to your place."

"Tami's taking me back," she told him, voice impersonal.

"Well, you can tell him you got something else fixed up."

"He won't like it. And, anyway, what's the matter with your nice-time girls?"

"Ag, those ... Don't talk about them." The disarming smile again: "I'm turning over a new leaf."

"Since when?"

"Today."

"Because of me? You've got a hope."

"I'm going to tell you something, Betty," he said, his voice rapid: "Don't answer me, don't speak. Just let me say it. You're the girl I want to marry. I'm not proposing, you understand? Just telling you that I've been looking for a girl like you – a woman like you. So even if I don't take you home tonight ... Where do you work?"

"In Lower Houghton," she replied, after she had overcome some of her surprise and irritation at this new madness.

"You mean a girl like you is a domestic servant?"

"Who eats dogs' meat?" she said crisply.

"No Madam would make you eat that, Betty. I thought you were a schoolteacher, or something."

She laughed. "That's only because of the way I look at you – when you're being drunk and stupid."

"But – I mean, why d'you do that kind of work? Hell, that's what you expect from sheilas who've just come out of the country."

"Do you think I ought to be a nice-time girl?"

"Of course not! But you should be working in a factory or something like that. Maybe even a secretary, if they have black ones."

"I used to – work in a factory, I mean. But I gave it up. Those wake-up girls make life difficult."

"Did they ...?"

"Oh, no!" she smiled. "Not me, I can tell you that. I beat them up instead – when I had to. But I get tired of fighting, so I left."

"Yes. All this fuck– ... bloody fighting."

"I thought you liked it."

He gave a short, bitter laugh.

"Don't you?"

"No. But sometimes I can't stop myself. Lately, anyway. In the past I just did it because it was necessary to show die real manne that they weren't the only ones who could do it."

"You shouldn't, Philip."

"Retire – like you?" A bitter laugh. "Now that would really be the end."

"Of what, Philip?"

"Maybe you want me to come to die Avies and be a kitchen boy?"

She smiled indulgently. "You couldn't afford your cashmeres then, Philip. And them you definitely don't want to give up. What do you do?"

"Oh, nothing much. I drive a truck – a delivery van, really. They tell me I'm a salesman, just because they save themselves money in wages by making me take the orders in the location shops, instead of the white man I used to drive around."

"Well, that's not a bad job."

"So, then – you'll let me take you home?"

"Go and ask Tami," she instructed him.

She knew Tami would refuse, but she preferred that the refusal should come from him rather than herself. She was not sure she could refuse; and if she could not it would only cause unpleasantness with her over-protective cousin. Tami had adopted an attitude that an elder brother would have, if there had been one in her own family. He did not object to her having boyfriends – she was twenty-three and, he reluctantly admitted, old enough to make such decisions – but none of them were ever good enough, in his opinion. And their intentions were always suspect, which she knew to be true but did not expect to be otherwise. He would object particularly to Philip, because he knew of Philip's conquests and did not want her to be counted among them. So many friendships broke up simply because the friend had made a pass at the other's sister.

It was humiliating to know one's sister – and a cousin was a sister – had been turned into just another casual skondaai.

In the weeks that followed, Philip Mokone turned out to be a persistent but considerate suitor, a completely new role for the well-known seducer and one he seemed to enjoy; like a musician who is suddenly allowed to exploit his unexpected talent for a new and complex virtuosity. He saw her as often as she – or her employment – allowed; and he did not irritate her with constant demands for her body, after her first good-natured but firm declaration that she did not intend to become another name in his roll-call of conquests. She liked him better than she had liked any of the men she had made love with in the past; but she was not going to bed with him as easily or casually as she had with them. Her pride would not let her, and her intuition warned it wouldn't be good for him, if she did. Not good for both of them.

He would be disappointed if she terminated his new-found role that he was enjoying with such pride and wonder at his own patience, and her easy seduction would confirm his cynical attitude towards women. He had said she was the kind of woman he had been looking for to marry; she was certain now that he had meant a woman he could respect and, perhaps, love.

After they had been seen together only twice, it was presumed they were lovers, a not unexpected assumption in an amoral community. And more so when the man – the *juba* – was this particular Brother Nice, the famous Nice Time Phil. Tami had been most annoyed, and had protested to them in a manner threatening to Philip; but was mollified by the change in Philip, who had abruptly retired from Sophiatown's skirt-lifting races.

On Thursday afternoons, when Betty had half the day off, she would wait outside the wholesalers who employed him and he would take her to the movies in Fordsburg, where the Indian owners gave Africans the worst seats under the screen. They spent her alternate Sundays off together, mostly out in the open and with the crowds, so they could avoid the excruciating frustrations of their curbed passion when they were alone. And he would sneak into her tiny room at the bottom of the Lower Houghton garden on the few evenings she allowed him – or allowed themselves the frustrations. Wrapped about each other, they'd converse, and when their passion flamed too high he'd depart, a questioning look in his eyes.

They clung together and kissed endlessly, softly, his hands wandering over the soft, voluptuous and warm body he was getting to know so well. She stopped him when he reached what she knew would be the point of no return.

He chuckled quietly one evening, after she had halted his five-finger sortie. She leaned away from him, examining the faded-brown handsomeness of his face, which was now childlike in its amusement.

"What's the joke, Philip?" she asked after a while.

"Me," he replied. "Me – Nice Time Phil. Nobody'd believe me if I told them about these passionate hours we spend together."

"You don't have to tell anybody anything."

"I don't plan to."

"Oh. Just because we haven't – yet …"

"No, Betty. I never will. Anybody. This one belongs to us, alone. You're the kind of woman – just the way you look and are, I mean – that any man would want to boast about. But I don't want to."

She smiled at him. "I'm glad, Philip. You'll be ready to have all of me soon."

"I'm in no hurry, Betty. I don't know why. I can't explain it even to myself, but I'm glad you're making me wait. I think I'm even enjoying it."

There was a teasing glint in her eyes. "You mean that. I wonder who's keeping you tuned up, while you're waiting?"

"You know they don't exist any more. Those cherries would only spoil the mood I'm in – have been in since I met you. I want you only on the day or night – the hour – when you want me too. Without any doubts."

"Then why these hot little fingers, my friend?"

He smiled back at her. "Just to remind you that I'm interested, madam. And to get the geography straight. Scouting. 'Be prepared,' we used to say."

"You know that I do want you, Philip? Right now."

"Then why –"

"You're not ready, Philip. You're about to be though."

"Did you feel that?" he asked, squirming. "And you think I'm not ready?"

"I can – I always feel it," she laughed. "I'm so sorry for him."

"You should be sorry for me," he laughed. "The trouble he gives me!"

"It's so nice to see you laugh, Philip," she said, tracing the curving lines at the edge of his mouth with her fingers. "To see you laugh so openly, and so often. When you forget you're a tough-guy klevah, and become just the nice human being you were meant to be."

"Is there such a great difference – a visible one?"

"You know there is, my dear."

"I don't know. I suppose I do know. But I try to forget it. Try to forget why things happen. Or why they shouldn't be allowed to happen."

"Why, Philip?"

"There's a lot of things everyone wants to forget, Betty."

"The small ones, yes. You don't even have to try to forget those. They just go. But the big ones you can't forget, my dear, no matter how hard you try. You must tell me about them. Maybe I can help. You torture yourself with them, you know."

"You see? I was right about you. You can read me like a book, as they say. As long as some lines or paragraphs remain blurred, though." He kissed her lightly. "Seriously, Betty, you are right. I do have some things that I should tell somebody." He paused, then added with wry bitterness: "Like the Ancient Mariner, who 'stoppeth one of three'."

"Who's he?" And as he smiled again she added with some asperity: "Or are you quoting again? Trying to impress me with your education, Mister Situation!"

He laughed. "I'm sorry. Sometimes I forget that – I mean, you're much more understanding than some of these intellectuals we have. They've got theories and theses, but you've got common sense. Intelligence."

"Anyway," she said into the silence, "what are these things you should tell somebody about?"

"You mean tell you? Not now, Betty," he sighed. "I mean, the burden of them drives me crazy – makes me torture myself, as you said. I feel like shouting them in the streets at times. Just walking up to a cop, to anybody, and committing legalised suicide. But I don't know if I can tell you."

"Why, Philip?"

"Because you're so – so good, Betty. I might lose you."

"You're going to lose me right now," she said ominously, "if that's how you think of me. Do you think, my love, my feeling for you depends on the marvellous things you've done? And what are these, anyway? Sleeping with all the women in Jo'burg? You haven't got me to lose yet, Philip."

"Don't be angry, Betty."

"I'm not angry. Can't you see? There's nothing you can tell me – now or at any time – that'll change how I feel about you."

"I'm sorry, sweetie. I didn't mean it that way. What I meant was I couldn't just tell you that – well, all right, then: I'm afraid to tell you.

Now. Because the person I tell ... It's not a matter of trusting them, or worrying that they'll despise me. It's just that I've got to be certain they'll understand. And from this understanding be able to help me – if that's possible!" he laughed. "Not just talk about it, although that might be all for the best. But help me to understand. If they fail me there'd be this thing between us, you see. I've kept it to myself a long time, now, and ..."

He sighed again, and she kissed his face.

"All right, Philip. Don't say any more. Wait until you're ready. Then you can tell me. And now, we're going to go to bed – together, here."

"Now?"

"Because I know something now: that this is the time."

It was a time, a night, that surprised and overwhelmed him with its strange but familiar newness. He had in his time slept with so many women that he could not remember all of them – their names, or that he had been with them. But this was as if it was his first time. He had subconsciously wanted it to be like this, but had not known how different – how exhilarating new and exciting – it could be. And there was none of the usual machismo resentment in him because she was not a virgin. Instead he was glad she was as knowledgeable as he was; not glib with expertise, but fluent in the expression of her emotions and feeling for him.

Afterwards he laid his cheek beside hers on the pillow, panting from exquisite exhaustion, staring with wide-eyed amazement at her serene, smiling face.

"I love you, Betty," he said in a breathless voice filled with awe and wonder. "I do love you, my darling. D'you know what that means? I didn't, before. But I do now – and always will, whatever happens."

"So do I, my dear," she said softly. "So do I, Philip."

Chapter 9

The tableau was set again.

They were at opposite ends of the living room, each reading under their own lamp. The pools of light left a gulf of darkness between them. They sat in their easy chairs reading, but each waited for the cue that would open a new skirmish in the conflict they were living through. They had not seen much of each other since the night she had pleaded for time to think. He stopped coming home for lunch, as he had done during the voluptuous days of their new-found love and awareness of the other.

How long ago was that? Jean Ryan wondered as she turned a page. And, now, he also came back late in the evenings. Just drinks with the boys, or something more? But tonight Patrick was early, after being away – how many nights? Saying gruffly he'd been away on another tour of out-of-town branch offices. Must've been given a promotion he's not bothered to mention. But perhaps he'd been in the city all the time. He'd not said much to her this evening, since his return. But she knew that he would speak tonight. The moratorium had come to an end.

"Jean." He spoke the name quietly. "Have you for God's sake made up your mind now? I've given you more time than you need. I've been waiting for you to tell me, but you've remained silent. You've got to get rid of it – immediately. It'll be dangerous soon, you know."

"I know the dangers, Patrick."

He could hardly hear her voice. He leaned forward, straining his ears to hear every word and nuance clearly. "What?"

"I know, Patrick. I wish you'd been firmer with me right at the beginning. I should have got rid of it the very day I found out. But now ... I'm more confused than I ever was, Paddy."

"There's nothing to be confused about, for God's sake!" He wanted to stop himself as he said the words, but it was too late. He had planned this talk so carefully; how he was going to be gentle but firm, how he would not lose his temper. But now he had lost it. So he went on:

"You're carrying a black rapist's child – remember? And there's only one thing to be done with it – this thing! How much simpler do you want anything to be?"

"It isn't simple, Patrick," she said slowly.

She was not going to lose control, she told herself. This was too important. I must make him appreciate what an awful dilemma I'm in.

"I so wish it was simple, but it's not, Paddy. Can't you understand that for the first time in my life I'm pregnant? I have in me something

I've prayed and hoped for – dreamed about for so many years … more years than we've been married, Paddy. Surely you must appreciate, just a little bit, how I feel?"

"You mean …" He paused, then began again, more slowly: "You mean to tell me you're actually glad that …?" He choked on the thought. He rose to his feet in the dark silence. "Jean! What's got into you? Are you crazy, woman? You must be stark, raving mad! You –"

The leash snapped off her temper and her voice cut him off.

"Damn you, Patrick Sean Ryan! How dare you!" She stopped and stared up at him, her face tense with the struggle to slip the restraining leash back on again. They glared, and she asked him in a muted, toneless voice: "Will you light me a cigarette, please?"

He did so with truculent reluctance, and after several puffs on the cigarette she spoke again, with deliberation: "Patrick. I'm not mad. Though there are times – there have been times when I feared I was going crazy. I'm not glad about anything. I'm not glad that I was raped, and I'm not glad that I'm pregnant as a result."

"Good!"

"But I am pregnant, Paddy. And the feel of it – the knowing. My whole being knows that I am carrying a child, at last. That's what I'm …" She paused and stared appealingly up at him. "It's got me all mixed up. Please don't interrupt, Patrick. Listen to me. Some nights I wake up in the dark and the knowledge floods my being with such an exhilaration. All I know, then, is that I'm pregnant at last. Forgetting how I came to be so. The word sings through me – pregnant, pregnant, pregnant … and I'm happy, Patrick. Then – then, suddenly – I remember. And I want to run out onto the roof and throw myself off. Not only because of the disgust this memory brings up in me, but because I want to kill myself for just having been happy for those few moments."

"I'm sorry, Jeanie," he said, crossing the gulf of darkness and placing a hand on her shoulder. "I'm truly, honestly sorry. I've been ignorantly selfish. Looking at everything from my side alone. I'm sorry."

"Patrick?" she said in a hopeful voice. "Paddy, darling, can't I …" The small, wistful voice hesitated then rushed ahead: "Can't I have the baby and then give it away? Just for the experience – to look at it once, my own baby?"

His lips twisted, and she hurriedly added, "I don't even have to see it, Paddy! I just want to feel those birth pains and that marvellous relief they say you get when it's all over. They can give it away immediately, for all I care!"

He had removed his hand from her shoulder and stepped back while she spoke. He stared down at her in disbelief, the disgust in his face lost in the gloom of the room.

"Jean! How can you even think it? You won't mind people knowing – seeing you bulging all over? What would they … no. What would I – d'you think for one crazy moment that I'd live here, day after day, watching you swell and swell with that vile, filthy thing? With everybody talking and pointing fingers? Good God, girl! Consider other people, man – and how I feel! Do you –"

"I don't care!" she exploded. "I don't fucking care, Mister Patrick Sean Ryan!" She, too, was on her feet, facing him: eyes blazing with a cold, furious light, and her voice a low, harsh sound. The leash had been thrown away.

"For the thirty years of my life, I've always cared what other people think. That's what you and they call being considerate, isn't it? An upright member of society! Well, now I care about me first. Do you know what I thought – I, not 'people' – after the first doctor said you were sterile? The doctor I wheedled you into seeing after you and your considerate family had been accusing me – oh, not in so many words, my dear, but it was there in their eyes! Do you know what I thought?"

She paused and her body shook as she sucked in breath. Her eyes stared blankly beyond herself; stunned by an anger that did not exclude wonder, contempt and pity. An impersonal portion of her mind distractedly asked if she realised the enormity and finality of what she was about to say, and if she really wanted to say these things. She felt somehow as she had on that night, she was carried along the alleyway by an unknown man. Except this time the mind – that noted the expression of his face, the room they were in, the sounds from the street and other apartments – was not in a state of paralysis. Its acute awareness was engendered by a fury at this known man and her past frustrations and humiliations. Her only fear this time was that she would not be able to articulate her feelings to her own satisfaction.

"You wouldn't believe the doctor. Just a quack – that's what you said. But I believed him. And you know what I thought? Find myself a lover. A stud! To give me the baby I wanted. Then I'd find you a real quack, who'd give you expensive injections and drugs. And one fine evening, I'd smile at you lovingly. 'I've been to the doctor, darling ...' That's what I'd tell you, and all the other things sentimental wives are supposed to say. You'd have believed me, wouldn't you? Of course you would! Your machismo back in place! And me? I'd have my baby. But no! Jean was a conscientious, considerate, upright member of society. It wouldn't be fair to you! And what would he think of me – the stud? What would people say, if they knew?"

She shook her head in wonder and pity at her naivety.

"I was a fool, Patrick. I should have done it. All men take their fatherhood on trust, don't they? What a fool! Then I'd have been home with my baby that night – or perhaps children, a lot of little bastard Ryans. Instead, I was out in the streets where that randy son of a whore could ruin my life. Rape me – and do in a few minutes what you couldn't do in years! On hundreds and thousands of nights when I've gladly, hopefully, opened myself to you!

"You know something, Patrick? I'm not confused any more. You, my darling love – my strong, firm, virile, adorable, considerate husband – you've made up my mind for me! I'm going to have this little bastard, whatever colour it is. Perhaps I'll even keep it. Who can stop me? It's mine, isn't it? The only thing I can ever really call my own. Yes, keep it! That'd be wonderful, wouldn't it? What would people say then, Paddy? About you being the step –"

"I'll divorce you, by God!" he cut in, his voice choked. "Throw you out into the streets where you belong! I'd – I'd ...

"Go to bed, Jean," he finished in a quiet, broken voice. "You're just upset and talking wild. Go to bed and we'll talk when you're all right again ... tomorrow."

I am going to have the baby, she told herself in the snug, comforting dark and warmth of her bed. Whatever he does or says. Whatever they all think. I am going to have it! She repeated the resolution with a deliberate defiance.

I'm going to have it. Produce a baby. Even if I do give it away afterwards.

Do you really mean it? Throw your crazy – which it is, my girl – defiance in his and all the other smug faces? Did you mean all you said? The lover – the stud; that was true. But what about all the rest? You don't have to.

He's given you a way out. He always does. Poor, irresolute Patrick. How many decisions has he ever made in his life?

Oh, now – don't be bitchy! He can be firm, yes. But when he was, was it for himself? Because he himself believed so, and wanted so? Selfish decisions? No, I don't think so. Firm where others have already beaten a track. The fearless and moral pathfinders. My people!

Ah, but are you any different? To suddenly be so smug, pitying, contemptuous? Don't you – didn't you – follow the same precedents? Only when they're right. Aren't they, now? Yes, but … no. Not really. Correct, maybe, but not right all the way. Motherhood is every woman's right, isn't it? Why should I be the only one who doesn't get a chance at it? Not the only one, but why should I give up the chance?

And after you do satisfy your maternal instincts and yearnings? He'll divorce you, of course. Nothing else he can do. Will you fight him in court?

Dear and Honourable Magistrate: an abortion was, and still is, against my religious belief and scruples. And against the law. He can't tell the court he asked me to. They can't say I should have. But maybe they can make you give it away. Take it away from its mother. Can they? Do you want to keep it? I don't know – whether they can, or whether I want to keep it.

He'll get it, though: the divorce. So why fight and heap dirt on dirt?

Chapter 10

He lay on the bed listening to the familiar sounds of early Sunday morning drifting into his backyard room from the street: cars and trucks roaring or squeaking past, the call of boys vending Sunday newspapers; and domestic noises from his neighbours in their one-room homes – a clatter of pots and pans, a thud of bare feet on concrete floors, a banging of flimsy doors into warped frames. The occasional, high-pitched laughter of kids playing on the packed earth of the backyard, between the barracks-like row of rooms he lived in and the sprawling warren of the main building that hid the backyard from the busy street. Almost all young voices, their elders still in bed on the only morning they could sleep late. But there was also the sound of tinny and cracked church bells calling out, demanding the presence of the faithful and pious to prayer and unending sermons made even lengthier by having to be interpreted into two or three languages. A long time since he'd hearkened to the call of any of those bells, or felt a pang of conscience at ignoring them.

He lay on his back and sniffed at the acrid smell of smoke from braziers that would cook the only proper breakfast of the week: a feast, but still nothing much. (Bacon and eggs a dream reserved for laanies, toast a white man's joke. Only Boykie spoke of them – boasted with familiarity from odd nights spent in the homes of particularly liberal friends, when he couldn't get a lift back to Soph'town after another mixed party.) A scratch breakfast to be followed by a heavy and even more festive lunch: boiled rice, meat and gravy, potatoes, beans, cabbage, beetroots that bled what was termed St Peter's blood over the whole lot.

His meals would also be ritually festive today – first time since he'd abandoned his mother's home to live alone; free to entertain whoever he pleased. Betty had been given the whole weekend off from a white kitchen, and had spent most of Saturday afternoon buying mountains of food he had to carry. Saying he could cook the remainder for himself during the week, which they both knew he never would. She lay beside him in the bed now, fast asleep and her warmth seeping into the left side of his body. Warmth, goodness – and she's mine. I can't be that bad, if she can love me. Doesn't think I'm bad. No worse than anybody else; thinks I'm even better than most of them. He smiled – I have a potential for good! Who, me? Yes, you, believe it or not.

Me myself, as Kirk Douglas said in that movie, beating his chest like he was Johnny Weismuller playing Tarzan, king of the apes.

Me, Philip Thabo Mokone. Twenty-eight years old, salesman-driver. Good pay complemented by some initiative with invoices and loading of the van. Good dresser and handsome – to hell with modesty, the cherries say it and some of the jealous majita sneer and call me Pretty Boy. A lady-killer who'd get his face kicked in regularly if die real manne didn't notch me. Keeping timing with them and, on a lower social level, die manne and way up to die really real manne: that's how safety was spelt in Kofifi and any other location. And also for acceptance, however reluctant by some, within the so-called 'decent community' of the law-abiding whose top level was the situations – and all of them victims of the wake-up manne. But their acceptance gave him self-respect while that of liberals – on their own terms – gave Boykie self-confidence.

Self-respect, okay; but still no past to be proud of, no future to look forward to, no individuality – not much, anyway, because then you stand out like a sore thumb that has to be amputated; thrown into prison by the powers that be ... just another black utility on the white man's treadmill. A cipher in the Census Register, a pass-book number. A Native without a soul he can call his own – kaffir, boy, Naturel. Not human, not mechanical, not animal. Just muscle that's marshalled, exploited, discarded.

Oh, you haven't done badly. Comparatively. You wear shoes every day, don't you? Remember the snot-nosed, barefoot, barely-dressed piccaninny running to school? Cracked soles burning in the hot summer dust and going numb on the frozen winter earth? Wiping off sweat with a grimy hand in summer, the snot with a shirt-tail in winter? Getting Education by rote: The Cat Sat On The Mat! Good boy, Thabo! You'll be a clever man and get a good job one day! Nine times nine is eighty-one. Good! Very good, Philip! The river Danube divides the capital of Hungary into the two towns called Buda and Pest and together they are called Budapest. Excellent, my boy! You'll become a teacher, a doctor or even a lawyer one of these days if you always study so hard! The Dutch trekked away from the Cape Colony because they wanted freedom from the British who forced them to give up their slaves with the Emancipation campaigned for by William Wilberforce. You're going to be an excellent scholar, Philip!

The history of what should've been his own land, according to an official textbook written by a white man called Whiteside.

Hey, Boykie! Y'know what? I got that bursary for secondary school! We're going to the same secondary – you and me!

Five years to go for the Joint Matriculation Board. Study hard, but don't let others think you're a bookworm. Work during the holidays, and don't look with envy at those few who don't have to but can still afford smart clothes. Exams – not really a breeze, but sailing through them with ease.

An annoying teasing of his hair by white fingers: You're one of the brightest students we've ever had here, Philip Mokone.

An attempt to avoid that big, white hand: Thank you, Father.

You should go to university, my boy.

Yes, Father Stephen; but my father has no –

Oh, we know that, my boy! Ha-ha-ha! D'you think you're the only poor boy here? Come on, Mokone – don't look so bashful! I'm sure the mission can get you a scholarship. It would be a great pity to waste that brain under this hair …

Cool – keeping timing – when he tells Boykie. Ek sê – hoor hier, my bitkaid. Father Stephen says they can get me a scholarship to go to Fort Hare and –

University! Hah! Why d'you want to waste your time there, Phil? Don't be stupid, man! What're you going to do there? Okay, you come back a teacher, eh? After another four years' swotting! And what d'you get for that BA and teaching diploma? A lousy twenty pounds a month! Not me, boy! A graduate – but still just a boy to these illiterate or semi-educated white bastards. I'm going to work, me. And make more money than any stiff-necked situation full of jaw-breaking English and all the other lah-di-lah laanie bullshit!

The irony was that he didn't even have the choice of going Boykie Nine Years' hardekop way or wasting four more years at Fort Hare – a bloody long way off in the bundu, but Wits around the corner was an almost white reserve.

Oh, I know, my son – I know, Thabo! But what can we do, ngoana wa ka? It is God's work, Thabo. Your father is gone, and now you are the man of this house. Your little brothers and sisters must also go to school and get a little bit of education. And of course I will always work, my son, but is there ever enough money from washing the white people's clothes and things? Hau! I wanted to see you a teacher or a doctor – wearing a suit and tie. But what can we do, Thabo? It has happened, it is God's work.

Yes, my mother. I too will find work and –

Thirteen years of exciting study gone down the drain. Just to become a driver for white salesmen – driving all over the country while they slumbered, and jumping to the click of their impatient fingers in shops and stores whose owners hardly ever looked at his face. Just another boy – a utility with the added ability of being able to read road maps and way-bills. Geography and literacy in three languages came in handy for earning an occasional pat on the back. Geometry came in handy for rolling the van round hairpin turns on mountain roads. Maths – ah, that had personal and profitable uses – fixing the grafts when he was promoted to salesman-driver in the locations. Fix those invoices so fast that Benade the dispatcher is left two years behind, chewing at his pencil. Not-so-bad wages and a fat graft. Double any graduate's salary. But no graft for Boykie Courtroom in a legal office – yet he wears a suit and tie every day like them; and better quality threads. Back-door stuff because he, too, is still one of the wake-up majita who notch and keep timing.

Boykie ... Nice guy, childhood pal – but so lost in the liberal world where he's patronised and accepted as one of the few, known members of the Black Intelligentsia. And you, pal? You know your way through the legal jungle apartheid's wrapped around us? If you did, you wouldn't have bothered with going to secondary school. Saved five years, and maybe the old man would've lived longer. Saved his health and a lot of trouble too. Stupid arguments with semi-literate whites like bloody Benade. Would've worked for the wholesale firm longer and made a pile by now. What d'you need trigonometry for? To load a truck? Shakespeare, Shelley and all the rest to fill out an invoice?

Stupid, frightened bastards! Even their women, the goddesses.

So, hey – you're the boy who smashed the truck, hey? Yes, Mevrou. Say Missus, jong! All right, now you must fill in this form for our insurance – it's called an Accident Claim Form. You know what that is, you cheeky kaffir. Can you write? Good, and do it so we can read every word, hoor. Now, what's this here about forty-five degree angles, boy? What d'you know about them, hey? Okay – I'll tell you what to write. Can't you say Missus, jong, when you talk to a white lady? Cheeky bloody kaffir! Go get me some cigarettes while I check this invoice, boy. Oh, I'm sorry, Sir, but – Don't 'Sir' me, jong! Baas, you hear? Baas – hoor jy my, fokken kaffer? That's what you call me! Where did you steal those nice shoes, boy? Who d'you think you are, looking at me like that, kaffir?

Okay – that's their fear which needs constant reassurance. But what the hell's the matter with this country – with them? Why are they so afraid of us all the time? Not just because we outnumber them. They've got all the guns, conquered the country with those muzzle loaders. Because they know deep down they're not really superior? I mean, if you are superior bastards, then you can't be afraid. Can you?

Something more, still. If they knew us – never mind what they really found out about themselves – and reconciled themselves to being the same as us, just people, they'd have nobody to look down on. And they need that. No, more than that – there's more to this whole thing. They'd lose their justification for what they've been doing to us these three hundred years. Bringing the Light and Civilisation – the start of our history, according to Baas Whiteside. The light that blinded us while their civilisation took our land and manhood from us. What's so civilised about them, anyway? The atom bomb and intercontinental ballistic missiles? A nuclear kingdom come – all of us frying together. Is that civilised? Is it – Whoa, now. No need to start diatribes against their technological civilisation.

Oh, boy! These jaw-breakers you're using this Sunday morning. Desmond would be most impressed. But it is – must be – because of their great and wonderful civilisation that they have this fear. Isn't it? We are not afraid of them – we, the savages. We know them better than they know themselves – and a helluva lot better than they'll ever know us. We have the worm's eye view. And we are not scared. Just oppressed. I know Benade, but he only remembers my name and face – first name only of this cheeky kaffir. We don't respect them, even while we call them Baas. What for – why should we? For the humiliations they pile on us? We just try to keep out of the way of their savagery.

That's it, pal: their savagery. After all, when they first came here we didn't show them a quarter of the savagery they've been handing us since we stretched out our black hands for the Bible and beads, listening to a sermon on Christian Love that passeth all understanding. Where was – where is – their Christian Love? It's supposed to be their religion, formulated by their messiah. Their European messiah, who was in fact a Jew in the Middle East.

But this still doesn't explain the fear. It is fear, isn't it? Not a physical fear, but something worse: a sickness of the soul. All right, Father Philip, the text of your sermon this Sabbath morning is: "And they haveth a sickness of the soul that maketh them so feareth their inferiors that they loseth their God."

Oh, stop it man! All this doesn't change the fact that you're a fucking rapist.

Okay. I'm a criminal. A refugee from the gallows. But do I feel like one? Don't think so. It's their laws that forced my ... To hell with them, then? It was, and is still, wrong to have done that to this poor woman. Morally. Whose morality? Do I think I did wrong, or do I feel I did wrong simply because that's how I'm supposed to feel? I don't think so. No, I wanted to do it, and I'm not sorry I did. So how can I feel guilty? But it is wrong to rape. Anybody. More than wrong, it's disgusting.

And Betty thinks I'm good. Would she if she knew? She said nothing I've done would change her love for me. But that doesn't mean she would sympathise – which is what you want, isn't it? Even if she continues loving you, she might not want to see you any more. Stop liking you. Yet I can't hide it from her any longer. She has to know. So she can judge me. And help me if she wants to. Which is what I want her to do, most of all. Help you do what? Absolve you of the guilt? There isn't any. But she might think there is – and more. Well, then, help me understand: myself, and my actions.

He sat at the table smoking his first cigarette of the day as Betty washed up after their breakfast – bacon and eggs that looked so clean, so beautiful on the plates; the yolks firm, so they didn't bleed all over the plate like they always did in that café at the bus terminus on Diagonal Street. But no toast because no electricity – and, anyway, he didn't much like the burnt offerings at that same café on Diagonal, or even at the Blue Lagoon down town on Von Wiellich. She was not the first woman to stand there on a Sunday morning as he smoked. But she was the first to cook him a laanie breakfast – not just porridge and milk – and, more important, the first one he was glad to have standing there like she belonged, and him feeling proprietorial and expansive, happy and contented.

"You're going to make somebody a good wife one day, sweetheart."

She turned to smile mockingly. "I thought it was going to be you, Philip? Have you forgotten what you said the first time we met at that stokvel of Tami's?"

"I was drunk – as you said," he grinned.

"I didn't say anything like that."

"Not with your tongue, but with your eyes."

"Or maybe you've changed your mind."

He laughed, luxuriating in the sound and its feeling inside his chest.

"That was the answer I wanted," she said. "And now I'll start cooking lunch. After you eat that, my dear, you'll want to marry me – tomorrow!"

"What would you say if I asked you to marry me, Betty?"

"Do you have to ask, Philip?"

"Tell me."

"I'd say yes ... and tell you to wait."

"What for? I'm getting old, you know."

"That's why you must wait. It would be very funny for a man of your age to jump into marriage like a little boy who doesn't know what he's doing."

"D'you think I don't love you? I mean, that I don't know –"

"Oh, I know you love me, my dear. But for the wrong things."

"What do you mean?"

"Do you really want to talk about such things today, my dear?"

He did not hesitate, knowing her question encompassed more than she would let on. Hell, why not? Maybe this is the right time. After all that early-morning self-analysis.

"Yes. Everything," he told her. "What are the wrong things?"

"You love me, Philip, mainly because I make you feel ... Well, I'm something like a mother to you, am I not?"

He told himself he should be angry, but he was not. He was too interested. "What d'you mean by that?"

"That's what you meant that day when you said I was looking at you like a schoolmistress. I'm not quite sure – I don't know how to say it,

Philip. But you seem to want me to punish you. You expect me to punish you, or maybe it's just to correct you. For what, Philip?"

He hid his surprise behind a wry smile. "For my sins."

"Which ones, Philip? Those of a Sophiatown klevah who steals from the people he works for like everybody else? Who gets drunk, sleeps with a lot of all kinds of women? Who gets into stupid fights and swears? Priests think of those things as sins; but you don't."

"And what about you?"

"I don't – not some of them. They've become too common. They're normal, these days. But those are not the sins you mean, Philip. It's something more than that. But you don't have to tell me."

"I want to, Betty."

"Then tell me."

"I don't know how – where to start and so on ..."

"Why, my dear?"

"I'm not sure – that it was a sin, or was really wrong ..."

"What did you do, Philip?"

He did not answer, and she continued: "You remind me of my cousin – your brikaid, Tami. Maybe you know that he killed a man two years ago? Very few people know. Even if they knew, it wouldn't make much difference. It was only a kitchen boy from the farms, and nobody would take the risk of going to court for him.

"But he worries about it. Somehow, he wants to be punished for it. He won't go to the police, of course. Even though they'd probably just chase him away. Too much work for them and too long ago, is what they would say."

"I haven't killed anybody," he said, feeling a tightness about his chest. Now! Now's your chance, now's the time. "But if I went to the cops, they wouldn't think it was a waste of time."

"Tell me, Philip."

"I raped a white woman."

They looked into each other's eyes in the silence that came over the room, blotting out the sounds from outside this sudden confessional. Her brown eyes narrowed in momentary pain, then softened with compassion as they studied the apprehensive but defiant gaze he kept steadfastly on her.

"All sorts of people rape women, Philip. But I –"

"You know it wasn't just lust, don't you?" he said quickly. "I don't have to rape women. You know that – you just said it ..."

"But she was white, and –"

"Yes. That's why I did it – but not because I was just another kaffir who wanted to fuck a white woman."

"The poor woman."

"You're sorry for her?"

"Of course. I'm sorry for all women who are raped. I feel for them – but not only because I'm also a woman."

"But whites aren't sorry for black women. Hey? Are they?"

"Philip, I feel what I feel because of what it does to me. Not because other people feel the same way, or don't."

"Don't you want to know why I did it?"

"You have started, you will tell me."

He spoke slowly, trying to recall his emotions in the hope that he would find some new clue that could help him explain his actions to himself. And as he spoke, she turned away from the puzzled hurt on his face. Betty peeled potatoes, washed the cabbage and made other preparations for their lunch. When he finished, they remained silent for minutes, and then she asked him:

"Are you sorry, Philip?"

"No – well, I don't know. I'm sorry for some things about it. But not for others."

"You're sorry for yourself."

"Yes, I suppose I am," he admitted slowly. "I'm also sorry that we live in a country where a man has to do a thing like that."

"What do you mean – when you say you had to do it?"

"Don't you see, Betty?" he asked, despair in the voice. "I was trying to prove something, when I did it. Something I wouldn't have to prove if I didn't live in this country with its stupid and savage politics."

"You must not hide behind politics, Philip."

"Why not? Politics is the most important thing in our lives – isn't it? They have made it so important. When I was born, it was a political event: another black bastard – a kaffir they had to oppress and suppress. Going to bed with you is a political event, too, because you might become pregnant and increase the number of kaffirs they have to fear. If it wasn't for the politics of this country, I wouldn't have done it, I tell you. White women would've been just like any other women."

"Do you feel sorry for her, Philip?"

"No. Why should I? To me she's only a body on which I tried to show how I feel. Just like to them we're nothing but another pass book."

"Yes," she sighed. "That is the trouble with this country. We're not people to each other. We behave like – like …"

"Like animals? Worse? But who started it, Betty? Not us – that's for sure! That's why we must show them how it feels to be treated like that – worse than their dogs."

"Can you imagine how she feels now?"

"Aah, the hell with her!" he said with sudden impatience. "Do they ever care how … All right, I know you're going to tell me I don't have to behave or think that way just because they do. Please try and understand, Betty," he continued in quick, half-pleading tones. "I wasn't doing it to her – can you understand that? It was to them – all three million of them. She was only important in that she was not just white but also obviously high-class. I wouldn't have bothered if she'd been just another poor-white. It had to be …" He paused and smiled ruefully. "Maybe," he said quietly, "I should've got the Mayor's wife, or the wife of a Cabinet Minister. Except they'd be too old."

"Don't make jokes, Philip."

"I'm not joking, Betty." He lit another cigarette as she watched him.

"Is this the thing you were afraid you'd lose me about?" she asked.

"Yes."

"You won't," she told him. "You need too much help."

"Can you give it to me, Betty?"

"I hope so. I'll try. But not by arguing with you. I don't have the education for that, my dear. I don't know how, but I'll do my best."

"Thank you, Betty."

"You don't have to," she smiled softly. "I'm doing it for myself, you see. I want to marry you, so I must help you. What about the police?"

"They'll never find out. I spent that night in the cells, and that's it: finish and klaar – for them, not me."

Chapter 11

"Hel-l-o, Jean darling!" the young woman said, smiling her way into the apartment and giving her sister-in-law an enthusiastic hug. "Ooh, it's been such a long time since I last saw you! Hasn't it, Jean my darling?"

"I'm glad to see you too, Sheila. Yes. It has been a long time."

Sheila was pretty, bright and breezy, and Jean spoke with a quiet wariness: not hostile, but watching the vivacious face with speculative eyes.

"Sit down and have a drink."

Sheila grimaced comically, then laughed and collapsed into an armchair, deftly arranging the skirt of her well-cut suit over shapely knees its length could not hide.

"I wish I could say yes, darling Jean. But I've made a new rule: no drinking before six! Have to watch the calories, you know. Till I hook myself a husband, anyway." She winked, then laughed: "I'll probably have to watch the old figure even more carefully then – to keep him hooked!"

She giggled, but Jean failed to react.

"Wouldn't want to lose him to these bright young things with ball-and-socket hip-joints!"

Jean almost laughed. "Is the competition getting you down already? I always thought you enjoyed these cat fights."

Another comical grimace from Sheila. Jean pressed the palms of her hands along her hips, keeping wary eyes on her sister-in-law.

"I wouldn't stand a chance with the competition now, with these hips. Fat like a cow. And I suppose that's what you've come about."

"Oh, Jeanie!" Sheila protested. "Do we have to go straight into that? I was hoping we could just sit around and gossip. And then – you know how sophisticated and subtle people do it ... just slide gently into this awful business. I got a detailed briefing from Patrick, but I suppose I'd never make a diplomat, would I?"

"You're doing just fine, Sheila," Jean reassured. "Very charming, disarming and all that. But what's awful about a woman being pregnant?"

"Nothing, darling – done the right way, with your husband."

She paused, lighting a cigarette. "But this isn't the right way, is it, Jean? Preggers from being raped? And by an African? I know there's no proof that it was one of them – it could just as easily have been your neighbour, for all we know.

"And personally, I don't stand for all this stereotyped bunk about the black, randy savages. But the chances are it was one of them. After all, they outnumber us."

"And it's worse if it was one of them?"

"Of course it is, darling. Not because they're inferior, dirty, smelly and all this other bull we good white women are expected to believe." A wagging finger, and naughty grin above it: "And let me tell you, sister-in-law, there's a hell of a lot who don't believe – because they know different. From personal experience – can you believe it? But don't let me get started on that! The important thing's that if it was an African, the baby's going to be half-and-half. Which is going to –"

"Make it inhuman? Aren't they people too? If your friends can enjoy fucking them – okay, maybe not your friends. But they, too, are human. Anyway, won't this half-and-half be as much a baby as any other?"

"Yes it will, Jean; but let's not get into race relations. I get enough of that from my liberal friends. Let's be practical. Don't be proud and mule-headed with me, darling. You know deep down that you've got to get rid of it. I can see you wanting to tease my dear brother – shake him out of his unearned complacency, let's say – but you're taking it dangerously far. There's nothing dangerous about an abortion these days, if that's what's worrying you; I know, dear sister-in-law. Personal experience. But it's going to be dangerous if you continue your complicated game much longer."

"'Thou shalt not kill', Sheila."

"Bosh! This isn't killing, darling. It's like an enema – ridding your body of an impurity."

Jean smiled. "You've said a lot of confused things, Sheila; you couldn't have been much good at debate. But still you do have good arguments. Good, impersonal arguments. But I can't discuss this impersonally. In fact there's no need to argue."

"Because the teasing's over and you're going to get rid of it?"

"No."

"You don't mean that you're really going to have this – this bastard?"

"I am. And I'd be very much obliged, dear sister-in-law, if you would be kind enough not to call my – my ... Oh, Sheila! Oh, Sheila! Can't you understand? You're a woman like me, damn it! Surely you can understand how I feel? How I need to have a baby? How I must be feeling after years and years of praying to have one? Of course I didn't want it this way, whether the man was black, white or yellow.

"But beggars can't be choosers, Sheila. All I know is that I want, for the first and last time in my life, to be big with child. And I am now. Why should I give up my only chance?"

Sheila attempted a smile. "You make me feel like a murderess, talking like that, Jean. Of course I understand, darling! I hope to have children one day. But this one's out of the question, Jeanie. Do you know what'll happen to you and your little, er – baby? I can't remember half my briefing, but you'll be an outcast. There'd be no place you could both stay, because of the Group Areas Act. No group that would – or could – accept you. Your little piccaninny would be like an albatross round your neck. Is motherhood worth all that?"

There were tears in Jean's eyes, and she shook her head irritably to get rid of them. "I don't know, Sheila. I haven't decided finally if I'm going to keep it. But I do intend –"

Sheila spoke quickly as she leapt into the breach – the chink in the maternal armour through which she might get that idea out of Jean's muddled mind. And perhaps get her to give up the whole project: "The police would hound you, Jeanie. One look at you and this, this baby, and they'd pick you up under the Immorality Act. Demanding to know the identity of your black lover – the father. Are you going to spend every day explaining to them and everybody else that you were raped? You'd be a freak, something that everyone could despise. You don't want such a life, Jeanie, and we don't want it for you either. Pat loves you, and none of us wants to give you up. But we – he would have to, even if you just had this baby and gave it away. Don't you see, man? He'd be ruined if he stayed with you through all this Mother Earth nonsense!"

So. We have it at bloody last, Jean thought in bitter triumph. Even with all her liberal talk – calling them Africans, not even just Natives like everybody else – she's still as much one of them. Only liberal when it doesn't affect her personally, is she?

"None of you have to worry, Sheila. I'll use my maiden name. I was a Griffiths much longer than I ever was a Ryan. I'll never ever say I even know any of you."

"Oh, Jean!" Sheila said in tired despair.

What is she trying to prove? Trying to be a saint? Suffer little bastards to come into me? At least she has guts – crazy, distended guts, but she has them. Sheila giggled inwardly at her word associations. I wonder if any of my professionally liberal friends would even fantasise about having them? Oh, now! Don't start admiring blind stupidity. Life's practical and you choose your sides accordingly.

Chapter 12

They sat again under their reading lamps in the barren silence that had become part of what had been their intimate home, and was now only a shared apartment. The pools of diffused light in the gloomy room appeared exhausted on the carpet, their strivings to merge and dispel the cheerlessness abandoned. She spoke into the magazine she was leafing through.

"I saw your future sister-in-law shopping on Eloff Street this afternoon."

"Maureen? Oh. That's nice."

He sat stiffly, looking down at his book, ready to look up and talk if that was what she wanted to do, for a change; hoping this conversational girder across the chasm would be the beginning of a bridge, over which the resolution he still hoped to hear from her would come marching towards him.

"No," she corrected him. "It was not nice."

"What? What do you mean?"

"We fought like civilised alley cats."

"Jean ..."

"Not literally, of course – not physically. I haven't lost all my white civilisation yet. Only fought with our bitchy tongues. Which can be worse."

"Did she insult you? She's got no business to –"

"Not actually, Patrick. You wouldn't understand the subtleties employed by the female of the species. She says they're having an engagement party soon."

"Yes. I know."

"You're going, of course."

"Well, I – I don't know yet. I haven't decided finally."

"Why not? After all, Mark's your brother. He'd be offended and everyone would be – well, you know how they'd be. You don't have to follow me beyond the pale, Patrick. Or take offence on my behalf."

"It's all such a helluva mess, Jean," he said, placing his unread book on the floor. "Maureen doesn't want you to come. And Mark – well, he wants you to come, but he doesn't want to quarrel with her over it. He's also afraid there might be a – er – some unpleasantness. And me – I ought to go, I suppose. But it wouldn't be right if I went alone. I mean –"

"You must go, Patrick," she said quietly, the bitterness washed out of her voice by his latest indecision and growing despair. "Don't let me be responsible for any ill-feeling between you and your family. Just go. Forget about me."

Three months to go. Oh, God! Why's time so slow? I can't stand it. I'm tired, exhausted, depleted. My head aches from the tension, the unending thinking, the resolutions taken and discarded, the decisions half-made then avoided. What's going to happen to me? What am I going to do? Oh, God, why? Why me? Why am I being so unreasonable, so bitchy, so stubborn? What do I want? What do I expect? I know what I want right now: him, Patrick. My man – I must have a man. I must! Oh, God! How I want a man, need a man, right this moment. A man …

She writhed slowly on the bed in the conjugal chamber Patrick had abandoned for the guest bedroom. Passing clammy hands that jerked in spasms over a body made strange to them by its girth. Squeezing heavy and taut breasts, the nipples excited and erecting at her touch. Caressing the drum-tight mound of her distended stomach and kneading between the spread of corrugated thighs.

I can't stand it! Why must all this happen to me? Why can't I at least have a man when I need him most between my – deep in myself? I can't! I can't stand it! A suggestion of movement in her belly, and she pressed hands against it – hard. Where's your fucking father, you little bastard? Raping somebody else while I suffer? Why isn't he here when even he – No! Not him! What the bloody hell are you thinking now? Sis! You must be off your head. Well, wouldn't you be? Of course I'm off my head. I want a man, damn them all to hell! I want his arms about me, his hands on my flesh – hard, gentle, knowing, squeezing, probing, rubbing, pulling and thrusting. His lips on mine, on my breasts, on my … I want the feel of him, the weight of him, the strength of him, the thrust of him.

I want to be fucked, d'you understand? And to fuck … I want a man to make love to me, hard, gentle, going on and on. I want to be had!

Her breath came in gasps, her hands fluttered over her body and her loins flamed and flowed with yearning. Oh, Patrick, Patrick! Come and love me, Paddy, my darling. Paddy. Paddy. Paddy. I need you, my darling. Come to me, please – pretend it's your own. For ten, fifteen minutes. Just pretend. You don't even have to kiss me or caress me. Just have me. Be cruel and hurtful if you want to, but have me. Please. Just this once, Patrick. Please, please, please, Patrick!

The bedroom door opened slowly. After a pause he tiptoed through and stood uncertainly over her bed, his eyes stricken as they passed over the heaving, grotesque mound under the disarranged bedclothes. They fastened with desire and revulsion on the thick, mottled thighs that stuck out obscenely from under the blankets.

"Did you call, Jean? Is anything the matter?" he asked in a hesitant whisper, afraid to wake her if she was only dreaming, or he'd been mistaken about the sounds heard from his bedroom.

A violent shudder galvanised her body into a tense arch when she heard his voice. She moaned: a soft, muffled, wailing noise. He placed a cautious hand on her sweaty brow. She knocked it away.

"Don't touch me! Don't bloody touch me, you – you … Please, go away, Patrick. I'm sorry if I disturbed your sleep. Please go. I didn't call; nothing's the matter. Nothing you can do anything about. Just go."

He stood smoking at the window of his bedroom, looking out at the quiet, moonlit night. Why are you still here? he asked himself. It's too late for an abortion now, even if she came to her senses. And she won't. Why haven't you packed and left? Almost everybody knows about it now. The whispers about your recluse wife have made the rounds, and they're wondering about you. You are too cowardly to stand by her, and you're too much of a coward to leave her. Are you waiting for her to kick you out? You want her to take the responsibility? What are you going to do?

Chapter 13

Patrick Ryan let himself into the silent Parkhurst apartment and walked quietly through the entrance hall and into the living room. No "I'm home, darling!" and the response that had not so long ago quickened his heart and loins.

She was not at her usual post in the easy chair at the window. Nor in her bedroom. He heard the sound of running water from the bathroom. What would she be doing in there at this time? What had she wanted stockings for in such a hurry, anyway, phoning him at the office? She had sounded different, too: relaxed, almost happy. He knocked at the bathroom door.

"Jean? Are you in there?"

"Yes, Paddy." The voice was loud and bright. "I'll be out in a minute."

There was something vaguely familiar about the atmosphere. As if he had lived through this before, or something similar. The unexpected cheerfulness, the early-evening toilette – her word for it last time, said with a mock French accent. When? He was going to have a surprise, he knew, and it would not please him. This he was certain of. Unlike the last time – when, he remembered, she'd demanded a night out on the town, and they'd watched that black-black man perform.

"I'll leave the stockings on your bed," he said through the door. His voice sounded strange, even to himself; as if he was reading lines learned long ago that demanded a certain tone of voice. "I hope they're the right colour."

He was sitting in the easy chair, jacket off and reading the evening paper, when she called him from the bedroom. The earlier premonition was aroused and grew stronger as he walked to the door and knocked. After her light-hearted response he opened the door and stopped abruptly. She stood before the full-length mirror, wearing a new, ankle-length maternity dress. Appreciation flitted through his startled mind – she looked marvellous – followed by alarm.

"Are you going out?" he asked. And knew what she would say before she turned around to smile and speak.

"We are, silly! To Mark's engagement party!"

His heart sank into the cold, gooey mess that was his stomach.

"But, Jean – you know you can't ... You're not –"

"Can't what? Not what?" she retorted, gaily. "Can't go to my own brother-in-law's engagement party? I'm going with you, Pat – I've made up my mind!"

She studied his appalled face and added, quietly: "Or alone, if you're too ashamed to be seen with me by your considerate family and friends. I don't care what any of them think, or how they react. I'm going. Isn't it time I made a public appearance? I've avoided everybody since ... that night." The voice grew stronger, determined: "It's time we had a showdown, instead of me hiding like an Indian woman in purdah!"

"Now, look here, Jean," he said in a deliberate, determined manner. Desperately trying to keep his voice from rising. A hysterical fury was bubbling to the surface within him, impotent in his knowledge that he could ever stop her from doing what she planned. "I've just about taken enough nonsense from you – and this is the absolute limit! You hear me? The limit! You're not going to that party under any circumstances." The fury reached the surface. "Haven't you caused enough trouble? Do you think we – I – will stand for this, too? Not a damn! I won't, y'hear me? Take off those clothes! Go to bed this minute!"

She stood with her hands on her hips, her back arched, her belly protruding in a grotesquely ribald manner. And her eyes glinting with a bitter humour and angry defiance. Flints of jade challenging, detesting, contemptuous.

"So!" she said in a harsh, sibilant voice. "There's been another and final family caucus. Of the Pure-White Citizens' Council! 'We won't stand it any more'," she mimicked. "Well, I, and I alone, am not standing any more either! I'm going there if it breaks up the party. I'll have it out with any of them who cares to – and I hope they care, Patrick, I do hope they do!"

They argued, quarrelled, cajoled. They turned red in the face, they blanched mottled white, they choked on their words, glaring at each other with mute hatred and despair. They said all that had been bottled up within them these months, purging themselves in hysterical anger and bitterness. Then they went to the party.

The cosy, smoke-hazed, cocoony atmosphere of the party shredded as Jean entered and was recognised. The bonhomie of celebrating an engagement disappeared, leaving a collection of individuals deprived of the protection from themselves that had been provided by the family and communal talk, laughter and tinkle of cocktail and wine glasses. All of it ceased at this unexpected, shocking entry of the least wanted guest. They were momentarily alone with themselves, reacting to her presence as their individual natures, or what was left of them, demanded. Eyes stared discreetly, necks craned delicately, heads swivelled imperceptibly.

She wore a breezy party smile, attempting to hide the vulnerability of her blooming and softly rounded face. Her green eyes flicked over blank faces, seeking that of Mark Ryan, her brother-in-law and nominal host. She found it suspended above the average-height crowd, frozen in a grin forgotten from some earlier pleasantry or congrats at his decision to get hitched. Among the faces in Mark's circle was that of his sister, Sheila, which was clouded with concern while she cursed vehemently and fluently under her breath. At the other end of the room stood Maureen, blue eyes glittering with hardening malice as they recovered from their initial surprise. The eyes of jade returned to Mark's face, which was thawing from surprise into embarrassed welcome. The party smile on Jean's face broadened into one indicating personal affection as she walked towards him, excluding from its vivacity the people she passed by and ignored.

"I'm so sorry we're late, Mark dear," she cooed prettily. "And congratulations! You're going to be the handsomest groom in all South Africa."

With her words, civilisation quickly reasserted itself in the crowded room; the barbarism of individual emotion receded, replaced by the accepted and expected expressions for such happy occasions. The laager was re-grouping. Heads came together for scandalised whisperings, eyes peered and politely veered, backs stiffened. A woman giggled, another clucked her tongue; a man swore, another shrugged: How shameless ... What cheek ... How dreadful! How embarrassing ... What a shame! Poor thing – poor Patrick ... So it's true ...!

Mark Ryan embraced Jean, but only briefly. And Sheila Ryan took Jean's arm and led her away. The cloud had lifted from her face.

"You know how much I like you, Jeanie – even love you," she said in a soft, conversational voice whose tone indicated emotional exhaustion. "But you're being a damn, bloody fool. I've never thought there were any similarities between courage and masochism."

Jean smiled gently at her sister-in-law. "I had to come, Sheila. And let me tell you something. It takes more than courage. But it isn't masochism."

Patrick drifted away from Mark after slapping his shoulder in congratulation. He slipped a defensive smile onto his face as he headed for the half circle of male backs beyond which he knew would be the liquor. The men in the corner smiled carefully at him as he poured a stiff drink; they spoke to him in voices hearty with barely disguised embarrassment.

Maureen marched directly to her fiancé as soon as Patrick moved away from him. She exuded indignation as she dragged him into another corner and whispered insistent demands. He imperceptibly shook his head in slow regret and firm denial. The blue eyes glared murder and vengeance into his grey ones. When he finally patted her shoulder reassuringly, her body stiffened in rejection and she wheeled away.

I – must – not – get – drunk! Jean repeatedly warned herself, accepting a drink from a tray held high by black hands hidden in white cotton gloves. Patrick can take that way out, hiding in the corner. Just a few drinks, not too many. Be defenceless if I do get even just a bit whoozy. Then these bitches – especially those clustered around Maureen – will tear me apart.

Rape me. Emotional rape. She giggled, and Sheila stared sharply at her. These sex-starved vultures! None with the guts to say anything yet, definitely not openly. Oh, no – too genteel for that. I'm not going to take offence at their sly, bitchy digs; I'll wait for the real McCoy. Then – wham! Show-down. They'll try it soon enough, they will. Just go on smiling, talking, drinking ... It'll come, the open attack. And the counter-attack. Just wait. They've got to do it soon, the blood-thirsty creatures. They've just got to! Why not now, eh? What're you waiting for? Soon, damn it! Please God, soon. I can't wait very much longer. Soon! Before I drown this foetus in alcohol. Drinking for two is not such a good idea.

But time was necessary for final decisions to be made by those who dared; time to build up indignation against the pariah, or compassion for the victim.

Maureen stalked through her guests, holding a brimming tumbler in her hand, her eyes bright and the smile exaggerated. She came to a swaying halt before Jean.

"Here's another drink, darling," she said – slurred – loudly, holding out the tumbler towards Jean. "Enough to save poor Sheila all those treks to the bar. And there's plenty more where this comes from, you know."

"Thank you, darling," Jean said.

Their eyes remained locked together as her fingers wrapped themselves around the glass brimming with whisky, or whatever the bitch had poured into this poisoned chalice. Now, she breathed, her throat constricting. Now! A shudder vibrated through her swollen body as she pulled the tumbler away.

"Will you join me?" she asked sweetly – and threw the contents into the pretty, smiling face.

Maureen screamed, just once, stumbling back. Glasses fell out of hands and broke, people scattered, drinks slopped, talk stopped, faces peered, heads turned.

Patrick grabbed Jean's arm and led her from the room. She leaned against the wall in the long corridor outside the apartment, her body spent and weak. It's over, she told herself. The nightmare's over. Everything's over. She shivered jerkily, and her teeth came down hard on a drink-numbed lower lip. Now it's all done.

"I'm sorry, Patrick," she said in a dull voice. "I'm truly sorry. For you. I was drunk, I suppose. Not just the liquor. Forgive me if you can. I ask nothing else."

"Come on!" he snapped in a hard, flinty voice. "I'm taking you ho– to the flat."

The next day he sent a chauffeur from his office with a formal letter.

It was brief and instructed her to give 'the boy' the ready-packed suitcases waiting in the guest bedroom. He was moving into a hotel and she could contact him at the office for anything she needed. The small black man kept his head down throughout the silent transaction. He stopped at the door and looked up at her, his shoulders dragged down by the suitcases.

"I am so very sorry, Madam," he said. "Mr Ryan – the boss – not be the same since ... Since that time in Hillbrow. If I get that black –"

"Shut up, you filthy swine!" she yelled at him, voice grating in her throat. "D'you think you can make me better by saying that? You want me to give you money for saying that, you – ? Then walk out laughing, hey? And how do you know it was a black? How do I know it wasn't you? How do you – Ag, just go away, you bloody kaffir!"

Chapter 14

They sat in the front seats of the double-decker bus, silently watching the brightly lit panorama of the white world approach, and then flow past and around them. Philip Mokone only used the red double-deckers when visiting the occasional girlfriend who was a domestic servant. Yet the novelty of sitting so high up in the air, with something of a bird's-eye view of his surroundings, remained within him. Also the quiet and cleanliness of the trolley buses, which were so different from the dirty, crowded, roaring rattle-traps that served the townships. And then to have a white conductor and driver too – almost like being served by them, although they made quite certain their manner towards passengers on the Slegs Nie-Blankes upper deck did not suggest they were serving: Kom, jong, betaal!

White men and white men's buses put at the disposal of the black man – to the advantage of his white employer of course, Philip reminded himself. But this night, he'd not be sneaking in through a side gate to a room at the bottom of the garden. Through the front gate and door tonight, boy! Boykie Courtroom offered his cigarette case, and Philip quickly flared a match before his friend could flourish a matching lighter. They sat back and smoked in silence for a few minutes, then Boykie spoke:

"How're you feeling, boy?" patting his knee. "You're not nervous or want to change your mind about coming?"

Philip smiled past his immediate irritation. "I asked you to do me a favour, didn't I? I've always wanted to see how the better half – quarter, fraction – lives." He laughed, a short bark. "Social research, you see."

"Well, don't make it too obvious, whatever it is you're after. The trouble is I don't trust you, boy," Boykie half-grunted. "I hope you're not doing this just to make a fool of me. Now promise me that you won't – well, you know what I mean."

"Disgrace you by guzzling down all their free booze too fast?"

"Aah, you know I don't mean that, Phil! Even if some of them watch us, just waiting for us to make a wrong move like that. What I mean is that you'll be polite, friendly – you know, behave like they're people just like you."

Philip laughed. "You mean, so I'm accepted as a person – well, almost – just as they are?"

"You know what I mean. Don't twist my words."

"Okay, Boykie. Sorry, my ma se kind. The truth is I've suddenly become full of curiosity about these mixed parties. I want to look at them from close up, you know what I mean?"

"Well, there'll be all kinds of people to look at from close up – black, white, coloured and Indian. Quite a few. But the important thing, Phil, is they're all nice people. So there's no need for you to – you know what I mean."

"I know, Boykie. Don't worry. Will there be a lot of women?'

Boykie laughed and slapped Philip's thigh. "You bastard! Is that why you want to come? Well, don't believe any of these fantasy stories you've heard, pal!"

"What stories?"

"Oh, they'll be there, all right. But they're not pushovers – I mean, not like the nice-time sisters in the shebeens. It's a different technique you have to use, boy; and even then you've got to pick the right ones. The married ones are easier," he winked. "But most of them are just cock-teasers who'll lead you along for the kicks and then suddenly remember that there's a law against it."

"You've been doing all right, though, haven't you? They even come to your room in Soph'town."

"Well," Boykie said expansively, pleased, "you know how it is, boy – luck and technique, man. Maybe I can fix you up. I know one –"

"Oh no, don't worry about me," Philip said hurriedly. If he wanted a woman – any woman – he could do it all for himself. And he didn't want any of these liberals looking for kicks. He'd had enough trouble from just one unknown. "I told you I just wanted to do some social research."

"Well, if you treat them right – you know, make an impression on them," Boykie advised, "they'll invite you to more parties. Then you'll be in, boy."

They walked down a silent, tree-lined street and turned into wide gates set in a tall hedge. The huge house stood brightly lit before them, surrounded by what looked like acres of lawn and flowers. Philip slowed down to take it all in. Boykie patted his shoulder in encouragement and led him up the gravelled drive crowded with large, shiny cars. They could hear the intimate sounds – the rise and fall of murmurs – that denoted a party which had gone beyond the first hour of loosening up. Boykie had told him that they must not arrive too early: they must make an entrance, boy, when it was already swinging.

Boykie paused at the foot of the steps leading onto the veranda, where a few people were gathered, then stepped resolutely ahead. It seemed to Philip that during that pause his friend stepped out of the guise of a Sophiatown klevah – Boykie Courtroom – to reveal the well-known, enthused-about Black Intellectual who went by what was a common first name, but unusual for such an educated person. Boykie waved casual greetings at the guests on the veranda, stopped just inside the door and looked around the room crowded with talking, laughing, dancing people. A broad smile was plastered on his face, and his lips stretched further off his teeth when the first shouts of recognition and welcome rose above the general hubbub.

A tall, languid white woman who had to be the hostess detached herself from a group and floated towards him.

"Oh, there you are, Boykie! We were beginning to fear you weren't going to turn up after all!"

They embraced and kissed each other's cheeks and Boykie reassured her that he could never miss any of her parties. Give up the chance to hold such luscious curves in his arms? Never! Then he turned to Philip, his arm still about the woman's waist.

"Darling, I want you to meet an old pal of mine – Philip Mokone," he said – announced, as Boykie placed a hand on Philip's shoulder. "You haven't seen this Native before, because he's only just shed his racialism!"

Through their laughter, Boykie introduced him to their hostess.

They made slow progress across the room as Boykie shook hands, patted backs, had his own pounded, kissed cheeks and placed his arm about naked pink shoulders. They laughed at everything he said, as if his remarks were cues. Philip shook soft, pink hands, murmured the correct responses and smiled politely as Boykie introduced him with facetious comments that annoyed him: Hi, Mike, how's the boy? Meet another civilised Native, my friend Phil ... Oh, h-e-l-l-o, Phyllis – watch out for this nice-time boy from Kofifi! ... Margaret, sweetie, where've you been all my celibate life? ... Hey, white boy, how're you making out? You've got competition, tonight! ... Jimmy – meet my friend, who thinks we should cut all the throats of you white exploiters!

They all think he's funny, Philip thought; amusingly rude. Pleased they can laugh at his insults; but too loud, the laughter. But it's all so – well, he repeats the same lines, and though they seem to have heard them before and are expecting them, they still roar. Philip wanted to look more closely and carefully at the faces and story-book luxury of his surroundings, but he was distracted by all the talk, stares and brittle laughter. Seeing them so close and from such a different perspective was – well, admit it: overwhelming. Shaking their hands for the first time, too – no, he reminded himself. There were the missionaries, when he was a kid. But far from the same thing.

He drifted away from the laughing group about Boykie, who was already recounting anecdotes about stupidly brutal policemen, easily flattered white racists, and the cunning of the black man in avoiding the confines of the laws and stupid prejudice. Philip found the permanent grin – that grimace! – on Boykie's face infuriating; and the ersatz eagerness of his audience humiliating.

He stood apart, trying to efface himself while he observed. Didn't want any of them to feel obliged to talk to him. His fingers were getting numb from holding a crystal glass of whisky-on-the-rocks – the best moonshine he'd ever drunk – and his elbow stiff from holding it up, when he saw Desmond approaching.

The younger man came weaving with lean adroitness around the little groups, a pleased but jeering smile on his thin, angular face.

"What are you doing here, klevah?" he shouted at Philip above gay din. "Don't tell me you've also offered yourself for civilised corruption!"

"Hi, Desmond," Philip grinned. "A little social research. That's all."

"So what d'you think of the circus?" the reporter laughed, waving a hand that held a tall glass at the room. "Just look at them! Christ, what a funny lot!"

"Everything's always funny to you, Desmond," Philip smiled. "Maybe I'd find it funny, too, if I had your sense of humour – or if I was as used to it as you are."

He wanted to ask questions, discuss his impressions with this boy from PE who never seemed to be impressed by anything. But he decided against it: he did not want to sound naive, especially to this strange boy who had something about him that irritated, making him feel inarticulate and artless.

"Well, I hope you don't get used to it," Desmond smiled back. "Just take one good, long look – your first and last!"

"What d'you mean?" Philip asked quickly, anger stirring within him at the suspected sly insult.

"No-no-no, boy. Don't get mad at me – that look in your eyes!" Desmond protested. "You know I'm scared to death of all you klevahs, man. What I mean is, you should do us both a favour and not get hooked on this drug. The cherries and the doped booze in the townships – that's good, clean fun. Stick to it, boy. I know what I'm talking about because I'm hooked here. But, thanks be to God, not as badly as Boykie. That boy's so far gone he doesn't even realise they've hung him up in the display window like prime beef. Look at them, Phil. Don't they all look like nice, friendly, charming people? All those pink and red faces smiling at the black and beige ones, those white arms around black shoulders, and vice versa? And the girls are easy – some of them, anyway! But not necessarily because they like us, which is a moot point. But because there's some mystique about getting screwed by one of us. A sort of campaign medal they hang on their scented bosoms for their part as bedroom guerillas in the Struggle for Freedom! And of course they think it's our freedom they're struggling for, not their own!"

He laughed loudly, a sardonic look in his eyes, amused by his own verbally italicised discourse. Desmond sipped from his frosted glass and continued:

"Maybe there's some kind of expiation too in that. But why worry as long as they're willing? What more can we ask for – they think – with all this legally exclusive stuff available? That's the question Boykie thinks of as a statement. To him, this is all – everything! To me, it's plenty; but I still know that I wish I had the strength or ignorance to reject it. This is all poison you see here, Phil – so's the atmosphere we're breathing, and this booze in these beautiful crystal glasses. More poisonous than the mahog mixed with methylated spirits we drink in plastic glasses at the shebeens. Well, maybe not you, Phil – drinking korea is not your style, eh, klevah."

The look in Philip's eyes made Desmond decide to grin, and take the sting out of whatever insult this touchy guy might find. Yet he couldn't stop or slow down his sermon to the barbarian knocking at the gate, seemingly demanding entry into the white man's civilisation.

He jabbed a finger at Philip: "But – do you know why?"

Philip did not answer. He was looking quizzically at the boy – this laaitie who loved words and spouted them faster than he could write them for his rag of a newspaper. Standing awkwardly but relaxed, with long and skinny legs twisted around each other at the knees. What's he trying to tell me with his lecture?

He'd noticed people staring: some walking slowly past to get a couple of words of what Desmond was on about this time, but for some reason loath to interrupt. Sneaking glances at the pair of black men who preferred a private chat to talking to people who were leading them out of the darkness cast by apartheid. Desmond caught his wandering eye and began to ease Philip out of the glare.

"I'll tell you why," Desmond was saying as they abandoned a reception room larger than any Philip had ever seen in Sophiatown: larger than some pondokkies that housed families of a dozen, but strictly for partying, here in suburbia.

Desmond's insistent voice was not deflected or deterred by Philip's wandering attention. They went out and onto a stoep dimly lit for dark intrigues under a romantic moon.

"Because, Phil, you lose yourself, your being, in these luxurious dens of character thieves. Look at Boykie – look at me! All this intellectual talk, brotherly sentiments, poking fun at the government, screwing and flattery … Hell, man! It makes you want to be liked. Of course we all want to be liked – even Verwoerd, in his own crazy way. I mean, you want them to approve of you. Don't we all want approval? Yes. But this approval is on their terms. They've already decided how an Educated Native should talk, behave – the lot! Even how he should fuck: virile as a stud horse and all that stuff. And we, the poor weaklings, the Black Intelligentsia – we conform to their stereotypes! The complete antithesis of intellectualism. We conform – some knowingly, some not. I know that I do. And so far, I can still shock and hurt them – disappoint them – with departures from the mould they've locked us into. Of course this honesty – my attempts to escape – is coming in less and less frequent spurts, I might add. Maybe one day I'll be like Boykie – the perfect stereotype. God forbid!

"I'll tell you something, Philip … Don't look at me like that, boy," he laughed. "I'm not drunk. I've drunk, but I'm not drunk. Yet! I'll tell you something funny – maybe you'll think I'm crazy, but I'm not, either. D'you know we'd all be much safer with the Afrikaners, away from these liberals? The more ignorant, brutal and prejudiced they are – the better for us kaffirs? Man, they don't have any liberal preconceptions about us. No, Sir!"

"Of course they don't," Philip interrupted the flow. "And now I suppose you're going to tell me Boere are better because they don't pretend?" He grinned and shook his head. "I've heard that before – in non-intellectual shebeens, Desmond."

"I wasn't suggesting it was an original thought, Phil," Desmond laughed. "The important thing about them is they believe we're the children of Ham. Their God-given hewers of wood and drawers of water, as their predikante reassure them every Sunday. We're to be chastised for presumed laziness as a matter of course, and flogged when we begin to forget these divine facts."

"And that's so good for us?"

"No, boy, but listen. To them we're just crazy, half-human, unpredictable animals. That's the key word – unpredictable! This means that whatever we do, they're not surprised, shocked, hurt or disappointed, like these liberals. They just shrug and get the sjambok or rifle down from the wall."

Philip laughed. "Ah! I see," he said, the tone almost sarcastic.

Desmond smiled; his eyes saying they knew what was going on behind Philip's sardonic face. Yes, I might sound crazy – but you know I'm not, whatever you pretend. He drank the dregs from his glass and chewed the remaining ice cubes.

"But instead," he continued as he crunched, "here we are actually being grateful to these liberals. They have such firm ideas about what we should – Oh, hell, what's the use of bothering with the endless list of their demands? You know what I mean. Anyway, all these crazy ideas make them missionaries. How I despise those bastards I'm supposed to be grateful to for the education they gave us!"

"I don't."

Desmond ignored the dissent. "So what do these latter-day saints in and out of dog collars do? Every time I try to express myself – be myself and not what they think I should be – they cluck their tongues and start missionarising me. That's why I say they're character thieves. Then there's their blackmail: if you rebel too strongly and persistently against fitting into the mould they're trying to press you into with every pat on the back, you get the cold shoulder. No more invitations to dinners, to parties – end of liberalism! So? Well, I don't want to give up the chance to talk intelligently – sometimes they do forget the missionary role, you know. And, anyway, why should I give up all this free booze?"

While Philip stood wondering how much of this monologue he should discount as the ranting of a near-drunk, a young woman came smiling towards them, her skirts swinging around a small, compact body.

"Which sermon according to Saint Desmond are you preaching this time?" she asked, smiling up at him. "No, don't bother to answer that or I'll get an earful," she laughed. "I've been watching, you know, and – No. Bad manners." She turned towards Philip. "First, Desmond, you must introduce me to your friend."

Desmond made the introductions with a flourish Boykie would've been proud of; and then Philip watched and listened, noticing their bantering tones and ease with each other. He realised that whatever scorn Desmond might feel towards the rest, this white girl, Vivienne, was not included. He enjoys talking to her. He likes her, as a person. Not one of the thieves listed in his little black book.

Then Desmond drifted lankily away, leaving them alone on the veranda.

She asked questions, of course, and he was not pleased with this Vivienne. Too earnest and intense; almost like a real missionary. Some of the questions annoyed and embarrassed him. But she was quick to realise her mistake, and instead told him about the voluntary case-work she did in townships as practicals for her social science studies at university. She did not have to go into the townships, she said, but she liked it – not really liked, but wanted to help in any way she could.

"And I want to know, Philip; that's why I'm so nosey. Asking questions which upset you. It's just that I wish to know people – especially Africans, who're a closed book to us – as individual people, not just a 'socio-economic group' and all that stuff the textbooks go on about. You see?"

"Yes, I think I'm with you, Vivienne," he said, rolling the name in his mouth; tasting its foreign – French? – resonances. And I'm here to do my own social research, baby, he wanted to tell her.

His wariness receded, and he was able to divert the conversation from the suffering of his socio-economic group without making her think she'd offended him with her naive probing. Her questions had been an invasion of his privacy, her actual knowledge of black squalor and frustrations an impertinent peeking. And discussing these with her would be like a cripple exhibiting his deformities in self-pity, begging for sympathy. But what else could they talk about? Whatever they tried somehow touched on politics. Couldn't even really discuss movies, because most of those she had enjoyed were deemed subversive, or too adult for any Native, by the Board of Censors. The stage plays he would never see.

Yet, somehow, they found narrow, tortuous, conversational bypasses. When the conversation lagged, he felt embarrassed for her, stuck with him. He wanted to tell her to go away. Find somebody who'd be knowledgeable about culture and interested in racial politics. Go talk – no, listen – to Boykie. She didn't have to stand there smiling brightly up at him, being friendly.

He would be quite happy on his own: leaning against a wall at the fringes of this party and observing white people in their natural habitat. Well, not quite natural, with darker skins dotted among them. This couldn't be their normal behaviour, either: too heightened a consciousness of what they were doing and saying. But he would be sorry to see vivacious little Vivienne go: like Desmond, he liked her.

She took him round – let's circulate, now, she suggested – and introduced him to her friends among the guests. And deflected those of their questions she knew wouldn't be welcomed by her adopted charge. They avoided joining the gaggle around Boykie, who were listening avidly to their guru – no, boy, he corrected himself: their guide into the nether world where we skulk, and from which a fortunate few emerge occasionally into the glowing, liberal world.

He noticed that Desmond returned to the stoep with a woman; but he was not lecturing this time. His monologue was intimate. And then, at some time he wasn't aware of, the pair discreetly disappeared.

As the party wound down after midnight, and Boykie wandered from one small group to another – a not-so-ancient Mariner who stoppeth three or four, not one of three – Vivienne offered to drive them home. The invitation was aimed at him, Philip felt, but Boykie was not to be excluded. "You drive into Kofifi at this time of night, Viv?" Boykie asked, his smile knowing and fixed with a confidential brightness.

"I know my way around, Boykie – even in the dark," she snapped, but with a mischievous grin on her face.

They said their goodbyes amid final and impromptu dinner and party invitations – "Bring your nice friend along, Boykie!" – and found her car, desolate beside a huge expanse of moonlit lawn.

Boykie spoke most of the way to Sophiatown: bright, clever talk that seemed to Philip aimed more at impressing them with his knowledge and fluency rather than conversing. And there was a vicious streak in his boyhood friend, Philip realised. When he did bring Philip into the conversation, there was an undertone of patronising spite in Boykie's remarks: "What d'you think of our silent friend here, Viv? Has he told you what a lady-killer he's regarded as in all the locations? A sharp dresser and talker, with his expensive, can't-get imported outfits?"

She answered in monosyllables, which would've discouraged anybody else but Boykie, he thought. The Soph'town sophisticate seemed impervious to any subtlety this evening. Maybe he's drunk, Philip wondered – unlike the brikaid he knew, who prided himself on keeping timing under all circumstances. Philip was surprised that he found a quiet satisfaction in Vivienne's manner towards Boykie Courtroom.

As they approached Sophiatown she turned towards Boykie, who sat beside her, with a bright smile that was belied by her slightly brittle voice. "I know where you live – so we'll drop you off first!"

"Oh …?"

She remained silent, and Boykie overcame whatever it was he felt – surprise, disappointment? Philip could've laughed at him, right in the face beside him in the crowded front seat of the Chevvie. But his own excitement at her proposal, and its possible suggestion, was fraught with – what? Fear?

"Yes, er-hum!" Boykie was saying. "Of course, sweetie pie!" His tone condescending, amused and knowing now. "You'll – er – do just that, won't you?"

"Clever boy!"

She tried to keep her voice bright and light, but the annoyance broke through as sarcasm. "Then Philip can show me where he lives." After a pause she added: "My good deeds for the day."

"But the night is still young, sweetie pie," Boykie retorted.

The car came out of the dimly-lit side streets of Westdene, the nondescript poor-white suburb, and rolled, starkly exposed in the dazzling, bluish moonlight, onto the road that crossed a featureless no-man's-land separating white workers from the black labourers of Sophiatown. All was breathlessly quiet about them.

"Are you – er – sure … I mean quite sure, sweetie – your good deed will be all you'll be doing on this beautiful, moonlit, romantic night?" Boykie persisted. "After all," he added expansively, "it's only two a.m., you know!"

The Chevrolet – her father's car? – entered Edward Road, which for the first time appeared sinister to Philip in the weak flare of occasional street lights and the glow of moonlight. The street was deserted, the widely spaced lights ineffectual and forlorn. He heard a dog bark, and its echo return from somewhere in the ghostly clutter of crumbling buildings and lopsided shanties that were home to him. But quite strange, after a night out in die Avies …

And a pretty white woman taking him home. Her warm thigh pressed against his own.

This is stupid, he said to himself. What's Courtroom trying to prove with all these clever, spiteful remarks? If it's that obvious to him, must he try to … Aaah, leave them alone. They know each other – they think. He thinks. They're the sophisticates and all that nonsense: full of clever insults and insinuations.

"Good boy!" she snapped at the legal clerk's last witticism. Runnels of acid now, in the voice she was barely trying to keep friendly – civilised, Philip corrected himself wryly. "Getting cleverer by the minute, aren't you, Boykie?"

"W-e-l-l …" Boykie said lamely, the warnings now evident to him. "You know how it is – you know what I mean."

"I'm sure I don't."

They're your friends, not mine, Boykie. But don't you ever for even one minute – one second – think they like you all that much, pal. They'll always set limits. And you, you'll always go a step too far beyond them. Then they'll slap you back into place with those civilised smiles and honeyed voices. You get too enthusiastic, boy – drunk with it. Keep timing, Boykie, play it cool. All night you've been behaving like I've never seen you. Bursting with wit and all the clever, civilised things. But d'you really like each other? Not a damn. Just what you do for each other, that's all. So bloody pleased at being able to associate across the colour bar – and in defiance of it – that you hardly see each other.

This one tries to be an individual, though. Vivienne. A bit too intense, but at least breaking out. Still a kid; a fresh immigrant without full citizenship yet in this sophisticated, liberal underworld. Earnest blue eyes still showing through the encroaching glaze, a trembling about lips still blundering towards what they want to really say, and not what they're expected to trot out so glibly ...

Oh-ho! Getting romantic and poetic now, are you, eh? Philip the after-midnight poet! Maybe you are right, Boykie, with these insinuations. I thought so too – hoped, even, against my new way of looking at things. At them. A kid, but old enough; not such a kid, really. She can vote, can't she? And I can't.

The Chevrolet drifted to a stop at Boykie's gate in the high, corrugated iron wall. He leaned across Philip in the crowded front seat and pulled his lips off his teeth in the grin that had annoyed and humiliated Philip at the party:

"Want to come in for some of my famous coffee, sweet?"

"No, thanks." Her voice impersonal, polite. "I've got to be up early tomorrow. Good night."

"Well, don't ever say I didn't offer you my gracious hospitality," Boykie said, making a final bid to break through her icy reserve. She did not reply. He placed a hand on Philip's knee and squeezed, rattling the door handle with the other to cover the words he whispered as he leaned sideways to slide out of the car. "There it is, brother!" he said in Sesotho. "Don't leave it. Kwela phezulu!" he added in Zulu.

Irritation flared up momentarily within Philip at the suggestion in Boykie's tone that he had arranged all this for his benefit. The car swept forward as soon as Boykie was clear.

"You'll have to direct me, you know." Her voice was uncertain and impatient.

"Oh, sorry," he said, coming out of his reverie.

He gave her directions. Now go on – say something more, something personal, something intimate! Make conversation, dammit! At least be sociable, if you can't be seductive. You might still be in luck.

She might … But do you want her? Boykie thinks it's on a plate. He ought to know. Do you? All right, yes! She's a woman, isn't she? Crap! Do you really? Of course! Doing my research. Or continuing what you started that night in the Hillbrow alley?

"I hope you won't get lost getting out of here," he said. "It's not a big place, but people do get lost."

"Oh, I know Sophiatown. I come here quite often. I think I told you about my practical research. It's an interesting place."

"Amusing."

"Oh, now! Don't let's always be so touchy, Philip!" The snap turned into a sigh: "You ought to know by now that I'm not like that. If I want to be amused, I go to a National Party rally – one of the big ones, where Verwoerd or some other big-mouth preaches on about our divine right to rule, and our mission to enlighten the black savage at the point of the boot."

She laughed. "Then I get mad! Silly, isn't it? I must be a masochist."

"I'm sorry. I don't know what I – well, maybe I'm still trying to take advantage of my first opportunity to talk to white people like we both belonged to the same human race."

"Another bitter one," she remarked lightly. "I hear Boykie was like that too, at the start, when my mother first met him. Searching out the insult and slight in everything said or done. Now he's – well, I don't know."

"Desmond was telling me, before you joined us, that all this liberalism was a drug we – he and Boykie, anyway – were getting hooked on. We even forgot what we were being consoled for by you people. At least I think that's what he meant."

Well, you're not doing to badly now, you see. It's not scintillating conversation, but it's something, even if it's getting back into abstract politics – and no kind of politics is your line. You don't know the hip phraseology: 'Economic Insecurity', 'Sexual Fear and Jealousy', 'Baasskap Mentality' …

So what do I do now – when we get to my place? Ask her in for coffee too? She told Boykie she was in a hurry. Just angry with him, that. Ask for her telephone number? Aah, forget the whole thing! You've done your research, haven't you? Shaken white hands, danced with their silky women, drunk cocktails and talked to them as equals. So why don't you just crawl back where you belong – and stay there, as Desmond advised? You don't want to be like Boykie with your body in Soph'town and your heart and soul in Lower Houghton. Or like Desmond, suspended somewhere between the two in a world echoing with cynical laughter.

They were still some distance away when he pointed out the large warren of rented rooms behind which he lived. She turned off the ignition immediately, and the Chevrolet glided silently forward, headlights blinking out as she swung it off the street and onto the sandy space between the dark, crumbling house and the street. The car came to a stop in shadow, and only the barking of a distant dog could be heard echoing in the bluish silence.

"Thanks very much for offering to drive us home. It was very kind of you."

She laughed quietly, quickly, nervously.

"Is that all the thanks I get? Aren't you going to ask me in for your famous coffee?"

He wanted to cough, to clear his constricting throat of the phlegm suddenly stuck in it. But a cough would rend the silence like an explosion; wake somebody beyond the crumbling brick wall. He swallowed.

"Well?" Her voice was soft and teasing. No: encouraging. Nervous but encouraging, he decided.

"No – I mean, yes! If you really want to I'll be very happy."

"But – you know – the neighbours?"

His mind had already calculated the odds. It was too late for anyone to be still awake, wandering about the yard: they used potties instead of trying to find their way to the outside lavatory. The car had come up quietly – what a cool chick, he smiled in the dark as the penny dropped. His room was behind, and separate from, the warren that housed a tribe of one-room tenants; in a low, flat-roofed, box-like structure, with only Joey in the other room. Joey had heard him bring in girls at all hours before, and wouldn't be curious.

Go out first, maybe, and scout around. Then we walk soft and fast, scarf over her head, hiding the white face and flowing hair? No, can't leave her alone out here – can't show I'm worried or she'll be nervous. Keep timing, and hope for the best.

Chapter 15

He locked the door behind them, and lit the paraffin lamp standing on the table. She was standing close to the door and, after squinting in the sudden harsh glare of his matches, the blue eyes darted about the small, neat room. The lamp flickered, then glowed into a brilliance that revealed his home. His eyes followed hers, trying to see the familiar furnishings as she saw them. Not as smart and sophisticated as Boykie's place, but comfortable. Adequate for me. Not even half, maybe a third, of the books on Boykie's shelves, and mine hand-made shelves and second-hand books. No reproductions of famous paintings on the walls – not even photographs, just a calender and posters.

Won't impress, my ma se kind ... So who wants to impress her, dammit! A wave of anger and resentment surged through him. This is all she wants: another glimpse of How The Other Side Lives. All right, white girl. This isn't rich and posh Lower Houghton, Parktown, Illovo or wherever the hell you live. This is Soph'town, baby – Kofifi! The Black Spot your people – your government, anyway – make us live in because we're supposed to enjoy squalor, just like pigs enjoy rolling in mud. And now they want to wipe out the Black Spot for the benefit of our poor-white neighbours in Westdene, Newlands and all those other suburbs that are like a laager around our location – that term reserved for black habitation. Go on and –

"Don't look so angry, Philip," she said softly, and walked across to the table where she placed a hand on his arm. "'It's – it's a nice room. I like it."

"Well!" The tone was bright, after a moment of bemused eyes staring at the hand on his arm. He rubbed his hands briskly together. "There's the Primus stove – so let's get the water boiling for a cup of my infamous –"

She stopped him with the tone of her voice and the pressure of her fingers. "Philip. Dear, poor Philip!" The voice was tender, impatient, chiding.

He looked down into her face, examining it slowly and deliberately for the first time. He'd avoided looking directly into her eyes and face, and into those of all the other smiling women at the party. Afraid of what they might detect in his eyes; not certain himself what showed in them, but afraid of what they might see. Perhaps they would interpret whatever they found in their deep brownness as the covetous lust they'd been brought up to expect in all male eyes the colour of his own.

His arms went out and clasped her firm, compact body, and he bent down to her smiling face. When their lips met his body shuddered briefly. Nervousness and a remembered frustration and anger. This is not the same, he fiercely reminded himself. You didn't even try to kiss that one. This one wants you to; and more than that … everything. And this nervousness – it's not that, it's excitement. Your first white woman – that's it! You're excited. For the first time in your life you're kissing one of them, and you're going to have her in your own bed. Because she wants you.

But is there anything different about this kiss? This body trembling in my arms? Just another woman, with my eyes shut. Like others before her, right here in this miserable room. Except for the hair, tickling my nostrils, brushing my cheek. That's new. And the taste of lipstick. He opened one eye, slowly. Hers were shut. He opened both eyes wide, stared fixedly at the pinkness before them. A white woman! A white woman. He repeated the phrase deliberately in his mind as their tongues explored; and waited expectantly for the three words to evoke some unknown thrill. Yet the knowledge and the sight still did not in themselves excite him.

The yielding softness of her fragrant body, the thigh pressing between his: these excited him, and he could feel the familiar tingling down the backs of his thighs and the hot flush in his crotch. But the fact of her colour added nothing special of its own. I have in my arms the greatest treasure of White Civilisation: the White Goddess who rules with smiles and favours. The unattainable perfection kept from us black savages by the guns, laws and venom of their jealous, frightened worshippers. Does this make me delirious with joy at this great achievement? It doesn't mean anything; it's nothing in itself, this dangerous, forbidden achievement. Like that night, but so very, very different. That night I lost something, and tonight I must not, I must gain, I must learn something!

"Wow!" she gasped, pulling her face away and laughing up at him. "I was just about to pass out! I – you look funny, Philip. That expression on your face ..."

"What expression?" he asked, wiping it off with his smile. "Didn't they teach you in kindergarten that we have just one expression – the ingratiating grin of the vacuum-headed savage?"

She smiled doubtfully, hoping he was only teasing. But even this hope failed to make her feel completely at ease, even with their arms still around each other.

"Sometimes – sometimes you do so worry me, Philip. And your humour – all these concentration-camp jokes everybody seems to love telling."

"Boykie and Desmond."

"Yes, them. Only yours have an odd kind of bitterness to them."

The smile that lit up his face was spontaneous. "I was trying to follow in their footsteps. Mistake number one, noted and never to be repeated. Just wait until you know me, baby," he said, passing his hand down her cheek. "Won't be any time to worry then, or listen to jokes – you know what I mean? Just be a good, patient girl, drink your coffee – and then we get to really know each other, hey? How'd you like that, babe? Am I right or am I right?"

She started to laugh but suppressed the relieved merriment into a giggle, remembering the likely consequences of white laughter being heard in this place at such a time.

"Now that's a very optimistic line you're shooting, my boy!"

She winced, looking inquiringly at his face for the reaction to the last word. But he smiled and nodded.

"I am your boy – or going to be. Is that being optimistic?"

It was suddenly as if they had known each other a long time. The kiss had not been a greeting or a promise; it had taken them beyond this sensuous anticipation, ensconcing them within an intimacy in which their personalities fused and were of little individual importance. They were Man and Woman, and that was all that mattered. There was already rising between them the assurance of lovers confident in their potent ability to please; secure in the knowledge of their own emotional power over the other.

She was laughing, cooing, at his dry, soft-voiced humour, pleased that she was loosening this man from the grip of frustrations that had made him impotent – but only with rage against the system! Pleased by the intuition that had directed her to the gentleness beneath the withdrawn façade and had led her to the bed on which she now sat. But she didn't realise that she hadn't demolished his barricades; that Philip had only removed a few bars from them. The companionship that glowed as he prepared the coffee – keeping timing, not rushing her, he was pleased to tell himself – involved only his sensual being and that portion of the mind required to communicate and titillate. Beyond, lurking in a dark corner of the room, was a detached being, watching the performance and listening to the sensuous inflections in the words and voices.

He was going to make love to her soon; but he didn't really desire her. She was a nice girl, a warm woman, and so he wanted to make love to her. The excitement would come from these feminine attractions, and the hope that their act – okay, fucking – would help in his search for his real self. She was the means, and he would use her: fuck her, but with gratitude at her providing this step in what he hoped would be progress to salvation from the devils born from apartheid.

Even if she had been a beauty – ravishing, alluring and all that – he knew, now, that he didn't desire her for herself. Perhaps in the future, if he was successful in his search, he might. Not now. This was what made her a white woman, different from all the other women he'd had here and elsewhere: so many beds, so many heaving bodies. He'd not desired the other one either, of that he was now certain. But this certainty had raised a new question: what is it you want to know? What do you hope to find out from this woman?

Afterwards. Maybe I'll know then. The answer will be there in bed beside me.

A chill thrill shuddered up his thighs and into his crotch as he watched her take off the party finery. And then stand before him, easy and confident in her nakedness: watching his face for approval. Proud of her small, high-breasted body, yet not brazen. This too was a new experience: even nice-time girls were shy about their bodies, unless drunk. But she was not being immodest, standing there – only proud to show off what she would be giving him. And with a familiarity that came from the assurance they felt in each other.

The shudder had risen from the resentful question he could now ask. As his manhood responded to the sight of her naked body, he could now ask the resentful question in all earnestness: what is so special about these bodies, that we must be hated and humiliated in their defence? That we risk – I have risked – the gallows for them? Are these shades of pink and red and white so much more sacred than the smooth black and brown?

She lay on the bed as he undressed: pleased, frightened and excited by the intensity of his stare. He decided to leave the flickering lamp on as he joined her.

In the caught-breath silence of the first kiss shared by the whole of their bodies, the detachment evaporated. His body tingled hot and feverish in its desire for the promise of her confident nakedness. When he opened his eyes, smiling blue slits were looking into his face.

"D'you know that you're handsome?"

"I've heard something to that effect – I think."

He combed fingers through the reddish-brown hair: slowly, carefully, luxuriating in this other new experience. Silky hair that blew in the wind and bounced on their heads when they ran. Just the effects least wanted by African women who spent money and patience, and suffered discomfort straightening hair they wanted to perch like curly helmets on their heads: don't touch, wena! He placed a hand against her cheek, fascinated by its fuzzy growth, and watched intently the contrasting colours of their skins. But there was nothing specially – titillating in having the freedom of all her skin.

Maybe just touching the face isn't doing the trick. Try something more intimate. He brought his face down and his lips wandered over her up-tilted nose, cheeks, chin while the hand slid along contours until it rested on her breast. He watched the fingers, as if they were not his own, caressing and squeezing the warm, yielding, flattened mound and the rose-tinted peaks of their nipples ... Only the old pleasure: nothing special in seeing my hand there.

"Philip – darling. Do you mind if I ask you something personal?"

He looked into her eyes and smiled. He'd wondered if she would. "Only if you'll answer the same question."

She giggled like a little girl caught out in a prank. "You see? You are perceptive, whatever you might say. All right, I'll answer first. No.

And now don't ask me what's made me change tonight. After all, there has to be a first time for everything."

Good, he told himself, the muscles of his legs stretching warm and confident. Good. Not such a habitual kaffir lover.

"I have – once," he told her. Don't lie, you bastard, jeered the voice he'd heard that night in Hillbrow. "… but nothing like this. I couldn't call it making love."

"What d'you mean, Philip?"

"Don't ask for any explanations or details. Please, Vivienne."

He watched her car wink a lewd orange eye at him as it turned the corner of the street, and returned to bed. But did not try to sleep.

Well, at least there's somebody who thinks I'm the – what did she say? Quote, the most marvellous lover in the world, unquote. How the hell would she know, poor kid? Can't have sampled many, even if university students are said to be – no, she's not one of those, even if she did … seduce you? I wasn't going to try anything like that on any of them, so I suppose she did seduce me. Well, make me an offer I couldn't refuse, like so many others. Nice Time Phil never says no, if they're presentable and desirable. But it's great to be told – to be thanked.

An enthusiastic performer, that little one. But all of them can't be like that – generalising, like they do about us. Also learned some things, tonight. Like that I "make love so innocently, darling"! Nice Time Phil, innocent! But now I know, baby; I believe you. But don't spread the word around. Glad you don't do it innocently.

Whoever was it who said they're cold fishes? A rumour put about to lead us up the garden path by their worshippers. Weak-kneed and frightened in their adoration, that's who and why. Devout instead of virile. What a waste. No wonder Boykie's prepared to renounce the black world after what he's learned from them about themselves. Did you enjoy it, anyway, apart from learning a few tricks that Betty will never stand – lie – for? But most definitely, my brikaid. Even though …

A renegade portion of his mind had remained maddeningly detached from the act, observing it all from beside the bed – and yet still feeling it. Glorying in his ability to give this woman so much pleasure. Just like with her nakedness, nothing self-conscious about her: groaning, gasping, drowning, thrashing and exploding – not just once, either – with a wanton vibrancy she muffled in the pillows. And, the renegade whispered: give it to her, boy! It's you, and you alone, giving her such a good fuck. Not quite making love, but more than just another fuck ...

But then where does Betty fit into all this? he wondered, inhaling the scents and odours she'd left behind. This one – Vivienne, dammit, she's got a name ... All right, Vivienne was – I'll say the word: marvellous. The multitudes are just easy lays you don't think much about afterwards; sometimes can't remember their names, and don't even want to remember anything about them. To skep them against all rivalry from the envious in a shebeen, at a party or wherever was what counted most among die manne.

But Betty – oh, Betty Nkosi my beloved. I didn't skep you, but waited for you. Because I love you, my sweet. With you there is no portion of my mind keeping aloof from our passion and joy. All of me is involved. With you I thank God, I praise balimo ba rona that, at long fucking last, such release is possible on this earth.

I must confess, though – a funny thing. It was watching you prepare, with your – what? Wifely? Anyway, with your usual modesty, to come into this bed, Betty, our bed – that made me decide I must do it. Get up the pluck to have one of them properly. I can now admit it to myself that I really did want one of them. Whatever I thought and said to Boykie, that's what was on my mind, at the back of it, anyway, when I asked him to take me to these mixed parties.

He had lain in bed watching Betty undress with that odd and dignified modesty that allowed him a view of her breasts and thighs, but mostly her back. And never the bushy spring of her being. He knew, now, from past experience that she would blow out the paraffin lamp before taking off her panties. On other nights she slipped into a night dress before taking them off – a signal that she wasn't in the mood, as she termed it. I have never seen all of her; caressed, yes, but not seen. No feasting of mine eyes. Nor has she seen all of me, because only if she stood naked before me would I be able – allowed – to do the same. There would be an awkwardness, standing erect and erected before her partially naked self. Perhaps embarrassing her.

He watched her bend over the table and blow out the lamp. And his body was suffused with a weakening tenderness.

This is the woman I love. It is not a complete immersion in love, but as much as I will ever feel.

Complete love – what would that be like? Something more than this. Something that makes you look at others with a patronising pity that they do not share what you and your woman have. Something that makes you look over other women, thinking that they're definitely more than desirable and should be good in bed; but you'd rather keep to your own.

Even when they give you the glad eye. What was Nick Romano's hands-off expression, in that novel set in a part of Chicago as rough and tough as this? Take a good look, baby, but you ain't getting any.

Keeping faith with a woman you love shouldn't be a conscious rejection of all other women. It should simply be that you don't want these other women. I'm faithful to her, but not with my body.

How does that line go from another, older – ancient – book? O Cynara, I am faithful to thee, in my own fashion … Something like that.

Still fucking a few others when she's not available or not in the mood when she does come around. Keeping myself in tune, as she once said while I waited for her. Ah, if only she knew how much more I love her afterwards! When I want to kick them out of bed, scrub myself and bleach the sheets.

Chapter 16

Jean Ryan sat uncomfortably, sprawled in the easy chair that had become her daily outpost for vaguely watching the world outside. Eleven o'clock and already tired, exhausted. And another three weeks to go before she could hope to be comfortable in any position. She looked down wearily at the sloping bulge couched in her spread-out lap. So big! It moved. Strong and restless bastard, kicking me. What's it going to be? A girl, I hope. Finished with men … Except when you writhe and pant for them in bed, eh? That's over too, now. Not important, any more.

What colour are you going to be, little one? Little orphan, sired by an unknown, mystery father – animal, brute. Benoni: child of my sorrow. A nightmare mystery which I hope, and you must too, little one, will never be solved. We don't want to know him, ever. He deserves to hang. Hung and quartered. Boiled in oil. Don't ever want to know anything about him. Best forgotten. Just the two of us to face this awful world, overcrowded with horrid people. My people! You and I alone. Should call you – what's it again? Naomi ... no, Deborah? Not right, either. Forgotten the Bible completely, heathen. Oh, yes – Ruth. Whither thou goest, I go. Is that right? Your people shall be my people – like bloody, fucking hell! Whoever they are. They, all of them, will never let you be, little one. I should be your Ruth. Except I don't want your people either. If they're what everybody thinks they are. You might want to go to them when you grow up. If they'll accept you. No: then it would've all been for nothing. We'll stay together and fight them. Everybody.

But what shall we be, in this mixed-up country? What will we do? How do we fight them all? Tell them to go to hell and leave us alone. But they won't. Everything must conform or they won't let it alone. Everybody must be catalogued, classified, pigeon-holed. The Population Registration Act will say who you are, the Group Areas Act where you live. The Immorality Act will tell you whom you can love. The Mixed Marriages Act will say whom you marry. The Job Reservation Act where you work, and what kind of work.

The – I'm boring you, little one. Hush, now. Don't kick so hard. Mummy's tired.

But perhaps you won't be a half-breed after all. Not a Bushman with peppercorn hair. White – as lily white as the blessed Volk. What a joke. Even a bastard member of The Race is superior to the most legitimate kaffir or coloured born in holy matrimony. That would really kill them, wouldn't it? You could even be Mister bloody Patrick Sean Ryan's own son or daughter. Doctors aren't all-knowing, are they? The ways of God are ... But would that make any difference? Would I – could I – take him back? And everybody else? Slip back into the old life, secure in my superiority over all lesser beings. Are they lesser beings? No, at least I've learned that: people, too, once you look at them as such. Like that guitar player at the restaurant.

Though I don't or can't look at them, behave towards them as such. Like with the boy – man – Patrick sent round to pick up his suitcases, the coward.

I'd be a heretic within the old fold, if I go back. If I want to. Do I, child? I don't know.

There was a knock at the door. She did not stir from her torpor. After two more knocks, each louder and more impatient, she remembered that the maid she'd been forced to hire was out shopping. She pulled her legs carefully together, then heaved slowly to her feet. She waddled to the door. I feel awful.

"Good morning, Mrs Ryan." The caretaker – white, short, wizened, ferret-eyed with a cunning, lewd and toothless smile. "How are you this morning, Mrs Ryan?"

"Good morning."

"Haven't seen Mr Ryan about for some days now – weeks. Very nice man, your husband. Has he gone on a trip, hey?"

"He'll be away for a while."

"For a while, eh? Looks to me like he's been gone much longer than that already. You going to invite me in?"

"What do you want?"

"Gone on a trip for a while, eh. But I'm sure I saw him sitting in his car across the street just last night. Are you sure he's gone away 'for a while', hey?"

"If you damn well know he's –"

"Uh-uh, Missus Ryan! Not so hoity-toity, now. Other women, yes, but not you! Why's he left you? I've made a few enquiries, you know – talked to the caretaker at the Hillbrow flat you left." He clucked his tongue and shook his head, chiding and pointing a horny finger: "I know what you carrying in there. I can have you kicked out of here, you know!"

She slammed the door, knocking him back and out of the doorway he'd been insinuating himself into. Out, and across the corridor. She locked the door and leaned against it, her breath coming in heavy, shuddering gasps. The door rattled against her back, and she could hear his cursing. Please help me, God. I'll kill him! I'll kill somebody! Going mad!

She tried to walk back to the living room, but her knees would not support her weight. Her ankles were painful. There were sharp stabbing pains in her stomach and back. She bent forward, but a violent pang shot through her abdomen, straightening her body with a jerk. Sweat popped out on her drawn face, frightened eyes staring; frantic fingers clutching at the air. And then, her body stiffly erect, she tried to sink onto her knees. Kneecaps hit the parquet floor with a loud thud. She held onto a side table, waiting for the pain to pass from the knees and the nausea to ebb out of her body. She wanted to go down on her hands and crawl forward – like that night! a voice yammered in her head. But the bulge would be in the way, and she was afraid of the pain and strain.

So she walked forward on her knees, holding onto the wall, a chair, a table. Pain, aches all over. Weak, sobbing, sweating. A doctor! The phone! Something's wrong, terribly wrong. Oh, God, don't let me die! Please help me, help me, help me ... She paused inside the entrance to the living room. The telephone sat on a little carved table diagonally across the large, airy room. So far!

She tried to ignore the pains, aches, exhaustion. Sweat trickled into her eyes, blurring vision. She planned how to get to that telephone. Quickest way, straight across. But there was no support. She looked at the alternatives, along the walls to her left and right – first the long one, then the shorter route on her left. Going round all that furniture. Too far. Much, much too far and long. Die before I get there. What am I going to do? I am dying! Just stand here – kneel here? Must do something – can't. Miriam! Where's the woman? Oh, please come Miriam. Come and help me, please! Help, help, help ...

She fell slowly forward, her body cringing away from the impending impact, her mind and nerves yelling warnings – stop! Don't fall forward! Fall sideways! Sideways! Don't ... For a moment her body balanced on her distended belly, feeling it give, and then she rolled slowly, majestically onto her side, then onto her back.

She was still on her back. But the floor was not hard through the carpet. Yielding. She moved: slowly, cautiously. Must be a bed. She opened her eyes, squinting against the light. Grey ceiling – not my ceiling: that's blue! Fear surged into her body as she looked down her nose, over her toes and a white bed-rail.

A hospital! Have I been raped – again?

Oh, God plea– Hey! No belly! Flat as a – my baby! I've lost it! Oh, what's happened? Please, God, good Lord – what's happened to my baby? I can't have lost it! No! I can't, not after all this … Please, no! Nurse!

The nurse heard a moaning croak from the emergency case in Bed Eleven. She came over quickly, starched uniform rubbing against her legs.

"Good afternoon, Mrs Ryan," she said in a light, pleasant voice meant to raise the spirits of even the lowliest patient. "Almost evening, in fact! How do you feel, now? Drowsy, eh?"

"Nurse … My baby … where is she? Did I lose her? Is she all right? Please, Nurse –"

"Ah, you've been cheating, Mrs Ryan," the nurse broke in, placing a dry, cool palm on the sweaty brow. "You were supposed to be unconscious, and here you are knowing it's a girl!" She laughed soundlessly. "You must have wished very hard, hey. It is a girl, and as lovely as any baby can be. Even though she was a little early, she's perfectly healthy and kicking."

"Can I – can I see her, Nurse? Now?"

"Not tonight, I'm afraid. Tomorrow, first thing in the morning, if you're a good patient and go to sleep now. You need to build up your strength to feed her."

"What colour – what colour's her hair? Her eyes?"

"Her eyes? Now, let me see – greyish, I think the sister said. But of course they'll probably change. Go back to sleep, now, like a good mother."

As she drifted back to sleep one disappointed thought held Jean's receding consciousness: I missed it! I didn't feel it born! I missed it …

What colour is my baby? Greyish eyes. Anybody can have those. Coloureds have them. A coloured man – rapist – then? Rare around Hillbrow or any suburb in Johannesburg; but it could have been. So what? That doesn't make any difference: still a half-and-half. Will I love it? Do I love this unknown, unseen baby? Now that I'm a mother – now that my womb has nurtured its fruit and presented it to me? Do I feel more feminine, suffused with that glow of motherhood they talk about? When I hold it – her, my albatross – in my arms, will I look and feel beatified, like a Madonna? Don't even remember any of the beatitudes, my girl; long time since you even picked up a Bible ... Or will I just feel like plain, misused and defiled Jean Griffiths, who's soon to be divorced? The defiant Jean Griffiths, the bitch without a family, without a place in the catalogue of this society.

Hell, it's still my baby, isn't it? The innocent fruit of my defiled womb.

She leaned forward in the wheelchair the nurses had insisted she use, staring intently through the plastic side of the tent. She kept her face non-committal as she examined the tiny, wrinkled body within the canopy.

The small, olive-skinned nurse who'd pushed the wheelchair stood aside, inquisitive eyes on the mother's face: searching for the merest flicker of a sign below the blonde hair that would confirm her suspicion that this baby was not white, and the mother must know. But no idea what to do should there be any confirmation. She knew what she ought to do, but did not know if she could. Would it mean, Beth asked herself, that the father was not white? Or that she was not – that this baby was a throwback, and this creamy-skinned, green-eyed, yellow-haired beauty was one of her own, secret tribe? That schizophrenic tribe contemptuously called *venstertjies* because they were forever gazing quickly and furtively into shop windows when they spied a familiar, darker face on the streets?

Beth believed she'd report such a confirmation directly to the matron: another of the many furtive acts she and the secret tribe performed to prove to their preferred half-cousins that they, too, were pure-white and Defenders of The Race. That they couldn't bear the thought of any trace of the tar-brush contaminating their protected world. But instead, as she watched the mother's face intently, she felt an odd sort of pity for this woman. A melting pity she could not define or explain.

Behind the withdrawn, beautiful mask a mind whirled in confusion, trepidation and resignation. Well, it's not white – but hello all the same, my little one. She's going to be pretty, a knockout. They were right, after all. But you're mine! Oh, the black swine! I've fought so hard for you, my baby. You'll never know him! How I've fought for you to grow in me, be born, breathe, live – to hell with all of them, your father most of all! I'm your mother, baby. I'm all you have, you're all I have. We'll fight them all ...

"She's lovely, isn't she, Mrs Ryan?" Beth asked, perplexed and a little impatient at the pity she felt. And spiteful at this unrevealing face. "With those dark looks, she's going to be a stunner."

Jean turned her head slowly, with trepidation, and looked into the pretty features of the nurse. And suddenly, in a flash, knew this snub-nosed girl's secret, and the knowledge sent a pang through her heart. My God. I'm becoming one of them, if I can spot them just like this! Just like she knows about my baby.

"Yes," she replied quietly. "A dark beauty. Like you."

They stared at each other with hostility, pleading and understanding. A truce replaced what was first in their eyes. Then Beth looked away, and her voice was impersonal when she spoke as she moved behind the wheelchair.

"Shall we go back to the ward, now, Madam?"

Jean had just finished a heavy breakfast – eating for two – and was preparing for the day's leisurely boredom, when the telephone on the table of the definitely pure-white duty nurse burred. The nurse picked up the instrument and listened, her eyes wandering to Bed Eleven. Her starched skirts rustled against heavy thighs as she walked over to the bed.

"That was reception, Mrs Ryan. Your husband is outside and wants to see you. We don't normally allow visitors in at this time, but he was here yesterday after the ambulance brought you. But he couldn't of course see you then because of your delicate condition."

"I don't want to see him," Jean replied quietly. "Not today, tomorrow or any other day. I don't want to see anybody."

The nurse's eyebrows arched slightly and were quickly drawn back into regulation order. "As you wish, Mrs Ryan."

As she turned away from the bed, her eyebrows shot freely up into an arch, and the grey eyes widened in mock dismay. And then became speculative: Why was she hiding from even her husband? Any substance to Beth's veiled insinuations about the baby – blonde mother, but with dark hair? Like her own. Doesn't mean anything, that. No rules of genealogy for new-born babies …

Patrick Ryan made no other attempts to see her during the days she spent in the private room he was paying for at the hospital. But his brother Mark did – twice, then gave up. Their sister Sheila was more persistent, and only gave up after the fourth attempt. On that last time, she left a bundle of gift-wrapped baby clothes and a change of clothes for her sister-in-law. And when Patrick Ryan was officially informed of the day and time for his wife's discharge, he said he would send a car. The telephonist just stopped herself from asking if he wasn't coming himself: she'd heard the rumours.

Jean was fully and stylishly dressed and straightening the seams of her stockings when the senior duty nurse approached her. She held a file folder to her left breast, silent on rubber-soled shoes, skirt starchily rustling about her legs.

"Glad to be leaving us, Mrs Ryan?" she smiled, eyes admiring the beauty and elegance of this taciturn patient with the sadly defiant face. "One last formality and you'll be free of us," she continued. "Just sign these forms, please … Thank you. Here's the birth certificate."

Jean glanced at the certificate, then read it slowly and carefully as the nurse walked back to her station. Her eyes came out of focus after she had read it twice, a ridge of concentrated thought and decision rising between them. The information was straightforward: Name – Beatrice Ruth; Mother's Name – Jean Cora Ryan; Mother's Maiden Name – Griffiths; Father's Name – Patrick Sean Ryan. And there lay the question and the decision, in that paternal line.

She stood for a long time bent over the paper before walking over to the nurse at her little table. The nurse looked up with friendly enquiry in her eyes.

"I'm afraid this is not quite correct, Nurse," Jean said in a voice devoid of inflection. "I'm sorry, but this is becoming an increasingly important document these days, isn't it?"

"What's wrong with it, Mrs Ryan?"

"My husband is not the father."

"Oh?"

"Yes."

"Who – who is the father?"

"Does it matter?"

"But you realise we must fill in all the details, don't you?" The tone hardened. "If you want to be so honest, why –"

"Can I speak to somebody responsible about this?"

The Matron was a short, stout woman with a round, beaming face that was trying to hide the concern and curiosity that showed in every wrinkled line.

"Do you really want this known officially, my dear? Surely you know –"

"My husband knows. Everybody knows."

"Oh, I see. What a pity. Does the actual father know you want to use his name? You realise he could –"

"He doesn't know, and I don't know his name. It'll have to be 'Father Unknown', if you really must fill in that line."

"Oh, dear. Dear me! This is really getting beyond me, my dear. And you aren't being very co-operative, you know."

"I was raped."

"Oh, no …! How terrible! How – how absolutely awful . . . I'm so sorry, my dear. You must be a very devout woman to have – you know."

"Not really."

"Who – ?"

"A Native or coloured, I suppose; from the colour of the baby. One of the paler ones if it was a Native."

"This does complicate everything, doesn't it? You realise, don't you, that this baby shouldn't have been born here?"

"Where else, Matron? In the Non-European section?"

"Now, now! Let's not bother about that problem. I suppose I ought to make a full report – oh, why bother them! That is, if you haven't told anybody else here?"

"I haven't."

"Good. Now, let's make out a fresh certificate. What an awful business," Matron clucked. "What a shame … These Natives! Well! Now, you'll want to know how to – er, give it away? You should have told me right at the beginning, you know. But I can still –"

"No, thanks, Matron. I'm going to keep her. She's mine."

"But, my dear!"

The woman who would from that day call herself Jean Griffiths was helped out of the hospital by Beth, the nurse who had chosen to live apart from her officially classified race. She wanted to carry the baby, but the mother wouldn't allow her: their final confrontation. A black limousine – not quite an undertaker's car, Jean reassured herself – was waiting outside, and its uniformed chauffeur hurriedly opened a rear door for his passengers, mother and child. And humbly took the suitcase and parcels from the uniformed nurse at her peremptory command.

Jean tried to smile at him as he slid behind the wheel and asked for her command about their destination. Pleased that he wasn't the man from Patrick's office who fetched his suitcases and attempted to apologise for a rapist he, also, assumed was from his own race. He'd been right, after all – they all had been.

Beth watched the limousine drive away and essayed a wave, fingers fluttering.

Chapter 17

Mid-fifties and hardly a decade since a landslide victory at the polls for die Volk. But foreign tourists were starting to look doubtfully at the travel posters urging them to Come to South Africa, Land of Sunny Contrasts! A land of fabled mineral riches, whose black savages will stamp their calloused feet in primitive, war-like rhythms for your amusement at gold mine compounds on Sunday mornings, after your Saturday night's entertainment in plush, sophisticated night-clubs; where melon-breasted black women stare vacuously at you in their barbaric nakedness from the edge of the road, and tanned, regulation-contoured white goddesses in bikinis give you sultry smiles on golden beaches; where you can see wildlife raw in tooth and claw in its natural splendour from the comfort of a safari vehicle in extensive game parks; where you can, if you insist on being eccentric, be safely conducted round garage-sized, raw-brick boxes so magnanimously built for the Native in urban locations. Such an improvement on primitive mud huts – but unfortunately, they prefer living like pigs in these modern dwellings, you know!

And then view with astonished admiration the skylines of the City of Gold, the Jacaranda City, the Mother City and all other monuments to white resourcefulness and ingenuity against barbaric odds on the Dark Continent. You'll feel safe at the comforting sight of hard-eyed policemen patrolling city streets in search of the cheeky and criminal kaffir who, given half a chance, will cut your throat, steal your valuables – and rape your women.

Other posters exhort South Africans – who are, naturally, white – to Know Your Own Country. The citizen who heeds this advice does indeed come to know this magnificent land: seventeen hours in a good car for the thousand miles between Jo'burg and Cape Town; a pound a night at that pleasant little guest house near Komatipoort if you can't make Lourenco Marques in one go; that unfrequented beach on the South Coast with fantastic surf; all those flowers and trees along the Garden Route. He knows his country without knowing where his servant or employee lives, how he gets to work, what kind of roof he sleeps under; those are the nauseous abstractions of locations which no decent person could ever wish to know or hear about. As long as they turn up on time, which they seldom do – the loafers.

Enough to see these locations from an aeroplane or train: unsightly smudges that are, fortunately, at a healthy distance from white cities and towns. That was enough to make one sick – people content to live is such slums. How can anybody ever want to live like that? My bloody dog is a thousand times cleaner!

The City of Gold is a microcosm of this land of contrasts. Crowded with proud and upright citizens; their rejected, part-white coloured cousins who are graded higher than all these Natives who want to be called Africans; and these coolies who ought to be sent back to India – that's where they'll get their freedom, dammit! And, of course, the foreign Natives imported to dig up the gold.

A mixture of races, but not, by parliamentary decree, a melting pot. They work together and for each other, grubbing gold from deep down in the miracle reef, and conjuring it out of each other's pockets in the shops, in commercial houses and on the streets. They come warily together every morning from their classified ghettoes, grudgingly dependent on each other in material intercourse, uncoupling hurriedly with the approaching dark to scurry back into those racially defined compartments. Any natural preference to live apart in racial enclosures, encouraged for colonial centuries, officially proclaimed a historic necessity for racial survival and termed apartheid. A doctrine which raised the height of the bar and nailed legal spikes into it, because even die Volk cannot be trusted to do what is necessary to maintain its superiority and survival. But between poor whites teetering on the verge of losing or abandoning that superiority, and coloureds who are a constant reminder of those colonial days when the bar was so low it didn't prevent, or even encouraged miscegenation, the social divide is blurred and disappears into a one-sided mating game.

Just as the white man's labour is worth very much more than that of any darker person, so is the spending power of his money more valuable. Yet, even with the divine prerogative to live off the fat of the land, the white man can still be dirt poor. But his poverty is equal to the prosperity of middle-class Non-Europeans, whom he still demands address him respectfully as Baas and Missus.

And because landlords can be colour-blind when there is profit for themselves – the sanctions and proclamations of apartheid cannot reverse economic reality – there are blots on the landscape of white superiority. A soiling of the escutcheon in older, crumbling suburbs where the half-cousins are forced to live together, if not at peace then under a truce.

These eyesores include Doornfontein, Jeppe, Malvern and Bertrams: respectable suburbs during the gold rush, but now slums or near-slums. Here, poor whites are the unhappy neighbours of the middle-class coloured and Indian families that have the financial means to be refugees from the ghettoes proclaimed as their designated areas by apartheid.

The poor whites are unhappy with, and some abhor, these shameful circumstances that contradic their divine superiority; but many of their unwanted coloured neighbours are flattered at having to some extent achieved a cherished aspiration: association with whites. When the pragmatic landlords can be persuaded to show colour consciousness for their lesser brethren, white families live in the front portion of the crumbling houses. Their coloured half-cousins stay out of sight in the backyards – and can, with some elasticity of the mind, be imagined to be servants.

They live together, but with a too conscious disregard of each other; they know each other, but they are not friends nor enemies. Like suspicious strangers on a train, politely or grudgingly passing matches and self-consciously exchanging magazines. The elite among coloureds – school-teachers, artisans, clerks – despise their neighbours for being poor despite the state's efforts to uplift them. And sneer at the boorish behaviour of these Boers; but envy them their paler skins, straight hair and the privileges that go with them. Still, friendships are made: inspired by necessity and mutual advantage. The white housewife can borrow a cup of sugar, a bowl of rice, while exchanging gossip; and her man can offer the sharing of cheap wine or buy some illegally for the unprivileged neighbour. Their son has the chance at a seduction that should flatter, and flatten, any hotnotsmeid: which is how the half-and-half race came to exist, anyway.

For the Coloured genus in these relationships, the major role is to always give when asked; and their dividend is the privilege to talk casually but familiarly of their white friends and neighbours in seemingly amused and derisive tones.

Within these neighbourhoods drift those venstertjies who cannot afford the security of pure-white suburbs, where the chances of recognition by their rejected, darker brethren is greatly reduced. Some only play white during working hours, but the more confident or daring immerse themselves in the white world, even marrying white – but fearful the offspring could be a throwback to their darker genes. They are jeered at, laughed at, and condemned by those without the necessary amount of white genes to bleach and escape; yet when they achieve fame in the white world, mainly in sport, the condemnations turn to gleeful smirks.

Then there is the small, smelly minority of the comparatively free who shuffle and stagger about these neighbourhoods, and the city itself, with a demanding hand held open to all and sundry. These are white dronkies and hoboes, who are seen to not have any pride about their associations, and are occasionally hauled back onto the correct side of the official bar with despair, anger and fear by their own: scolded and bribed to stay. They cunningly and blearily recognise the strength of their embarrassment to their race, and use it accordingly. They threaten to disgrace die Volk by staggering across the colour bar if the bribes are not satisfactory and regular; and they threaten to withdraw the prize of their whiteness from coloureds if their welcome is not warm and generous enough.

Jean Griffiths moved into this borderline world a week after her discharge from hospital. She set up home with her baby in Doornfontein, which was indeed to be her personal fountain of thorns.

The chauffeur who fetched her from the hospital had given her a document couched in stilted legal terms. It informed her that the front portion of a house owned by the estate agency in Doornfontein had been prepared as a home for herself and her offspring, name unknown; and a monthly allowance would be paid into an account opened on her behalf at a nearby bank. Should there be any emergency she could not cope with, she was advised to inform the solicitor whose name and other details appeared at the top of the said document.

The decree nisi of her divorce from Patrick Sean Ryan would be finalised soon. Goodbye and good luck, yours sincerely.

The house was on a quiet, tree-lined street north of the railway embankment.

At the turn of the century the colonial-style building and the others along the street had been fashionable residences of successful men working the gold mines; now, only a shoddy pretension about their gables and other ornamental features survived. But this house had been newly white-washed, unlike its equally solidly-built neighbours. A paved walk ended at seven semi-circular steps leading onto a narrow stoep, screened from the street by creepers. There was a smaller gate at one end of the wooden fence, opening onto an unpaved path that led to the back of the old house where, the legal document had informed Jean, lived a coloured family: fairly decent as they go, was the implication.

On her arrival in this unknown suburb with a funny name that rang a faint bell in her mind, Jean opened the broad, heavy front door, whose upper half was a mosaic of fading, multi-coloured glass panes held together by writhing snakes of lead. Beyond the door was a corridor blocked off part-way down its length by a brightly-painted brick wall – in case you walked into it and apartheid, she thought with bitter amusement. The first door on her right led into a large living room with new, comfortable furniture: must be Sheila's other contribution to my new half-life in my first home on my own. No – with my first and only baby. To the left was a door to the only bedroom and a bathroom: a new addition, the document had boasted. She asked of that instructive document: Am I not to be allowed overnight guests, Mister Lawyer? No, silly – you're not expected to have any friends. And past the living room was the last door before the dividing wall, which opened into the kitchen.

She stared at the brick wall with curiosity and some trepidation. And she could hear faint familiar household sounds and accented murmurs. She wondered what they were like – and found out within an hour.

There was a knock at the front door. Jean stopped rearranging furniture to listen, wondering with rising panic who it could be, so soon. The knock came again, louder. She walked towards it, and the green eyes staring wildly at the door spotted the judas hole within the leaded glass panes. And the blurred outline of a female body on the stoep. She closed one eye and peered though the peeping hole, and was confronted by a circular segment of lined, yellowish skin. After a hesitant, puzzled moment she opened the door.

A short, blowzy, older coloured woman stood on the veranda, an apron around a thick waist. Small brown eyes probing boldly and lips stretched in the beginnings of a smile. She wore a gaily patterned doek on her head, but tendrils of greying hair escaped its sweaty edge and hung over her eyes and ears.

"Yes?" Jean asked in a breathless voice.

"Good afternoon, Madam!" the woman said, too loudly, in a hoarse voice that seemed unable to speak at a lower pitch. "How're you? Is going to be so nice, having a lady like you living here, man! My name's Janey, and me and my old man and kids live round the back."

The cigarette-hoarse voice galloped on: "Ag, you jus' don't know how glad I is to see you looking such a lady, Madam. I was so worried, man! That we going to have some bad persons living out front here."

Jean hardly listened to the woman after the first heavily accented words. She was used to the slow, broad vowels of black servants, and this clipped, hurried, sing-song was strange and difficult to understand. Perhaps because her mind was also frozen between the immediate reaction of wanting to slam the door in the face of this grotesque hag, and the frightening realisation that she could never again do such a thing. This was her neighbour, and there would have to be some goodwill between them – which is what this woman was offering.

You ought to be smiling, a voice said in her head. This one can turn mean and nasty; make your life a worse nightmare than it already is, or has been for months. This one is obviously a gossip, so be friendly and smile – be neighbourly!

She twitched a smile onto her pale face, nodding her appreciation of whatever the woman was still gabbling – something about other people living on the street. Do I have to invite her inside? No, that would be taking neighbourliness too far, maybe just too soon. Sit with her on the veranda's second-hand wicker chairs? No. But she can be of immediate use! Show her my lovely Beatrice now. Then everybody will soon know about us. Save a lot of bother.

And on cue, Janey asked the sly question: "How's your baby, Madam? I think I saw you with a baby when you arrive just now?"

This Jean heard, or recognised from the sly look on Janey's face after a pause in her gossipy monologue. Now she was waiting for an answer that would send her rattling off on a new tack.

"She's fine – just fine!" Jean said, too heartily, too quickly. "A lovely baby girl. Beatrice. And – er – oh, sorry. I'm Jean – Miss Griffiths, I mean, because I'm divorced, you see. Or going to be, soon."

You didn't have to tell her that, silly! Now, how to show her Beatrice, without making it into a drama … A muffled wail on cue from the bedroom saved her the need for stratagem. "Oh, that's her!" she said, turning away from the door. "Just hold on a minute and I'll fetch her."

She returned, smiling fixedly and holding the baby bundle close to her body.

Janey cooed but stared long and carefully at the infant bundle, then turned her face slowly up – the smile wider, and the previous curiosity in small eyes now turned into recognition and a welcoming glint.

"Ag," she cooed. "Such a very nice and pretty little baba! Such a mooi skat, man! Wat is haar – what you call her?"

"Beatrice. She is lovely, isn't she?" Jean replied, amusement in her voice. She waited with bated curiously for whatever Janey would now say to supplement the message in her eyes – and those few words of Afrikaans.

"We'll all be very proud of her, Madam – I mean Miss Griffiths! Man, our kids is the prettiest in the whole world, man! I always said so, 's true's God! Die Here hoor my! And when she's got a mother like you – I mean, how can she be ugly?"

"Thank you, Janey."

"What about her father?"

"Oh, he's around."

"Well, I know he can't stay here by you. But I just hope he not going to play the fool like some people I know. You know, I got a good husband; but he still just like all of them! Drink! They always sop, and –" She stopped and smiled. "But he can't be like that, I'm sure! Not a man who – You too nice a lady to take a man like that, hey? Trouble is only this stupid government, you know! Why they try and treat us like Naytiffs? We not like they is, man – we got white blood same as you!"

Janey passed the amazing gossip to neighbours. Coloured women smiled with knowing irony and laughed with spiteful glee. And white women glared at the messenger, and clamped thin lips tight. Or were too incensed to refrain from venting their anger about so intimate a scandal to this gabby woman from a lesser breed. When they came home that evening, older coloured men grinned and nodded knowledgeably – they'd always known these things happened, man; while the eyes of younger men turned speculative, mutely asking: Why not me, now? White men were disgusted, angered and frustrated by this latest betrayal, and by a fokken woman, at that! But a few also wondered: If with one of them, then wragtig – surely with me, now?

Only Sannie Fourie showed any sympathy for this traitor who had come to upset the fine balance between blerry hotnots and fokken

Boere – as they cursed when there was an imbalance, and the customary giving and taking was suspended for the duration of hostilities. She was a tall, large-boned woman from that hardy stock of Great Trek tannies, who did as much as their men to conquer a vast land and subdue its savages. She radiated so much maternal confidence and a cosy feeling of protection that she was Tant Sannie to all those known to her – which meant most of Doornfontein.

She had listened to Janey's exciting and scandalous story, icy blue eyes seemingly amused by the relish with which her informant embellished a few facts.

"Poor child," Tant Sannie said when Janey could find nothing more to add to the little she knew. "Must be crazy mad or too blerry brave and sommer stubborn for her own good – anybody's good. I surprise you, hey Janey?" she asked, the pale flesh about her eyes crinkling to see the other woman's disappointment. "I can guess – I know – what they all said when you told them, these good Afrikaner women. Like that Grieta de Wet, hey? She – oh, no. I mustn't tell you anything, hey, Janey? You talk too much, you hotnot; more than die blerry Uitsaaikorporasie on the radio!"

"Me?" came the dismissive response. "Only to my friends, man!"

Sannie joined in the laughter. But I know how she feels about this poor girl, she thought.

She was feeding the baby while Janey, who had summarily installed herself as cleaning woman at a salary still to be fixed, bustled about: dusting, sweeping and forever talking. Hardly a week, but Jean had learned to let this flood of words pass over and through her, with only a few relevant bits of information seeping into her conscious mind. She'd firmly assured herself that she was not afraid to go out onto the streets; she was only waiting for the initial curiosity about her arrival to die down. Then she would walk the streets like any of them. And if they spoke, she would be polite but keep her distance: didn't wish to go native, even if they weren't black. If they insulted her, she would remain withdrawn, cool and aloof – make them all realise their social inferiority.

The only fear that she admitted to herself was the possibility of any of them invading her home to confront her with insults; or being overly familiar, assuming she was at their level … And now here was somebody knocking at the door.

"Janey – someone at the door," she said, body tensing. "I don't want to see anybody. Tell them I'm too busy, whoever it is knocking."

But Janey made no attempt to stop the tall, heavy, grey-haired woman with a skin coarsened by too much of everything and a face radiating self-confidence. The woman drove Janey back along the corridor and into the living room, where she smiled at Jean over her cleaner's head.

Janey turned round to face Jean, an inquisitive smile on her wrinkled face. Instead of an apology for not obeying instructions, she announced: "This is Tant Sannie – er, Miss Griffiths."

"That's enough from you, Janey," a deep voice rumbled from the woman looking down at mother and child. "Now, just leave us alone, hey? No, not hiding in there with your ears flapping. Go out to your own place, jong. Jou ou skelm!"

Janey walked out meekly, but her face was clouded with resentment and disappointment; her short, wide back stiff with hurt pride. Then the large woman settled herself slowly on the couch, which groaned. No waiting for a bloody invitation, Jean noted. The woman read her face and smiled.

"I suppose with that name you English."

"Welsh, actually. My grandfather was a coal miner in Wales, and thought he'd make more money as a miner here when the gold rush –"

"Ag, just the same," the Afrikaner woman said, brushing away her history with a dismissive hand. "Engels … So jy praat nie Afrikaans nie?"

Jean shook her head in mute reply: if I'm bloody English, why does she expect me to speak her 'taal'? Enough to know enough to understand the question.

"Ah, yes – of course not," Sannie nodded, still smiling despite her reading of the resentful face. "I thought not, but I had to try, you know. My English not so hot, hey, and you people laugh when we try to please you."

Jean bent down quickly to kiss Beatrice and avoid showing her easily-read face, that was now rising scarlet with embarrassment.

"I am Sannie Fourie, my kind – you know what that means?"

"'My child'."

"Oh, good," Sannie laughed. "But you call me Tant Sannie, if you like."

"Auntie Sannie," Jean said, looking up.

The heavy voice chuckled: "Even older people call me a tannie, you know. Everybody's aunt. I live down the street from here, and Janey told us all about you and your trouble. You angry with her?"

Jean shook her head.

"That's good. I hoped you have enough sense – even if you done some pretty damn stupid things."

Jean was alarmed and fascinated. She'd been waiting with dread in her heart for just such a meeting. Now she was confronted by this blunt-spoken but still strangely comforting person – everybody's agony aunt. She had stood at the window these past days, hiding behind curtains and waiting for one of them to turn into her gate and storm her house in the name of all that was white, holy and decent. But they had trundled past, turning brief, contemptuous stares at her windows and then passing on, staring stiffly ahead. She had willed one of them to turn in, damn it, and get it over with.

But they had not. Now she listened to this gruff voice, fascinated by the quiet confidence she had thought only strong men – not bloody Patrick! – could possess. In her mind she replaced the faded black dress and veiled Sunday church straw hat with the floppy sun bonnet and flowing dresses of those Voortrekker women portrayed in heroic paintings of their mythologised search for a new land they could rule as they wished, away from the verdomde Engelse who boasted they ruled the waves, and so the world.

Jean could imagine this hard old bird crouched behind a barricade between ox wagons set in a defensive laager. Mowing down kaffirs with a rifle with the best of the bearded men – not loading the rifles, like the other women cowering in the background.

"'Stupid thing,' you say – meaning my baby?" Jean asked, brushing away the Great Trek tableau.

Tant Sannie nodded. Jean rose and brought Beatrice over for inspection. But the older woman only stared matter-of-factly at the baby, asleep in her mother's arms.

"That's a nice healthy-looking baby," she observed. "What's her name?"

Ah-ha! Jean thought. Friendly and all that, even if blunt, so I let my guard down. No way, old bird. "Beatrice," she replied. "And I'm Jean Griffiths."

"Don't look so defiant, kind. So ready to fight – me, everybody, the whole world! There's nothing for us to fight about, if you're sensible." She chuckled. "But so far, you're not sensible. Foolhardy is the word, I think, hey? But it takes sense, too, to be foolhardy. So, we're not going to fight; and I'm the only person who'll talk decent to you around here.

"Of course, all these kleurling-vroumense like Janey will try to get familiar – she's already established a listening post for them. Hulle Spioenkop, hey. But don't worry about her, or about them. They're empty drums – just talk and nothing else."

Jean showed her a small, hesitant smile.

"Thank you for the advice, Mrs – Tant Sannie. You are very kind. I wish everybody else could be as nice." She'd rather be left alone, but felt she had to say something pleasant and appreciative.

"Moenie worry nie, skat, if that don't happen – and you don't want it to happen because you don't want to know them. Ja?"

"Ja, Tant Sannie," Jean was surprised to hear herself saying.

"You see?" Sannie grinned. "You're learning already, even though you come from a different class, and a different race which refuses to learn other people's languages. Why not? Because you despise all the rest of us – and, no, don't say anything or shake your head. Everybody's got the right to despise anybody they think is no good. What I also mean is you won't understand them, your new neighbours, and they you.

"If they try to be nice, then I bet you, they trying to use you. They – we – are poor people. So we use people who got something we need – and then hate you and skinder about you because you got more'n we got. You're in such a position. They despise you, Jean Griffiths," she said, pointing a large finger at mother and child. "And not only because you got a half-and-half baby."

She stopped, fumbled in her bodice and withdrew a crumpled packet of cigarettes. Sannie lit one, took a deep drag and continued:

"You don't understand, eh? You see, we're like the Natives."

She laughed at the surprise on Jean's face. "My people'll kill me – shoot me stone dead – if they hear me say that, hoor? But it's true: we're like them. That's why we get on so well under the hatred. We got a – a chip on the shoulder – that's what you say, eh? We got it because we hate you Engelse from the old days, when you forced us to trek up here from the Cape. The Natives hate us and you, because of what we done to them. So! That is why they – your new neighbours, I mean – will hate coming to you to borrow money or salt. Because you got this piccaninny, they never come to you. And they never forgive you, hoor. To them, you disgrace us all before die swart volk en hierdie kleurlinge. You don't hide that you done things some also done – doing it for years, man, since Jan van Riebeeck: his burgers with the hotnots, even after their wives come from Holland … Or some just tempted, but got no pluck. Hoor jy my, my kind?"

It was the first of many visits from the redoubtable Tant Sannie. She did not ask questions about how Jean came to have this baby. She talked, knowing that when she had won this young woman's confidence she would hear it all. She laughed, chuckled and lectured, and from what she said Jean felt newly justified in the decisions she'd made since that horrible and terrifying night in Hillbrow. There was nothing this awesome woman said she could quote as justification, but from all the gruffly spoken words she drew an understanding of herself and the people around her. And it made her feel like the only other sane person in an asylum.

Yet it was some time before Jean could tell Tant Sannie the truth, the whole truth, of her circumstances: the first person to hear the full story. Everybody in Doornfontein assumed Beatrice was born of an illegal and, worse, adulterous, affair with a coloured man who'd since abandoned her. For this they despised and hated Jean. But at the bottom of that bubbling hatred was another emotion, which she felt vaguely in what Janey told her of the local gossip and the tension she felt on her sporadic, defiant flits to the corner stores: trying not to scurry, to stroll tall and proud; but without Beatrice.

She vaguely suspected that, somehow, the women who glared out of cold, baleful eyes envied her the freedom of the defiant choice she'd made. But why did they all presume the father was coloured and not black? Because Beatrice was such a beautiful, honey brown? After all, they must all have seen, if they dared or bothered to look, light-coloured Natives. Africans. And Janey had hinted she would lose face among the coloureds if the father – no, damn it, the rapist – was African. Then it dawned on her that whites hoped he was coloured, which would somehow reduce the enormity of her betrayal: coloureds had white blood after all, as Janey couldn't help reminding her. And the presumption mollified coloureds because it made her a trophy they could point at with pride: one of them had conquered, despite the odds. And they could be right. But what would they think, how would they react, if they knew the truth – that she'd been raped? Perhaps show a little sympathy – but then want to know why not an immediate abortion. A rapist had to be a kaffir – sies! And sies tog.

But I'll be damned if I'm going to try explaining that again – and to strangers.

Sannie, though, would be too sensible to pity her. And the tannie might even understand. Jean hesitated, still. But knew she had to tell somebody, a person she could talk to and be understood. And after she'd finally worked up the nerve and told Sannie, Jean felt deliriously light-headed. Purged. The words had tumbled from her lips, and she'd several times had to pause and start again, slowly.

"I'm glad you've told me, my arme kind," the motherly woman rumbled into the silence that followed. "And flattered," she smiled. "Good for you too, of course. But it's better I know – just me, Sannie Fourie. I will not tell anybody, and neither must you. As you are now, as they think of you now, is better. Beter. They have some kind of good feeling for you, deep down. Most got someone in their family in what they think is your position."

"Really?"

"That is also why they so angry with you: been honest to yourself, they believe. And these people they know – they not been. Nobody likes anybody who is better, my Engelse skat."

Sannie fumbled in her bodice but Jean was much quicker, offering one of her own cigarettes. When they had lit up and taken the first deep drags, the blue-eyed woman spoke again, a cynical grin playing about her lips:

"Ag, we live in such a blerry mixed-up world, you know. I despise these kleurlinge and kaffirs as much as anybody – no, more, because I know my feelings clearly. I know they are inferior, I don't just believe it or like to think so. But I don't hate them. Do you hate a half-friendly dog, or a piece of shit on the pavement? No. The difference between me and most of the others is that even though I despise these volk, I don't forget that they're people too. With feelings – met 'n hart. The others, they try and treat them like they're not even useful animals. But now and again, they realise these are also people – people they want to naai – fuck, you know?"

Jean stared in amazement, but nodded.

"Then they get so die moer in – very angry – at themselves and hate them even more!" She rumbled a laugh: "Trouble is most times they think of them as people is when they want to naai with them!" The laughter grew louder, and the huge body shook and quivered. But the blue eyes remained shrewdly intent on the bewildered face with green eyes under the yellow hair.

"One time, I was talking to our MP – I'm a member of the National Party, of course – and I asked him: why, if we're superior and don't want to mix with these people; why must we have all these laws like the Immorality Act? You know what he said to me?" She chortled, shaking her head.

"He said, 'Tant Sannie, we must of course protect the weak among us!' Wragtig, my skat – that's what he told me! The blerry weak! Like the Prime Minister's secretary, caught sniffing around a kitchen girl's bloomers – not even a grown woman? Hey? I tell you something, Jean Griffiths!"

"What?"

"You know who's really free in this country? The only ones? Not you and me – oh, no. White man and black woman! If one of our fokken goats wants to get between those fat black thighs, he just has to ask – simple. Only very, very few black woman will try to report die Baas to the police. And when these whores want our men – well, if they not interested, they just tell her to voetsek, and that's it, my girl!"

"Oh – I see ..."

"And remember, they make the laws, our men. But can we ask a black man for a fuck, hey? Of course not – if we got any decency.

Because we're white, and because woman not supposed to ask even white men. And if a woman is crazy enough with lust for a darkie, and maybe he is too, she will have to ask him. Because he knows the risks – crimen injuria and all that if he's wrong – and he's not going to make the first move. You see? Anyway, skat. Just leave them to go on thinking you've done what some of them would like to do very much, the randy bitches."

It was an ethnic education of sorts for Jean Griffiths.

Chapter 18

Sheila Ryan was being proselytised, and not for the first time; but from an unexpected side of the racial divide.

She was regarded by her family and their circle of wealthy familiars as something of a liberal – not a Communist, of course, God forbid; but a young lady with some odd – well, let's say eccentric – ideas and beliefs in her pretty head. Such as insisting on calling these Natives Africans, which as all sensible people knew was the English for Afrikaners, and one had to respect the government's insistence that they were the only Africans. Anyway, it was their Voortrekkers who made the country what it is today, not the Natives. And anyway, who could ever dare to confuse those political protagonists: idealism against kragdadigheid? Might is always right, you know – and we have the economic power.

Sheila's liberal friends tolerated her as a free-thinking conservative on the left wing of the United Party; but not one of those straight-laced fogeys who debated the Native Question, but viewed Africans in the same way that 19th century missionaries had as they traversed the Dark Continent: heathens in need of enlightenment. Sheila could, given time, be won over to their liberal views on the Race Problem. A free thinker, they thought, but a political dilettante.

If she had ever bothered to analyse her feelings on these weighty matters, Sheila would have decided that she was only exercising an intelligent curiosity about the land she'd been born in because an Irish ancestor had fled the potato famine to seek his fortune at the southern tip of Africa. So, she attended liberal mixed parties – "lovely to see you again, Thabo!" And there, she was sympathetic to most criticisms of the Nats in government – "those stupid Afrikaners!" And laughed uproariously at the stories African guests such as Boykie and Desmond told about the farcical aspects of apartheid. But she was amazed, and some times annoyed, by the familiarities Africans were allowed on these merry occasions.

She'd never been to Sophiatown, like some of her liberal friends, and had in the past only driven through Doornfontein along a bleak main street lined with shops, bioscopes and other impersonal public buildings. She shared the general abstract knowledge of this fountain of thorns – or thorny fountain? – being a white slum; but that knowledge had not prepared her for what she saw as she drove slowly in her sports car through back streets, seeking the address of her rogue sister-in-law.

Realising the bleak main street was almost smart and metropolitan, compared to the back streets, she was appalled by their stark realities: can white people live like this, despite the fruits promised them by apartheid? She'd of course known there were poor whites – seen hoboes on the city streets; but they had so far not impinged on her own life. And this is where Patrick's dumped poor Jean! This is the neighbourhood Jean's forced to acknowledge as home, because her bloody stubborn maternal instincts have led to a defiance of everything that's decent!

For the first time there was sorrow in Sheila's heart as she realised how this beautiful, bountiful country brutalised itself and its people. Especially those it arbitrarily decided were not fit to share in its largesse – the coloureds who were gathered in small groups at corners and lounged at the gates and on the stoeps of horribly dilapidated houses.

This time the proselytising was not in arguments and debates within smart houses in the northern suburbs; but in what was before her eyes.

Janey fussily admitted Sheila into the freshly-painted house. At least, Sheila thought, Patrick did do something to make it homely. Jean stared at her from across the living room for what seemed ages. It was their first meeting since the last weeks of the pregnancy, and Sheila noticed definite changes. The most arresting was a tense quietness about Jean's person – that of a woman who is at all times expecting the worst, but has passed the point of being frightened by the prospect. The compassion that began to well up within Sheila was suppressed by another discovery: the serenity that showed behind the tension, and made any feelings approaching pity seem mean.

She began to feel a grudging respect and admiration for this new Jean Griffiths, who wasn't her sister-in-law any more. Patrick had found no difficulty getting his divorce, whatever lies he and his lawyer had concocted to avoid scandal.

"Hello, Jeanie," Sheila said quietly. "How are you?"

She wanted to be bright and cheerful, but felt it would be patronising and resented. Jean turned towards Janey, who was lurking at the back of the room.

"You can go home now," she instructed. "I won't be needing you until after lunch. In fact, I'll call if I need you at all. Go, Janey – and get one of those loafers outside to keep an eye on Miss Ryan's car."

After the short, fat and unkempt body had followed the thwarted face out of the room, Jean turned to the guest who'd telephoned – the first call since her arrival among the thorns – and smiled. "She's useful, but an incurable eavesdropper and gossip. Please sit down, Sheila. And I'm fine. How are you?"

"Desolated," Sheila replied as she sank into a chair. "And ashamed of myself for not having come to see you sooner. To think you have to live in a place like this!"

Jean smiled again. "It's quite a pleasant house – old, but comfortable. I'm getting to like it, in fact."

"But this area, Jean!" Sheila exclaimed. "These mean streets, these neighbours – and a smelly, frumpy servant like her!"

"I don't have much choice, do I?"

"Oh, it's horrible! Jeanie, you don't know how much I –"

"No, Sheila!" Jean cut her off sharply. "I don't want your pity or sympathy. I chose this life for myself. I didn't know exactly how it would be, but I chose it without anybody's help. So let's not start on that, please."

Sheila watched her for a long moment, before she spoke again.

"Are you happy, Jeanie?" she asked. "I mean – relatively?"

"Happy? How d'you spell the word? Oh, I'm sorry, Sheila. I shouldn't have said that. At least not to you. Though I don't have to answer that question, and you shouldn't have asked. But I will. No, Sheila, I'm not happy, nor am I unhappy. I live, my baby grows, and I love her."

Sheila hid her surprise at this last statement by quickly asking, "What's her name? I don't even know it – my own niece!"

"No, Sheila. She's not your niece. No sacred Ryan blood in Beatrice."

After a moment's embarrassed silence, Jean spoke matter-of-factly about Beatrice, but the detachment in her tone lessened, and its edges softened. Her voice took on what Sheila recognised as the beginnings of that indulgent tone mothers adopted when they complained of the sleepless nights, the illnesses, the wet nappies and other problems brought on by their adored offspring. She was surprised, pleased and at the same time shocked that Jean was really developing love for this ill-begotten child. Perhaps it was just as well; but so soon?

As she mulled over what she was learning, Sheila realised the meanness of her past attitudes to Jean's problems. An attitude she had, then in ignorance, regarded as magnanimous. What could she do to make up? To help – no, not that, because Jean didn't seem to need anybody's assistance. To somehow make herself a part of this tragedy; by being useful?

"And who's this woman – Janey, you said?" Sheila asked.

"Oh, her. She's my inheritance." Jean smiled – that resigned smile again. "I inherited her with the house. She lives at the back, and has installed herself as my housekeeper. She's quite infuriating, most of the time; but useful."

"I don't like her."

"Neither do I, Sheila. Especially because she thinks I should like her. We're both mothers of coloured children, you see. So we should like each other!"

"She thinks –"

"Oh, she doesn't think – she knows! They know that I'm one of them. I think the current stories are that I'm a play-white who married a white man, but whose first child was a throwback. Or that I am white, but cheated my husband with one of their very handsome and desirable sons, brothers or cousins. So we're all sisters under the skin."

"You must get a proper servant, Jeanie – an African nanny. These people don't know how to look after children or even themselves. You only have to look at them and their families."

"Oh, it doesn't matter that much, Sheila. I look after Bea myself."

"It does, Jeanie," Sheila insisted, exploiting this opening to be useful. "And you don't have to worry, if you think the search is too much bother. I'll do it all – get you a nice, clean girl who'll sleep out. Okay? One of the good ones from the locations who speaks passable English and you don't have to supervise all the time. With a bit more than some education."

There were various methods of acquiring domestic servants. The simplest was to ask friends' reliable servants to bring forward acquaintances who were as good, and a choice could be made from the hopeful recruits. Sheila, though, was going to be unethical in her strategy: she was going to steal a friend's servant! She giggled when the idea ballooned in her mind. A girl who'd stood out among the many she'd come across, from the first time she'd seen her serving at the friend's home.

Unusual to notice any of them, as every home she visited had servants who were regarded and evaluated with the same impersonality as other utilities in the house. Many were straight from the bush and without much of a clue about lifestyles in the northern suburbs; but this one was a location girl.

She had the expected superior intelligence and cleanliness of her type over the country girls, who accidentally – but sometimes deliberately, she'd heard at the mixed parties – broke precious glasses and crockery in the kitchens: and pinched wailing babies in nurseries.

Betty – was that her name? – also lacked the forwardness, the cheek, of many location girls who so often behaved as if they were doing their Madams favours. Yet this girl – yes, Betty! – was not obsequious: she was withdrawn and sort of dignified, but not unfriendly. A sort of female version of how Sheila visualised an English butler.

This was definitely the girl for Jean. With her reserve, she wouldn't ask nosey questions or behave with the familiarity she'd spotted in Janey. A familiarity which, in the average location kitchen girl, could worsen to disrespect for a white woman with a coloured baby.

Thursday afternoon was known as 'sheila's day' – afternoon and evening off for domestic servants – and Betty Nkosi stood close to the wall of a building near an intersection in the city. Five o'clock, and an avalanche of homeward-hurrying drones shuffled and eddied about her: tired faces, withdrawn faces, bright faces, serene faces, angry faces; black faces, white faces, off-white faces, Asian faces.

All intent on their destinations: bar, shebeen, beer hall, club. But all home, eventually. Home. The broad street Betty was facing and the narrow one intersecting it to her right were jammed with slow, solid lines of cars daring jay-walkers to squeeze between them and have their legs crushed. Inside the cars were the same faces as on the pavements – the whites alone or in twos and threes; the blacks in crowded jumbles.

An occasional black face surfaced from the stream, smiled or leered: "Hi, sweetie pie!"; "I got a cold bed needs warming, sugar!" The smiles, voices, eyes and wolf whistles didn't penetrate her mind. These were the noises of the city, the sights of the city, the phenomena of the city that was her home town, and they were part of her life. And the upright, forbidding carriage of her person was her best protection against any harassment.

Her eyes finally lit up in recognition, their expectancy fulfilled. Philip Mokone sat at ease in the high cab of the huge van: bored brown face above khaki dust coat, eyes squinting into the sun under the jaunty visor of a checked, five-piece cloth cap. He gunned the engine of the three-tonner and swung the vehicle into the entrance of the building across the street from where she stood. Blue smoke spouting a final raspberry to the world from its exhaust.

She still stood – very well-dressed, upright, handsome and disdainful – when he jay-walked across the traffic jam towards her. Dust coat abandoned, dressed in sharp clothes, the cloth cap replaced by a coconut-brown, narrow-brimmed Panama hat.

"Hello, sweetheart!" he said, a small, breezy grin playing about his mouth. "Nobody worried you?"

"Hello, Philip," she smiled and shrugged. "Just the usual things. You know."

He chuckled. "I'm surprised – the way you look, baby. Like a million dollars!"

Her smile was shy and reproving. As much as she enjoyed his extravagant compliments, she had a problem with this one about looking like a million dollars. He'd nagged and cajoled her to meet this guy he knew who worked in a ladies' fashion shop and could get her the best – better clothes than your Madam can afford, baby; but back-door. He would introduce her to him, and then all she had to do on one of her Thursday half-days was go to this shop, select what she liked, give this guy the nod – and the outfit would be delivered in Sophiatown.

Yes, she knew everybody did it: everything from socks to bedroom suites acquired through the back-door. But she had doubts, and not all of them moral. What if some envious policewoman arrested her – or a store manager recognised what she was wearing today, and demanded to see a receipt for clothes he knew were too expensive for a kaffermeid to buy across the counter? Philip had laughed and reminded her that his own sharp clothes, and those of most klevahs, came the same route: out of the best stores in town.

Of course the cops and store managers knew what was happening. But they didn't have any proof, did they? And there wasn't any law even in this country that kaffirs had to carry receipts with them all the time. Only their damned dompas reference books. Just look at the quarter-million boys, driving very slowly around in their open-top Cadillacs and Buicks, baby. Has anybody asked them where they got the money for these can't-get limos?

"Okay for tonight?" he asked, stroking the expensively fashionable silk that covered her arm.

"Yes, my dear. Did you get the tickets?"

"Oh, yes – one guinea each! What d'you think of that, eh?"

"Oh, Philip!"

"That's all they had left, sweetheart," he said, leading her into a maelstrom of the homeward bound. "Boykie made the connections – and you know how he is: no cheap seats for him! He's also fixed for a car. That," he turned and grinned, wryly, "is another twelve-and-six."

"That's a lot of money, my dear – for just a few hours."

"Ah, it's nothing. What's money for if not to enjoy ourselves? I drink more than that on a – sometimes," he smiled apologetically at her. "And for this show it's worth the two guineas, Betty. That's if you want to believe situations like Boykie and Desmond. Can't stop talking about this concert, those two!"

An American troupe touring the country had been begged, inveigled or shamed into giving a performance that Africans could attend at the University Great Hall. The only proper venue – not a small, inadequate Slegs Nie-Blankes hall such as the Bantu Men's Centre at the downmarket end of Eloff Street, the city's main drag for shoppers. A great hall where the races could mix colours and watch the same show. But with the seats in carefully colour-coded and separated blocks.

They arrived with Boykie in the car he'd fixed with a mutual friend. The courtroom wizard put on his big grin for mixed parties, as they climbed the broad steps into a foyer crowded with white faces. The crowd were in their night-out best, the women in strapless gowns and clouds of perfume. Philip had kept his fingers crossed, but Vivienne was there, with a few other liberals he recognised from the party he'd attended in Lower Houghton. And it was impossible, discourteous, for him to avoid his mentor in blatant passion – and more …

They met in the crowded foyer, and Vivienne smiled her mischievous understanding when Philip introduced her to his friend, Betty Nkosi. Almost two months since the mixed party and their first and only meeting. Vivienne would want to know why they'd not met again; why he'd not called the number she'd given him, or responded to the messages she'd passed on through Boykie. The messenger's grin was even broader, as he observed the encounter. But Philip knew he could not tell her why he'd forsaken her wanton body. He was himself not clear about the reasons, and he didn't want to give her the chance to ask. Now that he saw her, he did want to talk to her again; and make love to her again, too, if she wasn't too miffed by his silence and this introduction to his beloved. But there were still too many fears chasing round in his head for him to do it – ask her for a date. Not yet.

The show was a musical, the songs were familiar and popular, the packed audience gave the American troupers a standing ovation at the end. And Boykie failed to persuade Philip to go to an impromptu party – "She'll be there, boy, and Betty won't notice your reunion in the merry crowd!" he'd whispered. Boykie Courtroom was, of course, excited at the prospect of meeting members of the troupe – from America, land of all his dreams.

Philip mumbled excuses and they returned to his room in another friend's car.

"I didn't know you also knew these white people, my dear," Betty remarked as he sat smoking while she undressed – her usual, shy striptease, he thought, remembering Vivienne unselfconsciously flaunting her charms.

"Oh, I don't really know them. I just went to one of these liberal parties with Boykie. About two months ago."

"But that girl, the short one with red hair – she knew you, Philip … She even looked interested in you."

"Oh, Vivienne? That's where I met her. We had a long chat about things. Politics and all that – you know how they like to talk about that … But interested – in me? I didn't notice that!" He was uneasy, and barked an abrupt laugh. Ashamed at himself for what he felt he had to say, now: "You know what they are, those liberals. Maybe she's found out that black men are good screws."

She turned, and he got a better eyeful than normal of pendulous breasts. She looked carefully at him before she spoke.

"Have you found out how good they are in bed?"

"Me!"

"Never mind, Philip. Don't tell me. I know I'm not the only woman you sleep with, even now. In our bed."

"Oh, now, Betty! How can you –"

"I'm not worried, my dear. And I don't blame you, Philip. You don't like sleeping in the backyards, eating dogs' meat. And I can't come here enough. And you're a man – a popular man."

"And you know you're the only woman I love."

"I know, Philip. But it's all going to change, now." She spoke with determination, but smiled at the expression on his face. "Don't worry, I'm not asking you to marry me, Philip."

"You know I want to. I'm going to marry you."

"When you're ready, my dear. What I mean is that from next month I can come and sleep here as often as you want me. I can even come and live with you, if that's what you want."

"That's not what I want!" he protested. "I am going to marry you. But – I mean, why? What's happening next month?"

"I'm leaving this job. I've been offered another one in Doornfontein."

"What? You work for those poor whites? Those –"

"No, my dear. Not a poor-white family. I don't know much about her yet, but it's a woman who's living there with her baby. She's a friend or relation of this woman who asked me – Miss Ryan, who often visits where I work now. So she can't be a poor white. And I'm going to get more money than I can ever get from these people in the rich suburbs. And I'll be sleeping out. At home in Orlando … or here, if that's what you want."

"I see," he said, working out the odds between what he wanted and how he wished to live, free and fancy free, in this room. Maybe a reunion with Vivienne? "You'll stay with your family in Orlando, then?"

"If that's what you want, Philip. I can even get a room here in Sophiatown, if you only want me to be nearer."

"No – go home to Orlando, baby. You'd be too close – no, I don't mean it like that, Betty, but …"

"I know, Philip."

"You don't know anything, dammit!' he burst out. "Don't you women understand anything? It's not because if you stay in Soph'town I won't be able to do whatever things you think I want to do – fucking all the bitches around here, or whatever's on your suspicious, female mind. It's just that – well, you'd be so close and I'd want to see you all the time. Then I wouldn't have time to be by myself and think! Get myself together so we can get married. Don't you see?"

"That's all right, my dear," she murmured, blowing out the paraffin lamp and sliding into bed. "I can wait. Until you are ready. Remember the waiting before I let you get into a bed with me? Put your arms around me now, Philip – and fuck me. That bad word you klevahs like so much …"

Chapter 19

Betty slipped quietly into the domestic life of the only freshly-painted house in a back street of Doornfontein, and she learned not to shudder walking down the street past loafers of all colours. She performed her duties as instructed by Miss Griffiths, who refused to be called Missus in the normal, prescribed style. She asked few personal questions and accepted what she was told by the remote lady, without concerning herself with what lay beyond the taciturn replies. Her tasks were simple, and she could cope with them easily in the ten hours she was expected to spend daily at the house.

It was an odd household, but she accepted it on its own terms; it would only be a waste of time to concern oneself, as so many girls did, with the intricacies of the lives of white employers. They were different, all of them, and none of her business as long as they were decent to her and paid promptly. And this was an employer whose difference was – well, different from any of the others she'd worked for: but fair and respectable, even though she lived in this terrible area with a daughter who was pretty, good and cheerful, but clearly not of the same race.

A woman who would arouse anybody's curiosity. Betty had heard of white women having coloured babies, but she'd never met one until Miss Ryan – "You can call me Sheila, you know" – brought her to this lonely house.

Jean found herself uncomfortably aware of the constant presence of this servant whom, as Sheila had promised, was very well-behaved. She'd grown up among servants from the time of her birth, and had come to regard them as necessary fixtures for the comfort of her life. As mistress of her own home in Hillbrow, she'd treated them with a vague and detached politeness which they gratefully accepted as kindness compared to the treatment they received from other Madams. But now, in the third home of her own, she was acutely aware of this efficient girl, as silent as herself – which for some stupid reason made her self-conscious.

She wondered if, perhaps, the inquisitive and gabby Janey had been a better choice – which it had not been, a choice. Janey popped in and out during the day, but Betty was in the house for too many hours of the day.

Maybe she just wasn't ready yet to have one of them near her. That was why she'd adamantly refused to have one of them when they moved to Parkhurst, and Patrick insisted in his weak way that she needed to rest and let a Native do all the work. Maybe she'd surrendered to Janey's self-imposed ministrations for this very reason.

Her uneasiness had begun after Sheila telephoned to tell her when she would be bringing the girl for an interview. She'd caught herself preparing for the meeting as if she was the one who had to make an impression. Sheila brought Betty round in the sports car, and the interview was brief and really quite unnecessary because Sheila was bossily in charge. Jean had been content to let Betty do most of the talking, referring occasionally to The Missus for confirmation of her expected duties.

This feeling that had grown into something approaching trepidation on the first day of the month, when Betty knocked at the door. And a feeling of something else, not really panic, when Betty suggested quite reasonably that she should have a key to let herself in without bothering Madam – a title she'd instantly rejected.

She'd wondered about the girl's first reaction to Beatrice, and whether she should show her the toddler at the interview. But finally, and angrily, she decided to let the introduction take care of itself when this girl started work. Why should she bother so much about a mere black servant? In the end, Betty had not seen Bea during the interview because she was conveniently having a nap.

At their first meeting, she had carried Bea on her hip out of the bedroom, watching Betty's face closely for its reactions. But from long practice, there had been none of any consequence.

"This is Beatrice," Jean said, with defiance.

"Hello, Beatrice," Betty responded, approaching mother and child with a smile, a hand rising towards the baby's chubby-cheeked face.

Jean turned jerkily away to place her body between her baby and herself. "There's no need for you to have anything to do with Beatrice – she's my responsibiilty," she snapped – but smiling brightly. And then the challenge: "You can see she's coloured, of course."

"Is she, Madam? You cannot be sure when they're so young ..."

Jean had felt ashamed and angry at herself for going to these lengths – and then outraged at being offered reassurances by her own kitchen girl. Being pitied by a …

"I'm telling you, not asking you!" Jean snapped.

"I'm sorry, Missus."

"And don't call me Missus – or Madam!"

"Yes – er, Miss Griffiths … But she's still a very nice baby."

"Oh, I'm sorry – I didn't mean it like that, Betty!"

Actually apologising to one of them!

For weeks, Betty hardly saw Beatrice: Mummy was playing with her in the bedroom or on the stoep to, she was told, avoid the dust and noise of the vacuum cleaner. Other times Jean took her out for a breath of fresh air in the park – hat jammed around tiny ears to hide the dark, curly hair.

And on the odd occasions when the toddler crawled or staggered in her direction – dribbling and gurgling happily, tiny arms outstretched – Betty was discouraged from picking her up, not by direct prohibitions, but by Jean's possessive manner: "We mustn't spoil her, must we, Betty?"

As the weeks drifted by, Jean relented and the guilty hostility petered out. She could not, however, get over her awareness of this girl – Betty, not a girl – whenever they were in the same room. Betty noticed the uneasiness, but could not understand it. Or, rather, did not try to understand. She came to the simple conclusion early on that the woman was ashamed of herself and her baby, and Betty wondered why, then, she was insisting on bearing the cross of her mistake. And so possessive with Beatrice.

She asked Philip about this mystery, but he was off-hand.

"Obviously she likes it – this baby, her situation," he replied. "Nobody's forcing her to keep it and live in Doornfontein, instead of Parktown or somewhere. I bet they, her family, have tried to force her to give it away."

"I feel so sorry for her, Philip."

"That's right, sweetie," he said, his tone a cross between a snap and that Soph'town jeer and sneer. He attempted a wry grin to disguise his impatience with bleeding hearts. "Go on – feel sorry for all these laanies and masters of the world! Even when it's their own laws which catch them out and make them suffer for a change!"

Her bit of workplace gossip vividly reminded Philip of the one he'd raped. All thoughts of her and that night must be kept firmly in the recesses of his mind. He was going to spend as little time as possible thinking about that 'incident' – which is what he preferred to call it – after the magic worked on his troubled psyche by Betty's love and compassion; and Vivienne's demonstration that they, too, were just women – and what they could be like in an affectionate embrace. Courtesy of the two ladies, that night was fading into a shadowy memory. Not a problem gnawing at his nerves like toothache, any more. He was damned if Betty's gossip was going to arouse the monkey on his back, not that it was starting to doze off rather than jumping and yammering as it had the first weeks. Betty Bleeding Heart feeling 'so sorry for her', just because she was getting a lot of mazooma working for this crazy one who'd sacrificed the good life!

The only white woman he would allow himself to think of with a guilty tinge was Vivienne. He'd treated her badly by breaking off what could've been a relationship because of Betty; end of social research. But now they'd met again, and squeezed hands in the crowded foyer of the Great Hall – well, a man's a man for all that, as the mad Scotsman wrote. Seen her once since the concert: a short, uneasy chance meeting in the street, when he promised to call her. That had to be the major – no, immediate – reason he'd insisted on Betty going back to living with her family in Orlando. But he hadn't called Viv; not yet. But he would, and soon.

Vivienne the redhead just might blot out the memory of the unknown blonde in that dark, smelly alley. How long ago, now? Well over a year; about eighteen months. She must've – no, not forgotten that night, but submerged the experience. After all, they're pretty good at living the good life while knowing about the misery and suffering of their servants – their 'boys' and 'girls' of all ages …

After months of Betty's quiet and reserved ministrations, Jean had allowed her to attend to Bea in small ways. The presence of this girl she knew little about beyond her name and address in Orlando was still somewhat unsettling. And creating excuses to avoid being in the same room with her for more than a few minutes was wearing Jean down. She decided it must be a general restlessness: she had been cooped up in the house so long, hardly ever going beyond the corner store and what passed for a park. This was no life, just mooning about in captivity; but where could she – should they – go? All the people she wished to visit belonged to the past.

Tant Sannie provided the push out of her coop on one of her casual but regular visits. She remarked on the excitement created by a new department store in the centre of the city, even right here in Doornfontein where there's no money. She was astonished to learn that Jean didn't know that an old and well-known landmark had been pulled down to make way for this new building.

"You didn't see them knock it down – all that construction work going on for so many months?"

"No, Tant Sannie."

"Magtig … So when did you last walk down Eloff Street, my child?"

"Oh, I can't remember. At least – maybe two years ago."

"But why? You haven't been living here that long."

"Well, I stopped going into town about the time I knew I was pregnant – began to bulge." An embarrassed pause: how much should I tell her? "Except for one or two trips to buy maternity things. You see, I somehow felt self-conscious of my size – as if everybody would know how I came to be like that."

"But you aren't now, are you? Hey?" the old woman scolded. "You look just like any other young woman – prettier than most, I can tell you. So why don't you go? You think you've got the mark of Cain on your forehead, hey?"

"Of course not," she said tartly. "I've checked in the mirror often enough. In fact, I suppose I should go; I really do need some clothes. So does Bea, growing fast as she is. Though I've hardly worn street clothes – smart street clothes – since … since – well, since I started bulging out."

"So? Then why don't you go and do some shopping? You're not going to spend the rest of your life just hanging around in this slum."

"Yes, but – well, I've got to look after Bea, you see."

"Bosh!" Sannie Fourie grunted. "What you got this Native girl for, if you got to worry about that, hey?"

Still, Jean relinquished the baby in slow stages to Betty's care. The first time she went into town, she was back well within the two hours she'd said she would be away, and full of questions and concern about Beatrice. Gradually, she began to stay away longer, even returning almost too late to relieve Betty so she could go home.

On that first excursion, Jean was filled with trepidation. She walked too fast, instead of strolling like her shopping peers – former peers, she told herself. Nervous and sensitive to the vari-coloured faces taken for granted in the past: they seemed larger than life, their hues exaggerated. And they registered individually, instead of just as fragments of the mass. She felt like an outsider who was seeing all these people, these buildings, these cars and streets for the very first time. Beneath this spooky awareness lay the remnants of the dread and fear she'd known during her pregnancy: subconsciously searching for known and familiar faces, and ready to administer her own snub at them before they wielded theirs at her.

And almost expecting to see him – recognise his brutish face, even though she'd not known his colour in that dark and smelly alley in Hillbrow.

The black faces loomed largest and clearest, with an individuality that startled and was disturbing. For the first time she was aware of the watchfulness that lay below what she'd always regarded as their sullen, closed faces. She could note the misery and desperation beneath their smiles and jaunty manner, the tension that passed for detachment and insouciance.

The white faces, too, were far from relaxed as they drifted with stolid matter-of-factness about the streets. There was a grim and guarded quality about them which was heightened when their eyes locked momentarily and unwillingly with those peering out of darker faces. I'm not the only frightened animal here, she told herself. They all are – we all are. And I better get back home to Bea, who's yet to be scared of anything.

This strange awareness of everything, as if they were all under a super-analytical microscope, upset her and increased her trepidation. If they were all so insecure, how could she even hope to regain some form of composure in her new life? This unsettling realisation confirmed her plight but also pleased her, in a spiteful way. It gave her a sardonic attitude to these people who'd made her an outcast from what was so patently a panic-stricken camp. Shoring up its defences against the unknown but palpable peril by expelling dissidents – when it was too late. The rot had already festered within the laager.

But the spiteful pleasure was short-lived; it only added to her confusion. So she rushed back home earlier than intended to seek comfort from her daughter, and cower within the walls of her own prison. She now knew it could never be a sanctuary.

Chapter 20

Philip Mokone jammed the coconut-brown Panama hat with the flowered band firmly on his head, and leaned out forward from the narrow door of the bus as it whined at speed up the hill back to Sophiatown. He grinned over the rattling engine compartment and shouted at the driver enthroned in a glass-walled cab. The driver was a young man who wore his uniform cap jauntily over one eye against the blaze of the westering sun, left foot wedged negligently against the base of the windscreen. He turned a cocky head towards the shout, lifting an enquiring eyebrow at a fellow majita. Philip stretched out a hand, palm down, and moved it slowly up and down. The driver grinned, nodded and the whine of the greasy, heaving diesel engine exposed between them became a growl as the Putco bus slowed down in the line of fast-moving rush-hour traffic.

With a salute at the driver and a cheery farewell to other klevahs crowded in the narrow doorway, Philip swung with nimble grace off the bus, still growling at some speed, and ran in a curve away with mincing steps, dissipating the momentum of his leap with the jaunty elegance expected of a staff-rider. He loosened the hat and walked along an uneven pavement towards the red neon sign of the restaurant.

Fordsburg was an inner-city home to coloureds, Chinese and Indians. Streets lined with shops of all sorts, selling everything from saris to tribal blankets and *muti*; and dotted with a few curry cafés. Some of these actually restaurants, like the one he entered: a chrome and glass heaven made fashionable by the odd fact that it was patronised by whites, against all the strictures of apartheid supposedly enforced by the police station just across the busy street.

That privileged patronage alone had made this restaurant particularly popular with Indians and coloureds, who came from afar to eat in the same room as members of that envied race – and perhaps even chat. Now their eyes looked up from plates and dalliance to stare at the new arrival – some with indifference, a few with casual resentment at a Native who dared to presume he could patronise a rendezvous they would prefer to remain exclusive to white patrons, an their own sort-of-superior races.

He glanced about him, and Vivienne's red-haired head popped up from the farthest, high-backed booth. Smiling a welcome and waving a hand. Male Indian and coloured eyes widened and watched with grudging envy as he made his jaunty way towards her.

"So!" she said, as he settled down across the narrow table from her. "At last we meet again – alone!" The last word spoken in a conspiratorial whisper.

He smiled, warming to her eager and unselfconscious pleasure.

"Not quite alone. What about all these – er, baleful and curious eyes around us? And their flapping ears?"

"Oh, don't worry about them. They're getting used to us. This is becoming a favourite hands-across-the-colour-bar meeting place, you know."

"Even with Fordsburg police station just across the street?"

"The marvellous anomalies of our beloved apartheid, Philip," she laughed. "Are you nervous?"

"Me? Not if you're not. I'll take your word for it."

"How are you, Nice Time Phil?"

He grinned at her teasing and looked up as a waiter stopped and hovered over their table. They ordered coffee; too early for any curry for him.

"Exhausted," he said as the Indian waiter departed after staring down at the cleavage revealed by her summer frock. "But recovering," he added. "Now that I'm basking in your lovely presence."

"Oh – thank you very much, kind sir! I won't mention the fact that you've been avoiding me – and after seeing much more of me than the waiter has just peeked at."

"He's got taste."

They chatted about inconsequentials while the coffees were served; and – of course, he sighed – she asked questions. Wanted to know everything about what he'd been doing. He was relieved she asked nothing concerning Betty Nkosi. The sixty-four-thousand-dollar question came after they were served more coffee.

"Well, Mister Mokone," she drawled, leaning forward. "What are we going to do? Can't drink too much coffee, you know, or" – a girlish giggle – "it could keep us from getting any sleep tonight!"

He laughed, remembering the nice-time girls who sneered at flagging lovers: I would've stayed home if I wanted to just sleep!

"Well," he smiled lazily, "that's up to you, Vivienne."

"Not 'baby', like the other night?"

"If I said what's on my mind, you'll accuse me of having a one-track mind."

"Again I thank you, kind sir." But said without a coy smile, and the tone just very slightly rebuking. "Glad to hear you're back on track, Nice Time Phil."

"Will you do me a favour, baby?" he asked, tone sober. "Let's not talk about that – not just yet, anyway. Let's be relaxed and happy, Vivienne. And to hell with everybody else. The people in here and those cops across the street!"

They dawdled over more coffee, talking about everything and nothing.

An unspoken but impatient waiting for the dark.

"I think we can go now," she said later, making patterns on the plastic top of the table with foam from her espresso: funny-looking stuff he'd refused to even taste. Drinking so much ordinary coffee was bad enough when, back in Kofifi, he could've been sopping the right stuff – mahog with beer chasers …

"Yeah," he sighed. "We've been here a long time." Then laughed, in reaction to the expression on her face: "They'll begin to think we don't have anywhere to go."

"Your place?"

He hesitated, calculating the risks: a lot of people on the streets till really late – and around the backyard where he lived. All of them trying to get some fresh air on a summer evening before locking themselves up in overcrowded rooms.

"We can go to my place, if you like," she told him.

"Is it safe?"

She shrugged. "As safe as any place can ever be, Philip. Quite safe, in fact. An anonymous block of flats. We'll have to go in separately, of course." She smiled and made a comic face to mitigate what she had to add: "You'll have to use the servants' entrance and sneak up."

"I don't mind, Viv. Life-long training for that kind of – well, thing."

But it took him some time after she'd locked the door behind him for his breathing to return to something that passed for normal. He took her clumsily into his arms and kissed her, too hard, too hungry. And when she responded his hands started fumbling about her body, searching for entrances through her clothing. She broke away from him, and shook her head, slowly.

"Not yet, Philip," she said softly. "Not that blind and hurried – that easy. There's a lot we have to talk about, first. Really talk – about things."

"What?" Resentful.

"Everything – whatever you feel you can tell me."

"About what?"

"Oh, Phil! Why do you want to make it more difficult than it already is, my darling? All right, then," she said into his silence. "First, tell me why you've been avoiding me. Didn't you like the way I make love?"

"I don't know how to explain it, Vivienne ..."

"Did you decide I must be a nymphomaniac, some kind of tart, to throw myself at you like that? Or just another white liberal out for kicks?"

He shook his head quickly, noting the pain in her eyes: "No, Vivienne. Not that – whatever Boykie and especially Desmond say. But it all happened so fast – flattering, but I've been trying to work it out ever since."

"It might've helped you to sort it out by seeing me again."

"Possibly. I don't know. You see, for the past year – almost two years, now – I've lived in a state of confusion. Before that, white people were objects of hate: a simple, straightforward reaction. But now, I regard them with mixed feelings. Individuals, I suppose. Differentiating one from the other. I hate them, I pity them, I'm afraid of them, I despise them, et cetera, et cetera. Think of it, and I've felt it."

"What caused the change?"

He looked at her intently, a crazy impulse upon him. Wondering if he should tell her and pass some of the burden onto her shoulders. He decided against it: no – another way to legal suicide.

"I'm not sure what it was, Viv. But whatever it was doesn't matter. What matters is that I have changed. More confused than before."

"Before what, Philip?"

He shrugged.

"Is that why you suddenly made an appearance in what Desmond calls our corrupting, twilight world?"

"Yes. I wanted to know whites. As people, not –"

"And what awful thing did you find out? What decided you against coming again to the parties and – well, things?"

"Nothing. I mean, I don't know."

"Was it me?"

"Well," he said slowly, "you must have something to do with it."

"What I mean is – was that all you wanted? To sleep with – no, to fuck – a white woman? You must've heard the stories about what easy fucks we are. So you got what you wanted from innocent and ignorant me. And couldn't be bothered to" – a bitter snigger – "come again. Inside me. Right?"

"Don't be like that, Vivienne. You know it's not –"

"How should I know? That's what you want tonight, isn't it? After all these weeks, you've decided you want to fuck a white woman again. So you ring me, the easy fuck. And now here we are, and you're raring to ride – and then vanish again. Until you want me again in another couple of months."

They had sat down across her living room as they talked – as she interrogates me, he thought with some resentment. Now he got to his feet. He should be angry or insulted, but wasn't. Just suddenly felt tired.

"I suppose I'd better go," he said quietly.

She looked up at him from her perch on the floor. After a long moment, a smile tugged at her lips.

"Sit down, Philip Mokone."

He sat down, she scrambled to her feet and fetched him a drink. Whisky, and no questions this time about his needs.

"Okay," he said slowly after a thirsty gulp. "Let's say you're completely right. Where do we go from here? That's the thing I've been –"

"It's no great surprise if that's all you were after, Philip. A lot of the girls – white girls – go to these parties for that reason. Now, if that's all you wanted: were you satisfied? And if you were, what did you want to prove?"

He took a couple of thoughtful sips from the glass and swivelled it, making the ice cubes swirl and tinkle against its frosted sides.

"I went to that party because, as I said, I wanted to really know white people, not just as unfriendly or aloof faces in the streets and offices. Masters of my world – the whole, bloody world! – that I was expected to treat with a humble respect. Even the stupid ones, no real education, when I thought they were inferior to me. Well, I hardly made a beginning in getting to know them at that mixed, liberal party."

"Why not?" she asked, a glimmer of a smile on her lips.

"Because while I was busy observing and trying to learn, you – baby – came along."

"And distracted you from your socio-political research."

He smiled thinly at the word. She had to have been talking to Boykie about him. He remembered his flippant explanation to that other interrogator.

"Let's say you concentrated my interest from the general to the particular."

"My apologies for asking, Phil; but where did you go to school? And why, with your education are you just a –"

"That's another story, Viv. History. Let's stick to this one you're interrogating me about now. You showed an interest in me, the unknown. And I – well ... Ever read Peter Cheyney?"

"Who?" she asked, surprised and annoyed by the switch.

"An English guy who writes bang-bang detective books with titles like 'Farewell, my Lovely' and 'The Urgent Hangman'. Stories about hard-boiled guys: an English private eye called Slim Callaghan, and an FBI Special Agent, Lemmy Caution, who's always quoting the wisdom of his grandmother who lives in a hick town called Oshkosh."

"My goodness ..." Mock awe and a grin.

"Yup," he grinned back – a mock cowboy accent courtesy of Gary Cooper in High Noon. "And he calls them 'seven-minute eggs'."

"And are you hard-boiled too, Philip?" she asked, staring. Then: "No – let's not get into that right now. Point is, my boy, it's you who's digressing now!"

"No, Viv," he said earnestly. "You see, Peter Cheyney has these guys – his creations – believing that behind any mystery, there's almost always a woman. So, their policy for solving crime mysteries is cherchez la femme."

"Ooh! I am impressed – French as well, mon petit brave!"

She tried to make light of her amazement, but was indeed more surprised than impressed that this man who'd come into her life out of nowhere – this delivery-van driver – knew at least one French phrase, however trite, and pronounced it almost perfectly. She couldn't read his tight grin, but feared he'd read her thoughts from her tone and face. Oh, damn – don't spoil it, now, bitch; but how can he ...?

"Don't worry, Vivienne" – rolling the French pronunciation on his tongue – "I had to look it up, the meaning and pronunciation, in a dictionary at Boykie's place. And checked his atlas that there is a hick town in the States – Michigan, if my memory serves me right – called Oshkosh."

"Okay – apologies, darling Philip."

"As you said, my lovely Vivienne: that was a digression and I, too, apologise. Mea culpa." A wicked grin and a pause: "My one and only Latin bit." Another pause, and then without irony: "To finally answer your question, query, allegation, accusation and, well, et al," he said, laying it on thick – give you a few more surprises, to add to your damned amazement that people like me can have some education. "The idea was there, somewhere at the back of my mind: to sleep with a white woman. Though, of course, I didn't have any idea how to go about it. Klevahs from Kofifi don't quote Sakespeare to romance ladies, you see."

Her wicked grin: "I took care of that. I seduced you."

"I – slept with you. I cannot honestly say I made love to you, Vivienne."

"Just a convenient phrase everybody uses, Philip. Not shocking like 'fucking'."

She rose from the floor again, poured a whisky for herself and freshened his; then sank down on the same sofa, but at its other end. Raised her glass in a toast.

"And so," he picked up the theme, "we come to your question: What was I trying to prove, and did I? Well, I think I was trying to find out what was so different about you that the government hangs us for it."

"Six months for both of us under the Immorality Act."

"Hanging – die hangpaal – for rape. No option."

An odd, flitting look from her and he warned himself to be careful.

"And what did you find out, Phil?"

"Nothing – no difference."

"Ah!"

He smiled, looking her straight in the eye: "Only a few new ways to – let's say make love."

She laughed, blushed and looked away.

They ate a scratch meal standing at the kitchen table, Philip looking moodily out of the ninth-floor window. Down into Joubert Park at the bottom of the hill, with the lights of the city scattered beyond. Seldom been so high above the city except in those locations in the sky – one just a couple of floors above him now. And then without a chance to gaze out in leisure and comfort: tiny windows if any in the servants' quarters on the roof. And this was where it had all started, in Hillbrow. Where would it end? If it could ever end. It was life, it was living. This wondering, this continuing analysis, confusion, despair.

Maybe he should marry Betty right now and forget about it all. Go back to being just another dom, uncomplicated Native; but different – too much education, and so a cheeky kaffir. And in his haunts, een van die manne, to save him from the vulnerabilities of being a situation. Get hitched, and protect himself from everything with Betty's love, compassion and understanding. Little as she knew.

After the scratch meal, Vivienne again joined him on the couch and they sat smoking, silently engrossed in their thoughts and aloneness. She crushed out her cigarette in the ashtray and turned to him.

"Do you still want to make love to me, Phil? Or just fuck me?"

A quick glance at her, then away. Yes, whichever it was: he wanted her, but that was only his body's customary reaction.

"I don't know," he said slowly. "I desire you, yes; but I don't know if I want to – not fuck you or with you, Vivienne. It'll be more than that after these many hours, this amazing evening."

He turned fully towards her, and stretched out an arm. She shifted, and he placed it about her shoulders. "Vivienne, I –" He stopped, eyes open and intent on her face.

"Yes, Philip?"

"I was going to say I loved you."

"Then you changed your mind. Because it wouldn't be true."

"Yes, but not just another line. I am fond of you – quite sure I am. You're right. 'Love' would not be the truth. Just a way of saying thanks."

"What for? What have I done to be thanked for?"

"Just being yourself, I suppose. For the first time in my life I'm not thinking of a white person as white. I'm looking at you now, and I can see you're white. But you know what? It doesn't matter! You're just a person – a nice person. D'you understand? Really, really notch – understand?"

She hugged him: "Oh, yes – I do, Phil! I do!" And laughed: "Ek notch, my brikaid – my ma se kind!"

Surprised, looking down into her happy and mischievous face: "And where did you get that from?"

"I do my practicals in the townships – remember? So I've picked up a bit of die tsotsi-taal. A lot of it filthy, of course."

"In answer to your earlier question, my education – what it was before I had to drop out – came from the missionaries. And yours – your supplementary education – comes from the ghettoes."

"We all of us have to learn about each other – remember, Mister Researcher?" she whispered, hugging him tighter, kissing his lips and face and eyes. "You are learning, and so am I, my darling. And maybe I'm just a bit more than just fond you, Nice Time Phil!"

It was a long time before they slid between cool, starched sheets – fresh, he thought: was she expecting me between them? And when they did made love, the self-satisfaction at his male potency that he had thrilled at so much in his own room did not encompass him. They wrestled gently and with passion, and when the first of many moments came for him to come, he uttered a sound that was an anguished groan as well as a cry of triumph and happy release.

Never done that before, he told himself. That's not keeping timing, when I come from ... And, he grinned before they fell asleep, she's like a string of fire-crackers. Both of us un-in-hi-bi-ted, he rolled the word on his lips and tasted its sweetness. Free, and in a kind of paradise!

But tomorrow morning? Very early? Sneaking out and down the service lift, of course. Just another Native coming down from the location in the sky to earn a crust from the white-man-boss ...

Chapter 21

Life in the house in the back street in Doornfontein took on a smoother rhythm after Jean Griffiths made her partial surrender of Beatrice to the servant. Betty Nkosi's constant presence during the day was no longer so unsettling. She arrived every morning at first light, six days a week. She made tea for her employer, and warm milk for the toddler whose steps were getting more confident by the day. And after tidying up the suppers she'd prepared for mother and child the previous night before returning to Orlando, it was time to cook breakfast. Jean, who was now up and wrapped in a silk dressing gown, would read the newspapers that Betty had bought on her way. Then Betty washed the breakfast things and cleaned the house – thoroughly and painstakingly, although it had received a similar going-over the day before – while Jean played with and read to her baby.

Later, when Betty had strapped Beatrice into a stroller for their daily trip to the shops, Jean would have an indolent 'toilette', as she referred to it in a mock French accent. On their return from the outing, Beatrice would stagger, run, hop – and fall – about the house that was really an apartment: gurgling and grinning broadly at her energetic successes, and demanding the consolation of warm bosoms after the falls.

In the afternoons Jean would often go into the city, following Tant Sannie's stern advice: window-shopping, the cinema – never 'bioscope' to her! – or whatever took her fancy. But carefully avoiding all the tea-shops she'd once frequented with other young matrons on such expeditions. No longer the proud and insensitive Mrs Patrick Ryan. Occasionally she dared go for a walk about the neighbourhood, but wearing her plainest dresses. Tempted to take Beatrice with her for their mutual exercise, but the thought of questioning, incredulous and indignant stares discouraged her from that adventure.

The days of open defiance to one and all were over.

But the secret of Beatrice's conception remained a closed book into which only Tant Sannie had been allowed to peek. The redoubtable old lady still visited at least twice a week, and read more in the face of the beautiful but madly stubborn Engelse vroumens. To the rest of the neighbourhood, she was the eccentric woman – had to be English, man! – who insisted on a shockingly public payment for fucking with some cheeky darkie: kleurling or Native, made no difference, hey?

She would keep this secret from all of them, nosey as they were. Not asking for their sympathy, and they could think whatever they pleased. Curse as much as they liked under their breath when she walked past the damned loafers.

But the secret was not to remain exclusive much longer. Other's shameful secrets had been uncovered by coincidence, spite, mistakes, indiscretions, accidents or sheer carelessness by their keepers. Hers came to light through the group lust of the young men who speculated about their chances with her: a beautiful and shapely woman, a stuk that would normally live in a different world, beyond their wildest dreams of sexual access. But no man ever visited her, and she must just be gasping for it, hey. She would surely welcome any fokken lover, man!

All the coloured boys believed that once a white woman got a taste of true virility she would not want to bother with white men. And that belief was a nightmare for white men: the cause of murder, mayhem and lynchings. Still, some of the young white bloods who roared down the streets on motorbikes and in jalopies wanted to do the bitch a favour. After being stupid enough to give it to darkies, she'd be just too grateful for the privilege of being fucked by a white man again. Both groups prepared campaigns, and some actually set about putting them into action. She froze into retreat all those who called: an icy and polite aloofness was her only and best defence.

But one evening, when she thought the battle against all comers was won, Jean lost her temper with a belated campaigner. He was curly-haired white with the overbearing build of a rugby second-row forward. Walked past a bewildered scrum-half at the door and flopped into a chair in her living room. She sat on the edge of a settee near the door, ready for flight or a fight, and listened to the lengthy, autobiographical monologue of this proud king of the jungle.

Then he rose to his full, majestic height and plonked himself at the other end of her settee. After a discreet glance at a watch on a hairy wrist, he started wriggling closer. Big brute has a time schedule, Jean thought, and wondered why she'd put herself in this vulnerable position: on this most inviting of all the seats in the damned room. He was still talking about himself when he placed a muscular arm round her rigid shoulders. The heavy forearm bowed the shoulders – and she leant forward and slapped his cheek. He laughed softly, chidingly, and brought his other arm round.

The encirclement was too much, and Jean lost her temper. The hairy arms protruding beyond the rolled-up short sleeves of his sports shirt triggered all the loathing that had been building up at his oily, loud-mouthed bragging about athletic prowess on the field and in various beds.

She slapped him much harder and then wrestled him. They fell off the settee and onto the floor, and he rolled on top of her, his breath coming in short, excited gasps. For a moment her body went limp and numb. The weight, the heavy breathing, reminded her of that night in the alley.

Oh, no! her mind shrieked through the numbness. Oh, no ...!

And the limp body convulsed into thrashing legs, arms around the broad, muscular neck. She pulled his head down, and as he relaxed the neck muscles to accept with a smirk what he thought was a wild-eyed kiss – she sunk teeth into his meaty nose. A sadistic satisfaction at his scream and a stomach-churning revulsion at the sweaty object in her mouth and the foul breath exploding into herself. When she let go he leapt to his feet and held a hand over the bleeding nose, the eyes above it agonised, shocked and homicidal.

He stomped out of the house swearing muffled vengeance.

A week later, on a Thursday afternoon, she opened the door to an authoritative, door-rattling knock that would've been familiar to Betty and most of her neighbours. She walked to the door, annoyed, and swung it open with a sharp rebuke on her lips. It took moments to recognise the boastful sportsman and too-confident swain.

He wore a nasty smirk on his face, the peak of his khaki cap almost touching the inflamed nose. In a policeman's uniform, complete to the pistol at his hip. Two other uniformed young men stood behind him, their large bodies crowding the veranda. He was impersonal and abrupt: it had come to their official attention at the police station that she must have contravened the Immorality Act and was now living here with the issue of the said contravention. She was to come to the station with them immediately.

She looked up at him, dumbfounded. Body stiff with fury and mind chilly with a contempt that blazed out of green eyes. But she was afraid under the outrage, and it was this fear he recognised and smirked at with a cold triumph, ignoring the fury and contempt. So this was to be the vengeance he'd threatened – bastard! He is not ashamed: I'm not a white person any more, worse than a slut, something to be used to satisfy his ego and punished for resisting.

Is this how they treat their despised victims, Africans? A cold apprehension flooded her being, and the dignified stiffness ebbed from her body. What would they do – what could they do? She'd heard stories of police atrocities, but had only shrugged, like a few other millions: terrible, but not her concern.

But the voice stayed level and aloof when she responded to the summons:

"You will have to wait a few minutes while I arrange for somebody to take care of my daughter. It's my maid's afternoon off, as I'm certain you are aware."

The triumphant smirk turned into a sneer on the meaty face.

"Don't worry about that – Exhibit Number One, hey! Bring it along!"

Inquisitive faces stared from windows, doorways, gates and the street corner as she carried Beatrice down the semi-circular steps, along the short paved walk, through the gate, across the filthy pavement and into the police car waiting at the kerb. The bulky young policemen squeezed into the front seat, as if they would not contaminate themselves by sitting with her and the offensive Exhibit Number One in the back.

The black-painted car's engine was revved, its body jerked away from the kerb and it roared, burning rubber, down the street. Tall antenna snapping in the air like the sting of a scorpion – the township nickname for the Flying Squad.

Several white women waited at a tram stop outside the police station. They turned as one at the sounds of the approaching car, and stared with the stolid curiosity of those who'd seen and heard it all. Their eyes widened and elbows nudged at the sight of a white woman, pale and withdrawn, slide out, carefully carrying a coloured toddler in her arms. People along both pavements stopped and gaped.

Jean followed the constables, her tormentor leading and another in the vanguard, through the gate, up a flagged walkway bisecting neat lawns, and into the charge office. The would-be lover bursting with importance at the questioning stares directed at them and their prisoner.

"What's the matter with your eyes, Sarge?" the constable grinned, elbow on the counter. "White woman, *boesmankind* – evidence of contravening the Immorality Act, hey?" Then turned to the contravener, happy grin replaced by a sneer. "Stand over there!"

The balding sergeant behind the counter studied her with cold, brown eyes.

"That your baba?"

"Yes."

"Where did you –"

The constable cut in, barking a rephrasing of the question: "Where's the black bastard you've been fucking with? Or has he –"

The impact of the sergeant's angry brown eyes on the back of his muscular neck stopped him.

"Name?" the charge sergeant asked.

"Jean Griffiths."

He scribbled slowly on a buff charge sheet, grunting "Engels".

"Address?"

She recited.

"Age?"

"Thirty-one – no, thirty-two ..."

The sergeant grunted again as he wrote, then looked up. "Pretty girl like you should've been married a long time ago," he grumbled.

"Huh! She prefers giving it away to –"

The brown eyes restrained the constable again.

"I was married ... Divorced."

"Is dit so, hey? When – this divorce?"

"Nearly two years ago."

"Any other children?"

"No."

"Sien jy? You see, Sarge? You hear? I told you she –"

The cold eyes flickering with impatience stopped him again.

"He divorced you because of this, hey?"

"Well, yes ... In a way."

"His name?"

"Patrick Ryan."

"Address?"

She gave it to him: Patrick had moved from the apartment in Parkhurst – polluted by their few weeks of passionate love, Jean had thought when she heard from Sheila Ryan, her only occasional visitor.

"I wonder why he didn't report you," the sergeant grumbled. "And where's the – the father of this – this ..." A grimace, and gnarled finger pointing.

"I don't know."

"What's his name?"

"I don't know."

"Answer the blerry question, you fucking bitch!"

"Konstabel Piet Strydom! Shut up!" the sergeant barked, his cheeks and bald scalp reddening. "Bly stil – hoor jy my, jong?"

"Why're you so blerry polite to this whore, Sarge?" Strydom protested. "Talking to her like she's still a – she's just a fokken hoermeid for all these hotnot bushmen bastards always calling at her place!"

"Why didn't you arrest them, Constable?" she spat at him. "Conspiring to contravene your Act is a charge too, isn't it? Or were you waiting until you –"

"Shut up, you! Don't talk like –"

"Piet! You shut your filthy mouth – hoor?"

Jean's voice was cold and hard when she spoke again. "Sergeant, I don't see why I should stand here and listen to all these insults from this – this boy!"

The sergeant smiled in slow amusement. "Just as you say – er, Miss Griffiths. Just a boy, an excitable boy." The constable bridled, the sergeant grinned at him. "Now, what's this boy's name? I mean your – ag, the one who ..."

Beatrice had been lying quiet in her mother's arms, sucking a thumb and staring around in bewilderment. Now, suddenly, her mouth stretched wide – and she shrieked. They all stared in surprise at the small, tensed body and convulsed face, waiting for the wide-open mouth gasping for air to burst into another, louder shriek. She did, and other shrieks followed in a fast, ear-piercing rhythm, ricocheting off the low ceiling and walls of the charge office.

"Take it outside!" the sergeant shouted in disgust.

Jean sat on a bench, leaning her back against a rough wall.

She sat deathly still, eyes staring blankly at the gaping faces beyond the fence. She held tight onto the bawling child, a tinny ringing in her ears and tears in the corners of her eyes. She wanted to cry – loud and long, like Beatrice. Bawl out, too, for the first time against her Calvary: this needless and spiteful public crucifixion. Burst the dam and release pressure she'd been resisting for almost two years. Scream her hatred, despair and anger.

Then she shook her head violently, the yellow hair sweeping out defiantly. She turned to her Beatrice: jogging her on a knee, cooing and kissing, oblivious of the disbelief and horror on the watching faces.

Then a sudden, skirted tornado whirled round the corner, through the gate, up the flagged pathway and into the station with only a glare at the cooing mother and sobbing child. Tant Sannie's voice boomed out of the charge office and into the street, but only a few of the curses could be distinguished. Then there was a silence. After a few minutes she reappeared in the doorway.

"Kom!" she snapped at Jean. "Inside!"

Constable Piet Strydom stood a little away from the counter, staring self-consciously out of the barred window. And the sergeant was busily shuffling buff forms on the counter. Sannie led Jean past the raised flap in the counter and on into an office behind it. A uniformed officer stood irresolutely behind his desk.

"Tell him!" Sannie instructed. "Sit and tell him!"

By early evening the story was common knowledge among her neighbours and beyond Doornfontein, her thorny fountain.

Chapter 22

Betty Nkosi arrived at the house early the next morning, as usual; and let herself in, as usual. And, as usual, Jean and Beatrice were still in bed. The only change she noticed when Jean came into the kitchen for breakfast was that the face was pale and drawn, and her eyes glittered with a hard light. And she hardly spoke – not that she'd ever been a great one for conversation with kitchen girls. She glanced quickly through the newspapers Betty had, as usual, brought with her; then settled back into a chair with a sigh of relief at not finding whatever she'd been searching for with anxiety. And when Betty prepared for her daily shopping expedition, she was told not to take Beatrice along for the usual breath of fresh air and healthy sunshine.

Now this was unusual, but Betty did not question the instruction. She met Janey at the gate, which was not unusual. But the bright smile Janey turned on her was, most definitely. They had ignored each other elaborately after a short and sharp confrontation when the coloured woman from the back rooms of the house accused the Native of stealing her job – and was warned that another word would unleash physical retribution.

"Hoe is sy vandag?" Janey asked and then switched from her native tongue to English: "How is she today, hey?" Glancing slyly towards the front door. "Is your Missus okay, hey?"

"Ja, sy is goed. Waarom nie?" Betty replied.

But Janey preferred to show off her grasp of English: "Where were you yesterday afternoon, then?"

"My half day. What about it?"

"Ag yes – sheila's day. But you work every day except Sunday."

"That's got nothing to do with you."

An accusing finger, pointing: "You asked for it, hey? So you not here when it happened!"

"What are you talking about, old woman? Have you forgotten what I told you before, eh? If you want a –"

"You Naytiff girls think you so fly, hey?" Janey cackled – and then quickly added, as Betty moved ominously closer: "Don't try that, my girl, or my Basil will give you a moerse klap! You get very bad trouble you touch me!"

Betty stared, the anger past and replaced by a puzzled curiosity: "What are you talking about, Janey?" she asked with deliberate patience.

"Her, of course! Don't you know she was arrested yesterday?"

"What!"

"Oh, yes – she was and I see it all! That nose-in-the-air Engelse lady! Flying Squad car pick her up, all right, and the baba. Immorality Act!"

"Oh, I see," Betty said slowly. "And that pleases you, eh? Because she sacked you for talking too much – and being lazy!"

"Hah! You think I worry about doing a Naytiff girl's job?"

Betty ignored the insult. "Then why are you so glad?"

"Because now everybody know God's truth, man!"

"Which is what? Look, old woman, I don't have time to waste with your skinder. If you got something to tell me, speak."

"One of your brothers did it – raped her! That's God's truth, man! That's how she come to be staying here with us!"

Janey laughed at the stricken expression that came into Betty's eyes. She turned and hurried to the backyard of the house, her own domain.

Betty walked slowly up the street, trying to analyse her reaction to what she'd understood from Janey's gleeful gossip. The frumpy woman was a malicious skinderbek, and this knowledge made Betty doubt the veracity of what she'd said. The doubt was important, for it stopped her from accepting the conclusion to which her mind had immediately jumped. She told herself that even if Janey's story was true, it did not have to be the woman Philip raped. Johannesburg was a big city, and plenty of other women were raped.

Whoever had, she felt an overwhelming compassion, and a new understanding for Jean Griffiths. Strong emotions, but of minor importance to what she felt for baby Beatrice – poor child!

Was this Philip's baby? Was that why she had felt such a strange affinity with this luckless child from the very beginning? No, that was like believing in miracles. Miraculous coincidences.

Philip had finally – when he was ready – confessed the guilt bedevilling him. Told her the rape was in Hillbrow, so it would had to have been a woman who lived in that very laanie suburb … She knew a girl who worked in Hillbrow, near Clarendon Circle where it happened. She must find her and ask. But it was a long time ago. And what was Miss Griffiths going to do, now?

This woman was so obviously out of place in Doornfontein among these poor whites and coloureds. There had been an atmosphere of a fortress about the house when she started working there. A state of siege: mother and child keeping themselves to themselves, even with herself at the start … And this morning, that same atmosphere. Surely they could not remain indoors year after year because of – no, can't be my Philip! Move? That wouldn't solve anything. They would be found out again, or the story would follow them. Move again after that? Oh, Philip – Philip! What have you done, Philip?

No. She must not accuse him before she was certain. Even then, accusing him would be the wrong thing to do. He'd been close to tears when he spilt out his anguish …

Betty was still mulling over her doleful thoughts as she returned from the shops, and did not see Tant Sannie until the large woman barked out her name. She looked up into the broad, high-cheekboned face.

"Goeie môre, Missus," she responded.

"What're you looking so – so sorrowful about, Betty?"

"Oh – I'm not looking like that, Missus."

"Don't lie to me, my girl. I got eyes to see. You heard I suppose?"

"Yes."

"So?"

"It is very bad, Missus. I feel so sad for the Madam."

"Hah. I believe you. Even if I don't know why you should be sad."

"I'd feel sad whoever it was, Missus."

"Because it was one of your boys did it?"

"No, Missus. Just because it was done."

"Hah, I do believe you. You're a strange girl, Betty. Any other girl would be grinning like a monkey and cackling like a hen laid a big egg. Just like Janey."

"Yes, Missus."

"Now you see why our government must hang your people when they do a thing like this, hey?"

"Yes, Missus ..."

"You agree?"

"Well – I don't know about these things, Missus."

"Hah! What do you think they should do about such things?"

"Hanging is too much, Missus. And they don't do it when – when ..."

Appreciative laughter rumbled in Tant Sannie's big-breasted chest.

"Well? Why don't you say it?" she demanded. "They don't hang white men when they do it to you?"

"Yes, Missus."

"That would be the day, all right. You hear anything in the locations about this? The time it happen, hey?"

"No, Missus."

"Hah. You wouldn't tell me even if you had. Not any one of you tell the truth."

"Missus? Where did she live before – the Madam?"

"What? Oh, in Parkhurst, I think."

"I see. Is that where it happened?"

"So you know something, hey?"

"No, Missus. I just wanted to know."

"Well, it happened in Hillbrow. That's where she lived, then."

"I see ..."

"Well? What d'you know about that?"

"Nothing, Missus. These things happen all the time."

"Yes – the horny, black bastards. But the Madams aren't all so crazy they have the babies ... All right, Betty. Now you go back in there – and be good to her, hoor? Don't say a word to her about anything."

The conversation with Sannie Fourie convinced Betty that, indeed, Beatrice was – could be – Philip's child. Would that make her Beatrice's stepmother after they married? she wondered, distracted.

Still, she visited Hillbrow that evening and talked to several kitchen girls in the area around Clarendon Circle. The approximate dates and descriptions tallied, but the names did not. But the surname mentioned was that of the woman who'd offered her the job – Sheila Ryan. They were sisters-in-law, maybe ...

Betty went home late to Orlando, on a train crowded with commuters who were preyed upon by tsotsis. *Izigebengwa* studied her manner, nodded and pushed past: not just any moll, this one, but a cherry with the right brothers, cousins and friends – a juba who was one of die real manne, maybe, to look down her nose at them.

She would think it all out first, before she met Philip again. Her beloved juba ... Couldn't face him, otherwise. Decide if she was going to tell him. And if she was going to tell him, when – and how.

A new, subtle tension developed imperceptibly between the servant and mistress. Betty was by nature a direct person, and the impulse that rose in her after she heard the tragic story was to commiserate immediately with Miss Griffiths. She suppressed it on instructions from Tant Sannie, but still had to constantly fight the urge, sensing that Miss Griffiths would, anyway, reject the sympathy. And fearing that she might herself say too much in any attempt at consolation. This made their usually sparse talk more clipped and forced.

What distressed Betty most was the new clarity with which she perceived Jean's every action – which was more a lack of any action. A clarity brought on by her compassion – and guilt by association. Beatrice brought out a different and more anguished reaction. Every time she was alone with the child, which was seldom and briefly in these taciturn days, Betty felt like bursting into tears and smothering the chubby cheeks with kisses.

Jean had realised as soon as Betty returned from the shops the first morning that she'd heard the gossip missing from the newspapers. This she'd expected, and had resolved never to allow her servant any opportunity to bring up the scandal in any way. She was taken aback, though, by what she saw of Betty's silent reaction – mourning – when she entered the house. The large brown eyes which had in the past looked respectfully past hers when they spoke – as she gave instructions and received their confirmation – now stared her fully in the face, filled with a compassion which showed unexpected depths of feeling. She told herself with irritation that this should not surprise her: she'd known for some time now that they too could have depths of emotion. But that this girl should care so much about her plight moved Jean, although she remained annoyed and humiliated.

Occasionally – until she forced herself to stop noticing – she caught Betty looking at her with eyes filled with such a sad understanding and sorrow, that her defences against any invasion of her privacy were almost breached. The impulse would rise in her to throw herself upon that comfortable-looking bosom, and assuage her anger and despair with a flood of unchecked tears. And so absorb all the compassion brimming in those dark eyes. Here was one who cared and understood.

But this she would definitely never allow. She could dismiss the girl; but that in itself would be an admission of defeat. She need not employ anybody. There was not really so much housework that she couldn't cope. But what would nosey Sheila say on her next visit, whenever that would be?

Living without a servant would tie her down completely. It would provide an excuse not to go out among the people who'd disowned her; but she needed to go out and observe their unrecognised or sublimated terror of 'die swart gevaar'. Watch and learn to live with her own.

Betty sat on the edge of the bed in a night-dress she kept in Philip's room, watching every move he made as he undressed and carefully hung up his clothes in the narrow wardrobe and on the peg behind the door.

"Philip."

"What is it, sweetheart?" he asked, her tone making him to glance at her.

"I think I'm going to leave that job."

"Why? Too much work?"

"Nothing like that, Philip. It's just that – well, I can't go on working for her."

"What's the matter?"

"I feel sorry for the poor woman."

"There we go again. Betty, she's doing what she wants! She made her bed, as they say, and has to lie in it. You know what I mean?"

"Yes I know. But it's not what she wants, the way we thought. The poor woman!"

"Oh, come on – look, Betty," he said, sitting down wearily on a chair by the lamp-lit table. "I know you've got a very big heart, sweetheart; big and forgiving. Which is why I love you so much. But all this opening it for the whole world is –"

"It's your child, Philip."

"What!"

"She's the woman you … raped."

"Hey?"

"It's true, Philip. I've checked."

"Jesus Christ!"

Awe in his voice tinged with disbelief, amusement, excitement, bitterness … Then he laughed. Loud, long, gasping and gagging laughter that was torn out of his heart. Tears clouded his bulging, staring eyes. He bent over on the chair, held his knees – and he laughed. The sound that was not really laughter died slowly from his lips, but the hysterical merriment continued within. Distorting his face, splitting his sides and weakening the tightly-held knees. When he stopped, the silence was abrupt, the effort painful. He gasped, and then stared at Betty with hooded eyes. He knew what she was going to say, the bleeding heart.

"You must not laugh, my dear. It's more than sad."

"You think I'm laughing?" he asked in a voice hoarse from the sounds that had erupted from his being. "Do you call that laughter, Betty?"

"It is terrible, Philip."

"Why must you leave her?"

"Because – because she and I … We feel something very strong and difficult between us. You won't understand and I can't explain, Philip. But it is there. And then there's Beatrice. Your child, Philip."

"Tell me about her – the child."

"Do you want to see her?"

"No."

"I can arrange for you to see her when I take her out for a –"

"No, dammit! Didn't you hear me?"

"A father should know his children, Philip."

"Oh my God, Betty! What kind of animal do you think I am? Eh? Do you really think I don't care?"

"I care, too, my dear – for all of you with my big-big heart. That is why I cannot go on seeing the two of them six days a week. If I do, I'm going to say or do the wrong thing one of these days."

"What a bloody, fucking awful mess!" he said angrily, lighting a cigarette, blowing smoke at the roof without a ceiling and keeping brooding eyes up there. "Just when – when I thought I was getting there … Getting to where I could forget it all! I wish you hadn't taken that damned job, whatever the big money!"

"Don't you wish you had not done what you did instead?"

"What?" he asked, turning about with a jerk to glare at her. "Not done it – raped her? I don't know, Betty. Maybe I do, maybe I don't. I just don't know, dammit." And then grinned in amazement. "But this is all crazy! Why did she have the baby? She could have got an abortion, easy. What a crazy bitch!"

"You should be sorry for her, Philip."

"Oh, that I am, my sweet. That I definitely am. I am sorry for her – and for myself, too," jabbing his chest. "And all of us in this mad country! She was crazy to follow through like this, and I was crazier to do what I did to her, the craziest woman among them! But am I sorry? Is she sorry? If you can answer those questions, Betty Nkosi, you'll be the wisest person living."

"She must have wanted a baby very badly. She didn't have children before."

"And of course I must have wanted a white … Oh, never mind. Never mind, Betty!"

At the end of the month, Betty gave her notice. She did not explain why she was leaving, and Jean did not ask. She paid her a month's salary in lieu of notice, and told her she should leave immediately. Just before Betty left the house, the two women stared at each other from across the living room. For a long, silent and communicative moment. Then Betty walked quickly away from the front door and towards her former mistress, but at the final moment she hesitated and instead kissed the baby Jean held in her arms.

Philip retired into the shell he had been emerging from. He found it a different shell, more confining, and pinching at the raw edges of his conscience. The woman had come back to haunt him again. Not a nameless, faceless ghost, but a human being like himself. With a known name and a personality. Now there was the baby too. His baby. His own flesh and blood. The fruit of his hatred and vengeance. Different from the others he had disowned and shut out of his mind. He hoped and prayed he would never, ever set eyes on either of them.

Chapter 23

Philip walked through the gate in the corrugated-iron fence that had been corroded by years of neglect into a flecked, rusty colour streaked with its original prison grey. He made his way across a yard that was always muddy to the door, guarded with jealous pride, behind which was a room without any trace of Sophiatown, but an atmosphere of suburbia. The room in which his childhood friend held court, he thought with ironic amusement – at the pun, and at Boykie Courtroom's isolation from real life.

Saturday afternoon, the first full day of the weekend: another surcease from labouring for Whitey. He should still be drinking among his peers in the Syrian and Lebanese shebeens of the city slums – cheaper and better booze than those in Kofifi – and catching up with the week's wake-up gossip. These were fairly neat shebeens owned by honorary whites, and nothing like this smelly *s'godi*, where a few skokiaan drinkers were already dotted about the yard. Renegades who risked arrest by refusing to drink in municipal beer halls: dedicated soppers who insisted on a decently potent brew, even when it was called 'kill-me-quick'.

And they could insist, he grinned, that boozing here was a defiance campaign, since beer-hall profits from weak kafferbier went to the municipality, local arm of the Nat government, and so funded bloody apartheid.

He was back in Sophiatown this early after a morning's labour to avoid the rude camaraderie of his peers. Afraid that mahog or any other alcohol he swilled would only heighten the new anguish that had settled in him after the shattering news delivered by Betty. Maybe loosen his tongue to tell any gathering of klevahs that the mother of his latest child was white ... Bragging all the way to die hangpaal inside Pretoria Central – 'new lock' as oldies called that prison.

Boykie wore old clothes and had been on his hands and knees, polishing the linoleum floor of his cosy room. Jazz pulsed from the radiogram, and the furniture was in an ordered disarray: chairs piled one on top of another, the coffee table lying with legs in the air on the bed like a dissatisfied nice-time girl.

"Hi, klevah – how's it, man?" he asked cheerily when he opened the door after demanding the identity of his caller. "I don't know about you, boy, but some of us got to do housework too at weekends. Just like the aunties."

"You're doing some schoolgirl out of a few bob, Boykie."

"You don't use them, wiseguy! The nice-time sisters clean up for you, don't they? Or maybe now it's only Betty – who's a professional, and can do an excellent job. Well, I also like a good job done, which no lazy, don't-care-a-damn schoolgirl or even location girlfriend is going to do."

"Aah, you're just too fussy," Philip replied, placing his hand on one of the chairs in the pile. "Can I use this?"

"Not yet, boy. Better sit on the bed. I'll be finished in a few minutes."

They talked desultorily as Boykie completed the polishing, and carefully wiped each single piece of furniture before returning it to its precise place. Then he put a new batch of records in the player and made tea: too early for booze, according to his suburban clock. They sat sipping tea and listening to music.

"So, klevah … How's your love life, eh?"

"Oh, it's there, boy. It's there, my brikaid."

"How's Betty?"

"She's fine."

"And Vivienne?"

"Saw her a couple of weeks ago."

"You want me to change the topic?"

"No, Boykie. It's along those lines I want to talk to you … I got a dog on my back I need to shake off." Maybe bitch, but 'dog' was Boykie's phrase.

"How's that?"

Philip smiled, a lopsided grimace. "It's a big, black dog – no, a big, white bitch. And it's going to need some serious shaking off."

"Vivienne? What's she done? Or have you, you fucking moerskont –"

"No, not Vivienne. She's done nothing and I've done nothing to her – we like each other too much for that. It's – well, some other white woman."

"Oh? Do I know her?"

"No."

"You mean you've been operating on your own?"

"No, and I better end the suspense there. This is a woman I've never met – I mean, like you meet people, you understand."

"Like the real English say," Boykie grinned, holding out a hand to be shaken: "We haven't met, have we old boy?"

"A white woman I raped about three years ago."

"You!"

"That's right, Boykie. Me, Nice Time Phil with the cherries chasing me."

"I can't believe it! I mean, you're not a fucking hooligan, man!"

Philip shrugged and started: "Walking through Hillbrow on a dark night. Near Clarendon Circle."

"And …?"

"I saw her. And I raped her."

"Just like that?"

"Yes. I was so angry about what went wrong with the kitchen girl, you see."

"So you – no ... Tell me more, boy."

"Quiet street, nobody around. Dragged her into a dark alley – I think she was just going into it. And raped her."

"Jesu Christo, Phil!"

"The usual things followed, of course. The gattas picked up all the usual suspects they could find within a mile. Including me, in a basement shebeen. Gave us a really rough night. But she couldn't identify anybody – didn't even come round for an ID parade. So the bastards released us. But I haven't been – released, I mean. To myself, you understand. I'm not going to hang for her; but I'm in a worse prison than death row."

"And it's taken you this long to want to talk about it ..."

"I thought I'd got rid of it – got so used to this prison inside me. Maybe, I've been telling myself, it wasn't there any more. Or been released, by Betty and Vivienne. I was looking for the key when I asked you to take me to that party."

"I see ..." Boykie said softly, examining broad hands and their spatulate fingers. It was a while before he spoke again. "I should be shocked and disgusted, but I'm not, Phil. Not really."

"You mean you expected me to do a thing like that?"

"I've been expecting you to do something – to blow up."

"Why?"

"A lot of little things, Phil. I can't explain ..."

"Do you think I was – well, wrong?"

"It's still a crime, isn't it? Of course you were fucking wrong! Isn't that why you want to talk about it today? So long after the – dastardly event?"

"I suppose so, boy," Philip said in a weary voice. "But I'm not sorry I did it, my ma se kind. Oh, I'm sorry for her, of course. Now – now, I really am sorry for the bitch. When I did it – well, she was just standing in for all these white people I wanted to avenge myself against. She didn't matter."

"But she matters now?"

"Yes."

"Why?"

"I have – I've heard … Never mind about that, Boykie. But tell me what you think about a guy like me doing such a thing to –"

"Get back at them? 'Vengeance is mine, saith the Lord', my broer. I'm not a Bible fan; but that's right, Philip Mokone. It doesn't work. Maybe that's why you say you didn't get what you wanted from doing it. But explain that first."

"Well, just doing it was enough revenge. In a way. I dragged one of their spotless queens into the gutter, through the mud. I had to do something to show them. That's what I wanted to do. But I also failed, Boykie. I expected to get a helluva kick from it. And I didn't get anything like that. Just guilt and misery. A new look at life, I suppose you can say."

Boykie Courtroom said angrily: "Did you really think you could hurt them – all of them – by raping some poor woman?" They've already forgotten all about it, Phil … But I bet she hasn't forgotten!"

"That's why I'm sorry for her. When I think of her as a person."

"A-ha! Those are the key words, my friend. It's all different when you think of her 'as a person'. Not as a – a representative of the oppressors. But it's taken you almost three years, you say. To think about her that way."

"No, that's not correct. I have thought about her in that way before. But she didn't mean a thing, even then." A rueful grin: "But now she's even got a name."

"Wasn't her name in the newspapers at the time?"

"I don't know. I didn't look to see."

"No, of course not. The names are always kept secret … You want me to speak my mind, Philip? Tell it like I see it, boy?"

"Okay, Boykie?"

"I don't blame you for doing such a terrible thing. No. This country's so criminally mixed up there's justification for almost anything. You were wrong, but you were justified – sort of. Like our big-shot hooligans wielding three-star knives and guns around here, preying on other victims. I don't condemn them for the God-awful things they do. They're not really responsible."

A wry smile pulled the corners of Philip's lips at being compared to tsotsis.

"You're more complicated than they are, of course," Boykie added.

"Now I am. Before, I was just another klevah who –"

"Don't kid yourself, pal! You were not – ever! Not with all that missionary education in you. Remember? We shared that education – reading their books about schoolboys in England while we lived in locations. You're much more frustrated than those bloody tsotsis. Just like I am."

So he knows himself – a bit, anyway. But that wasn't a subject to chase after now, Philip decided. He was the one under the microscope.

"Well, I used to be uncomplicated then – I believed. I just hated them. Okay, maybe more than other klevahs. Mine was such an intense hatred it used to give me cramps in the stomach and strike me dumb – unable to talk to them. Like when I was arrested for a night special pass, or something stupid like that. The rest of the boys could talk their way out with the usual flattery and stuff. But I couldn't. I was full of hate. I wasn't afraid of getting beaten up, you understand. Just afraid of the – the humiliation … defiling me like I wanted to defile them. D'you know what I mean? That they'd do something to me, after which I'd be too ashamed to look at myself in the mirror."

"I understand, boy," Boykie said quietly. "Emotional emasculation. No man wants to be emasculated; he'll give up anything but never his balls."

"Well, maybe that's it. Anyway, it ended that night – the fear. After I raped her. You remember that Sunday I found you here with Desmond – when he congratulated me for my liberation? After I said I pitied white people? I began feeling like that after we were picked up that night. Kicked into the charge office and jammed into cells. I wasn't angry or ballsed up any more. I just pitied them."

"Yes, I sort of remember. I didn't understand what you two were talking about – then. But I worked it out."

Did you really, Boykie Courtroom? He wondered.

"So the good news, Phil, is that you did get something from doing such a terrible thing to an innocent woman."

"But at what a price, Boykie? Three years of twisting and turning, trying to get this dog off my back!"

Boykie grinned, clasped his neck with one hand and swung the other in the air.

"Twisting in the wind, boy – hung out to dry!"

Philip was not amused. "Desmond said I was free. But free to do what? How long d'you think I'd survive if I started behaving like a free man? Behaving like a white man? That's what they'd call it, even if they aren't free themselves."

Boykie smiled his appreciation. "You can still surprise me, Phil. I mean, I've come to think of you so much as just another bright klevah I forget you can be – well, let's say profound. And cunning – asking me to take you to the party, to get an idea how supposedly free people live and behave!"

"Something like that, Boykie."

"And what did you find?"

Philip smiled. "Just another prison – a big, luxurious solitary confinement area. Where everybody's – what's the phrase? Not stir-crazy. Jail-happy."

Boykie took some time before responding.

"Maybe you're right, Phil. Fresh eyes and a different perspective – that kind of thing ... But was that all? Was screwing Viv any help?"

Annoyance passed at the question. Vivienne was one of those rare girls whose intimacies he did not want to discuss with anybody.

"In a way," he replied. "It showed me that I wasn't just after that other one's white body, her whiteness ... Do you remember when you were a kid and had to drink castor oil every Saturday morning? I had to, anyway. And afterwards my mother gave me a spoonful of sugar to get rid of that awful taste. Vivienne was like that for me – sweet, but the taste of castor oil remained. Belching it out now and again."

"Ja, I remember that horrible after-taste ..."

"At least," Philip grinned, "not the first time, but later."

"And what gives between you two now?"

"Nothing – I don't know. She's done something else for me. She broke down the wall of my prison. That's what she said she wanted to do, and she did. But it's been repaired, now," he added bleakly. "Rebuilt. Reinforced."

"How? What's happened?"

"I can't tell you, boy," Philip said listlessly. Then he smiled slowly, slightly. "At least, not now. Not yet."

He stood up, bright, cheerful and rubbing his hands briskly.

"So – Boykie Courtroom?"

"Don't call me that. Not here, not now when we've been discussing –"

"To hell with that! Why don't I go out and get us a bottle – real moonshine, no korea about it? Hey, my ma se kind? Warm up and be merry, because tomorrow ..."

He shrugged and shook his head, angry.

"I think that's a very good idea, Phil!" Boykie said quickly. "After all, it's the weekend and" – a glance at the clock on the wall – "the sun's about to go below the yard-arm, as they say in the Royal Navy!"

Chapter 24

The first gaggle of girls from garment factories hidden in back streets across the city centre, in Doornfontein and those other white working-class semi-suburbs he avoided, came noisily round the corner towards the line of silent buses waiting to take Sophiatown's workers home. The women were laughing and talking aloud, but the sounds became muted and coquettish as they approached the loose bunch of bus conductors, drivers, dispatchers, queue marshals and inspectors in Putco dust coats; and the klevahs, die manne and die real manne who'd completed their day's business, legal and illegal, in the city and were now dressed to kill in wake-up outfits. They hung about the terminus for whatever diversion it could offer, and to spot new talent from the factories.

Philip was leaning against the wall of the row of Indian-owned shops, the coconut-brown Panama hat at an angle to keep the sun out of watchful eyes. He glanced at his watch as the cherries approached, nodding at the men they knew and casting speculative looks at those who interested them: potential *mashetla.* Friday afternoon, and high jinks about to start in Kofifi. Quarter past four, fifteen minutes after the clothing factories closed. He began walking slowly up and down the long queue, searching for her face, hoping he'd recognise it.

The queue's convoluted length had disappeared around the corner from Diagonal Street when he finally spotted her.

"Hello, Maggie," he said in a quiet voice.

She recognised his voice and held her head stiffly for a moment; then turned it slowly to face him. The big eyes in her smooth, plump face gazed at him with wary surprise.

"Hello, Philip."

"I want to talk to you, Maggie."

The shoulders stiffened, and a resentful light came into her eyes. "What about?"

"I can't tell you here," he said in a voice that tried to hide its plea, eyes flicking at the flapping ears ahead and behind her in the queue. "Come and have a coffee or something with me in the café."

"Hah!" she said, tone hardening and voice too loud for his liking. "And lose my place in this queue?"

"I can fix it with the inspectors to –"

"Anyway, I haven't got time for such things. My children are waiting for me."

"Please, Maggie. I must talk to you."

"What about, after all this time? I'm not a nice-time sister, you know."

"I know that," he replied, holding back his rising impatience. He remembered the days and nights when she was one. "It won't take long. But it's important."

"Say it here."

"Oh, come on, Maggie! We can't talk here with all these people –"

"I don't have time!"

"I'll put you in a taxi, Maggie."

"Have you forgotten that I'm now a –"

"Hey, klevah! Leave her alone!" A hard, challenging voice behind Philip. "Don't you know she's somebody's wife?"

Philip turned warily, body tensing, and looked at the speaker. A young man he knew only by sight; one of the real men, and not a particular enemy.

"She was just going to remind me, broer," Philip said in a flat voice. "But not yours – right?"

"Then why don't you leave her alone? You can hear she doesn't want to talk – not to you, anyway."

"Look, broer, she's a grown woman. She doesn't need your help."

The man's cold, spiteful eyes moved from Philip to Maggie, then back. "That's right, isn't it, klevah?" he jeered. "You want all the grown women, nice-timer!" His eyes turned to Maggie: "Do you want to talk to this klevah, my sister?" he asked. "Just say the word and I'll be too glad to get rid of this moerskont."

Philip sighed and stood back, the people around them shuffled farther away.

"Look, man," he said, voice harder. "I don't want to make dust, okay? You don't know me, and I haven't done anything to you."

The man laughed. "I don't know you, eh? But never mind – you've done something to her, moerskont. Or have you forgotten, pretty boy? She's a respectable, married woman these days. A nice ousie who doesn't run after klevahs any more. I don't want you spoiling her name with your sweet talk, jy notch. So scram."

Philip turned to Maggie, a question in his slitted eyes. Her large brown ones reflected unease and embarrassment at being the centre of so much attention. Also a growing fear that she would be involved in violence that would do as much to spoil her name as anything else.

"Maggie, please!" he whispered, urgently. "Let's get away before ... I must –"

"I said scram! Vamoose, klevah," the voice, turned sibilant, cut in. "Unless you want some dust flying and then the hospital – if you're lucky."

The young man tapped Philip's shoulder – hard.

"I don't want a fight with you," Philip said slowly, eyes casting over the curious and expectant faces that had formed a ring about them. Not one that looked like it might intervene. "I'm finished with that kind of thing."

"Oh, is that so?" the man sneered. "Then do what I say."

"Okay, Philip," Maggie said hurriedly into the strained silence. "Let's go."

A sigh rippled through the disappointed crowd as Maggie pushed her way through the circle, Philip behind. He felt weak and light-headed with anger and mortification. As they walked away, he heard running footsteps behind and swivelled violently, resigned to a fight that was now inescapable.

He relaxed, relieved, when he recognised the running man: Boykie Nine Years, face congested with fury.

"What's the matter with you – you fucking bastard?" Boykie demanded, disgust knitted into his face. "You let a punk like that – just a tsotsi – Come! Let's go back and fix him!"

"No, Nine Years," Philip said without any hope of explaining himself. "I don't want to fight him. I don't feel like fighting anybody."

"You can't do that, Phil!" Boykie exclaimed in a shocked voice. "You can't let a loud-mouth bastard like him talk to you like that. I just heard, man. What about your reputation? What's going to happen when –"

"Never mind my reputation, boy. I just don't feel like it."

Philip turned away, walked into the café – rickety tables, faded and cracked or with torn plastic covers – and across to the table where Maggie was already seated. Curious glances at him from customers who couldn't help overhearing the furious distress of Boykie Nine Years. They sat in silence while he tried to regain his composure. He fetched them cups of lukewarm coffee.

"You've really changed, Philip."

"Maybe."

"I thought – I heard you'd come to like fighting."

"I don't need that any more."

"But you may still have to fight that one. They're not going to let you forget it – you know that. Everybody will be talking. And you have spoiled my name, Philip."

"I'm very sorry, Maggie."

"For the second time," Maggie added. "The first time was bad enough."

"That's what I wanted to talk to you about. The first time."

A short, bitter laugh broke from her heavy lips.

"What about it? I've been hearing you've got a girl from Orlando, now. Not a Soph'town rubberneck, but a serious girl. And you might even marry her. And without making her pregnant first – what you did to stupid me, and maybe a dozen others."

"Please, Maggie." He said softly. "I'm sorry for a lot of things I've done, and that is one of them."

"Don't forget the others – if you can even remember their names."

"How is she?"

"Who?"

"My daughter."

"Your what? Your daughter? She's mine, Philip – me and Tommy. When he married me, she became his daughter! You lost interest when my belly –"

"I want to see her, Maggie. I've never seen her."

"Never! Not if I can do anything about it."

"Please, Maggie, I'm asking you with all my –"

"No, Philip," shaking her head, resolute. "You leave us alone."

"It's important, Maggie. I must see her; talk to her. Please."

"Why?"

"Because she's my –"

What? he asked himself. Because she's my flesh and blood? That's just why I didn't want to see her, or any baby. When she told me about her pregnancy, when any of them told me … I didn't care; wanted to forget.

"I don't know how to explain, Maggie," he went on, avoiding her hostile stare – not so much hostile, he hoped, as forbidding. "But it's important. For me," he ended in a lame appeal.

"That's too bad," she said, voice sharp and rising from the table. "Suddenly, after all these years, you remember that you're a … Are you going to try and see all the others too? If you still remember their mothers and where they live, now? I'm going now, Philip. And don't worry about the taxi. I can pay for it myself."

He was not surprised at her refusal; she was right. When she'd brought him the news, frightened and lost, he'd fobbed her off. At least he'd not denied the baby was his, as he already had done with others – the done thing among klevahs and other seducers. He'd paid the damages demanded by her distraught parents, and convinced himself that payments ended these episodes.

He would now have to take up her departing, jeering challenge: meet some of his unknown offspring, after all. One or two, anyway. If he could find them. Had to get at least a glimpse of what his own offspring had blossomed or wilted into. Just a glimpse, an inkling – if he was lucky. He'd see nothing if the mothers were like Maggie. Maybe find them and observe from a distance …

The remains of a barbed-wire fence drooped, and all that was left of a gate were rusty iron posts – which also drooped at discouraged angles. Beyond was a long, narrow stretch of hard-packed earth, with a dripping tap at its centre. Stretching along two sides of the yard, and blocking its end, were what appeared to be dilapidated barracks; but open doors and tiny windows indicated they were one-room homes. Mothers sitting beside the doors and fanning themselves as they gossiped with neighbours and visitors; listless children playing in the yard late on a sultry Saturday afternoon.

Philip turned into the yard, which was littered with smoking braziers on which suppers would be cooked. Nearby were heaps of ash and piles of coal; broken toys and other flotsam from the crowded lives of families crammed into the single rooms. He ducked past wet laundry flapping from rope and wire lines that criss-crossed above the barren earth. Grinned and avoided little girls in torn dresses chased by tough little boys, who already modelled themselves on Soph'town's street-corner heroes.

He watched the boys closely, knowing – fearing – one of them was most likely his own son. Miniature tsotsis, he shuddered. Hundreds of them all over the Golden City's townships; unknown thousands. And he'd never before been disturbed by their existence – kids, but with faces as old as slum time. He called out at one of them, hoping this sneer-faced little bastard was not his own.

But what can you expect – when you ditched them?

The boy stopped warily at a safe distance and hard, inquisitive eyes quickly, but cheekily, examined his face and then his can't-get clothes. The Panama hat with a floral band just like Frank Sinatra wore in the movies; the off-white cashmere cardigan; the colourful shirt patterned with palm trees that could only be from Hawaii, where half-naked cherries shake their hips doing the hula without a hoop; tan trousers designed for holidays in Palm Beach, Florida; and those two-tone Florsheims seen on the feet of smart-sharp Yanks in *Esquire* magazine. The boy grinned up at Philip.

"Heita, my groot brikaid – een van die real manne!" the boy piped up in what he believed was a gruff and tough voice. But fluent in die tsotsi-taal. "Howzit there, my brikaid?"

The wake-up greeting he himself used all the time, and had heard from even younger kids than this precocious one. He'd found the make-believe amusing in the past; but now it, and the tough-guy manner, only annoyed him. But he smiled down, holding back an impulse to slap the face. Definitely no angel with a dirty face.

"Ja, my laaitie," he responded. "You know Meisie?"

"Sure, that door," the boy pointed. "But she don't sell mahog or anything, you know," he added knowingly. "The shebeen's over there – but not for majita like you – just KB and that kind of kaffir –"

"Thanks, sonny."

"Aah…!" the boy drawled, pulling a face. "Do yourself a favour, groot man. Don't call me 'sonny' or laaitie. Jy notch, broer?"

"Why – my laaitie?"

"You get killed for that kind of thing."

"Okay, tough guy," Philip said, shaking his head and walking towards the door the boy had indicated. I wasn't like that at his age. Nobody was. The door was slightly ajar and he knocked.

"Kena – come in!" the voice of an elderly woman said from within.

He took off the Panama hat, pushed gently and slowly at the door and entered the quiet gloom of a room crowded with dilapidated furniture. The woman sat on a grass mat, fanning herself, under the open window which provided some ventilation.

"Good afternoon, Mama," he said in respectful Tswana.

"Dumela, ngoana oa ka," she responded, but her watery eyes not expressing any maternal feeling towards anybody's son. Seen everything already, Philip thought: tougher than that bloody laaitie …

"What do you want?" A pointed demand, but spoken with caution.

"I wanted to see Meisie, Mama."

"Meisie?" Not surprised, just wearily curious. "She went to the shops. Who are you, my boy? Do I know you?"

"Philip – ba mpitsa Philip Mokone, Mama. Maybe you remember –"

"Ah-ha! Y-e-s … I thought you looked – I knew it was you." The tired voice reproving. "Sonnyboy's father, eh? What do you want with Meisie this time?"

"I just want to talk to her, Mama."

"If you are thinking you want to give her another child, go away. Some other tsotsi has already made her pregnant again."

"Oh. I didn't know."

"Of course. Gone for years. Too busy with some other poor woman's stupid daughter who cannot keep her bloomers on. Well? Are you going to wait here?"

"No, Mama … I'll come back another time."

He met her at the gate that didn't exist, holding a heavy, brown-paper shopping bag to her chest. Melon breasts beneath the bag, covered by a maternity smock that was too small, too tight and had seen duty elsewhere. Face and body bloated, legs spindly. She smiled her surprise at him.

"Hello, nice-time boy!" she said brightly. "What are you doing here?"

"I just thought I'd visit you, Meisie. See the boy."

"Well, well! Philip! You really surprise me. How did you know where we stay now?"

"Oh, I asked around. But nobody told me you were pregnant."

She laughed. "That's not news in Soph'town. You know that, klevah!" The word spat out with amused contempt. And then a cynical grin: "Were you hoping that maybe – just maybe – with some of your sweet talk you might –"

"Your mother's already asked me that. No." He tried to keep the distaste out of his voice and eyes; but she flinched and looked away.

"Oh, I see. Ek notch, pretty boy. Just suddenly feel like a father. Is that it?"

"Well – you can say so, Meisie. Is he around?"

"Yes, playing over there – chasing girls like his nice-time father. Sonnyboy!" she shouted, voice changing pitch into the habitually strident tone of a mother who is forever calling after an errant child.

"Okay, Meisie, okay, man – I'm coming!" a somewhat familiar voice yelled back behind Philip.

He did not look round to watch the boy he knew would be slouching towards them – hands stuffed in, or hanging from, ragged pockets; the stiff walk of a gunslinger seen in too many cowboy movies at cheap matinees in the Odin cinema. He kept his eyes fixed above Meisie's head, hoping and praying that the insolent voice he'd just heard did not belong to the toughie he met earlier.

He sighed with short-lived relief when he saw a different boy walk past him and rise on short legs to plunge a grimy hand into the shopping bag – "What you got for me, Meisie?"

A thin but tall boy who looked older than the seven years – or was it eight? – since Philip had renounced him before birth. Dressed in a ragged but not too dirty khaki shirt and tight, patched blue jeans above naked feet. Still just another tsotsi, Philip thought and his relief faded. Even with Meisie as his mother he doesn't have to be like this. My son, my son! But the inward chant did not mean anything.

"Well?" Meisie asked. "What d'you think of your tsotsi?"

The boy looked up at the strange, sharply dressed man with little interest in his eyes. Philip felt the right thing to do would be to go down on his haunches and perhaps pat the boy's head and talk fondly to him. He could not do it; no way …

"How're you, kid?" he said softly.

"Sweet – dolly," the boy replied and turned around to look up at his mother. "Who's this one, Meisie? Is he your new –"

"No, Sonnyboy," she grinned. "He's –"

"I'm going to tell Bra James, if you were double-crossing him!" the boy cut in with an ominous threat. He turned to Philip with a warning: "Do you know Jimmy Luger? He's got one of those – and bullets. So watch out, klevah!"

Meisie laughed. "You see? My own son spies on me. James," she explained, "is the father of this one," patting her large belly. "This is your father, Sonnyboy. His name is Philip. Nice Time Phil, I hear he's called."

The boy looked up with new but casual interest.

"Are you my father?"

"Yes, I am, my laaitie," he replied, trying to make his voice friendly, if not quite paternal: no pride, no affection in the tone.

"I haven't seen you before."

"Well, I didn't know where you lived, you see. I just found out."

"What do you do – in Kofifi, in Jozi? You look like a klevah, but," with awe and pride, "Bra James is …" A skinny shrug. "Well, I told you already. He's got plenty of ching – mazooma – money. And he doesn't have to work. He says only cattle do that!"

"Then I'm just cattle," Philip said, smiling and thinking: but Jimmy Luger doesn't spend it on your mother, does he bright boy? "And I hope you're going to work too, Sonnyboy. When you grow up. Then maybe you'll never go to jail like this James."

Must be a small-timer if I've never heard of him.

"Me?" the boy queried, aghast. "Go to –"

"Yes – you!" Philip snapped, surprising himself. "D'you go to school?"

"Aah, she makes me go!" he replied, gesturing at Meisie.

"Shall I leave you two alone to work out the future, Philip?" Meisie asked wryly, voice amused but with an edge.

The idea of being left alone with this boy who was his son appalled and frightened Philip. What would they talk about? They'd already quarrelled. He had no right to give the boy any advice about how he should lead his life.

"Eh – no, Meisie. I'm in a bit of a hurry," he said quickly. "But I'll come back to see him soon. Maybe take him shopping in town."

"That will be nice, Philip," she said, stressing will and avoiding would or maybe. "You can see he needs clothes. Not sharp like you, but just a boy's clothes for school."

She was watching her lover of teenage times closely, enjoying his discomfiture.

"Of course, you paid the damages; but fifty pounds didn't go far, even in those days, you know."

"Yes, you're right," he said, hastily pulling out a pigskin wallet from the hip pocket of his Palm Beach slacks. He drew out all the currency notes and passed them to her without a glance.

The hell with it – definitely not going to look for any more of them, Philip decided as he hurried down Gertie Street. Failed to trace two, so can justifiably give up searching. Nowhere to be found, Betty, my beloved bleeding heart ... All growing up somehow, wherever they are and however they're going to end up. You can't complain – you fucking rapist!

Maybe they would meet one day, when they're all grown up. Maybe hate and fight each other, and then victimise him in his doddering middle age. Murder each other, because he'd fight back; not walk away like with the snot of a tsotsi at the bus terminus on Diagonal Street. Would that be fratricide?

Or one of my boys – oh, yes, my boys! – will rape one of my daughters. Like father, like son. And their coloured sister in Doornfontein will look down her snooty nose at them as she taps down the city streets on high heels and tosses her hair back in slinky disdain as they stare lustfully after her.

The scattered tribe of Philip Mokone. The wild oats sown to grow into a jungle. They won't know me, either. And I won't know them, ever. No recognition some Friday night when they rob their ageing father of his miserly pay packet – the good days of being a klevah gone and almost forgotten.

Patricide? They'd laugh if they knew. Maybe kick me harder: Well done, pal. A great nice-time fucker and father ...

Chapter 25

Philip was standing at the table in his room when he heard approaching footsteps in the backyard which he always passed through as fast as he could to avoid other tenants. He waited, unseeing eyes on the paraffin lamp that stood on the table, ears attuned to the various noises outside, isolating those footsteps. The plain deal table and the bed behind him were littered with the garish sleeves of long-playing records he'd been restlessly shuffling through, searching for music he could listen to; but without success. He didn't know what kind would suit his mood.

The footsteps stopped, then a knock at his door. Damn!

The knock came again, and the door started opening, hesitantly, before he could respond in some fashion: Who is it? Go away, fuck off, I'm busy ... Can't say that without knowing who the hell it is disturbing Lonesome Phil.

Vivienne walked shyly into the room, the smile on her small, homely face apologetic and apprehensive. Before his surprise and dismay had fully registered, Desmond's thin grinning face appeared above her thatch of reddish hair. Philip stood very still, staring at the unlikely intruders – Vivienne, anyway.

"Aw, man! Don't look so dramatic, klevah!" Desmond laughed, pushing her gently farther into the room. "What's so surprising about a friendly visit? I never thought you were so anti-social – that's Boykie's bag, Philip. You wouldn't even answer the door! I mean, just to tell us to go away."

"Hello, Philip," she said.

"Hello, Vivienne ... Desmond."

"Look man, we're going to sit down even if you don't appear to welcome us," Desmond said into the silence, and sat down at the table; but she remained standing.

Philip smiled and placed the record he was holding onto the table.

"How are you, Vivienne?"

Pleased his voice struck the right note of casual interest. But damn this kid reporter and his meddling. This cheeky laaitie out of the bloody bundu – okay, Port Elizabeth – who thinks everything's a fucking joke!

"I'm fine, Philip."

She took her eyes off his own and looked around the room:

"What're you doing – all these records all over the place?"

"Polishing the grooves and gloating over the sleeves. Don't you know what these jazz buffs are like? Worse than a miser – a Micawber out of Dickens! – counting his treasures."

The grin about Desmond's wide mouth in the angular face was mischievous: eyes darting from the yellow-brown face to the pink, flushing towards puce.

"Aren't you going to shake hands – at least with her – Philip? Or just grab and kiss her?" he asked, on the verge of more laughter.

"I was trying to find something I wanted to listen to," Philip told her, waving one hand vaguely over the jumble on the table and bed.

"What kind of music did you want to listen to, Philip?"

"I don't know." He shrugged slightly, still impatient and irritated.

"That's life, brother – that is life!" Desmond declared. "We don't know what we want, what we are, what we're doing, where we're going, how we're going to get there ..."

She glared, sighed and sat down – on the bed and possessively so, Philip thought. About the same age, but she's a helluva lot more mature. Or just selfconscious.

"But at least I know what you should play, Phil," Desmond proclaimed, rising from the chair and starting to flip through the record sleeves on the table. "That's because I'm not a jazz buff," he explained. "I don't get mixed up by knowing too much." He held up a record: "Play this baby: Billie Holiday. Lady Day, as I believe The Prez –" turning and grinning at Vivienne "– that's Lester Young to you, Viv, named her. I do know something about the legends, you see! Now that's a chick who knew what she was singing about, boy."

"How've you been, Philip?" Vivienne asked in a soft, intimate voice that excluded Desmond from the room.

Desmond glanced up from the record he'd slid out of its sleeve, and looked at them. "All right," he said. "Okay! I get the message. I've done what was wanted of me. And so – I'm off, now."

Vivienne smiled at him. "Life is tough, Desmond – as you've been lecturing us. But thanks. Come back for me in about an hour."

"An hour?" he asked, trying to sound and look shocked through his toothy smile. "Is that all?"

"Buzz off, you fuck-minded situation!" Philip said in a measured, hard voice.

After the door had closed, Philip turned worried eyes towards her. "I don't think it's safe, you know. Coming here in daylight – I mean us here alone."

"Don't fuss, Philip," she smiled. "All we need do, if you insist, is leave the door and curtains open. Then they can't accuse us of contravening their silly Immorality Act, can they? It's quite simple."

She laughed, rose from the bed and straightened its cover: "See?"

After he'd taken the prescribed precautions, he returned to the table and began gathering the records, keeping busy eyes on them.

"I haven't seen you for a long time, Philip."

"I know." He looked up. "I didn't want to see you again."

Her lips jerked at the corners in a failed attempt at a rueful smile.

"That's not very complimentary, is it? Am I that bad? I thought, after the last time – in my flat ..."

"No, Vivienne. And you know that. Maybe that's part of the reason."

This time she did smile, and not ruefully: "Oh, Philip! You don't mean you're afraid of falling in love with me?"

"It's not that simple. Nobody falls in love because of a good time in bed. A very good time. Anyway, why did you come today?"

"To see you, of course. And talk to you. I've been doing a lot of thinking. About you – not us, but you. I want to help you, Philip. I said I was going to break down that wall around you, remember? And I thought I'd succeeded – partially, like the way this door here is open. But now I know from the way you've avoided me since the last time, that I didn't even make a crack in your armour."

"Is this part of the field work for your social science degree?"

"Oh, Philip!" she snapped. "You know you need help … Don't you?"

"I'm sorry, Vivienne. Yes, I need help. But –"

"Good. I'm glad you feel that way."

"Vivienne, how old are you?"

She laughed. "Does it matter? Do I have to be grey-haired like the tribal elders at the khotla for you to talk to me? I'm twenty-four."

"A very intelligent one score and four. Though that's not why I asked – or what I mean. You're still a kid, but you're – you're …"

"Sympathique. Remember? I told you there was no English equivalent for it."

"Yes. Maybe that's the word. I don't know." He sat down opposite her at the table. "Do you want a drink? There's a joint in the yard here that sells good stuff."

"No, thanks, Philip. Do go on."

"You think it's a simple problem of adjusting to apartheid and all its madnesses, don't you? It was once; but not any more."

"Tell me everything, Philip."

"I said to you the first night in here something had happened which made me what you called perceptive. It's done more than that, really. Changed my life. Before then –" He opened his arms wide, holding them away from his body as if he was trying to lure an elusive idea into himself.

"What, Philip? What happened?"

"No … I can't tell you."

"But how can I help if you don't? Are you ashamed?"

He smiled thinly, shaking his head. "No. Not ashamed. But I did something which the law, the Bible – every and anything – says is bad, is foul and evil. But I'm not ashamed. I've – well, come to ask myself a lot of questions. Ask the world."

"That's the beginning of knowledge," she smiled encouragingly.

"I know. But the misery I feel isn't so much from knowing about myself. It's because I've realised just how crazy, evil, brutalising – any and all and more of those adjectives – apartheid is. You see, I've learned that I'm not inferior. I've become convinced, in fact. I really know I'm not. And I know your tribe – they aren't as sure as they pretend that they're superior to me. To any of us."

"Of course not. I could've told you that without you … Go on."

"But this is the danger now, Viv. The danger: where do I go from here?"

"How do you mean? If you know you're equal – as against belief, which I think is what you mean – you've got nothing to worry about. Have you, Philip?"

"It's just the opposite, Vivienne. Now the worrying really begins. What d'you do when you suddenly find out that – that all these years you've been forced to drink poison? Maybe you believed it was poison before. But now you know it for a fact! Do you continue drinking it? Eh?"

"No, you don't. You refuse the poisoned chalice."

"But that's just what I can't – cannot – do, don't you see! Apartheid says drink. Or else!"

"So you have to find an antidote? Or pretend you're drinking when you're not?"

"That's right!" He spoke with an excitement that surprised him. "You've hit the nail on the bloody head, baby!"

She smiled, relieved to have understood him and shown him a way out.

"I've got to find a way to go on living here without going crazy."

"Can't you just ignore it – apartheid?"

"How? Who can?"

She shrugged. "I've always thought Boykie and Desmond did. And Desmond doing so quite successfully."

"Desmond … That boy. A jolly cynic who laughs at everything all the time. A circus, he calls it. But laughter can kill just like poison, you know."

"But he's not the only cynic. There are millions all over the world."

"That's why I know there'd be no point in trying to leave this country – Boykie's dream. I'd still have to find my own way. And Desmond's laughter isn't the solution, Vivienne. He's going to be the man who jumps off the top of Anstey's Building – laughing his head off before it crashes into the pavement."

"What about Boykie? Where does he fit in?"

"Boykie!" he laughed; a quiet, mirthless sound. "My poor, childhood friend, my ma se kind … Boykie! He doesn't – doesn't fit in, I mean. He's in a class by himself. Resigned. His body's still in Sophiatown because of apartheid, but his heart is in Lower Houghton. And his soul is in orbit somewhere."

"Poor Boykie," she said. "Like an internal exile."

"Yes. Or, if you'll allow me another cliché, there's a white man inside him yelling and clawing to get out of his black skin. And yelling, kicking, biting, using that sharp tongue of his, and clawing at the black people around him that he believes are holding him back."

"It's so sad."

"Yeah. This is the poison I can't drink any more."

"Nobody should have to."

"But what the hell am I going to do now? The cup's pressed against my clamped teeth, and I can't just push it away or there'll be a police bullet in my head. Or I'll be swinging at the end of a hangman's rope … As I should have been already."

Her eyes jerked up and stared into his face with fear and new awareness.

"You mean that, don't you?" she asked in a hushed voice. "That you should have been executed? Already? Was it that bad – darling?"

He looked up at the tender endearment. She held his eyes.

"What was it?"

He looked into the disturbed blue of her eyes for a long moment, wondering if he should tell her. Oh, fuck it, he decided. Confessing into Betty's soft and comforting bosom had not been enough – only sent him on a futile and shaming search for his illegitimate brood. Maybe this one: mature beyond her years, but understanding. Trying to understand, anyway.

"I raped a woman – a white woman."

"Philip!"

"You're only the second – you know what will happen to me if this gets about."

"Oh, Philip! I'm not even angry that you should think you have to warn me – remind me ..." She placed a hand over his fists on the table. "But why, Philip? A man like you who –"

"That's what I've been trying to explain to you."

"Who was she?"

"I don't know – didn't know her from Adam. Eve... Until recently. It wasn't so bad before I knew who she was. But now I know her name. She's more of a person."

"What are you going to do now?"

"What can I do?"

"But you want to do something?"

"Like what?"

"I don't know. But that's what you're looking for now, isn't it? The only way you can break down this wall completely. Out of your personal prison and find a personal peace."

"Yes, peace. What did the Ancient Mariner say?"

"A lot of things. What, particularly?"

"About peace, which he said came down with the rain from heaven like ... Oh, the hell with poetry. A damned long time since I had to drop out of college. But I don't expect to find any kind of peace. Don't want to end up always stopping one of three to tell my tale. I'm doomed, Vivienne – fucking doomed!"

"Don't say that, darling."

"But it's true! Isn't it? Unless I take the simple way out by giving myself up to the cops. Not to be shriven, but to be –"

"Don't ever think of doing it, Philip."

"No. That's something which I'm not going to do, crazy as I am."

"Thank goodness."

"Not goodness, Vivienne. I haven't told you the worst yet."

"Go on."

"She's got a child by me."

"Oh, no!"

"That's what I found out recently. Why I've been avoiding you. Why I'm back where I started, but with a vicious difference."

"Do you know where she lives?"

"Yes."
"Shall I go and see her?"
"What would you tell her? That I'm such a nice person that you call me darling? That she shouldn't mind too much what I did to her? And made her do to herself, the stupid bitch? No – sorry. Just another crazy person. Like me."
"I wonder why she didn't have an abortion."
"Stupid, but not a bitch. If she had 'done the decent thing' – which I'm damned sure she was told to do by everybody ... then I wouldn't be in this mess."
"Poor woman."
"Don't forget me. We're both victims, you know."

Chapter 26

Midsummer, and the December sun glittered in the high, blue glare of a sky without clouds, its rays bouncing on the Highveld in a shimmer of heat waves.

West of the City of Gold, the slum cluster that was Sophiatown lay frazzled and somnolent in the heat. The silence of a working day was broken by the echo of barking dogs and the yipping cries of ragged children playing in desultory fashion on the narrow streets, their calls to each other dying away listlessly on the hot air. The stillness of the day was only occasionally shattered by the grating roar of a diesel engine that reverberated half across the tight little location. The sound of the bus climbing the rise of Toby Street on the eastern edge of Sophiatown changed from a guttural grunting to a disgruntled pitch as its bored, sweaty driver manipulated the pedals and shifted gears. The dispatcher smoking in the shade of a corner store at the terminus half a mile away could, from the familiar sounds, follow its progress up Toby, and knew the moment it reached the top of the boundary street and turned left into Edward Road. Minutes later he heard the rattles and squeaks as it coasted down Gibson Street, engine whining against the braking change to low gear. And, finally, the ageing Putco wagon careered triumphantly left into Victoria Road and its engine sighed as the driver applied brakes: end of a journey, and pointing east again in the general direction of the city it had left some twenty minutes earlier.

The driver waved negligently at the dispatcher, switched off the engine, which shuddered and gasped into silence, and leapt out of his cab. Grateful to get away for a few minutes from the smell of a hot, steaming diesel engine that had been rattling all the way, its cover pulled open to avoid over-heating. He pulled a face – a bit of relief at last – and fanned the face with his uniform cap.

The dispatcher checked a clip-board on his knee before climbing to his feet in the shade of the store's veranda: on time, he noted on the pad. Then adjusted his uniform khaki dust coat and dragged himself a few feet to the shabby green bus with a broad, yellow stripe under its rows of grimy windows.

The driver held out his waybill to the dispatcher, who mumbled, "A bit late, eh," for want of anything else to say. The driver ignored him and walked stiff-legged into the shade, still fanning his face.

The dispatcher turned listlessly to check the tickets of those few passengers who hadn't already alighted and wandered homewards.

"Heita, Philip – is hoe daar? Hi, Betty," he greeted as the couple came down the metal steps in the narrow entrance. The bored look on his sweaty face was replaced by a smile. "I'll be there, Saturday, my brikaid," he told Philip. "Nee, man – ek lieg!" he laughed. "Everybody will be there, my ma se kind. So you better have plenty of booze around, boy."

Philip smiled back. "See you there, then, Rick – if I still got some ching."

He turned back to Betty, who smiled indulgently at the crack about money she knew was aimed indirectly at herself. They strolled along Victoria Road, loaded down with packages bearing the logos and names of the city's best-known fashion shops. They did not speak much – too hot, and they were tired.

"How about coming round tonight?" he asked, after a block.

"I have a lot to do, my dear."

"You can get away for a couple of hours."

"Oh, Philip ..."

"You haven't – we haven't ... more than three weeks, now."

"I can't, my dear."

"Ah, come on, sweetheart. After all, your people know all about us."

"It's not that."

They walked half a block towards the home of the 'your people' he'd referred to before she continued: "You must wait till Saturday night. When we're married. But you'll be too drunk then, I suppose. It's – you see … I don't know how to say it. But I decided, that first Sunday when the banns were read in church. I decided that until we're married we won't do anything. Maybe – well, perhaps I'm trying to pretend that it'll be the first time on Saturday night."

So he'd endured three weeks without the comfort of her presence. Sleeping alone – like a snake, as the saying went – wasn't the problem. He'd done that after they met – and surprised himself by being prepared to wait for her to invite him into herself.

They were at the end of the block of dilapidated houses before he spoke:

"That's all right, Betty. I can wait, baby."

She glanced at him out of soft, brown eyes. She spoke after a few more strolling steps: "You can wait because …" She stopped. When she began again the resigned bitterness that had crept into the four words she had spoken was replaced by a quiet plea.

"Philip. You have said that after we're married, you'll never even look at these Sophiatown bitches again. I know it'll be difficult because they chase after you. But I trust you. I'm not talking about that now. But tonight … I want you to do something. When I decided that Sunday of the first banns, I wanted to tell you. To ask you to also – these location girls …! But I couldn't. Something stopped me. I suppose you've been having them these past –"

"No."

"From now, today, I want you to stop. So we can start off fresh."

A soft, slow chuckle dribbled out of his mouth.

"You know, Betty, you should be glad you're a location girl yourself. These babes are afraid of you, did you know that?'

"Good!"

"Or just respect you, I don't know which. Of course I've also warned them. They know what'll happen if they tried something funny with you."

"I can look after myself, you know."

"I know. But I must tell you something funny – and don't get angry, sweetheart. I haven't played around for a long time, but I had a date for Friday with one of them. A nice doll who said she wanted to be my last."

"That's why I want us to live somewhere else and not in that room. It's full of too many – things. That's why all this time I never asked you when you were going to marry me. I knew I had to wait until you were ready. You are ready now."

Philip glanced at her, shook his head and grinned.

"I hope you're right, sweetheart, because I don't know. I think so – hope so. As ready as I'll ever be, Betty. But you don't have to worry about the cherries. That's over."

Saturday morning, traditional morning for weddings. A cloud-flecked but sunny day, with the final word-of-mouth invitations passing around Kofifi. It would be a big wedding, as Rick the dispatcher had declared. Nice Time Phil was well-known and they all wanted to witness and celebrate this amazing change in his status. He was popular and accepted by the various strata of Sophiatown society, including uptight situations who wondered why such a bright young man with a fairly good education from a decent college ... his 'situation' was cut short by economics, of course. Why he preferred to live like, and associate with, the underworld.

And that world was surprised, pleased and somewhat flattered by Pretty Boy Phil's style: a brikaid who'd not abandoned his roots, my ma hoor my.

Die manne had a grudging respect for him because he didn't take kak from anybody and was pretty good in a dust-up, even if he didn't carry a gun or even a knife. The klevahs had welcomed him as a comrade who spoke their lingo but could also talk like a white man. Die real manne who proclaimed that only cattle worked for the white man regarded him with friendly patronage even though he refused to buy back-door goods taken in violent robberies. And die really real manne who robbed only banks and payrolls to pay for their convertible Cadillacs and Buicks: they, too, would be at the wedding. Congratulatory smiles, jeering a little at this majita who was signing away his freedom to a kitchen girl, of all cherries – from Orlando, of all places. But she'd graduated to a factory worker since meeting the nice-timer. A majita who'd be withdrawing – maybe only partially – from their orbit by marrying this moegoe of a girl who didn't notch nice times and would try and keep him away from the wake-up people.

But the situations would be pleased that Philip Mokone was settling down, at last – and with a decent young lady. Ill at ease at being thrown socially together with these various manne, yet worth the risk to witness the salvation of a man who should've always belonged exclusively to their circle.

The girls – the cherries, the molls, the nice-time sisters – would also be there to witness the abdication of Mister Nice from their world. Eyes jealous, admiring, envious as they examined and evaluated the unknown bride's gown and make-up, the bridesmaids' frocks and the waitresses' matched aprons.

Ten o'clock is the favoured hour for the commencement and Philip, with his best man Boykie Courtroom Modise, and two groom's men leave his widowed mother's home on time. Women ululating, singing and shouting parental advice, and a few lewd suggestions; little boys calling out his klevah names and jeering, little girls giggling, waving tiny hands and staring through excited, dreamy eyes, young men waving a last farewell at a hero about to be domesticated; husbands shouting warnings about what lay ahead. The four men in formal dress – grey, striped trousers and black jackets – look like English butlers in blackface.

With a flourish of gloved hands, Boykie opens the door of a red, highly-polished Buick convertible with gay streamers fluttering across its bonnet. A grin wider than usual as he mockingly bows the groom into its soft seats. The driver is dressed like them in the immaculate wedding uniform – and owns his outfit, as well as the limousine, since for him this is a weekly, well-paid ritual.

He grins as they settle onto leather seats amid the ululations: "How's the hangovers, eh, boys? What a booze-up that was last night, man!"

The door thuds shut, and the Buick ticks into life, a hum that's just audible from a well-maintained straight eight engine. The driver glances behind to check that Philip's relations have all climbed into the two shiny sedans that complete the ceremonial convoy. Then the red limo erupts into a powerful murmur and surges forward, horn blaring the traditional declaration of its cargo and mission. Down one street, up another, along another; doing a quick, noisy tour of Kofifi to spread the glad tidings before heading for a church whose minister will only perform the nuptials because Philip's mother is a devout member of his congregation. Other cars join the procession. People rush out of homes, lean over tottering walls and fences, stop and stare on the streets; smile recognition or just for the fun of it – wave, shout and whistle: There goes Nice Time Philip getting married! Can you believe it! Wonders will never cease, I tell you!

The Buick and its followers – other cars have joined the procession – slow down, hooters moan and sigh into silence at the church gates. The four men alight and glance at waiting faces: grinning, smiling and emitting more of the ululations that have followed the convoy. The wedding men are erect, solemn and self-consciously proud of themselves in their stiff, hired outfits. They straighten trouser creases, check the shine on brand-new black shoes, tug at blue-striped cravats strangling their necks, and pat at fresh white carnations with the tips of fingers clad in grey gloves.

From the gathering come whispered jokes and congrats, nods, admiring and rude comments. Philip and his men walk stiffly along the corridor left by the crowd, through the gates, crunch up the gravelled walk and into the cool, quiet and crowded church. Women in gay hats, smart dresses, men in dark suits and their sharpest can't-get clothes: they all turn to follow the procession up the aisle.

Then the seemingly interminable and stiff-legged waiting below the altar: ten minutes late! Women – all the same! Twenty minutes ... Why do they always ... and then, at long last, the sound of blaring hooters drifts into the solemn silence. About time! Ululating outside, a sigh inside the church, and the fidgeting stops. A shuffling of feet and muffled voices at the door. Except for those of the four men staring rigidly at the altar, all heads turn toward the sounds, eyes peering.

Here comes the bride, all dressed in white ... Demure, radiant, proud, beautiful. Flash-bulbs pop and flicker. The glide up the aisle. The father hands over a beloved and dutiful daughter to a dubious, klevah. They stand together before the altar, now waiting for the priest in his vestments and his servers in their surplices to enter from the vestry.

The nuptial ceremony begins. Singing and praying. Vows and unspoken promises. The ring. Blessings. Signing the register in the vestry. Her hand in white lace gloves on his arm clothed in black, they glide down the aisle past hundreds of eyes and congratulatory smiles.

Singing and ululating outside. More flash-bulbs in the blinding sun. Cheering, pushing, shouting. Rice and paper confetti. Smiles, handshakes, pats on the back. Bridesmaids fussing around the convertible Buick and their bride; pulling, patting, adjusting. Doors thud and slam shut. The Buick ticks back into life and sighs away from the crowded kerb. Horns blow, crowd cheers, and the motorcade to the city and photographic studio rolls ahead. A slow drive through Soph'town – an exhibitionist procession escorted by yelling, running, waving children. Heads pop out of windows and doors, bodies spill out onto the streets.

Every Saturday the red convertible bears its exhibits for admiration; and every Saturday the motley audience gapes, recognises, admires and shouts its congratulations.

The Buick and its convoy weaving through heavy Saturday morning traffic in the city. White faces turn and stare: Bloody ostentatious Natives! Where do these kaffirs get the money, hey? Steal it from us, of course! The limo parks, the curious gather: black, white, half-black and Asian. Just look at that dress! Must've cost a packet! Maar sy's 'n mooi kaffermeid, hey. Live on pap and water – 'n bietjie vleis when they can afford it – for a year to save for this waste of money!

Back west to Sophiatown for the wedding lunch and reception in a school hall. All welcome to feed from what the big, black, steaming pots had produced over open fires in the courtyard, started the previous night while the groom and his brikaids caroused at the bachelor party. Droves of big, black, sweaty women fussing over the pots, aprons getting in the way.

Long trestle tables inside the hall covered with crisply starched cloths borrowed from friends and relations; pretty waitresses in smart frocks and dainty, matching aprons shuttling about with trays: heads held carefully high to keep shiny, processed hair in place. The tables crowded with guests, humming with talk, exploding into laughter. Loud music from the combo in a corner, near the bridal table on a platform so everybody can admire the splendour of these newly-weds. Huge platters of meat, rice, vegetables, dumplings, jelly, custard are carted high over heads by hurrying, harried men in too-large wrap-around aprons. Stacks of greasy dishes are carried away, sheaves of knives and forks and spoons bundled away. A steady stream of guests taking the seats vacated by those who have eaten and must make room.

The music stops, the serving stops, loud voices are hushed and the people outside crowd and shuffle inside to stand along the walls and crouch in the aisles. Speeches from uncles: "You must look well after her, my boy"; former teachers: "He was a very bright boy and should've gone to university but unfortunately his mother was only a poor widow"; and friends: "Keep timing from now on, Phil, you've got a beautiful wife, you lucky spy!" Applause and laughter.

And now, ladies and gentlemen – The Groom!

Philip rises slowly behind the table on the platform, sweaty from the heat and liquor, feeling disembodied and barely smiling. Bated, expectant silence. Ladies and gentlemen, my wife and I thank you for – the expectant grins burst into roars of laughter, quickly hushed, at the standing joke of this first domestic proclamation: My wife and I!

A toast to the happy couple, long on rhetoric and heavy with sly and clever quotations, from best man Boykie. And the master of ceremonies takes over the microphone again: It is time now, ladies and gentlemen, to clear the tables and move them out of the way for – wait for it ... The dancing!

Applause again when the bride and groom step out onto the bare concrete floor and dance to the combo, now free to play as loudly as they wish – and revive Philip's hangover headache. And the wedding party departs.

Those who wish to show off their dance steps – and wedding outfits, of course – take over the floor. The talk is louder over jazz, the laughter explodes more often and more uproariously, tongues loosened by secret booze furtively poured from half-jacks under table-tops.

Then the blare of car horns outside again. The bride and her maids re-enter in afternoon frocks, under startling and demure hats; the groom and his men swagger in on loosened limbs and wearing brand-new lounge suits; smiling loosely and waving exaggeratedly from the fuel consumed in the interim to see them through the rest of the day. Fresh applause and inspecting eyes.

The groom leads his bride back onto the floor, and this time they jive to jazz after earlier dancing to a waltz. Watched with critical approval by an audience seated on the few available chairs, and standing on stacked tables and benches lined against the walls. Applause again, and a streaming onto the floor to congratulate the couple with handshakes, kisses, hugs, pats on the back … Desmond grinning ferociously as he leads Vivienne forward, and Philip making an effort to appear relaxed and not surprised. But open and surprised stares, then amusement and a clapping of some hands as this white woman kisses Philip, then Betty – on their lips! Boykie is besieged by urgent, whispering younger men near the door and he glares: "Jesus Christ! What's wrong with you – eh? All this 'where's the s'godi?' Eh? Can't you bastards wait until you're invited?" They know Courtroom and his idiosyncrasies too well to take offence. He turns to a bruiser whose eyes glower, but a thin smile plays around his lip: "Hankie – tell these bloody tsotsi baadjie-vangers to go to the nearest shebeen if they can't wait!"

The younger men grin and wait.

More and louder music, more frantic and flirtatious dancing. An hour goes by, and the wedding party departs for the last time. The bright-eyed young men who form the inner circle smile and stream away in the wake of the party. They've got the word from Hank, after all.

The wake-up and klevahs, as well as some of die real manne gather again a few streets away at Hankie's *dladla* to make up for all the orange squash they'd been forced to drink at the reception. Hankie – very large, pitch-black and ugly enough to scare most people – shouts belligerently at the baekie-vangers. He slops whisky, gin, brandy, beer into glasses, tin mugs and plastic beakers.

The groom and his men join them after a while, and the congrats go up: Hey, Philip – you got plenty of good stuff here, boy – who's your *gweva*, eh? He grins and will not reveal the name of his bootlegger. And the lewd jokes: Who's going to fuck all those nice-time sisters now, eh? Ek sê, my brikaid, who was that weebit – die laanie cherry who kissed you right on the mouth? You mean you're getting into them too, Pretty Boy? Watch out, boy – wives can smell it on you, laanie perfume or the back-door stuff, if you don't walk the straight and narrow! Ha-haha-haa! Hey, don't forget, man; she's Tami's cousin and he won't take any kak thrown her way by his new swaer!

Tami? Man, he was really *meshugen* last night – and he warned this nice-timer to keep timing with the babe! Yeah? Where? At Boykie's bachelor party for Phil, klevah! But why wasn't I there too? Eh? Aah, you think Boykie invites tsotsis like you? Ha-ha-ha! Ag, I didn't miss anything – just wine, I bet you: just like fucking water! Hey, Buller – when is your wife going to produce something for you, eh? Two years and still no kids? He's too small for her, man! Ha-ha-ha-ha-ha!

Hell, you guys – what's happened to all the moonshine? Boykie! Hankie! How 'bout more booze, onse brikaids? A case of whisky and you spies are still not satis? You got to gazaat now, if you want to drink. No more free booze – ten bob a man! Okay, okay – okay, Boykie! Just don't get shook-up, Mister Courtroom. We'll bloody gazaat, all right! Say – got me an idea, boys. Why don't we get some hot – really hot-hot – babes in here?

After midnight. The last of the elderly revellers – relations and their close friends – talking quietly by the brazier fires outside Betty's aunt's home. The red Buick sighs to a jerky stop at the gate, and three men alight and walk with exaggerated care into the yard. Where's my wife, Auntie? The erstwhile groom slurs respectfully. Ooh! Look at him – the groom! Our brand-new mkonyana! Drunk as a … What has my poor niece married? I only want my wife, Auntie, not – not your … Take it easy, Phil. His brand-new brother-in-law Tami is stern, but also slurring – and his mother shakes her head. Your wife has gone to her Auntie's Martha, my boy. You forgotten you're sleeping there tonight?

The three men wander away from the blowing braziers, out of the yard and back into the limo in which the bleary-eyed driver is waiting.

The contract for the wedding has expired, but these majita are his pals, his brothers, his brikaids.

Say, Phil – why don't we go to Kort Boykie's midnight party first, eh? Still early, man! Yeah, man. After all the nights you already spent together – No! You go. I want to see my wife. That's all I want! Ag, man – You go, but take me to my wife first! Aah, you're starting too early boy – wife, wife, wife! Watch out or she'll have you in chains, boy. You got to show her right now that you're not – No! All I want is my wife – you deaf, eh? Ag, man – come on, Philip! It's still early, dammit.

Sorry, boys, but all I want …

A loud, off-beat knock at a door. The door opens and she stands with the dim and flickering lamplight behind: face in darkness, its indulgent smile hidden from him.

"Ah, my darling Betty!"

"Ssshh – thula, my dear!"

He enters, she closes the door and he notes the reason why he must remain silent: two bridesmaids from Orlando sleeping on the extended studio couch in the living-room-cum-kitchen. He tiptoes across and into the borrowed bedroom. He squints in the brighter lamplight and can see Betty, looking more woman than ever in her wedding nightie, smiling quietly.

"How are you, Philip? Not too drunk, my dearest?"

"No, sweetness, heart of my heart. No, my darling wife!"

He blinks as the bedroom tilts: about to start a familiar, dizzying whirl in his head. He quickly plonks himself on the bed and slowly, carefully shakes his head.

"You're my wife, now, aren't you, sweetheart? We're going to go through this damned life together – and to hell with their poisons!"

She watches as he rises from the bed – carefully, slowly, head at an angle – and fumbles with the smart, new suit that's already seen better days. Holding himself carefully upright.

"You want me to –"

"No! I'm fine. I can handle myself."

"So we can talk?"

He pauses, a suspicious glance at her. "What about?"

"I've been thinking about something, my dearest."

"Tomorrow."

"All right, Philip. Just lie down, now, and I'll try to help you."

"No! I told you –"

"But, my dear –"

"Oh, no! Don't start spoiling me. Don't start treating me like a – like – like …"

He crawls into the strange bed in his underwear, ignoring the new pyjamas she has laid out. He nestles into the soft pillow – Jesus! He sits up quickly, his eyes wide and staring. Then slides hurriedly off the bed and sits on its edge, feet firmly planted into a small rug. The room stops spinning and tilting about him. Jesus! I am really drunk! Blotto, poegat! Really stinko.

"What's the matter, dearest?"

Smiling knowingly, but still concern in her voice. She sits beside him on the bed, an arm round his shoulders.

"Nothing much – don't worry. Just water, that's all. I need to drink some water."

She leaves the bedroom, and returns holding a tumbler brimming with the stuff of life that should dilute the alcohol. And sits beside him again and puts the tumbler to his dry lips. He sucks in the water with an urgent greed, then sighs.

"Sorry, Betty. I shouldn't have drunk so much."

"It's all right Philip. You only get married once."

"Yes, I know – I hope, I promise. Just once."

"I am glad, dearest."

"You better go to sleep, Betty. It's going to take time before I can lie down."

"No. I will wait with you."

He turns his head, slowly, and looks at her.

"What did you want to talk about? We might as well talk now."

She is silent for long moments.

"This morning in church, dearest," she says softly. "It suddenly came to me as we made the vows. I don't know why … I was so happy, you see. Then it came. Miss Griffiths. We are getting married, I thought. And she – she has lost a husband. She is divorced. Because of you, my dearest."

For one crazy moment while she spoke, he'd wanted to throw his hands up and laugh. But the urge passed, and when she stopped he was depressed.

"Miss Jean Griffiths! Dear, poor, stupid, crazy, defiled Miss Griffiths. You know, I'm beginning to wish I'd done it to some other, sensible woman – any other woman but your dear Miss Griffiths."

"She is a nice woman, Philip."

"Nice! Nice? Ha! You're telling me – nice. Too bloody nice to have an abortion! Oh, everybody's nice to somebody. But they are not nice, not where we are concerned. Nice! They're nice to their cats and even their dogs. But us they hate – they fear, Betty. The poor, stupid bastards. Superior? They've got such an inferiority complex, Betty, that they ..."

A glance at a wife with too much compassion.

"You are too sweet, too good, too considerate to be living in this crazy place, my dearest. How have you done it, Betty? How have you missed the cup?"

"What cup, dear?"

"The cup they pass around, full of this poison they want us to guzzle like it was the best mahog. Not Mellow-wood – no wood is good for them," he grinned.

"Talk sense, Philip."

"Haven't you ever seen their cup? Smelled and tasted this awful brew? The problem – maybe your luck – is that you refuse to see evil, my darling wife. You're blind to such things. That's why you marry a man like me. And that's why I need you in my life. Can't you see the evil in me – the evil from that poisoned chalice, like ..."

No; not the time and place to quote Vivienne.

"I sipped from that cup with my mother's milk, Betty. My birth – like yours too, even if you don't know – was a political crime: another kaffir to reinforce a majority that must be crushed under the heel of their boots! And from that first day, I had to sip and then guzzle this poison from their cup. For the rest of my life. All our lives, the drinkers. Trying to wash away the taste – immunise against the effects, Betty – with mahog, moonshine and stinking, flavoured gin!

"And what do they – everybody, the good people – call us for trying that chaser, that remedy? Drunks, dronkies, *matahoa*! Just for trying to chase away the damned poison. But you've been lucky, Betty.

Missed the infection that's in me and swilling all around the rest of us. Well, fine – for you."

"There's nothing fine –"

"Shut up! Marvellous if you have avoided that cup, and aren't just well-trained to be one of the meek who'll inherit the earth, one day. Well, baby, heaven can't wait, far as I'm concerned. But even I can see good too – that's why you are sitting here beside me. As my wife. I love you, Betty; but more than that I respect you."

He looked up at the ceiling and grinned again.

"In fact, I'm afraid of you."

"Afraid of me? Why –"

"Oh, not of your muscles, my darling wife. I hope you're not going to try and push me around, because ... It's because with you beside me, I feel more at ease living and surviving this evil, this poison. We know each other, me and their devil. Old pals, that's us – brikaids. But it's still a rotten life, sweetness. And you've got to be – I have got to be rotten to live and survive. But I don't make sense to you. I'm drunk."

"I understand, dearest."

"No, sweetheart, you don't begin to understand. How can you understand something you don't even know exists? That's what scares me about you – your goodness. How could you ever begin to understand why I raped a white woman? You couldn't, Betty. And you'll be shocked when I tell you that I'm glad I raped her."

"Oh, my dear!"

"And even glad she became pregnant. Glad she, your nice Miss Griffiths, was so stupid and crazy enough to have the baby."

"Yours, dearest."

"And become an outcast. Because she's so nice. Shows just how stupidly evil they are, making her, an innocent victim, an outcast."

"She is suffering, Philip. Living there in Doornfontein with all those low-class, dirty Boers who despise her. And those coloureds who want things from her but laugh behind her back – pleased that a white woman has ..." She shrugged. "Poor woman. I really pity her, my dearest."

"Amen. Poor us all – that's who you ought to pity, Betty. This country and all who live in it. If it's really living."

Chapter 27

How long can one defy the world? Refuse the easy solution, refuse to return to the fold? There was an observation in a book she'd read at school that suffering can be endured beyond all expectations: even under torture – a Red Indian smeared with pig's fat and pegged on an anthill could still fall asleep, despite the continuous pain. In other places, at other times, it's termed heroism, this stubbornness that had left her chained to Doornfontein, this fountain of thorns. Joan of Arc shouting defiance from a burning pyre ... Why not raise the white flag? Tell the enemy what it wants to hear, or know, and get it over with? What is this heroism? What holds you back? Principle, courage, resignation? Honour and duty? Pig-headed defiance? Hatred? Or just plain stupidity, lack of imagination? One of these factors, or some of them together. When the body or the mind – both? – make their peace with the tormentor, go numb, accept unquestioningly, learn to live with the unremitting pain. Past caring.

You don't care any more, Jean Griffiths. You've suffered this much, so why not go to the bitter end? There's nothing to gain from surrender. You only lose, that way. And they'll still despise you. Gone beyond the point of no return – of any recall, in their eyes – and then trying to sneak back. Damn them all.

You learn things about yourself, all right. A greater resilience than you ever dreamt possible. You look at yourself in the mirror of your mind with awe and a frightened wonder. Amazed: is this really me? A new pride in yourself. But how long can one remain resilient without snapping? No rule there, my girl. Just go on and maybe you'll even be happy some day. It's only a new and different life.

But why are you prepared to suffer, Jean Griffiths? Why insist on continuing this torture? Out of spite, defiance, bravado – or out of love? I do love Beatrice, yes. Millions of mothers have loved babies born deformed and – but she's not; she just happens to be the wrong colour. They forced me to love the only baby I was ever to have, married to Patrick Sean Ryan. Really? Perhaps you wanted to; made yourself want to have her, to keep her and love her. Those were acts – no, decisions – of a defiant person. Or an angry one.

If Patrick – they – had not been so stupid! If they, he had only been understanding. But how could poor Paddy? How could they, any of them? Even my staunchly supportive sister-in-law Sheila – former sister-in-law. She doesn't really understand either. "It's my baby too!" you yelled at them, persuading yourself the rapist could burn unto eternity in hell, but what was growing in your womb was your very own and yours alone. Oh, it definitely was, and still is yours alone; just like a cancer can be yours.

But no sensible person chooses to keep the cancer.

And now you're trapped. By this love you force-fed into your heart. The defiant love that has mellowed into a splendidly beautiful emotion: love without any qualifications. Yes – perhaps unfortunately. To spring the trap I'd have to give Bea away. But not now, if ever. Oh, yes, you could; that's just your stubborn pride. Go back to the matron at the hospital and tell her …

But could I really? I don't know, dammit! Which mother ever knows that she'll dash in front of a speeding car to save her child? Nobody knows for sure what they'll do. You're trapped, my girl.

And where's her fucking father? Where is your father, Beatrice, my love?

Her eyes wandered across the room to the honey-coloured child who smiled and babbled happily when their eyes met. Beatrice abandoned her toys and rushed over to climb onto her mother's lap. What kind of a man – brute – is he? Such a beautiful, lovable child. What kind of a – no! Don't start that. Forget him. May he be roasting in his own perdition.

She went to answer the knock on the door carrying Beatrice on a hip. A white woman in her early twenties smiled at her with some hesitation across the threshold.

"Good morning!" the young woman said brightly. "May I come in for a few minutes?"

Another curious and inquisitive one, but what the hell. When they were seated, the girl – no more than that, can't cause much harm or distress – made baby noises at Beatrice, who gazed at her with more reservations than her mother.

"That's a beautiful child. Whose is it?"

"She's mine."

"Oh! I'm sorry – I didn't mean to pry."

"I'm used to it. But I suppose you'd already heard about us."

The girl shrugged and smiled. "Well, as a matter of fact a woman down the street – one of these ware Afrikaner harridans – suggested I should try you. But she didn't explain – just said you'd be sympathetic to my appeal. Which is why I'm in this unlikely –" She stopped and started again: "What I've come about – donations for our Fund, you see. But I truly didn't have any idea what she meant."

"Now you know. What Fund is this?"

"I should introduce myself first," the girl smiled, an open friendly smile that relaxed Jean's tensed body. "I'm Velma Ellis, and I'm collecting money for the Treason Trial Defence Fund."

"The what? Oh, yes. Read about it somewhere. Hundreds of Communists appearing in the Pretoria synagogue."

"Only a few are Communists. On trial for ages, and the devil – that's our government – only knows how much longer the farce is going to go on. But these people have families, you know. And they can't work. So they and their families need money for food, clothes and everything else. That's what the Fund's for – not to pay for their defence counsel, you see. Just humanitarian. How much can you give, or pledge?"

"Didn't they think of all these difficulties before they started agitating for – for ... Knowing they'd get into trouble with the government?"

She stared at Jean in surprise.

"Well, we're all doing this, whatever any of us do, with our eyes wide open."

"And you presume I just have to be sympathetic. Because of my child – because of what you think I did."

"Oh, now. Please don't be so touchy. When I knocked at your door I didn't know anything about you. I've knocked at doors all over Jo'burg, you know. Even of rabid Nats like your neighbours. And been thrown out on my arse, sometimes. And well, after seeing you and her, you can't really blame me if I –"

"I suppose – of course not. I'm sorry I've been rude, Miss Ellis. And my name is Jean Griffiths. But all your presumptions about me are wrong. I don't care, nor am I particularly interested in whatever problems the Africans, coloureds or coolies might have. They're what they are because ... The only person of colour I'm interested in is my Beatrice, here."

"If you're interested in her welfare, what do you think's going to happen to her when she grows up? When she has to go out of here on her own, without your love and protection? When she goes to school, for instance? The first problem being which school? Is that what you want for your daughter? That is, if you can keep her that long – if you are allowed to do so. The Group Areas Act authorities are breaking their collective neck in their race to classify residential areas. What's going to happen to you two when they get to Doornfontein? If the Nats have their way, there won't be a place for you to live anywhere in this benighted country."

"South Africa isn't all the world, Miss Ellis. I can go overseas."

Velma shrugged. "If you can afford to, Miss Griffiths, good for you. But there's prejudice against black people of any shade even there, you know. Didn't you read about the race riots in London? But why should you have to go abroad? This is your home, your country. The only thing wrong is racist politics. Why should you, or any of us, run away instead of fighting for our birthright? Your freedom is tied up with that of other people of any colour. By oppressing one group, we also restrict ourselves."

"You sound like a – never mind. Is that the end of your lecture?"

"Sorry. I do get carried away. Anyway, all we're asking of you, now, is money. So that some of us can eat – and fight for the freedom for us all. Nats included."

Jean spoke in an indifferent voice: "You're right on some things, and wrong on others." A small, bitter smile slid onto her face as she added: "But I'll give you some money if it'll in any way delay the Group Areas Act officials from hounding me out of this thorny fountain."

"The what?"

"That's what Doornfontein means. Didn't you know?"

"No. My Afrikaans is ..." She shrugged again. "But, thanks; we're prepared to take anybody's money. Even those who can't see the light – the writing on the wall, if you like. For this humanitarian purpose, not everybody has to agree with us."

Velma Ellis was on the veranda when Jean stopped her.

"I suppose you'll be asking questions about me and Beatrice," she said in a matter-of-fact tone. "I'll save you the trouble. There's no mystery lover – nothing like that, as my neighbours also assumed at first. I have this child because I was raped. Probably by one of your comrades in the struggle towards this light you talk about so much. Goodbye."

The men lolled in the new easy chairs and studio couch, that gleamed from the polishing of a professional, and drank beer. The conversation was light and lazy, and had been drifting easily from one topic to another. The also new housewife Betty Mokone laughed and commented on what was said from the kitchen corner of the room, where she was preparing supper. The early evening sounds on the streets of Sophiatown mingled with the voices – angry shouts, loud laughter, screaming babies – and clatter of other tenants in the large house where Philip was starting married life in two rooms.

"Hey – hey, you guys!" Desmond cut in excitedly on the rambling anecdote Boykie was embroidering. "I almost forgot to tell you this one! A real scoop we got today. The front-page story of the year, that's what it could've been. The biggest of its kind since Regina Brookes appeared in court a couple of years ago!"

Boykie glared at the young and impetuous reporter, and hurriedly asked: "About that white woman?" Glancing quickly at Philip, then trying to stop Desmond's wide-open mouth with the toothy grin. "Hah! Who wants to be bored by that kind of a story? It's just –"

"Let me tell it, boy!" Desmond interrupted, laughing.

"You don't have to, you know," Boykie tried to warn the scoop gatherer.

But Desmond did.

As he spoke, dramatising and also embroidering the scoop when he could, Betty came out of the alcove. She wiped her hands slowly on a dish-towel and leaned against the sideboard across the room from her husband. Desmond wrung the story dry of all the humour and pathos it could be forced to surrender. Betty's eyes tried to hold Philip's, but he looked away, shrugging imperceptibly.

Desmond said that when his good friend Velma Ellis had telephoned and told him about Jean Griffiths, he'd thought it would be another sensation, like that caused by Regina Brookes.

Regina had achieved some fame – notoriety in certain quarters, of course – and made a few bucks telling her own amazing story. About actually marrying a Zulu cop the customary way out there on a farm in Zululand, and then coming to live with him and their baby in Orlando West. Spiteful mouths blabbed, cops got the word, the couple were nabbed under the Immorality Act. And Regina appeared in court wearing a doek over her blond hair, and the baby strapped to her back with a blanket just like any good African mother.

This woman sounded like a second edition from what Velma said: co-operating in giving his weekly newspaper her inside story. But, Desmond shrugged and grinned, what a sad mistake that assumption had been! This one had refused to let him and the photographer any further than the door. And when he'd explained who they were and what they wanted, she cursed them with a low and bitter fluency, using a few choice Afrikaans words clearly learnt in Doornfontein by what was really a middle-class English woman. But Willy – that boy never misses a chance, man! – had taken a picture as she cursed.

The flash of Willy's camera, a Speed Graphic with a round globe almost as big as some people use in rooms of their homes, stopped the bilingual curses, all right. She blinked in the sudden lightning flash, and the click of the camera's shutter was as if there'd also been a click in her brain – like they say in skiet-en-donder detective stories, boy. A hand went up to shield her eyes, and then she cried – wept, boy; and without a sound. Just tears streaming down her beautiful face. Then she turned away and into the house with her shoulders drooping; defeated. Didn't even close the front door behind her.

"Even my hard-boiled heart was touched, boy," Desmond grinned. "I should've followed her in, of course. But I got sentimental and left her – didn't even see this baby of hers. Like Duggie says, 'sentiment is the foundation of disaster'!"

"Don't look so bloody pleased with yourself, you barbarian!" Boykie spat out, his voice choking. "That's a damn sad story and nothing to grin at like a bloody hyena! Not to make jokes about! D'you realise the odds that woman's up against, you stupid, hard-hearted plaasjaapie! You moegoe! Jesus, man – she's living in a hell on earth!"

"Come on, Boykie – that's why I wanted the story," Desmond said, hurt by the imprecations, but still at ease. "It's a damn good story."

"You disgust me!" Boykie hissed, his broad face pained and eyes rounded. He turned and asked: "What do you think of this pig, Philip?"

He regretted asking as soon as the question was out of his mouth. From the moment he'd heard the story on the liberal grapevine that morning, he'd known instinctively this must be the woman Philip had once told him about.

Philip smiled slowly, hesitantly. And when he spoke into the silence his voice was harsh: "I think next time his so-called newspaper does one of its crime exposés, 'revealing' stuff we already know … I think, Boykie, we don't interfere any more. We just let die real manne beat him up and the rest of his gang."

"Hey, Phil – you can't do that," Desmond protested.

Philip ignored the protest and continued, voice icy with anger and contempt: "They're getting too fucking nosey, these so-called news hounds, Boykie. Maybe somebody should teach them a lesson about manners."

Boykie dragged Desmond away without the supper Betty had been happily preparing for the bachelors. The hungry duo left behind them a strained silence in the two-roomed home of the recently-weds. Late at night, neighbours beyond the thin walls were certain their new, and aloof next-doors were having their first serious quarrel – maybe even a fight, eh! No sound of blows, but the voices filtering through were taut with emotion, heightened by an attempt to keep them low.

Then came the muffled sounds of a woman's sobs.

"Oh, Jesus Christ, Betty!" Philip was saying in an anguished voice and glaring at the shaking shoulders. "I've told you I'm sorry for her – and I am! I've told you I'm even sorry I did it. If she's doomed and damned, how d'you think I feel? What d'you think I am? Even more damned, dammit! Not damned out of choice like she is – but I am damned … Oh, what the fucking hell! What d'you want me to do now? Go on, say it! D'you want me to turn into a Hollywood hero and give myself up to the cops? Tell them I confess! That would make a best-seller, if bloody Desmond got both our stories, eh? Jesus Christ! Don't you know they'd hang me? Or don't you care if they do string me up? Are you so fucking good that you want justice – justice, hah! – at any price? Do you want me to hang, Betty? Swing from a rope, shitting myself? Oh, you good people. You bleeding hearts!"

After weeks during which neighbours started laying bets on how much longer this glamorous marriage – convertible Buick and their very smart clothes – would last, Philip went back to Boykie. They talked late into the night, Boykie doing most of the quiet and intense talking.

Chapter 28

Sunday afternoon, and the city streets are quiet, echoing, empty; filled with sunlight and shadow, but no people. The workers are confined to their locations, except for a few men and women in long, blue-and-white robes, carrying Bibles, hymn books, shepherds' crooks and other paraphernalia of religious sects. And their masters are gathered round picnics and braais, bemoaning The Servant Problem in their comfortable homes in suburbia.

Bree Street is one of the broadest streets in Johannesburg; and not quite in line with those it connects to the north, as if it's never been in tune with the City of Gold. Die breë straat is steeped in the perpetual shade of a deep canyon created by tall buildings: gloomy and silent, perhaps a little chilly, in the Highveld heat. The ruthless gashes and scars of tram lines cut spitefully through its uniform black surface. Without the week-day bustling crowds, its disjointed intersections are like broken limbs, and the few Sunday loungers – kaffir loafers to even fewer white motorists – like gangrenous growths.

The traffic lights at the intersection of Bree and Von Brandis turn to green, and a panel van coughs apologetically and chugs across, bumping over tram lines. The fading letters on its sides advertise that it is the property of a wholesale company whose name is a house-hold byword, especially in suburbia. Philip is slumped behind the wheel, his eyes introspective. Now that he's been promoted to a proper salesman, but exclusively for the company's clientele in the locations, he has a perk of his own: this delivery van he's allowed to keep over weekends. The unexpressed theory is that he will use it to make new contacts, and perhaps – if it could be expected from one of these lazy Natives – even drum up a few orders.

"What happens if she has visitors?" he asks.

"We'll go back later, my dearest," Betty answers from the broken-down seat beside him. "I'm not forcing you to do this, dear."

His smile is slow, crooked and thin. "No, sweetheart. I know. It's me who wants to do this – thing. Forced by my conscience – the one I married. And, also, the one that's come back to haunt me."

The van turns to the right and dips under a railway bridge and chugs up the hill on the other side of Siemert Street. Out of the commercial city centre, now, and in low-class suburbia: Doornfontein which, further up the hill, changes its residential class and purifies the colour of its residents. Beyond the bridge, the van turns right again and then, after two blocks, to the left. Into a quiet, tree-lined street with big, solid houses: paint peeling from once respectable establishments that now glower on their seedy surroundings. The silence of this day of rest is broken by the sudden roar of a motorcycle in the distance, the banging of a nearby door, an explosion of drunkenly hilarious laughter from behind a crumbling wall.

Our superior half-citizens, Philip muses bitterly. For them every Friday isn't just pay-day but Christmas; Saturday is Boxing Day; Sunday is New Year's Day; and Monday is another year, another week, another hungry scrabbling for a living. But then, that's exactly what laanies – not those who live in this slum – say about us in Soph'town and the other locations.

The van rolls to a stop at the kerb on the silent street. He smiles bitterly: Enter – The Villain.

"Perhaps she's not in," Betty suggests, suddenly reluctant.

His smile turns encouraging. "We've come this far, sweetheart, we'll go on to the end. Don't be afraid, now. We're doing the right thing. The only thing, dearest."

She straightens his knitted black tie with nervous fingers, and they climb out of the van she'd suggested he give an extra-clean wash that morning. They look at each other with thinly disguised apprehension, checking over clothes they have chosen with great care. They –

he – must not look flashy, like one of the real manne. A charcoal-grey lightweight suit with the knitted black tie and a plain, white shirt; for Betty a filmy blue blouse to set off a grey gaberdine suit she had accepted with some reluctance from him, not asking any questions about its price.

"We must look like really respectable married people, Philip," she had said. "Like any married people. Otherwise she ..."

And now, he thought, we look like we're going to a funeral. His decision not to wear the coconut-brown Panama hat with the floral band was his own: he had no wish to doff his hat to her, if she did allow them into her refuge from their world.

Philip opens the gate and they walk past the narrow, neat garden, not just a patch of weeds like the neighbours'. And up the semicircular steps leading to a stoep discreetly screened by climbing plants.

He stops on the top step and looks back: a few houses down the somnolent street an old woman with straggly hair is leaning against the veranda wall and staring at them. Two teenagers in tight jeans and black leather jackets – oily hair in the fashionable ducktail cut – have stopped immediately across the street and are glaring at him. If I'd come alone, he thinks, there'd have been trouble.

Betty knocks timidly at the familiar door to which she'd once had a key. He impatiently signals that she knock louder. She does so – too loud, she thinks. They hear muffled footsteps inside, which pause at the door. She knows they're being observed through the judas spyhole set in the door; she can picture the expression on Miss Griffiths' face. The door-knob turns; and the door opens.

Jean Griffiths had seen nobody through the thick, round glass of the little judas hole, because her visitors had instinctively stood aside from the door after knocking. She had shrugged and opened the door all the same – what the hell. Now it took her a puzzled moment, looking out through the partially open door, before she recognised her former maid-servant. Another startled moment before she decided to smile – not too friendly a smile, only one of recognition. But only a quizzical look at the man standing on the other side of the doorway.

"Hello, Betty," she said, the door wedged against the right shoulder and her body blocking any view of the inside of her home. What does she want? And who's this boy with her? Shall I – no, of course not! Can't let them in; no back door either, damn it.

"Good afternoon, Miss Griffiths," Betty smiled.

"What do you want?"

"I – we wanted to talk to you, Miss Griffiths."

The smile became a fraction wider; amused and patronising. "Just as vague as ever, eh, Betty?"

What more can I say to her without being really offensive? What does she want, here? She was not frightened, just uneasy at these unexpected visitors that life-long training didn't allow through front doors.

"Where are you working now, Betty?" she asked, examining the smart gaberdine outfit and flicking a glance at his suit and foreign shoes.

"In a factory not far from –"

Philip cut off his wife, voice reverberating with a trace of the impatience he felt at these patronising and inane questions followed by respectful responses. He had let them go this far while his hooded eyes examined her body, and then the beautiful face, with a detached curiosity: willing this first, clear sight of the victim to transmit some emotion to his own body – a remembrance of the brutal sensuality, a satisfaction at his knowledge of her inner being. But he felt nothing. Not even pity. Instead he became impatient – and nervous like her, which annoyed him.

"We'd like to talk to you, Miss Griffiths, and I think –" He stopped himself. Why doesn't she tell us to voetsek if she doesn't want us in the damned house? Invading her – not privacy, but maybe seclusion?

Jean's eyes flicked briefly over his face when he spoke, refusing to acknowledge his presence: too smart and sort-of handsome, surely, for the boy of a factory girl. The green eyes fled quickly back to Betty's placid face, unnerved by the arrogance of the – yes, okay, handsome – yellowish-brown face. Handsome! Is that how you can think of a cheeky Native boy at this embarrassing moment? And who the hell does he think he is, talking to me like that; looking me straight in the eye? Who does he think he's talking to? Her lover, I suppose; living together in sin in somebody's smelly backyard, no doubt. Has to be smelly in a location.

Jean came hesitantly through the door, trying to smile brightly at Betty, eyes glancing swiftly up and down the deserted street.

"Why don't we sit out here on the veranda? It's much cooler than inside."

She led them to the basket chairs at the end of the narrow veranda, thankful for the flowering creeper that screened it from the street.

Well, at least it's not the kitchen, Philip told himself grimly as he and Betty sat next to each other.

"How is Beatrice, Miss Griffiths?" Betty asked as Jean stared inquiringly at her.

"Sleeping."

"I see. I hope she is well."

"Thanks for your interest." The voice without intonation.

"We are interested, Miss Griffiths," Philip said in a deliberate voice, the intonation as flat as hers. "Betty isn't asking out of idle curiosity, but because –"

"Who is this boy, Betty?"

"Philip is my husband, Madam."

"Oh. I see. Does he have a – where does he work?"

"Miss Griffiths," Philip said, stressing the difference between that politeness with the servitude of Madam. His voice hard, now: a tone which jerked Betty's head round towards him in alarm. He shook his head briefly and vehemently at her, and the mouth opening to stop him or apologise to the Madam closed slowly.

The white woman refused to look in his direction.

"Miss Griffiths," he repeated, "you don't have to patronise us. Even if Betty once worked for you, you don't have to ... We regret having to come here and place you in this embarrassing situation. We don't expect you to go out of your way to be nice to us, Miss Griffiths. All we hoped for was a decent reception. We're here because we had to come, and not because we wanted to come. We –"

"I don't think I have to listen to such talk from you," she snapped. A boy with too much education for his own good; never met one like him. "I only have to call those two men coming down the street to have you taught a proper –"

"Oh, no! I'm so sorry, Mad– I mean Miss Griffiths," Betty cut in, agitated by distress and a sudden fear. "Philip did not mean to insult you, Madam. Please don't be angry with us, Miss Griffiths."

"I'm not angry, Betty. He couldn't ever make me angry. I'm simply disgusted – fed-up with the kind of man you ... this husband of yours." She paused and stared accusingly. "Now, Beatrice will be awake in a minute. What do you want? I've got another girl and don't need your services."

"The child, Miss Griffiths," Betty answered. "It is because of Beatrice that we are here."

"What?"

"Miss Griffiths, we would like to take Beatrice away from you."

"Take Bea – what's that supposed to mean? You want to take my baby away? Whoever told you I was giving her away? And even if I was – what makes you think I'd give her to you – and him?"

"We don't want to just take her, Miss Griffiths. We want to adopt her," Philip said, speaking in a softer but impersonal voice.

"Thank you for that explanation, Mister Who-ever-you-are! And why do you want to – to adopt my baby? Can't you make your own?"

"You have suffered so very much, Miss Griffiths," Betty said into the silence. "I feel so very much for you. We must help you; it is our duty to do so. We must take – adopt – Beatrice so that you can go back to your old life. Go back to your people and be happy again, Miss Griffiths."

Jean wanted to laugh out loud. This was the very end – me patronised by Natives! But the hysterical urge passed quickly, and she looked into the compassionate black face: remembering the mute awareness that had strained their past relationship. Then she attempted to generate fresh anger, to neutralise any return of the emotional weakness Betty had engendered in her during those days. But she was curious about this amazing and preposterous offer to adopt Bea. Raise her in a location, of all places – as if this Doornfontein wasn't awful enough! When she spoke, her voice was quiet, almost encouraging.

"Why is it your duty to help me, Betty?"

"If you don't mind the – er, interruption, Miss Griffiths," Philip said in a voice as quiet as her own. "I'll explain. I'm the one who has to explain."

He'd overcome the intermittent anger she raised in him; no need not to keep timing, he should've expected her kind of behaviour. He suppressed the nervousness that was so irritating, but had welled up in him from the moment she opened the door and he saw her for the first time: a beautiful woman with tragedy written all over that face. But she had stared blankly at Betty, as if … Anyway, he could talk to her, now; and perhaps explain it all to her – and to himself.

"Please have some patience, Miss Griffiths, because this – er, explanation is going to take some time," he said, leaning forward as she shrank back. He shot the cuffs of his white shirt and placed elbows on his knees, over the sharp creases of his carefully adjusted trousers.

"You see, certain things happen. And people become victims – innocent people who can never understand why. And the victims are not just the obvious ones, or on one side. A man who's run over by a bus is not necessarily the only victim. Perhaps I should say he's only the ultimate victim. But the bus driver – the official cause of the crime, or accident – can also suffer. Sometimes, even more than the dead or crippled man. Let me make it clear that I'm not just talking about a bus accident or the driver and, er, casualty … I'm talking about the person responsible for any incident, criminal or otherwise."

Get to the point, you, she wanted to say; but beginning to dread the conclusion of this roundabout rigmarole. His wife doesn't understand all this either; but she knows what he's driving at. That's why she's looking so intently at her hands.

"Now, when he did what he did, doing it deliberately, he could've been under some compulsion. An impulse – something he couldn't fully understand, something he couldn't really stop himself from doing.

"Sometimes a white man, for instance – or several men, or even a white woman – assaults an African on the street. But they don't really know why, you see. They just see him or her, get the urge and do it. They'll give some excuse, of course: say they were insulted by the way he looked at them, something silly like that. But the basic reason, the motivation, is colour and race; a racial frustration, let's say. They feel that to justify themselves – to assert themselves, and prove that white skins make them superior to us – they must do something violent or humiliating. Well, black people can be like that too. We hurt white people, but usually in roundabout ways because we know the consequences of bucking this country's one-way justice. We do whatever it is – steal, do a job badly or too slowly; trying to prove to ourselves and to white people that you are not superior, but just as stupid and all that."

She crossed her legs and glanced at a downcast Betty.

"I'm coming to the point now; please don't be impatient. Now you, Miss Griffiths, have been hurt in that way. Maybe not in such a roundabout way, but the purpose of the act against you was complicated. You see, it wasn't just against you – the purpose was not so much to hurt you as to humiliate all white people, Miss Griffiths. Unfortunately, what happened on the spur of the moment has caused a lot of personal suffering to you. Alone. For that I am very sorry. Your suffering has made you stand out from the white crowd in the laager. It has been individualised, making it personal suffering instead of ..." He shrugged. "You have become a person, instead of a race against which the action was really directed. And that, Miss Griffiths, changed everything. That's why Elizabeth and I feel we must help you. To our way of thinking, the only way we can do so effectively is by adopting Beatrice. So you can return to the life you know and become just another white person again."

Jean's eyes wandered from the face that had mesmerised her, and tried to read Betty's face; but she was still looking down at her hands. The green eyes looked up and came to rest on the cross-beams supporting the veranda roof. Mind and emotions suspended away from her body, drifting up there and looking down on a tableau that did not concern her personally, as this boy, this man had said; but only as an interested party on the sidelines.

Then her eyes came down and returned to stare at Philip. She was not mesmerised, now, but didn't mind looking directly at him. Into his brown eyes, with her green eyes full of enquiry. Yet a perverse antagonism still remained, and would not allow her to speak to him without a certain malice.

"I wonder which book you picked up all these ideas from – and the vocabulary," she said coldly. "One of these do-it-yourself self-analysis ones, I suppose. I wonder if that book might also have told you that your setting yourself up to do penance for your race might be unnecessary? That I'm not going to help assuage whatever guilt you might feel, for whatever reasons you feel guilty? That I reject your seemingly selfless offer for the simple reason that I love my Beatrice? Why should I give her to you, of all people? Betty was a good girl, when she worked here – a very good maid, in fact. But what care could you give her in a location? I believe there are orphanages and decent coloured families who could look after her much better – if, that is, I wanted to 'give her away'."

"No, Miss Griffiths!" Betty said, her face and voice agitated. "You can't give her to them. You know me, Miss Griffiths," she pleaded. "I worked for you, and I worked well. You said just now you know how good I am. And you know I took good care of her when you went out. And she knows me, and liked me, maybe even more than – I must have her, Miss Griffiths. You cannot give her to anybody else."

"Can't I?" Jean snapped. "Why not? And why must you have her? Only you? Is that your duty calling again, Betty? My daughter's coloured, and should at the very least be brought up as one of them. Do you think I'd be happy knowing she was running around half-naked and with a distended belly on some filthy location street?"

"Your newspapers, Miss Griffiths," Philip began carefully, "understandably never publish pictures of healthy and well-dressed African children. Except overseas, as propaganda for the government – how good apartheid is for us. Yet they never explain to you how these sickly children they photograph grow up to be the healthy men and women that this country depends on for its strength.

"Maybe it's just our dom krag, we who the predikante and dominees say have been condemned in the Bible to forever be 'hewers of wood and drawers of water'." He half-smiled. "But still, strength ... And what's so special about coloured families? You see them around you here – clean ones and dirty ones, good ones and bad ones. Same with whites. Why can't there also be clean and decent African families? You say that you know Elizabeth – but only as a maid. I can tell you, Miss Griffiths, that she has all the qualities any husband and child could ever desire. You don't know me, but I'm sure I look as decent, and talk as well, as most white people. And we live better than your white neighbours around here.

"I promise you, we will bring up Beatrice as our own. She'll be provided for as well as by any coloured family."

"I'm not giving her away. And, anyway, how do you know what happened to me – and why?"

"Betty was working for you when it was –"

"I know. But that doesn't explain all these explanations you've been mouthing about motivations and impulses. How do you know why they – and we're talking about rapists, here! How do you know how they think, if they do? That it isn't just animal lust for something beyond their filthy reach? You impute such complicated and almost noble motives to the brutish scum!"

"I don't know about other –"

He stopped and looked steadily into the green eyes; the beautiful, angry and contemptuous face framed by golden-yellow hair. Must I? Do I really have to? What the hell! Why not? Still the high and mighty bitch. Give it to her between the eyes – not the thighs, this time. His lips twisted in distaste at the obscene thought.

"Go on," she said, eyes bleak. "You started to say something."

But she was afraid, now, the earlier dread rising in her throat. And a pressure behind her temples, a numbness about the face she wasn't sure she could control. Knees suddenly weak, but she wanted to stand up and walk away. She uncrossed the knees and stretched out shapely legs; but keeping them close together. The insides of her thighs quivered and jerked. She so much wanted to massage them.

"Earlier, Miss Griffiths," he said slowly, "you asked Betty – Elizabeth, my wife – why she thought it was our duty to adopt the child. Now I'll tell you. Tell you something which, at first, I thought I would want to shout at you and the white world. Shout out loud – wild with exultation at being able to fling it into your faces. But there's no gladness in the telling of it now. Instead I'm telling it with sorrow. What I did, I did because I hated bitterly – apartheid and everything white. The hate's still there, perhaps. And so I suppose I'm not really sorry. Only for you," he added when the expression on her face changed.

"But that hate's changed. The repercussions have changed that hate I was raised on. The consequences have made life miserable, I suppose you can say. But it has led to a new way of thinking. I've had to find something new to live by; I'm still searching. And I'm hoping that having the child, Beatrice, will help me find it."

He stopped and looked at a face that had shrunk as he spoke: now small and wan, immobile like cold marble. The only flicker of life – a flicker of hatred and despair – was in the green eyes.

"Who are you?" she hissed, then turned and glared. "Betty – who is he?"

"To put it baldly, Miss Griffiths," he said into the silence, "I was …" A shrug: "I am the father of your child."

With this confirmation of what she had been dreading but refusing to consider, her gaze fled to Betty's usually compassionate face. There was no deliverance there; those soft, big brown eyes were still downcast, the meek hands clasped in her lap. She stared back at him, but his eyes were hooded as they observed her reaction.

A drumming in her head, between pressured temples. Her face felt alternately hot and sweaty, then dry and sandy, then cold and clammy. The sensations spreading all over her body in quick succession. A bitter taste in her mouth, a gagging in the throat that made her want to cough; but she was too weak for the effort, and afraid she'd vomit if she did. Stomach fluttering and hollow, thigh muscles jerking and jumping in spasmodic convulsions.

She could see it and smell it all over again, flickering before her staring eyes: the dark, dank, smelly alley; the line of rubbish bins; the puddle she'd known to avoid. The grabbing arms, her bewilderment, the tearing at her dress and silk panties; the grunts and hot breath past her ear; the hand bruising her lips … And then utter exhaustion, crawling through the muddy puddle and back up the alley to islands of illumination on the pavement.

A hot flush shuddered up her spine and turned icy-cold at the base of her neck. He did it! He's the one! And now, all these years later, sitting comfortably on my veranda looking like – not the devil incarnate, but …

She ought to be wild with anger – fury: screaming accusations and spitting disgust; cursing, clawing out those hooded eyes, tearing at that too-fucking-smart get-up and raising the alarm. Calling for the police to take him away – boil him in oil, hang the brute!

Instead a listless acknowledgement of reality, and the first of many despairing questions. How could he, if Betty knew and still loved him; how could he do such a horrible, terrible, disgusting thing? Whatever theoretical justifications? Did he have to come here and tell me this? Not confess, but offer a trade? Barter my Bea as a penance for his damned soul – his barbaric spirit? The bait being my return to being a member of a faceless community that I've come to regard as a heartless, soulless society?

How dare he reveal himself, and blast down the wall she'd so painfully built between herself and that night! Now that he sat here across from her, the recoil of disgust she had felt at just the occasional thought of him was ebbing away. There he was: as human and as much of a man as anybody else.

The stare of green eyes refocused slowly, and wandered back to his impassive face. When she spoke the voice was weak and tired:

"You."

"Yes, Miss Griffiths. Me."

"You knew all this, Betty?" turning, the voice questioning but not expecting an answer worth a damn.

"Yes, Miss Griffiths. He told me."

"When?"

"Before I came to work for you, Miss Griffiths. Before I knew you and Bea. But all the time, I did not know it was you ... Until the police came here."

Jean sighed, and her body relaxed. She looked at them with fascinated, hopeless and enquiring eyes. She must know more, know it all.

"Why didn't you report him?"

"I love him."

The three words turned the knife in brain and body. Her voice turned bitter and nasty. The green eyes moved slowly to Philip's face.

"Why did you rape me? Why?" A note of hysteria, but she suppressed it and continued: "Why did you do it, to me? Wasn't Betty enough for you?"

The pain and remorse that had wrenched his stomach as he watched her absorb and then battle against the shock of the knowledge he had thrown at her – I am the father of your child – had died down, been overcome. And now he was calm.

"I've been trying to explain just that to you, Miss Griffiths. And not from any books. I learned the hard and painful way."

"None of that, please. Did you think that by raping me – any white woman – you'd suddenly turn white? Be as good as white people? Is that it?"

"Miss Griffiths. If you didn't understand what I tried to explain, there's nothing more I can say."

"You realise I could have you hanged? You know that you deserve to die, don't you? To hang until you're dead for the misery you've caused?"

"No, Miss Griffiths."

I have to keep on repeating this Miss Griffiths thing to be – not like Betty, but just to be nice to her, he assured himself. To show my sympathy, I suppose.

"You can't have me hanged. I'd deny everything. I don't deserve to die when white men only get ... I'm sorry I've caused you – you, alone – this misery. It has caused me a lot of misery too, you know. And I'm not the only villain. It's not just us who're savages in this country. We're all to blame. But you – your people! – more than anybody else.

"If it was just animal lust, then yes, I deserve to die: every such rapist deserves to die, not just us. But it wasn't lust, as I've been trying to explain. What I did had nothing to do with sex. Perhaps, as you say, this is a kind of atonement I'm asking for from you; I don't know. All I know is that I want you to go back into the crowd, not to stick out like this." A small, bitter smile. "And not to suffer – alone."

They sat there on the narrow veranda for long, silent minutes, avoiding each other's eyes and trying to avoid the thoughts; thoughts that each knew were rolling and tumbling in the other. Then she spoke again, a small tired whisper into the silence.

"I couldn't have you hanged, even if I wanted to. I couldn't ever bring myself to, you bastard. Because you are her father, after all."

The silence resettled about them before she spoke once more.

"Please go. Go away, now. I don't want to ever see you again. Both of you. I don't know what more to say to you, now or at any other time. I don't even know what I feel about you – about this whole thing. Just go. Please."

Epilogue

Philip Mokone, elderly chair of the Equal Opportunities and Gender Equality Portfolio Committee in the Gauteng Legislature, slowed his pace and tamped down his anger three steps away from its source, Boykie Eightpence. Had to behave like that dignified personage, even if he didn't feel like any damned chair, as politics insisted must be his title. After the 'fuck you too' to Boykie, he must now grin, smile, nod and shake hands with glitzy constituents at this glittering function. Behave like a politician, while seeking refuge among this mostly young and multi-racial – no, non-racial! – crowd. Refuge from ancient memories.

This was what he'd learned during the intervening decades since his days of boozing with the likes of all the Boykies he'd known: to play it cool, leaving behind a young man's quick-fire temper brought on by stifling frustrations.

It all started when Bontle was shot dead during the Soweto Uprising, and they found her body piled with those of other klipgooiers in the stinking mortuary. His initial hot and bitter anger – go out there and shoot the first cop – had been calmed by watching Betty's matter-of-fact mourning.

He'd decided the Yanks had something else right, apart from their can't-get clothes. Don't get mad, get even; that was their cold logic. So he'd gone into politics, become an activist and finally got more than just even. Apartheid was history and he was a man of respect, as much a master of his own fate as Meneer Heunis Swanepoel or anybody else in the ballroom. No – Heunis and his wife … well, they didn't quite kiss ass, but they now looked to him for favours. Sucking up to the one-time delivery-van driver – huh! He lifted a fluted glass from the silver tray of a passing waiter and raised it in a silent toast, pretending to the curious that he was only appreciating the colour of the blood-red wine – he's learned to enjoy that as well, after being raised on mahog and moonshine. A toast to Bontle, who'd been much more beautiful than the over-used name could ever tell the world.

But then, he reminded himself with an impatient shake of his head, there was the even older daughter, who'd been like an albatross around his neck. All those years ago, when Betty had believed that only adopting 'this boesman child of yours' could lift the crippling weight of guilt pressing down on his resentful shoulders. Bontle's birth had slowly lifted that weight. He even knew the older one's name, unlike others he might have sired during those nice-time days of sowing random oats among the nice-time sisters:

Beatrice Griffiths. No, married now, surely. But not to one of those amper-baas coloured boys in Doornfontein. And with a brood – family, now, watch it boy! – of her own. My grandchildren. How many others out there, Nice Time Phil? A tribe of ill-begotten children and grandchildren? What a damned stupid, poes-crazy goat you were, eh.

Unknown daughters who're now mothers, with children who have no idea I exist. And sons who've also seduced and, probably, raped: like father like son. The difference being that they may have done it – seduction and rape – to their unknown half-sisters. Remember that one you met during that brief search for your scattered seed? The snot-nosed boy who sneered and warned you to leave his mother alone? "Do yourself a favour," he warned me! The little so-and-so had become the keeper of his mother's morals and her only protector. Probably long dead, that tiny tough guy with attitude. Or more likely, wielding a Kalashnikov in hijackings: shooting from the hip – stupid, murderous bastards. Killing people ready to give up the cars, dammit.

But getting too old for that, now, if he has my genes. If he really were my son – and had to be a criminal – he'd have enough sense to have graduated from a foot soldier to planning heists: getting away with millions from armoured cash-in-transit vehicles. That's the same aim as white-collar criminals, after all: hit the jackpot.

But the sons that Betty and I have loved and succoured from the days they were born don't have any criminal tendencies. Only fantasies, like everybody else. The genes we nurtured in them – the morality they sipped with their mother's milk – has kept them on the straight and narrow. Aiming only for legitimate jackpots, and their aim getting better all the time. My two sharpshooters!

Selected Glossary

These slang words were the language of 'wake-up' and 'fly' young people in Sophiatown – to them, Kofifi – and other townships on the Reef. The basis of this 'tsotsi taal' was Afrikaans, but was little understood by speakers of that language because it comprised words and phrases from all other South African languages: English, Zulu, Sotho and even Yiddish.

Avies, die: abbreviation of 'the avenues' – tree-lined suburban streets.
back-door: stolen goods not bought through the front door of a store.
baekie-vangers: 'baadjie-vangers', literally 'jacket hangers-on' in Afrikaans – hangers-on in shebeens.
barberton: very potent home-brewed beer named after the town where it originated.
boesman: Afrikaans for 'bushmen' and a derogatory term for coloured people; *kind:* child.
botho: Sotho for the Zulu/Xhosa 'ubuntu' – humane attitude as in 'a person is a person (motho) because of empathy with other people'.
Boer: Afrikaans for 'farmer', and a derogatory term for Afrikaners.
bra: a corruption of 'brother'; *Bra:* a term of respect for an older man.
brikaid: a corruption of 'broer' – Afrikaans for 'brother'.
can't-gets: imported fashionable clothes not available in local shops.
cattle/oxen: ordinary people who work – slave – like cattle.
Charles Atlas: an American body-builder who claimed his programme built up weaklings so nobody ever again kicked sand in their faces on any beach: common advertisement in local journals in the Fifties.
ching: money.
die manne/die real manne/die really real manne: the underworld hierarchy, ranging upwards from 'the men' and 'the real men' to 'the really real' klevahs. All of them a social cut above *tsotsis* – common thugs.
dladla: the home of a klevah, equivalent to 'a pad' for the hip in Europe.

dog's meat: suburban madams bought cheap cuts for pets, and their servants, which were served to lovers — a domestic servant.
dolly (Dit is): 'It's fine/good' – after the singer and pin-up girl Dolly Rathebe.
duze (come): invitation to a woman to get sexually closer – 'baby, come duze' in shebeens.
gats: old-time American slang for 'guns'.
gatsak: from Afrikaans, meaning 'back pocket'.
gattas: derogatory term for police.
gazaat: clubbing together to buy alcohol in shebeens.
gweva: a bootlegger who sold alcohol illegally from a *s'godi.*
hangpaal: the hangman's gallows (pole).
Heita!: 'Hello'.
izigebengwa: Zulu/Xhosa for a thug – *tsotsi.*
jewish: anything good – clothes and attitudes.
juba: boyfriend, lover or husband.
keeping timing: to 'be cool' – not losing the beat.
klevah: a streetwise and 'wake-up' young man as opposed to *situation:* an upright and uptight man; law-abiding and often unfamiliar with 'tsotsi taal' and usually vulnerable to victimisation by klevahs.
korea: from the Korean war – alcohol doped or watered-down to increase quantities in cheap shebeens.
laaitie: a younger person – patronising or insulting.
laanie: a white person, but currently meaning anything up-market.
leshetla: a desirable man – plural, *mashetla.*
mabalane: a clerk, someone who writes; from the Zulu 'bala' – to write.
magoduka: a transient person – newly arrived in urban areas.
mahog: brandy, from the mahogany colour.
majita: 'the guys' or wake-up friends/comrades
makgoa: white people – 'those who shout' as the Voortrekkers were seen by Africans to do to the cattle pulling their wagons.
matahoa: drunks – *dronkies.*
mazooma: money, as in *ching.*
meshugen: Yiddish for crazy/confused.
moegoe: someone not streetwise like a klevah; in town from a rural area.
muti: traditional medicine, some of it for witchcraft purposes.
my ma se kind: Afrikaans – 'my mother's child', as in *brikaid.*

mzala: Zulu/Xhosa – cousin.
ngoana oa mme: Sotho – 'my mother's child'.
nice-time girls/sisters/boys/nice-timer: 'wake-up' fun people who frequent shebeens – the girls regarded as easy 'meat' for male *nice-timers.*
notch: to understand.
ousie: Afrikaans for 'big sister', a term of respect that can have undertones.
phola: where one rests or stays, as in Phola Park.
plaas-jaapie: Afrikaans 'plaasjapie' – same as *moegoe* and *magoduka.*
poegat: from the Yiddish – dead drunk.
s'qeda viki: 'finish the week' – a lethal concoction that kept a person drunk all week.
s'godi: a hole in Zulu/Xhosa but in the slang meaning the source of illicit alcohol provided by a bootlegger, a *gweva.*
se bapa le masenke: Sotho – 'staggering against/along corrugated/zinc fences' – too drunk to stagger on one's own.
shaandies: things that happen, usually unpleasant.
singali (Dit is): 'It's good/fine', as in *dolly.*
situation: uptight person – not streetwise, and despised by klevahs.
sheila/sheila's day: a domestic servant/her day-off, usually Thursday.
skep: to pick up a woman for the night; usually a nice-time sister.
skinker: a person serving drink.
skokiaan: another lethal, and illegal, home-brewed concoction.
skondaai: to fuck, as opposed to making love.
stokvel: weekend drinking party to raise money for member of a group.
timer: as in 'old-timer'.
tsotsi: a thug – low-class criminal despised by klevahs and all die manne.
venstertjie: Afrikaans for 'window' – a coloured who 'plays white' and peers into store windows to avoid being recognised by other coloureds.
wake-up: a streetwise klevah who is awake to everything around him.
war-timer: new arrival in Jo'burg – a *moegoe.*
weebit: a woman, as in *cherry* – from the Scottish 'wee bit'.
weetie: to talk, especially in slang.
wena: Zulu/Xhosa/Sotho for 'you'.

Author's note

This is my version of The Great South African Novel that we – the 'young, black intelligentsia' – were always asked when we were going to write by white liberals at their 'mixed' parties in Johannesburg's wealthy and leafy northern suburbs.

This novel was written in exile: started in Accra, Ghana, and completed in London, England. I had made a choice to abandon South Africa, believing, as the government proclaimed, that apartheid would survive for a millennium. Before that, only short stories were possible for me. A novel would be an immense task, living in the 'locations' of that period: the fifties, when apartheid was in its first decade and still spreading its bleak wings over the country.

South Africa was bad in that time – bad enough for me and many others to choose exile; never to return, we believed. The questions to which Philip Mokone and Jean Griffiths sought answers became more urgent and perplexing, and the answers less likely to be found.

But now, at the time of this second edition of this novel – the first was, not surprisingly, banned in South Africa – some answers have emerged, and some are still being sought: are we, of all colours and races, a single nation; or are we still enclosed in the suspicions and fears engendered by the imposed superiority of one group over all others?

I have returned from half a life-time in exile, and this edition has necessarily had to be revised to plant its perspectives solidly in South Africa. I have removed explanations that were necessary for a foreign audience, but retained those about circumstances unknown to a later generation of South Africans – or forgotten by those of us who lived through the worst of a burgeoning apartheid.

I have added a prologue and epilogue reflecting the post-apartheid era – the new dawn, as romantics might say. I have also revised this author's note, which was written for the first edition, published in London during 1976 as *Victims.* At that time all the reviews of this novel, in Britain and other countries, were complimentary. An Australian reviewer praised it as "the best out of South Africa since *Cry the Beloved Country*". A compliment, yes; but double-edged for me because I regarded that novel by Alan Paton, a classic white liberal, as patronising to Africans. But his heart was in the right place, or near enough. Like the hearts of all those liberals we met at 'mixed' parties and other events across the colour bar, as it was called before 'apartheid' was coined to hold full sway over our lives: victims, all.

Johannesburg, January 2000